This Year in Jerusalem

A novel by

Joel Gross

G. P. PUTNAM'S SONS   New York

Library of Congress Cataloging in Publication Data

Gross, Joel.
  This year in Jerusalem.

  1. Palestine—History—1917–1948—Fiction.   I. Title.
PS3557.R58T48   1983   813'.54   82-24081
ISBN 0-399-12812-3

Printed in the United States of America

Second Impression

This Year
in
Jerusalem

This book is for my grandmother, Rose Pearl,
and for the memory of my grandmother, Mary Gross,
and my grandfathers, Theodore Pearl and Milton Gross.

Chronology

(July) 1914–
(November) 1918:   World War I

1915:   Zionists contribute to British war effort. Jewish espionage organization formed behind Turkish lines. Weizman negotiates with British politicians.

1917:   Turks destroy Jewish espionage group. British government issues Balfour Declaration promising to "facilitate establishment of Jewish National Home in Palestine."

1920:   Arabs riot against Jews in Jerusalem. Haganah founded.

1922:   Transjordan truncated by British from mandated area of Palestine.

1929:   Arabs riot in Jerusalem and Hebron against Jews.

1930:   British impose restrictions on Jewish emigration to Palestine.

1933:   Nazis come to power in Germany.

1936–39:   Severe restrictions on Jewish immigration confronted by illegal Jewish émigrés from Hitler's Europe.

(September) 1939–
(September) 1945:   World War II

1945:   Death-camp survivors refused permission to emigrate to Palestine.

1946:   Irgun blows up King David Hotel. British Navy blockades Palestine, deports illegal immigrants to Cyprus D.P. camps.

1947:   (July) *Exodus 1947* refugee ship prevented from landing in Palestine. Refugees removed to Germany.

(November) United Nations votes to partition Palestine.

(December) United States enforces arms embargo to Palestine. Great Britain continues to sell arms to Arab states. Undeclared war between Arabs and Jews begins.

1948:   (May 14) State of Israel proclaimed.

If I forget thee, O Jerusalem,
let my right hand forget her cunning.
Let my tongue cleave to the roof of my mouth,
if I remember thee not:
if I set not Jerusalem
above my chiefest joy.

—Psalms 137: 5–6

Next year in Jerusalem!

—Traditional closing words of the Passover Seder.

This Year
in
Jerusalem

ONE

Diana woke slowly. A familiar pleasure lingered in her lazy frame. She became aware of his scent, of her own scent, of the thin sheet warmed by their bodies, but did not hurry to decide if these sensations were memories of the night before or the reality awaiting her on the other side of consciousness. The rhythm of his breathing grew momently louder, even as she became aware of the gray light, the drizzle of cold rain, the wet draft of air from the cracked window above their heads. It had been pitch dark, and very slowly she decided that her eyes were open, that a new day had dawned, that the man she loved was not simply a memory but was both past and present, the man whose touch she remembered, the man who lay beside her now.

Thoughtlessly, she reached out for him, her delicate fingers barely grazing the cleft of his chin, the red-blond stubble along his jaw.

David woke at once.

It was as if he had been kicked, and now awaited the next blow. His knees jerked toward his groin, his hands covered mouth and nose, his forearms guarded his broad chest. He was rigid, the muscles straining, his eyes wide open to no sight in the tiny room.

"Only me," she said in a small voice.

"Did I say anything?"

"No."

"I didn't cry out? Please tell me the truth. It's not your fault. I only want to know if I cried out."

He had lowered his knees and forced his arms to his sides, but the rigidity remained. In his pale eyes was not terror but despair, and even this he seemed to be now trying to blink away.

"I'm sorry," she said.

"Stop," he said. "You didn't do anything to be sorry for." He turned toward her finally, taking her face in his hands and kissing her. She knew that he was feeling no love at that moment, but she forgave him this, as she would forgive him almost anything. "Good morning," he said, exhibiting his smile, bringing his body over hers, but not allowing them to meet. "Now, are you absolutely sure I didn't cry out?"

"Yes."

"I didn't even say 'I love you, Diana!'?" Slowly he brought his body to hers, his handsome face not so much alive with pleasure as it was freed of horror. "Diana," he said, whispering now, as if attempting to bring back the peace of sleep, the peace before waking. He parted her hair with his hands, and he spread her thighs with his knee. He kissed her lips, her eyes, her neck, exhibiting his gentleness so that she would know that he was without fear. But whatever his motives, it was simple to forget them. He was amorous, he was passionate, and she could feel the desire behind his easy, unhurried touch. She began to believe in the love expressed by his body, and this love was beautiful, the mirror image of her own and therefore all-encompassing, inescapable. They made love and she spoke out his name, "David," saying it over and over again until it had no meaning, until it was an expulsion of breath, until it was a silent twisting of lips, until it was nothing but a pulsing rhythm in her brain.

It had been dark the first time she'd heard his voice. Or rather, she had been in the dark, a blindfold around her eyes, as a car door had been flung open on the road outside Tel Aviv, and David Stern had been let in at her side.

"I have a statement for the American press," he had said, and as the car accelerated quickly on the dusty road, she felt the force of his anger and impatience like a fresh wind in her tired face. "The

16

Haganah is the defense force of the Jewish settlement in Palestine. We are a secret force, but everyone knows we exist. We are not supposed to be necessary because the British are supposed to keep order in Palestine, but without us, the Jewish settlements throughout the Mandate would be threatened, attacked, and bombed even more than they are at present. We are not terrorists. We are opposed to the policies of the Irgun, though they are fellow Jews, and we can understand their anger; our policy is restraint, defense, and patience. But we will not restrain ourselves if the British continue to look the other way as the Arabs attack us; we will not restrict ourselves permanently to defense if the British Navy continues to viciously prevent the victims of Hitler's concentration camps from landing on our shores; and we will not be patient if the British promise to grant us a homeland in Palestine is postponed forever. That is the end of my statement to the press."

"What is your name, please?" Diana had said, knowing full well that he would not give it, but wanting only to hear his anger again, feel the strength of his convictions ring through the restricted space of the car.

"No names, no positions, no ranks," David had said. "A member of the Haganah on an unknown road in British-occupied Palestine."

"Since the Irgun has already directly attacked and killed British soldiers without provocation—"

"Without *direct* provocation," he had said.

"Functioning as terrorists," Diana had said, "as opposed to a defense force. And since you are showing your impatience, is it not then possible that your Haganah will soon be doing what the Irgun already is?"

"Why do they send women journalists?" he had said. "They are always so damned clever, much better than the men." She could feel him move around to take a look at her in the dark car. In a moment's absurd vanity she wondered if he could see how pretty she was in the bad light, with her face obscured by the bulky blindfold. "Yes, the Irgun are Jewish terrorists, but they restrict themselves to military targets. The Arab terrorists, who go by a hundred different names, attack British military targets too, but rarely. They prefer civilian Jewish targets, unarmed, defenseless. Ideally they like to blow up schools, nurseries, half-built kibbutzim when the men are away. But the Haganah is not terrorist. We will blow up a radar installation if it is being used to find Jewish refugees on the seacoast of our own country, but we will not indiscriminately kill the British soldiers manning it."

"But what if they shoot at you?" said Diana. But before she could elaborate, she felt the blindfold ripped off her face, and her head turned round to face the man she had been interviewing.

"Look, miss," David had said. "Roadblock. My name is David Stern. We are lovers. I met you in a café in Tel Aviv, and we are coming back to Tel Aviv after a picnic. You are mad at being stopped and questioned. What is your name on your passport?" Diana Mann told him. The car slowed down at the checkpoint of the Palestine police. "Kiss me," said David Stern, and Diana closed her eyes gladly against the shock of his momentarily seen beautiful face. They kissed, and she was too new to the country to feel any real danger about her, to believe in the possibility of a trouble too great to be solved by her press card and American passport; and when their lips met, she was able to take pleasure in the moment, and when she felt the response in his mouth, in the hands he had placed so gently about her cheeks, she took more than pleasure.

"Out of the car," said a brusque British voice.

Diana opened her eyes, then squinted against the harsh beam of a flashlight. But David kept his hands on her cheeks, so that she did not move out of the embrace. It was only the two of them in the backseat of the ancient Ford; their driver was already out and on his feet, showing them his papers.

"I said out of the car, you two, you don't fool me. I want to see your guns."

David let go of Diana, and nodded at her, and she quickly opened her car door and got out, while David did the same on his side of the car. There were five policemen, three of them Arab members of the force. One of the two British policemen was about to speak when Diana turned on him in a rage:

"Who the hell do you think you are, talking to me like that?" She was waving her American passport like a talisman now. "Do you enjoy breaking up five minutes of peace with my fiancé just to show how tough you are? What's your name, officer? My family is in constant communication with the High Commissioner, and I am dining with the Financial Secretary tomorrow, and I have letters of introduction to the Attorney General and the Chief Secretary of this police state and I want to know your name."

As it turned out, her family didn't know the High Commissioner, nor did she have letters of introduction to anyone in Palestine; but she did have a dinner engagement with the Financial Secretary— thanks to her family's influence in London's banking community— and this was the only reference the policemen checked. "We're terribly sorry to have troubled you, Miss Mann," she was told, and when they were all sent back on their way along the road to Tel Aviv, David Stern apologized.

"You have nothing to apologize for," she had said. "I'm a journalist, and I accept the possibility of danger when I take an assignment."

"That's not what I mean. I thought you'd be a coward," he'd said, and then he smiled at her and brought his hands back to her cheeks, and they kissed once again, this time not for show, but for romance. It took Diana months to realize how brave she must have appeared to him; because in the same amount of time, she had learned to be afraid. This was not a movie. This was a place where people were arrested, tortured, executed. From the time that they became lovers, till the moment three months later in his bed in Jerusalem, Diana was terrified lest he discover just how weak her character might be. If he had begun to love her—or even begun to appreciate her—this love, this appreciation, this respect, could vanish in an instant. She steeled herself in his presence: to be brave, to anticipate his desires, his anger, his action.

"Don't get dressed," he said.

"It's getting late," she said, as if he were teasing her, as if the very thought of any more lovemaking was simply not in the realm of possibility. But she dropped her skirt back on the foot of the bed and walked toward where he sat examining her across the room. "I didn't hear you get up."

"Naturally not," said David. "I'm a commando."

"My darling commando," said Diana, coming up to him for an embrace. But he held her at arm's length, his pale eyes severe, measuring.

"Look, put on a blouse and your underwear," he said.

Diana looked at him quizzically, with a sadness that never failed to infuriate him. "Please," he said. "I want to kiss you and I want to hug you and I want to do all the rest of the things you people do in

America, but for the moment, I have something to ask you and I don't know how you're going to respond. So please, this is not easy for me. Don't insist on my showing adoration at every instant of the day."

She could feel the headache starting up with violence, and its concomitant pains of guilt. Who was she to question this man's temper? It would have been lovely to have awakened a second time that morning to the same slow rhapsody of sensations, but as David insisted on reminding her, it was a privilege to have awakened at all. Even if it had been to awaken with a start, seeing the man she loved reassembling his revolver with quick, angry movements. She began to dress. "Not my skirt, that's all?"

"Please."

"I have a feeling this isn't about stroking my luscious legs," said Diana. As she spoke, she saw him pop a Novadrin pep pill into his mouth; he swallowed it without water, painfully. "Didn't you sleep enough last night?"

"Yes," said David. "But somehow I'm still tired." He stood up abruptly, and carefully put down his gun on the chair. "You should go back to America."

"I am going back. What do you mean?"

"I mean that you should go back for good. Stay away from here. You don't know what you are, you're not sure how you feel, and I don't want to see you killed under those circumstances."

"That's not fair. I know how I feel. And I've told you often enough how I feel."

"Come here," he said, and once again she crossed the room without thought, going to her lover. This time he embraced her gently, placing his cheek against hers, waiting for the apology to be felt before he voiced it. "I'm sorry," he said.

"I'm sorry for the way I woke you."

"Diana, please, for the last time," he said, his anger flaring up once again. "Learn to believe what I tell you. If you want to wake me with a kiss or a feather or by dropping a water balloon on my head, feel free to do so. I am the one who acted incorrectly this morning, not you. Do you understand?"

"Yes."

"I wasn't apologizing for the way I woke up, either. What I'm sorry about is . . . everything. The way I talk to you. Even now. I'm angry at you. All the time."

"I understand that you're under terrible strain."

"You don't understand anything. Diana, I can't help it. I'm angry at you because I want to use you. I want to exploit you. And I'm angry at you because I'm not asking you, because what I want from you is something that you shouldn't do, not if you're a reporter from America, instead of a Jew in Jerusalem."

"I don't think it's fair to be angry at me if I haven't denied you anything. What makes you think I'd turn you down?"

"You wouldn't turn me down," said David. "That's why I'm so angry." She began to speak, but he stilled her with his hand pressed to her lips. "Did you hear me, Diana? I know you wouldn't turn me down." He removed his hand from her lips and turned away from her, going back to pick up the heavy revolver from the chair.

"Please ask me, David," she said.

"I don't want you to do this for me, but only if you believe in creating a Jewish homeland. Not for me, Diana. For Eretz-Israel."

"Of course," said Diana, but he was hardly waiting for her answer, going back to her and placing the cold steel of the gun next to the outside of her right thigh. She stopped herself from speaking, from questioning. As he strapped the heavy weight to her leg, she found herself smiling. If the man she loved was asking her to hold on to a gun for the Haganah, he must therefore hold her in high regard.

"Put your skirt on, please."

The tightly strapped gun threatened the circulation in her right leg, and when she'd put on her California skirt and sat down on the bed next to David, an ominous bulge showed. "No one will see this when you're standing," he said, his blue eyes impatient, as if she had expressed an objection or voiced a fear. "When you sit, it will be at a café table, and you will be on my left. Very close, like this." David put his left arm about her shoulders and cupped her chin in his right hand. He kissed her tenderly, slowly, and in the heart of the moment drew his tongue back from her mouth and hissed, "Now." In a second, he had dropped her chin, lifted her skirt, and with his right hand viciously pulled the revolver free of its strap, tearing at the skin of her thigh in the process.

She stopped herself from crying out, not at the pain in her thigh, but at the ease with which he had feigned passion. Even with the gun strapped to her thigh, even with the coldness in his eyes, she had believed in his love as he'd put his arm about her, as he'd kissed her simply to practice for the moment when he might have to pull out his gun in a café crowded with enemies. "You pulled away from me, Diana," he said. "Lean into me if you feel that I'm going to go for the gun."

"I'm sorry."

"You look a little pale. Brighten up, now. Think of Beverly Hills, sunshine, movie stars. The British never search women, not even big ugly women. Nobody's going to search a California society girl with a press pass and a pretty face."

"I'm not a society girl," she said very meekly, afraid that he might try to shove her past down her throat again. But David was busy strapping the revolver onto her bruised thigh, lost in thought. He had called her pretty, complimenting her obliquely, not to bolster her vanity, but to give her confidence. When he had finished with the gun, he snapped out further words of instruction and inspiration, and Diana despaired at the coldness of his voice. How could he possibly love her? He had lost a wife to the Nazis, and much of his capacity for love had been burned out of his soul. She had not placed the six blue digits of the Auschwitz horror camp on his forearm, but because she had never suffered what his wife had suffered, what his parents and siblings had suffered, what he himself had lived through, there was an essential part of him that was closed to her forever.

"You're looking better, then," he said when they'd found a Jewish taxi to take them toward the Old City. "You can still say no, and I'll understand." Diana looked at him with amazement. He was stroking her hand, and his eyes were no longer hard. "I was a little afraid myself this time, and I thought you'd be able to help. But I can do it without you, I think, and I'll love you regardless."

"The Tommies don't even search big ugly women, remember?" she said.

"We need big ugly women," said David Stern. "All your size is good for is pistols. How are we supposed to get the big guns out with skinny little things like you?"

They left the taxi near the Jaffa Road, two short blocks from the great gate to the Old City, witness of petty commerce, political intrigue, and religious fervor. The cold drizzle had finally let up, and now, at a half-hour before noon, the streets were thronged with the endless variety of the city's people—saints and peasants, soldiers and businessmen, black water-carriers from the Sudan and fair-haired missionaries from Minnesota, Jewish survivors of the Polish resistance and Yugoslav fascists working for the Grand Mufti, Christians and Muslims and Jews of every denomination and subdenomination, more in conflict with the religious values of their co-religionists than with those of other faiths. The sun was weak behind a layer of clouds, but enough light filtered through to strike with magic the domes and towers looming behind the forty-foot-high walls for two and one-half miles around the ancient city of David. A far greater city—greater in size, population, resources—had been built up around this three-thousand-year-old core, but the new city of Jerusalem would have little meaning for its 160,000 inhabitants without its magnificent heart.

David was very animated as he walked toward Jaffa Gate, holding tightly to Diana's elbow, warning her in a loud English-accented voice about pickpockets, shouting unnecessarily in Arabic at beggars no older than six, or in Hebrew at merchants insistently selling their wares to the attractive young "European" couple. Within a block of the gate, still in the new city, the crowd of professional guides, sellers of holy relics, agents of archaeological treasures, grew thicker: there was an urgency to grab hold of their victims before they could be seized by the far greater frenzy in the Old City itself.

As they neared the checkpoint, David was gesturing to the walls and speaking so loudly that Diana felt his fear grow up and overwhelm his act of insouciance. Of the nearly hundred thousand British personnel in Palestine, about eighty thousand were with various military divisions, with most of the rest British police officials, bolstered with representative Jewish and Arab policemen. Even with this enormous strong-arm presence for a population of 1,200,000 Arabs and 600,000 Jews in the entire country, the sense of security in the Holy Land had all but collapsed. In February, two thousand British civilians were evacuated from the country; remaining nonmilitary personnel were virtually prisoners behind their own barbed-wire security zones, removed from most contact with Palestinian Jews and Arabs who had become in their minds a source of violence and murder. Some British soldiers were pro-Arab, that is to say, they espoused the cause of Arab nationalism and agreed that the Arabs should rule Palestine as a single sovereign state. Other British soldiers were pro-Zionist, believing that the Jews should have a share of their ancient homeland, if not the entire original mandated area—which included all of Transjordan—then at least a portion of the land west of the Jordan River that had been promised for decades as a future homeland for the dispersed Jews of the world. Unfortunately for the Jews of Palestine, the pro-Arab stance of the British military and political establishment largely filtered its way down to the rank and file. Jewish young men were far more likely to be stopped and searched at any of the checkpoints scattered through new and old Jerusalem than their Arab counterparts.

A young Arab boy in tattered shorts and an American soldier's fatigue hat was waved through the checkpoint by an Arab constable of the Palestine police. As the boy prodded forward his donkey, loaded down with tin oil cans filled with drinking water, one of the three British constables shook his head at Diana, who was next in line. "Another clear example of British favoritism of the Arab race," he said with sarcasm. "That boy could be carrying dynamite in those bloody cans, and we didn't even search."

"That's enough, officer," said the ranking constable at the checkpoint, a pink-faced boy of no more than twenty.

"This is an American lady," insisted the first constable. "One of the American ladies who pays for the Irgun. Pays for all their postage stamps, all their filthy scandal sheets, all their guns and bombs."

"I beg your pardon, miss," said the pink-faced constable. He barely glanced at her American passport, and looked hardly a moment longer at David Stern's Palestinian passport, embarrassed at the fright he saw in her lovely face. Any constable, by the law of the land, could arrest anyone on suspicion of terrorist activity and hold him for seven days without trial; the local military commander could legally elongate this detention period indefinitely. Diana had met a boy of seventeen who had been held in the squalid detention center at Latrun for four months on suspicion of handing out illegal literature— one of the handbills of the Irgun that some constables kept around to plant on Jews who spoke back to them at the checkpoints. She could hardly imagine what they'd do to her for carrying a real gun. They would certainly hang David, for they would know at once that they were together. But no, there would be no hanging. David would drop to his knee and tear out her revolver and shoot at least one of them before the others mowed him down. She wondered what she would do then. It would be incumbent on her to die, of course, to die by his side, fighting the enemy.

"I think he was quite taken with you," said David as they joined the masses going into the Old City.

"What did you say?"

"The Old City Wall is four yards thick on top, and ten yards thick at the bottom," said David. "And that I think at least one British constable thinks you incapable of any vile anti-Imperial action."

"I thought the first constable—"

"Is going to get his head handed to him by the second. Imagine saying 'bloody' in front of a lady. Wait till the Irgun hears about this. They'll have his bloody behind, won't they?"

"Should you be talking?" she whispered, still under the spell of the checkpoint. David put his arm about her shoulders.

"On our right, the Tower of David." He laughed. "Which really should not be its name, since it's been the Old City's stronghold only since the time of Herod." He steered her through the crowd, keeping his arm tightly about her as they followed David Street with its sellers of Bibles and Korans, canned food from America and fresh vegetables from the neighboring Arab villages, sacramental wine and surplus uniforms from a dozen armies. The stalls and carts and individual hawkers of wares were more crowded than usual, as the morning rain had kept shoppers at home; usually the early morning was the busiest time of day for the David Street markets. Dour-faced Arab men performed their husbandly duties shortly after their prayers, bringing home the daily allotment of food that their wives would spend the day preparing. "It's a very confused little city in the walls here, my dear, with the latest walls built in the sixteenth century by Suleiman the Magnificent, but they are far from the first set of walls, and perhaps not the last either. Still, our British protectors huddle up near the Citadel, just like the Crusaders, just like Herod and a hundred conquerors and defenders before him." They had come up to the crowded spice market on the way to the Christian quarter, and now David ceased his guidebook prattling. "We're going to walk a bit more quickly now, and you'll hold on to me very tightly, and all you have to do is talk about how tired you are from climbing up and down these hilly little alleys, in your best Hollywood English."

"I'm not the least bit tired," she said, standing up on her toes to kiss his cheek. "And I probably know as much about the Old City as you."

"Then you know this street," he said, just as loudly as before, gesturing to his right, where the Street of the Jews began its un-distinguished way into the Jewish quarter. "While it's highly unlikely that we shall have a problem, my dear, in the event that one of us gets lost in the crowd, I would like to meet you in the Johanan Ben-Zakai synagogue. It's Sephardi, you ask anyone once you're in the Jewish quarter. Will you remember?"

"Why should we get separated?"

"This is important, and I'm relying on you, Diana. The Johanan Ben-Zakai synagogue. Ask any Jew to direct you, and once you're there—listen—you must go to the Kehal Zion hall. That's where I'll be."

"When?"

"That's where I'll be if there's a problem," he said. "And if there's a problem, there's no telling how long it will take either of us to get there. Do you understand?"

"Johanan Ben-Zakai synagogue. Sephardi. I'll ask a Sephardi Jew to direct me. And then it's Kehal Zion hall. I'll wait as long as I have to, you know that. But maybe it won't be necessary. Maybe we won't be separated."

"In the café, remember to lean into me, all right?"

"What café?"

"In a moment, just remember. The Street of the Jews to the Jewish quarter. You're a rich tourist, happy-go-lucky Diana Mann from Beverly Hills."

"Sure I am," she said. He had taken her down a steep alley to their left, leaving the bustle of David Street for an unfamiliar part of the Christian quarter. They passed under an ancient marketplace, covered by crumbling stone arches a thousand years old, and an Arab woman—a Christian, as she wore no veil—shoved a gold watch on a thick chain into Diana's hands.

"Very much luck, miss. Very much blessings on you," she said. "Two pounds English, eight dollars American. Gold, all gold."

"I'm sorry," mumbled Diana, but David had already pulled her past, eliciting a curse. They climbed up a little street behind three mules bearing sacks of flour, prodded by two small children with switches. A small yellow handbill bearing the signature of the Irgun and sentencing various Englishmen to death in poetic Hebrew and imperfect English had been pasted to the gray stone wall of a decrepit stairway that seemed to lead into perfect darkness. David had stopped to get his bearings, and Diana read: "Wanted for Murder! For making drowning of Jews at sea . . ."

"This way," said David, leading her up the stairway, which somehow crossed over an adjacent alley, and then wound down to an almost pretty street, with black-robed priests walking in pairs, and children selling sandals and offering shoeshines in guttural lamentations. "For making drowning of Jews at sea," thought Diana, her eyes never leaving David's broad figure, observing the powerful stride marred by a tiny jerk in his left knee: this was her man, recognizing the slight wave of the blond hair at the nape of his neck, the swinging forward of his arms, both index fingers extended as if to claim the space ahead of him. She knew the way the sweat started up in the small of his back, staining his khaki shirt, the way his shoulders hunched forward toward any source of danger, prepared to fight. Because she loved him, and he was in the Haganah's full-time striking force, the Palmach, she sympathized with all his opinions—not only politically; he had changed her mind about which movies she liked, how sweet to drink her coffee. He would not like the Irgun poster running through her mind: the Haganah's job was to try to bring the survivors of the Nazi death camps to Eretz-Israel, even if it was in defiance of British law. While he would condone the blowing up of radar installations, communications lines, and other sources of British power used to halt immigration, he despised the Irgun's murders of British soldiers, their terrorist bombings that killed the innocent along with the guilty. Diana could imagine David explaining away the anger of the Irgun handbill as childish. He would tell her that the few Jewish refugees who had drowned trying to swim to shore from their miserably crowded immigrant ships, determined to fight the unknown undertow rather than face life away from the Holy Land, were heroes; but the enemies who had prevented their ship from landing became heroic when murdered in their rose gardens or curled up in their beds. The Haganah didn't want to fight the British, they only wanted to defend their people. The Irgun wanted to revenge more than defend, terrorize more than compromise. Diana knew that the gun at her thigh was not to be used for an assassination, but only for defense, and only as a last resort. How could she not agree with the restraint of a man who had so much to revenge, not only on the British, but on the world which had allowed the horror of his family's destruction?

"Thirsty?" said David, reaching back to squeeze her hand. His smile was uneasy, an attempt to be reassuring that did not succeed. The street turned sharply left, and then ran uphill, its old cobblestones marked with holes where a metal gate had once stood.

"I'm fine."

"You look like you could use a coffee," said David. Out of breath, she followed him over the rise in the street, and nearly slipped on a patch of wet stone as they began downhill. Tiny houses with elaborate awnings and fancy iron grillwork lined both sides of the steep street. Balconies sprouted trees and gaily colored chairs. A gorgeous white stallion stood quietly, untethered, at the bottom of the street where children played a game with bottle caps, and a man in European clothes smoked a water pipe, watching them approach with dead eyes. An Arab woman with a huge basket of fruit on her head ran past them, unable to slow her gait on the steep downward incline. Across the way, Diana noticed an Arab café, incongruously poor on the comfortable street. Three men, two of them wearing scarlet tarbooshes, sat outside on short wooden stools, balancing tiny bowls of Turkish coffee on rickety tables. The third man was red-haired, with a military posture and civilian clothes that looked like they were fresh out of the box.

"Shalom Aleichem," said the red-haired man as David and Diana crossed over the narrow cobblestoned street. He had the accent of an English gentleman, but like his clothes, it seemed put on for the occasion. One of the Arabs clapped his hands, and from inside the adjacent gray stone house a boy of ten or eleven brought out a tiny table and two stools. "You're prompt, Abie, but I don't see your number one anywhere," continued the Englishman.

"It's not wise calling me 'Abie,'" said David as he pulled his stool next to Diana's and sat down, lazily putting his left arm about her shoulders. Their backs were to the street, but they faced the three men who were arranged in a broken line about the front door to the inside of the café. "Not if you plan to do business with me."

"Don't get upset," said the Englishman. "I don't know your name, so I called you whatever came to mind." Slowly he took in David's forearm with its blue tattooed number and said without any sign of emotion, "You were in one of those camps."

"Isn't there a waiter in this café?" said David sharply, removing his right arm from the top of the table where it had been harmlessly on view for the three men. Diana felt his hand land on her leg, light and amorous and ready. The Englishman called for the boy in Arabic, and when he had appeared with the muddy Turkish coffee, sweetened past any Westerner's taste, he spoke again, exhibiting his impatience: "I didn't come here to risk getting blown up by the Jews just to meet your girlfriend, did I? Is he coming or what?"

"He's coming," said David.

"You don't look like one of those from the camps," said the red-haired Englishman. "I would have thought you the fighting type."

"We're not here to discuss me," said David abruptly. "If you wish to wait for the arrival of my superior officer before discussing our agreement, then I suggest we both remain silent until he arrives."

"Bloody cheek is what I call it," said the Englishman to Diana. "Imagine calling him a 'superior officer.' What does that make him, a soldier in the Jew army? I'll tell you something, miss, it's no bloody good trying to convince an English soldier that these Jews here are ever going to do any kind of face-to-face fighting like real soldiers. Just hit and run is what they know. Blow up their little bombs in the dark like the cowards they are."

"They're not cowards," said Diana, but David shut her up.

"Look," he said. "If you want to do business with us, you'd better change your tune. Otherwise, I'm calling off the meeting."

"Calling off the meeting, are you? I'll shoot you where you sit, you little murdering Jew-bastard." David decided that the man was not drunk, and therefore his provocations had purpose. All he knew about the Englishman was that he had twice before sold weapons to the Haganah, mostly Lee-Enfield rifles stolen from local armories, and that each time the sale was about to go through, the price had been raised at the last moment. That the man hated Jews was probable, but that he would present a threat to David's superior officer was very much in doubt.

"If you're trying to raise your price at the last moment," said David mildly, "you needn't go to the bother of racking your tiny brain for insults. You will tell us what you can and cannot do for us, and whether you will honor the original agreement or break your word once again. And then we will decide if we shall do business with you or if we won't."

"Is that how you spoke to the Nazis when they were stepping on your face?" said the Englishman. At this, one of the Arabs broke into a smile that was as broad as it was brief. Diana found herself staring at this man as he adjusted his tarboosh; at first she hadn't been sure that he could even understand English, but now his easy smile made him seem not only English-speaking but also capable of easy violence. Only a few days before, she'd filed a story to New York about the precipitous rise in the sales of tarbooshes in Jerusalem. As in the anti-Jewish Arab riots of 1936, Arabs were suddenly buying the distinctive scarlet hats so that they might not be mistaken for Jews. She felt the pressure of David's hand on her shoulder ease up, and she stiffened involuntarily, as if this might be the prelude to an outburst of gunfire. But almost at once she could imagine her editor explaining, as if to a child, why he couldn't run her silly story about tarbooshes: it was irresponsible to be so melodramatic, he'd say. What did a silly-looking Arab hat have to do with the threat of murdering the Jews of Palestine? As for David's hand on her shoulder, whether it squeezed her or pinched her or fell asleep from inaction, nothing would happen to her that day, no danger would cross her path.

One of the Arabs spoke, in Arabic, so that everyone but Diana understood what he said: "Someone comes, a stranger. In a *kaffiyeh*."

David didn't turn to look, because he knew it was Uri, the man for whom they were waiting, and that with the Arab headdress he would be wearing baggy black cotton bloomers and a black Syrian tunic. Had Diana or some other girl not been sitting there with David, Uri would know to keep on walking, that there would be no weapons under the table that were on their side. Even now, David could tell Diana to leave, that this was not a meeting that she would find entertaining, and as she would get up to go, Uri would continue on his way down the quiet street, passing them without a murmur or a glance.

"May I join you gentlemen," said Uri in Russian-accented English. It was not a question, but an explosion of syllables as he sat on the empty stool at the Englishman's tiny table, not even acknowledging the presence of David and Diana.

"So now the Jews dress up like Arabs," said the Englishman.

"I don't like business with redheads," said Uri, taking hold of the Englishman's bowl of coffee. "They talk too much, and if they're not very brave, then they are cowards." He took a sip of the Englishman's coffee, then spat it out onto the cobblestones. As the Englishman's face whitened in fury, Uri kicked over the tiny table with his knee, and standing up a full second before the Englishman could, he was able to drive the heel of his hand into the bridge of the man's nose.

Diana never saw any of that. All she was aware of was the shock of the stranger drinking the Englishman's coffee, and then David's revolver was pulled violently from where it was strapped to her thigh and she herself was knocked to the ground, apparently by David, who screamed words at her that she was momentarily incapable of understanding.

There was shooting.

Of course she had heard gunfire before; three months in Palestine had given her experience with the sound of rifle fire, pistol shots, even the distant explosion of a homemade bomb on Jerusalem's Number Two bus. She had seen amputees, dead men, bloody women and children, the blinded and diseased, the maimed victims of concentration camps and poverty and politics. But nothing had prepared her for the sight of the smiling Arab raising a revolver from under his abayah and pointing it directly at her.

But then she was on the floor, and of course the Arab hadn't meant to shoot her, but to shoot David, and as she turned about to look, David stepped on her back, so that she was flat to the ground, and even so she could see the smiling Arab tumbling toward her, his right eye gone, blood dripping through his shattered face. "Now," said David, as if this were the last of a hundred instructions he had given her and she had failed to heed, and in that second she could see that the Englishman was lying on the ground, his face pressed directly to the cobblestones in a way that she imagined must be exceedingly uncomfortable, and the stranger had joined David on the side of their overturned little table, and someone from inside the café was pumping bullets into the street.

"I said go," said David. "Run and get the hell away. Go now!"

She was wondering where the other Arab was, the other man in a scarlet tarboosh that she could perhaps now write a story about that her newspaper editor would publish. But she found herself smarting in pain, and tears came to her eyes as she realized that David had slapped her face, just like in the movies. But no movie had ever explained how loud the explosions of nearby guns were, how weak it made your legs, how stupid it made your every action.

Clumsily she backed away from David and Uri, and trying to run up the steep street, nearly collapsed on knees that wouldn't bend. A child had come out from one of the houses to hold on to the un-tethered white stallion who was rearing his beautiful head at the gunfire. But this she saw as if in a badly remembered dream. What she recognized was not the need for personal safety, but for following the instructions issued to her by David. She must not, she could not, disappoint her lover. It was not a question of being brave or cowardly, of running for her life. None of the sounds, none of the sights, none of the physical events that made her so clumsy, had any reality for her in those first minutes. But her knees understood, her heart understood, and the fear that had prevented her from thinking and acting now came to her aid as it forced her into following the simplest of tasks: she looked at the irregularly paved ground, she followed the twisting uphill street, she ran up and down winding stairs in the suddenly brilliantly sunny day. Fear was her tool, for it prevented her from thinking about the scene she'd left behind, from thinking about what would happen to David, what would happen to her if she was found with the black leather strap still attached to her thigh, where it had held the gun that had killed an out-of-uniform member of His Maj-esty's Armed Forces. Fear put one step after the other, one step at a time. She ran, because fear made her run, and when she'd crossed two streets, run up an alley, and emerged in dazzling daylight at a tiny square jammed with shoppers coming from David Street, fear made her slow down, take a breath, smile with idiotic grace.

She was near the spice market, and now she remembered quite clearly what she was supposed to do: find the Street of the Jews, locate the Johanan Ben-Zakai synagogue in the Jewish quarter. But this memory was no longer backed by a single-minded terror. Once again she was capable of thought, and even in the moment of thinking of the Street of the Jews, she remembered David's emphatic words: "Go now!"

And she couldn't go at all.

It was as if every man, woman, and child in the Old City was descending upon her now, fueled by the powerful fumes from the spice market, foreign and familiar at the same time. She turned around, as if looking for a sign. But there was nothing clear to follow. She was suddenly flushed, and faint, and along with the heady smell of spices came a torrent of phrases in Arabic, Hebrew, Persian, Turk-ish, and behind this wave of sound came a sea of faces, unwashed and dark, scarred and unshaven, leering and bold. She wanted to go to the Jewish quarter, but she couldn't move, she couldn't think; David had told her to go, and she wasn't doing what David had told her to do, and all about her was danger and madness and no way of going home.

"Pardon me, miss, are you by any chance . . . lost?"

An Englishman was looking down at her from what seemed at first like a great distance. She forgot that Englishmen were precisely from whom she was running, for this Englishman was tall and fair and young and he had taken off his pith helmet to smile at her with the full force of his youth. "What?" said Diana, her voice so high-pitched and unnatural that she immediately repeated herself so that he would understand.

"I don't mean to be impertinent," said the Englishman, who was dressed in a freshly pressed uniform of the Palestine police. "But seeing as you have that glazed look, and seeing as you're the prettiest pilgrim I've seen all day, I thought I'd ask you if you were in need of some direction."

"I'm looking for the Jewish quarter," said Diana, trying to sound grateful but coming out harsh and staccato.

"I don't like the British policy any more than you, miss," said the policeman in a stage whisper. "No need to bite my head off. Really."

"I'm sorry."

"You don't have to apologize. Just tell me one thing. If I wasn't a copper, and if you weren't in a bad mood, would I be the sort of man who could buy you a cup of coffee?"

"Yes," said Diana, speaking so mechanically that the policeman began to think she might be crazed, one of those endless emotionally scarred victims of the war. "Please tell me how to find the Jewish quarter," she added with emphatic dullness.

"Let me walk you, miss," said the policeman, and Diana didn't fight this suggestion, as fear had now fully returned to her, blindly channeling her actions. This man could arrest her, could question her, could find the leather strap that had supported the gun, could torture her into a confession of David's actions. This handsome young man was the enemy, and he was taking her along David Street to the Street of the Jews. "One more thing I'll say, miss," he said when they'd reached the street that would take her into the Jewish quarter. "It's not right for all of us to be judged by what the higher-ups do and say, is it, then? I was in the last war, and I've seen some things, and

33

maybe we all have, but one thing I know is that every country has its good and its bad, and I'm not the only Englishman who thinks it rotten that the Jews can't even come to Palestine after all they've been through. If you understand my meaning, miss."

Diana didn't, not at that moment, understand his meaning, but she followed the dictates of fear and feeling and rose up on her toes and kissed the surprised policeman on his cheek and walked off, like an automaton, down the Street of the Jews.

She took no notice of the filth and poverty, the clothing and customs of the ultraorthodox that had hardly changed in two hundred years. One old man recoiled from her when she began to question him in the tourist-book Hebrew that was for him a sacred tongue, but shortly after she'd passed the great Hurva synagogue, a young boy in a black caftan, black hat, and black side-locks directed her to the alley that led to the Johanan Ben-Zakai synagogue. A man in modern clothes—surplus army pants and a green sweater—sprang up from his seat on a nearby railing as she approached. He directed her into the Sephardi synagogue, shouting down the objections of an old man in oriental dress, and took her at once into the Kehal Zion hall, where David had told her to wait for him.

"I ask you nothing," said the man in the green sweater.

Like Diana, he would wait in the room as long as it was necessary. He could have told her of the room's treasure—the drum of olive oil and the ram's horn set on a high window ledge in this basement chapel. A sepulchral light filtered down from where the windows touched the ceiling, as if particular ghostly rays had been chosen to illuminate the bit of floor into which Diana stared. When the Messiah will finally arrive, said the legend of the room, he will blow the ram's horn of the Kehal Zion and use the oil in the drum to kindle the perpetual lamp that will once again hang in the restored Temple of the Jews. But the Haganah man who kept her company had little interest in religious stories, and sensed correctly that Diana would not relish stories about waiting for the Messiah when the man for whom she was waiting would either come very soon or very soon be discovered to be dead.

Later on she would learn that the crazy-quilt elements of the day made sense; that David could have taken an ordinary Palmach girl as his accomplice; that Uri had not counted on any special trouble until just before the meeting, when Haganah intelligence revealed that the red-haired English arms thief had been caught by military intelligence and had prepared a trap to get himself off the hook. But for the moment, nothing that had happened that day made sense. She had woken to love and fear and passion. David had been tender, violent, self-sacrificing. She had felt loved and despised. Diana had seen a man with a gun shoot at her, had seen a dead man with a hole in his head, had participated in murder, had run from men who were trying to kill her lover.

Sitting in the underground chapel, she could make sense of nothing. She wanted David, she wanted him to be safe, she wanted to be safe together with him. This is what she thought of as the fear drained away, only to be replaced by dread. In her mind, he died, he was captured, he escaped and was shot, he died on David Street, he died on the Street of the Jews, he died attacking the Citadel with a torch in one hand, his revolver in the other. He died slowly, all afternoon, as she sat in the fading light of the chapel, until finally the Haganah man spoke again: "Perhaps he is waiting for darkness."

But he wasn't waiting for darkness, for almost at that moment David Stern appeared, whole and hale, not a drop of blood on his sweat-stained clothing, and without a word he pulled her out of her chair and embraced her. She felt the tears on his cheeks, and for a moment she thought he had cried over her, that he had been terrified that she might have been hurt. "Your friend," she said. "Is he all right?"

"Yes," said David Stern, and then he pushed her away and turned his miserable eyes on the Haganah man waiting for him. "There were soldiers in the quarter," he said. "Waiting for us, checking everyone. We got the ones in the café, but we knew they were all around, the soldiers." Diana had never seen him so stricken with grief. This survivor of Auschwitz was openly crying, his eyes wide with desperate pain. She tried to hold him, to offer him solace, but he didn't want her embrace. David sat down in the chair in which Diana had awaited him for hours and looked from her to the Haganah man as if they both would loathe him, as if they would shun him once they had heard his words.

"We had to leave our guns," he said. "Both of us. We dropped them, and we ran, and there was no place to hide them, and they're lost forever. We lost two guns. I'm sorry. I'm so sorry, but we lost them and they're gone."

"David, it's all right," said Diana. "You're alive, that's all that matters." She had no idea how he could be so upset. He was her lover, he was brilliant and strong, and as long as he had life in him, everything was possible. She got on her knees to hold his sobbing head in her hands, talking to him as if he were a child. "It's all right, darling," she said. "You're alive. There will be other guns. I'll get you guns. Don't worry about guns. I'm going to America and I'm going to get you money and guns and anything else you need, and all that matters is that you're alive."

TWO

Two days later, Diana Mann caught the Trans World Airlines Thursday flight back to the United States. Her one-way ticket to La Guardia Field in New York was $607, or approximately twice the amount of money owed her for the half-dozen free-lance stories from Jerusalem her editor had been able to use. She had seen one of her stories—her first, filed three months before, a day after she'd arrived in Palestine—and had been appalled not only at the way her phrases had been truncated but also at how paltry and insignificant her dreams of journalistic glory had become to her. Her parents had sent her the tiny article—"Heat and Hot Tempers in Tel Aviv"—from Los Angeles, enclosing a congratulatory note and asking her if she needed any more money. Dr. and Mrs. Samuel Mann did not write that they missed her terribly or that they wished she'd take the next flight home, though Diana assumed that both of these things were true. It was not her family's style to state the obvious or to try to manipulate one another with an emotional display. Ever since Diana had been told, at the age of eight, that she was an adopted child—her adoptive parents were actually her aunt and uncle—they had attempted to disassociate themselves from any taint of overcompensation. Neither adoptive parent wanted to exhibit overprotectiveness or an excess of love, and in this way they were successful. Diana was loved, but this love wasn't stifling. Diana had access to money and introductions to powerful people, but neither was forced upon her.

Now she would ask for help, as much help as she could get. She would ask, she would plead, she would beg if need be, but somehow, somewhere, her parents would be able to raise the money to buy guns, and more important, have the influence to get them to Palestine.

She had last seen her parents in June, when she had left Los Angeles for New York, en route to Palestine and a chance to break away from the petty social reportage she had been sentenced to in Los Angeles. Even her parents couldn't help her land a job with a byline in New York, city of journalists, and understood her clearly ambitious reasons for traveling nine thousand miles away from them. In Palestine, in chaotic, explosive Jerusalem, her very presence had been a story. For once the fact of her femininity, of her Radcliffe manners and her twenty-five years, had been an asset to gaining a byline: from Jerusalem, Diana Mann had sent home the story of her own survival, and this had been news.

Diana hadn't made it through the maze of familial obstructions and government red tape in New York till late July, arriving in the Holy Land a few days after the famous *Exodus 1947* illegal immigrant ship had finished its wretched voyage to Haifa, and its tragic cargo of "displaced persons" sent back across the Mediterranean. But if she had missed this story, she had found others, and she had written them and filed them and hoped that they would be published. And then she had met David Stern, and suddenly everything she had ever written, everything she had ever desired, seemed small and selfish and without purpose.

The TWA DC-4 took thirty-five hours to get to La Guardia Field in New York City from Lydda Airport in Palestine, only two hours behind schedule. There were seven stopovers: Cairo's Farouk Airport, Hassani Airport in Athens, Rome's Ciampino Airport, Cointrin Airport in Geneva, Orly Field in Paris, Shannon Airport in Ireland, and Gander Field in Newfoundland. From Gander it was only seven hours and forty-five minutes for the plane to be refueled, sent into the air at a climbing rate of twelve hundred feet per minute, flown to New York at 289 miles per hour, and brought down from nine thousand feet to the blessedly smooth runway at La Guardia Field.

While most of the plane's twenty-five passengers—there were

nineteen empty seats when they left Lydda—had tried to focus on the next stopover, the next meal, the next break in the low-level turbulence, the next time the four 1,100-horsepower Pratt and Whitney engines would be stilled, Diana dreamed of David. Flying through space in a little insulated shell, stepping out for brief moments on the foreign soil of seven nations, catered to by two stewardesses who were also registered nurses, urged by a fellow passenger to chew the gum he kept pressing into her hands to counteract the pressure in her ears, Diana felt like a disembodied spirit, a shadow floating over her body, watching her take her meals, engage in loud superficial talk over the roar of the engines, sleep. But it was as if her mind never slept, not for a moment. There was an urgency to discover something, to unravel a piece of convoluted memory that would rest her unquiet soul. For all its noise and wild shaking through the sky, the airplane was safe. From the moment she'd boarded the plane in Palestine, Diana had been welcomed back to the world of her parents: for $607 and an American passport she had been transported from David's dangerous world to one of comfort and ease. She was not a Jew in British-run Jerusalem, she was an American with money in an American world. It was not David she was trying to remember; he was never long out of her mind. It was some part of her past that was not safe, that was not of a piece with the world of Dr. and Mrs. Samuel Mann, that would be able to help David. As she passed bleary-eyed through customs in New York, she realized that what David had asked of her, what she had promised to accomplish, was not possible from her parents. This was why she was distracted, why her mind would not quit searching for the memory she needed to take hold of.

"Go ahead, walk right past me, beautiful," said Richard Mann, Diana's handsome first cousin. She was struck by the somber black suit he was wearing, so incongruous against her image of him, the dashing young man-about-town with a flower in his buttonhole and an aspiring actress on his arm.

"I'm sorry," said Diana, suddenly remembering for the first time in thirty-five hours why she had to visit New York at this time. Her grandmother, her father's mother, Lydia Mann, had suffered her third heart attack and wanted very much to see her favorite grandchild one more time. "I didn't see you. How is she? You're in black. I didn't make it, did I?"

"The funeral was yesterday," he said, taking her arm. A uniformed chauffeur took charge of her baggage, and for a moment the shock of her grandmother being dead and buried, the sense of being dragged back fully into the events of her family and the orderly life it presented, diverted her attention. She made no parallels between the sixteen-cylinder Cadillac town car driving her into a perfect November day in Manhattan and the ancient Jewish taxis that skirted the Arab neighborhoods and British checkpoints on the way to Jerusalem; she thought nothing of the porter who ran out to assist the chauffeur in front of the Waldorf, where Richard had reserved her a suite. Fresh roses were arranged in a silver vase, a bowl of fruit from Florida and rich cheeses from impoverished Europe awaited her pleasure, and she hardly noticed; flowers, champagne, a peerless city view from a Waldorf Towers suite—these were ordinary, part of the background she never questioned about her life.

"Medicinal," said Richard, pouring her some champagne.

"I don't feel right," said Diana, but she didn't finish her sentence. The bubbles settled her stomach, and the familiar taste of the wine sent a glow of pleasure through her.

"You've lost weight."

"Food's rationed there," said Diana, but she put up her hands to stop all talk about Palestine. She wanted to know about her grandmother, how she had died, had there been pain, who had been with her.

"You don't want to know about it," said Richard with what he seemed to feel was manly restraint.

"How's your father taking it?"

"No problem. He's got a heart of ice from all those years at the shop." Diana's Uncle Stephen, her father's older brother, was the only sibling who'd chosen to go into the Mann family's investment-banking concern; this "shop" had been a Wall Street power for four generations. "Your father said it was all for the good," continued Richard. "The body shouldn't be made to suffer life any longer than practical, and all that rot—you know your saintly father."

"Hey, I'm just off the plane, darling," said Diana.

"Have some more champagne."

"Aren't they in mourning—sitting *shiva*?" said Diana, drinking her second glass of wine.

"After the funeral they went back to the apartment and partook of a

40

sumptuous buffet. Mrs. Stephen Mann wore a black Dior, and Mr. Stephen Mann had snipped off the bottom half of his tie in deference to ancient Hebraic custom. There were one hundred guests, dressed in drab colors, but whose appetites had been whetted by the windy conditions at the cemetery. There was a brief panic when the Scotch salmon ran out, until a maid returned, flushed from her trek to Columbus Avenue, with four more pounds of delectable fish."

"Richard, you're impossible."

"I want to write a gossip column. Everyone does something. *You're* a foreign correspondent. *I* want to write gossip!"

"Please be serious for a moment, Richard. Did Grandmother ask for me?"

"Yes. But it's all right. She kept saying she was going to see you in the Holy Land. Not in a superstitious way. She didn't lose her mind or anything. She just said she'd get better and make the trip. Grandmother couldn't get over the fact that you could fly through the air to the Holy Land in thirty-three hours. I think she thought more about that than the fact that you weren't at her bedside. I was there. Your parents were with her a month ago but couldn't come back for the funeral. I spoke to your father on the phone. He sounds okay. But there's no *shiva*. No real seven-days-of-mourning-and-let's-cover-the-mirrors-and-sit-on-the-floor *shiva*. There was a buffet after the funeral, and like I said, my dad ripped off the bottom half of his tie." Richard looked up at her, pouring a bit more champagne into both their glasses. "It wasn't necessary for you to make this trip," he said. "You don't get to see Grandmother, and you can't even find anyone here collapsed in tears."

But there were tears in his eyes now, whether of anger or of sorrow she couldn't know, but instinctively she reached out for him, and they held each other for a long while, remembering their grandmother. Room service brought up lunch a few minutes later, and then Richard left her: she needed a long nap, and a bath, and a chance to be alone. That evening his parents were having a small dinner for her; it would be her best chance to express her grief to Richard's father.

Just before Richard picked her up that evening, her call to Los Angeles came through. She heard her father's deep, intelligently paced voice through the bad connection:

"Welcome back, sweetheart," he said. "I hope you're not taking it too bad. Grandmother was very old."

"How are you?"

"You know me," said Dr. Mann. "I'm resigned to certain inevitabilities."

"I loved her very much."

"So did we all," said Dr. Mann. Her mother was nearby and took the phone from her father. Quickly she asked when Diana was coming to Los Angeles, whether she was flying or going by train, and if she would like anything special prepared for her arrival.

"And, darling," said her mother, adhering to form, "I hope you're not too terribly sad about your grandmother."

"Mother, I'm looking for a contribution to the Haganah," said Diana thoughtlessly. She wanted no more formula words of consolation.

"Well, if that's what you're looking for, dear," said her mother, "we shall certainly be glad to offer our assistance. And, Diana, just between you and me, I couldn't be happier that you're out of that place."

Later that evening Diana heard similar sentiments about her being safely home, away from "that place"—Palestine. Her aunt and uncle seemed to find nothing strange about holding a "small" dinner party for twenty-one people a day after her grandmother had been buried. After all, their darling niece was back from Palestine, and no matter how one mourned, it was still essential to eat.

Diana knew almost everyone at the dinner party: there were former patients of her father, cousins by blood and cousins by marriage, an investment banker who handled her mother's portfolio, a lawyer who invested her father's money in the risky new field of computers. Most were American Jews, and of these, many were descended from German Jewish immigrants who had prospered in the unregulated world of turn-of-the-century banking.

"I want you to meet someone," said her aunt, extricating her from Richard and bringing her across the enormous living room to a former classmate of his at Harvard. "I'd like you to meet Russell Glazer," she said when she'd brought her niece up to a blond young man with a military mustache and a banker's suit of clothes. "He's with the State Department."

"I hear," said Russell Glazer to Diana, as her aunt sidled off, "you're just back from Palestine." But Russell had little interest in hearing about her three months there; his comment had been an introduction to a speech about his role in creating American policy toward Hungary. "I understand you were at Radcliffe," he said, by way of introducing his career at Harvard. "You're from Los Angeles," he continued, by way of introducing his six-month saga in San Diego before leaving for glory in the Pacific.

"May I say something?" said Diana finally.

"Please," said Russell, convinced that his charm and intelligence were so far above the norm that no woman, save for a stray movie star or the wife of a rising senator, could help but fall in love with him. All he had to do was talk, to exhibit for two minutes that his beautiful clothing was a reflection of his mind, that his posture was no straighter than his moral sensibilities, that the wealth and position he so obviously enjoyed could not have been conferred on a more worthy soul.

"Why is the State Department so pro-Arab?"

"I beg your pardon, Miss Mann," said Russell Glazer, looking as if he had been slapped. "That doesn't sound like a question. A question might be, 'Do you think that State is pro-Arab?' That I could answer. But you're making an assertion. Besides, I deal with Hungarian issues."

"Do you?" said Diana, and seeing that he didn't understand, continued: " . . . find that State is pro-Arab?"

"Well, that's a very difficult question to answer. Not intrinsically pro-Arab, though there are many Arabists at State, some of whom were educated at Beirut and have a great deal of sympathy for Arab nationalist—"

"You're Jewish, aren't you?" said Diana.

"So what? What has that got to do with anything?"

"I thought you might be trying too hard to show you're not pro-Zionist. You're not, are you?"

"No. Not for reasons of being Jewish or not. A matter of policy. American oil interests rest with the Arabs. This has nothing to do with religious issues. I don't hide the fact that I'm Jewish. But neither do I pretend to follow the Zionist line. I don't. The greatest oil reserves in the world are in Arab hands. If America continues to espouse the cause of a Zionist state, we will be defeating our own interests as a country. There are Jews in America who will suffer if we are denied access to Arab oil. It's not a religious issue."

"So what you're saying is that the State Department is pro-Arab because the Arab countries have the oil?"

"Not exactly—"

"And that the issue of the ingathering of the Jews to their homeland is irrelevant to the bigger issues of money and power? And that you, as a Jew, feel no compunction in allowing the destruction of the remnant of the Jews in Europe?"

"No one's destroying them," said Russell. "The British have put the illegals in camps. That's unfortunate, but it's the rules of civilization. You can't just get up and go wherever you want, without money or a visa or permission of some kind. Look, you seem a little upset, can I get you a drink?"

"Go away."

"Miss Mann, please. I think you're overreacting to some statements I made without any special attention to detail—"

"To emotion," said Diana.

"I beg your pardon?" He followed her three steps closer to where the vast room's windows overlooked the dark expanse of Central Park and the framing vista of Fifth Avenue's party-lighted towers. "Miss Mann, if you'll only give me a moment. It's never a good idea to discuss religion or politics upon first meeting someone, and I certainly seem to have put my foot in it. I haven't read your articles, I have no idea what your political stance is, and as you asked me a question, I simply answered it before. The truth is, I feel very badly for the Jews over there. I am against partition, not only because if partition takes place the Arabs will blame the United States, but because the Jews over there can't possibly defend themselves once the British get out. Now, does that make me such a monster?"

Diana's aunt took that moment to intervene. "How are we getting on here? I hope you're not telling Diana any of your Hungarian jokes—she's much too serious for that!"

"We've been getting on famously," said Russell. "Harvard and Radcliffe, after all."

"Actually," said Diana, "Russell was trying to whitewash the State Department's anti-Semitic foreign policy, and at the same time tell me that I was overreacting. And I didn't even spill a drink down his shirt. I don't think I want to stay for dinner."

"I hope you'll ignore her, Russell," said Mrs. Mann. "She is not only staying for dinner, but sitting on your right. As for you, Diana, stop biting everyone's head off." Even without dwelling on the circumstances of her niece's birth, there were many reasons to forgive

Diana her rudeness. She was the adopted daughter of a man who had wanted a son, and of a woman who had wanted a child as quietly dedicated to the status quo as she. Besides, Mrs. Mann thought, all of Diana's roughness and anger could be blamed on her natural father's contribution to her makeup.

Before Diana could decide whether or not to run out and retreat to the Waldorf, dinner was served. Her aunt took hold of her elbow and steered her to the dining room. "Do you know I actually thought you were going to like Russell," she said.

"I can't stand him."

"Please, Diana. We're not on the battlefield. I know you're tough, you don't have to knock me down." Her aunt refrained from saying more on this subject; she simply looked down to Diana's high-heeled shoes, shaking her head at the needless two inches added to the girl's too-tall frame. Diana was beautiful, after a fashion, but it was not a fashion that Mrs. Mann found appealing, and she wondered how many men, home from years of war and deprivation, would be anxious to take on so angry a woman. Still, Russell Glazer seemed smitten. Even if what he truly desired was a little blond girl, a diminutive version of himself who would quietly adore him, this black-haired, green-eyed career woman had fascinated him. "And it's not necessary to look so superior. All the people here tonight are going to be pledging money to the Jewish community in Palestine. We're going to build a new hospital in your grandmother's name."

She caught her cousin Richard's eye across the table, and they shared a weak smile. It was not a traditional way of mourning the dead, but both knew that their grandmother would have applauded the rich dinner table, the well-dressed men and women, the raising of funds that would support her people and honor her memory. So Diana quieted, stopped herself from interrupting the political arguments running all about her. She thought of David, in need of guns, of money, of medicine. At least tonight she would do nothing to sabotage the good feelings of potential donors. There was no need to be rude to these people, to tell Russell Glazer that she'd carried a gun under her skirt for a man a hundred times better than he. That was not the way to aid her people. If she could sugar-coat her desires for the other dinner guests, tell them how the sight of blood and misery brought her to tears, how the fact of the holocaust of the Jews of Europe had reoriented her life, how she could not bring herself to reap the benefits of marriage and motherhood while Jews were being starved and murdered, even Russell would understand: Lovely Diana was driven to Zionism by her woman's soft heart.

Still, it was difficult to carry out her resolve of silence. Sitting next to Russell at the rich table, listening to poignant talk of the squalor of the Jewish D.P. camps in Europe, their miserable inhabitants denied entrance to Eretz-Israel by the British, unwanted elsewhere, Diana felt cheapened by inaction. She knew how her parents loved to talk about the poor and the dispossessed, even while praying that Jews without money or with accents would stay away from American shores. For all the tears collected in the bosom of Beverly Hills over the facts of gas chambers and crematoria, Diana had never felt any involvement in the torrent of words and donations.

"You'd best be careful, General," Russell was saying to the retired Army career officer across the table. "We have a fiery defender of partition sitting right next to me."

But Diana didn't have to rise to defend the right of the Jews to have their state. A woman every bit as pretty and sedate as her own mother burst into a tirade of indignation that was as informed as it was emotional: ever since the Biltmore Resolution of 1942, the British had quashed the hopes of the Jewish people. The resolution had called for the unrestricted immigration of Jews to Palestine, as well as the establishment of a Jewish commonwealth within the territory of Palestine. But the British had reneged on resolutions and promises and guarantees. The only reason that a Jewish state needed to be created at all, insisted the angry society woman, was that Jewish immigration was being denied, that the survivors of the concentration camps were left to rot in miserable D.P. camps.

"I am a Jew," said the retired general, "but the Jews have no business in the Middle East, and the British have a responsibility to the Arabs."

"You're no Jew," said the society woman.

"If it's Jews who blow up the King David Hotel, then I'm no Jew, okay?" said the general.

"Then you're right," said the little woman. "You are no Jew."

"I think it would make more sense," said Russell Glazer, "to think about what our response should be if partition does take place, which seems likely, if not definite." He turned slightly to Diana, so that she could better examine his erudite look. "I'm not attempting to foster a particular political opinion, though as many of you know, I am opposed to the plan of the United Nations Special Committee on Palestine. But if the General Assembly approves the plan, there will be war, blood will be shed, and lives will be lost, and we must be prepared for this."

This proved to be the opening that Diana's uncle had been waiting for. He stood up abruptly and began to drone on about the urgent necessity for a hospital to be built in memory of his mother. But his own son, Richard, interrupted him.

"The Jews over there can't defend themselves without weapons," he said, "and the British confiscate every gun the Haganah has."

"There are sound reasons of law for those confiscations," said the general.

A well-known financier at Richard's right hand asked what the point of raising money was if whatever good it bought was confiscated or destroyed.

"They need guns," said Diana.

Stephen Mann tried to bring the table to order, to try to recreate the graceful moment after a satisfying meal so conducive to the raising of funds. Richard interrupted him again, rudely: "Everyone here is going to be pledging money to the hospital. There's nothing wrong with letting them talk."

"We should give money to the Irgun," said the financier. "They don't let their weapons get confiscated."

"You see," said the general. "A terrorist sympathizer."

"My nephew was murdered in March by a terrorist, on a kibbutz that had no weapons because the British had confiscated them. He was probably killed by a gun that had been paid for by Jews and confiscated by the British to turn over to the Arabs."

"It's very simple," said the sedate society woman. "You either stay on your knees or you fight. The only thing we can fight with is our money—at least for the moment."

"They need guns," said Diana for the second time.

"Diana's just back from Palestine," said her aunt.

"It's one thing to be back from Palestine," said the general. "It's another thing to understand the realities of war."

"It's very simple," said Diana. "The Jews in Eretz-Israel must rely on themselves for protection. Once there is a state, they can buy weapons legally, they can arm their citizens in the open, their defense force will not have to practice in deserted schoolrooms armed with wooden rifles. But until partition, until the British leave, the Jews over there can die. They can lose. They can be murdered while the British look the other way, because Palestine is surrounded by Arab countries that have legal arms, and because the British do nothing about restricting the entry of armed Arabs into Palestine. They need guns. Now."

"You are advocating a total breakdown of law," said the general. He began to explain to her, and the table at large, the reason why sovereign nations—the Arab countries bordering Palestine—could and should be allowed to arm themselves, while any misguided arming of the Jews under British rule was a direct flouting of the Mandate set up for their own protection.

Diana looked down at the bowl of orange sherbet placed before her, trying not to say or do anything that would jeopardize the task she had promised to accomplish for David Stern. A professor of anthropology was trying to steal the general's thunder with a detailed explanation of why Guatemala and Peru had come out in favor of partition, while her uncle was trying to get the attention of the whole table without any success at all.

"Take me out of here, Russell," she said impulsively.

"Do you mean now? In the midst of all this sound and fury?"

"I want to go to a jazz club, and I'd like you to take me."

"A jazz club? Why on earth would you—?"

Diana stood up and put her hand on his arm. "I need an escort, and if you're not willing, I'll ask someone else."

"I'm willing, I'm willing," he said, not comprehending either her anger or her impatience. It took them another twenty minutes to make extremely awkward good-byes, saved only by her aunt's glad surprise at Diana's leaving with Russell Glazer.

"So you like jazz?" he said when they were alone in the cab lurching its way through light Central Park West traffic. He seemed to have twisted his face into a simpleton's mask, as if this would please the girl who had shown such waning interest in the violent discussion about the Jewish state.

"It's not that I like jazz, Russell," she said. "There's a club I've read about, and I want to go. King's—do you know it?"

"No," said Russell, not questioning her when she gave the cabdriver the address when they were already halfway to a club he knew on West Fifty-second Street.

"I hope you don't mind taking me. But I had no choice. I really wanted to go to this place, and there's no way I can go alone."

"That's not very flattering to me," said Russell. "I was hoping you had somehow succumbed to my fatal charm."

Diana had been incensed a few months earlier upon learning about a bill before the state legislature forbidding women without male escort to enter a bar or club or restaurant after ten P.M. Certainly most clubs already barred entry to single women or to women in pairs, and well before the ten-o'clock mark; but the notion that the state would consider institutionalizing the idea that women alone at night were prostitutes plying their trade was infuriating.

"I'm more interested in what you had to say about the General Assembly. Do you honestly think they're going to approve the Special Committee's recommendations?"

Hardly two months before, the committee had recommended an end to the British mandate in Palestine and the granting of independence for a new state or states based on democratic lines. Their easy recommendations had been for inarguable items like access to all holy places for religious pilgrims of any creed. But the General Assembly still had to deal with the 250,000 Jewish "displaced persons" in Europe, and the structure of a new state—or if partition would take place, two new states.

"The General Assembly will approve," said Russell. "And there are going to be two separate states, and the day the British leave, there's going to be war, all-out war."

"How can you be so sure?" said Diana. Now that they were almost at their destination, she felt somehow calmer. King's was a place she had long heard about, but the idea of her going there was exactly the elusive bit of memory she hadn't been able to dredge up before. The part of memory that was not safe.

"The State Department's been wrong before," said Russell. "But my family is very active in agitating for partition. They're just as mad at me as you are."

"It's your family that's made you sure there's going to be war?"

"Ben-Gurion met with my father the last time he was in New York. Almost a year ago. And Ben-Gurion knew then. And last month—don't print this in your newspaper, please—this very nice British-educated fellow, Eban his name is, he met with Azzan Pasha. In London. Just a few weeks ago. On the fourteenth of October. Anyway, they tried for a compromise, Eban, that is, and his people, but

49

Azzan Pasha said a peaceful compromise was impossible. If he made any compromises with the Zionists, he'd be dead in minutes. His own people would do him in. Everyone in the Jewish Agency seems to think partition is inevitable, and when it comes, the Egyptians, the Arab Legionnaires, the Syrians, the Iraqis, and the Lebanese are going to walk into the Jewish side of the country and annihilate it."

"They'll try," said Diana, "but they won't succeed."

And then the cab pulled up at King's, on Sixty-seventh Street, a little east of the Third Avenue El. Though quite a few jazz clubs had moved over to the East Side, including a number of the "black-and-tan"—interracial—clubs, few had ventured past Lexington Avenue. The last elevated train line in midtown remained on Third Avenue, and the tenements around this noisy and dirty thoroughfare excited the well-to-do patrons of the city's nightclubs with a sense of foreboding. Russell wondered how the rich girl from Los Angeles, via Palestine, knew about this club, and whether she had any notion what a bad neighborhood they were in.

The taxi fare came to forty cents, and Russell made it easy for Diana to see that he was letting the cabbie keep his cleanly folded dollar. But Diana's attention was not on Russell. She was steeling herself to be able to do what had suddenly occurred to her at the dinner table; she would be doing more than talking now for David Stern's cause.

"Look, once I'm inside, if you want, you don't have to stay," said Diana. Russell looked at her as if she'd really gone crazy.

"You don't suppose I'd leave a lady in a place like this?" he said as a tall man in a cheerful suit, not a uniform, opened their cab door. "You folks here for King's?" he said, and then he stepped with them to a street-level door, marked only with a king's crown above the address, and opened this with a flourish. As they entered, another man took charge of them, looking with pleasure at their well-cut clothes.

"Good evening, and welcome to King's. Have you a reservation?"

Russell reached into his wallet. "Regrettably, my secretary forgot to call, but I'm more than happy to . . . wait." He had taken out a five-dollar bill, far more than the occasion deserved, but even so the man didn't seem about to jump for the bait.

"I'm terribly sorry, sir, but if you haven't reserved, there won't be a table for at least an hour. I could put you both at the bar. It's quite a small club."

Russell took out a ten-dollar bill, and the man seemed genuinely

50

embarrassed for him. Before he could turn this down, Diana interrupted.

"Is Mr. Bernstein in, by any chance?"

"Our Mr. Bernstein?" said the reservations man.

"Marty Bernstein."

"Yes, miss, he is," said the man, looking from her face to Russell's as if for a sign.

"May I see him?"

"Who's Marty Bernstein?" said Russell.

"Who shall I say is asking for him, miss?"

"Diana Mann," she said. "'Diana' by itself may be better."

"Diana by itself," repeated the reservations man nervously. "Please, I'll be a moment." He opened the upholstered door at his back and slipped through, letting out a moment of convoluted sounds: the jagged braying of a horn, the broken laughter of a drunk, the clink and clatter of glasses. "That name is familiar. I know the name Marty Bernstein," said Russell. "How do you happen to know a jazz-club owner?"

The upholstered door was abruptly thrown open from the inside, and a tall man of about fifty came up to Diana, his lips slightly askew. "You the one looking for Marty Bernstein?"

"I'm Diana. Yes."

"What do you mean, 'Diana'? What Diana?"

"Diana Mann. From California. From . . . My parents are Dr. Samuel Mann and Karla Mann. Samuel Mann was Paula Mann's brother."

"What are you telling me?" said Marty Bernstein. He was very angry, inexplicably angry to Russell Glazer, who seemed on the verge of stepping between the man and Diana.

"We neglected to make reservations," said Russell, but only the reservations man paid him any attention. Marty Bernstein took a step closer to Diana and picked up his hands so that they were level with her cheeks. But he didn't touch her.

"Perhaps I should have written," said Diana.

"You even look like him," said Marty Bernstein, and slowly, carefully, as if he were afraid of breaking her skin, he brought his hands to her cheeks and pressed them.

"It was wrong of me not to write," she said, unable to think of anything else to say. She couldn't move, didn't know what sort of embrace to render this man. "It's not just my parents' fault, I don't want you to think that, it was me, I didn't know what to say really. There's really nothing I remember that far back, and I suppose when I was old enough to understand who you were, I mean that it was you who sent those presents, I didn't know what to write back. I'm sorry, Mr. Bernstein."

Marty still held her with his hands; and his eyes, as green as her own, never left her face as he spoke to the reservations man. "Clear the booth in the back," he said.

"Yes, Mr. Bernstein."

"Diana," he said. "You were wrong."

"I know."

"Shut up," said Marty. "It's enough already. We'll start over. It's day number one. We'll celebrate, like it's a birthday, right?"

"I almost didn't come," said Diana. She had begun to cry, and Russell had moved imperceptibly closer to the outside door. He had remembered who Marty Bernstein was, and now the raw edge of brutality that seemed to hover over the man's elegant exterior made sense. "I'm ashamed," said Diana. "I only came because I need help. Help I can't get from anyone else. I only came because I needed help." Marty moved his hands from her cheeks and pulled her into his arms. She'd needed to cry, and he knew that she needed his embrace. But he couldn't stop her from talking, and when she spoke, the words spurred her tears. "I never wanted to have anything to do with you—with him. And it didn't bother me, not so much, not all that much anyway. It was a whim to come here, do you understand? I didn't know it would be important. I didn't know anything."

"Louie was like that," he said.

"Like what? Tell me."

"I'll tell you," said Marty. And then he took her inside, and Russell Glazer followed them, much against his will, hoping to be dismissed. There were two dozen tiny tables, and a five-piece band, and every man on his feet seemed to be big and broad and threatening. It was smoky. The music seemed to be blowing through the smoke and the noise like a dangerous specter. Russell felt the rhythm rise up from the floor beneath him, sending fear into his knees. He heard Diana explain who he was to Marty Bernstein: a friend of the family.

"Not your fiancé, right?" Bernstein looked at Russell suddenly, just as he was about to join them in the quiet booth in the back of the club.

"I'm terribly sorry to have to ask you this, Mr. Glazer," said Marty Bernstein, but his eyes were anything but sorry. "I know this will seem incredibly rude, and I hope I can make it up to you by having you come by as my guest whenever you like. And you may stay tonight, for that matter, at the bar, or a table . . . or anywhere you like."

"Of course," said Russell, though he had not yet been asked to leave. He stood up a bit straighter, as if by slouching, Marty Bernstein might imagine him anxious to sit down.

"We—Diana and I—haven't actually seen each other in years. In twenty-two years. You see . . . My brother . . . Maybe it's not necessary to go into all this," he said, and Russell wished he could sink at once into the earth or vanish quickly through the low ceiling above him. Marty Bernstein had tears in his eyes, had tears as evident as Diana's, and rather than make him seem any more weak or vulnerable or human, it only lent a leavening of pure madness to the threat of violence about his every gesture.

"Russell," said Diana. "My parents died when I was three years old. I was adopted by my mother's brother and his wife. I don't remember my real mother or real father, but this man is my real father's brother, and I've never seen him, not since I was an infant, and I'm very sorry, but I have to be alone with him. Let me call you tomorrow, and I hope you'll forgive me, but this is my uncle, this is my Uncle Marty, and I have to get to know him."

They didn't watch Russell leave, but if they had, they would've seen him walk out with firm steps, erect posture, and a red face. The doorman insisted on finding him a cab, which he did with alacrity and considerable grace. Russell gave the driver his address on Sutton Place and shut his eyes. Diana Mann had been somewhat incoherent, and perhaps he had been too flustered to think clearly about what she and Marty Bernstein had said. But this much was clear: Diana Mann was related by blood to Marty Bernstein, and Marty Bernstein was the most famous unconvicted criminal in the United States.

THREE

In the spring of 1849, Aaron Mann left Cologne, Germany, for the United States. He had studied philosophy, and scandalized his merchant family by practicing revolutionary politics. In America, however, he forsook revolution for dry goods. Within a decade he had opened one of the first department stores in New York, and ten years after that, Aaron Mann was rich enough to open a bank to service the enterprising class of new immigrants. His son steered the family fortune into investment banking. Aaron Mann's great-grandchildren, Stephen, Samuel, and Paula, all born near the turn of the century, grew up with the advantages and disadvantages common to great wealth. Stephen followed his father into the "shop," the all-consuming firm that was the fountain of their wealth. Samuel studied medicine; he wanted to be a surgeon so that he could make his mark in the world without having to thank either his father or brother. Paula took a more traditional way to rebel: she refused to go to college, drank herself insensate, and drove her way from accident to accident with reckless abandon. Though beautiful and rich, she frightened away fortune hunters as well as the scions of the German-Jewish banking community pushed on her by parents and brothers.

But she didn't frighten Louis Bernstein, thirty years old in 1920, three of those years having been spent in Sing Sing for armed robbery, and the last seven of them spent organizing gambling clubs in New York and Chicago. Louis Bernstein thought of his clubs as legitimate, because he had policemen, district attorneys, and judges on his payroll.

"Everyone came to the Keno and the Private Life," said Marty Bernstein, twenty-seven years after the fact. "The mayor, the chief of police, railroad tycoons, movie stars, the works. And your mother. Paula Mann. Louis was so impressed. Hell, I was impressed. Don't get me wrong. We weren't mugs, you understand. Louie was a reader, and I even made a year of college—he forced me. But the point is—Paula Mann. I'm talking about white gloves and that debutante's voice. You don't have what she had, honey. I mean, sweetheart, you're gorgeous and all that, but you're a modern woman. She was old-fashioned, a crazy old-fashioned heartbreaker whose voice could melt you to a puddle."

Marty Bernstein had been a boy of seventeen when Paula Mann had eloped with Louie Bernstein six days after they'd first met. Sitting with his newly discovered niece in a brightly sunlit restaurant on West Ninth Street in Greenwich Village, he looked older than his forty-four years. He had all his hair, and very handsome teeth, but what had aged him in Diana's eyes was the weariness in his eyes, a fatigue that ran through all his reminiscences, all his joy at seeing his dead brother's child.

They had the $1.25 table-d'hote luncheon: fried chicken, soup, and salad, and though the food was wonderful, the dishes and silverware of fine quality, the service attentive and competent, Marty never quit apologizing for the inferior luncheon. "But I wanted to go somewhere where they wouldn't know me," he said.

"This place is fine, Marty."

"Call me 'Uncle Marty.'"

"Okay. Uncle Marty." Diana let the pause run on to alert him of her seriousness. Last night he had filled her with stories, memories, dreams. Today she would have to ask him for help. Diana felt cheap, no matter how worthy her cause. She hardly knew this man, her father's brother who had bounced her on his knee when she was an infant, but who had since then been kept out of her life by solicitous adoptive parents. Marty was ready, eager, willing to help with anything. But she felt his love for her unearned, his respect for her education and profession misguided. Diana wanted to beg him to forgive her for not having the decency—the curiosity—to look him up in all the years she'd been out from under her parents' influence; she wanted him to gather up the raw facts of her indifference and throw them in her face. But Marty had castigated her enough, and then only for a moment, the night before. That was over. Diana hesitated so long that her request finally emerged like a demand, clumsy and insistent.

"I need guns," she said.

"What?" said Marty, his smile freezing on his face. "You didn't say *guns*, did you?"

She felt David's presence behind her now, urging her to slow down, tell him the story, explain who and what the Haganah was; but Diana was clumsy under the steady glare of her uncle.

"If you're in some kind of trouble, honey, you just tell me. You don't need guns, then, you need some help from me. But what? Go on. Tell me, I'm listening. Why did you say you needed guns?"

"Last night," she tried again. "When I said I needed help—"

"And I said you'd get any help you wanted, you're Louie's daughter," said Marty.

"I think it can't just be for that," said Diana. "I have to try to make you understand why I feel the way I do about . . ."

"Just say it, sweetheart. I'm not going to bite your head off. Tell me what you want."

"It's about Palestine," said Diana. "The political situation."

Marty stopped her, punctuating the air with his cigar. "You know why my place is called King's?" he said.

"You told me last night—that you named it after my father."

"But your father's name was Louie Bernstein. He got to be called King because of what he did, not what he was born with. Once Louie won ten thousand bucks in one night—this is no lie, Diana—ten thousand bucks. It meant more in those days, before you were born. Anyway, the guy he won it from was a gangster. Not like Louie, because Louie was smart, he made friends, he covered his bets wherever he went. Anyway, this guy wasn't so smart. He was playing with money that didn't belong to him. He tells Louie to go double or nothing on one roll. Only the guy has no money. Louie refuses. The guy tells Louie all the favors he can do for him if Louie only rolls one more time. Louie says no, the guy's got no collateral. Finally the guy pulls a gun on Louie and tells him that he can't have the cash—the guys he works for are going to kill him if he doesn't show up with the money they gave him to carry. Louie says to shoot, he won't give him the money. The guy hesitates, and then Louie grabs his gun, breaks his nose—he was tough, your father, when he had to be. Anyway, he tells the guy to ask him what he wants. The guy's got a broken nose, figures he's going to be shot, either by Louie or by the guys whose money he's lost, and so he says he wants Louie to shoot him. Louie says just tell him what he wants, just speak it out. So the guy says, finally, I'm going to die if they don't get their money. Let me keep it. Louie says he understands—and he throws him the suitcase full of money he'd just lost. Ten thousand bucks. Everyone heard that story. He was called King by some people before that, but after that, everyone called him that. Even me. King. You're the King's daughter. You want something, ask for it straight."

"I promised the Haganah I'd try to get some guns into Palestine. It's illegal. The British can shoot you for it. I'm asking you to help me get the guns and advise me how to smuggle them out of the U.S. and into Palestine."

"Okay, Diana. Now I know what you want," said Marty Bernstein. "You want to help the Jews over there. Now tell me why."

Diana told him what she had learned during the three months she'd lived in British-ruled Palestine: how the Jews wanted a Jewish state and the Arabs an Arab one; how the British refused to believe that they would one day be pulling out of this strategically placed bit of earth, gateway both to Iraq's rich oilfields and the northern approaches to the Suez Canal. She had learned about Jewish nationalism, how the Jewish demand for statehood had been dramatically strengthened by the British refusal to accept the mass immigration of Jews to what had been perceived for two thousand years as the Jewish homeland.

Diana told her uncle about Arab nationalism too: the British had drawn lines on many maps, in many places in the world; the bogus "nations" that she'd created with a pencil, serving up great expanses of desert to sheikhs who had promised to return the favor of a kingdom for one of loyalty to the aspirations of the British crown, rested on foundations of sand. The original mandate over the land of Palestine—given the British by the League of Nations not as a fiefdom but as an obligation to bring governmental order to a troubled country—was arbitrarily whittled down to a third of its original size by the cutting away of the emirate of Transjordan. All the land east of the Jordan River that had been part of the original mandate of Palestine was lopped off, not because of any nationalist sentiment, but because the British wanted to repay the favors of the Hashemite family with a British-controlled kingdom. Transjordan was created, and with it, Transjordanians, even if their new king, the second son of Hussein, was new to the territory, an outsider in his own country. As much as Transjordan was a fabricated country with a puppet king with no other connections to the masses he ruled than a common religion and language, the nationalism of the Palestinian Arabs was fabricated, a reaction to a Jewish nationalism overwhelming the land on which they lived. Arab nationalism meant freedom from British rule, from domination by all the big Western powers wanting control of their oil. But the idea of a separate people, a "Palestinian" Arab, as opposed to a "Transjordanian" Arab, had no meaning for Diana, even after three months in the Holy Land. There was passion in the Arab masses, a desire for justice and for right treatment. But the concepts of national boundaries, of states forged out of the great wastes of Arabia, were the province of cynical leaders, rich and powerful Arab families who fostered the notion of separate nations where before there were only Arab peoples as a means to personal power.

"Let me tell you something, sweetheart," said Marty Bernstein. "That's all very interesting, and maybe I understand some of it, or even most of it, but that's not the *spiel* you're going to use when you want to go out and get guns."

"I was trying to explain why I'm so involved—"

"Hey. You're Jewish. They're killing Jews, right?" said Marty Bernstein.

"Right," said Diana.

"So what else do you got to say, sweetheart?" Marty smiled. "The Jews are going to get a fighting chance to get their part of Palestine when the British walk out, and you want my help to get them some guns."

"Yes. Until they're a state, it's not legal—"

"It's not legal, but it's right," said Marty Bernstein. "This isn't the only case of that in the world. Remember that."

"Okay, Uncle Marty." It was that simple. He was going to help.

"I don't want you involved in anything dangerous."

"Okay, but do you think you can help?"

Marty Bernstein looked at his niece from behind his cigar. "Sweetheart, if you want guns that aren't legal, you've come to the right place."

Marty Bernstein hadn't survived in the New York world of gambling and nightclubs simply on the strength of his departed brother's name. He always had an idea of what he wanted, in a relationship, in a deal, and he drove a hard bargain. If Diana wanted his help, she would get it, but only if she played by his rules.

"I'll do anything you say, Marty—Uncle Marty."

"Don't give me a promise like that. What if I wanted you to deliver a package to somebody in Marseilles on the way over there—maybe there's narcotics in there. Be careful what you say, what you promise."

"I know you wouldn't ask me to do anything that would get me in trouble."

"You're right. But you might not like my ideas to see that you keep out of trouble."

"I'll be happy to listen—"

"No. Not listen. You're going to do it, Diana, or there's no deal. Come on. Let's go meet Joey Marino."

They were driven up from the Village by one of Marty's elegantly dressed bodyguards, who drove his boss's Packard 12 with great attention to the ruts and the holes in the badly paved streets. "My first rule is that you tell none of this to your parents—you know who I mean when I say parents?"

"Yes. But, Marty . . . I was hoping to get some money from them."

"For guns? Sweetheart, you're not thinking. They may be rich, and they may even care about the Jews in Palestine, but they're not going to put money into something that's not an organized charity."

"But those guns—rifles, machine guns, pistols, grenades, all that ammunition—"

"Millions of dollars maybe. Or at least one million if you do it right. I mean, I can't send you to Las Vegas and have you come back empty-handed."

"What do you mean, Las Vegas?"

"I'd like you to go to Las Vegas to meet some guys. They owe me, and they owe your father—even after twenty years, they owe King." The Packard arrived at King's, but this time, no doorman rushed to their car. They waited for the bodyguard to come around from the driver's seat and open their door. "My second rule is that you go to Las Vegas with Joey Marino."

"Why do I have to go with anyone?"

"Because otherwise I won't help you, sweetheart," said her uncle. They walked into the club, standing quietly in the hallway before the main room while a singer finished her audition. From where they stood they couldn't see the girl who was singing, but only the dimly lit room she faced, so different in appearance from the night before. The two dozen tables were pushed into one corner, and a lone worker mopped the floor. Cigarette smoke drifted into the dreamy edge of the stagelight, coming from a man in shirtsleeves sitting a few feet from the stage. The singer's voice had a ghostly quality, touched with a sadness that faded in the high notes. Her accompanist on the tinny piano played badly, but Diana was touched by her song of loss, of a lover that returned from his war intact in body but without his spirit.

"It's beautiful," she whispered to her uncle.

"It's like my living room," he said. "Comfortable. That's the only reason I run it. A comfortable place so I can explain how I make a living."

The singer finished, and before Diana and her uncle could cross into the room and clap their hands, they saw the man in shirtsleeves stand up and pull the singer off the stage, so that they could see her— a pale young woman in black sweater and black pants. The singer's face was empty of emotion as it caught the light; as if the singing had drained her of love and desire. But the man in shirtsleeves didn't seem to notice this. He took her in his arms and kissed her passionately, pulling his head away only to laugh.

"Baby, you taste like a dead fish," said Joey Marino.

"Hey, I was singing."

"Yeah, I was here, remember?" Joey pulled her closer. "And I want to see a little more excitement in the act."

This time the singer responded, whether with passion or its facsimile, Diana couldn't tell. But the embrace didn't last. Marty Bernstein called out, "Hey, Joey, this is a clean joint we're running here."

Joey let go of the singer, his lips twisted into a broad smile. "Mr. Bernstein, what are you doing here?" he said, using Marty's last name so the singer would know who it was.

"It's my club, right?"

"Sure it is," said Joey, reaching for his suit jacket and slipping it on hurriedly.

"He didn't tell you it was his club, did he, Miss?" said Marty to the singer.

"Oh no, sir. Everyone knows who runs King's."

"I'm just checking. I don't want anybody to take advantage of such a talented singer."

60

"She's good, you like her, eh?" said Joey, very pleased with himself.

"We both like her," said Marty, gesturing to Diana, who had lingered a few steps behind her uncle, but now walked up to the pale circle of reflected stagelight.

"Yes," said Diana, aware at once at the distinctive educated shape of her syllables. "I thought you sang beautifully."

"Hey, that's swell," said the singer, looking up at Joey Marino as if he were indeed a prize, as if perhaps he had sneaked these people into the back of the room just so they might catch her audition too.

"When can you start?" continued Marty, captivating the singer with the sense of his authority. So focused was he on the singer at that moment, and the singer on him, that it was as if the two strangers, Joey Marino and Diana Mann, were alone in the dimly lit room.

"So who are you?" said Joey Marino, smiling at her the way she imagined he smiled at every pretty girl who came his way—girls on the subway, applying for jobs at the club, walking briskly along Fifth Avenue—smiled so that his eyes were winking, so that his face was lit up from inside. It was not so much a lecherous smile as it was friendly. He had black eyes, a cleft chin, black hair that needed cutting, and clothes a trifle too elegant for his young age. There was something about the playboy in him, but this was undercut by the too-long hair, by the inelegant accent. He had the enormous self-confidence of a young and handsome man with money in his pocket; he believed he had seen a good deal of the world and knew something about how it was run. Joey would have been amazed to learn how boyish and innocent he looked to Diana, even after his war duty in the Philippines, even after having grown up in a milieu of gangsters.

"What kind of talk is that?" said Marty. He laughed at Joey, and shook his head at Diana. "'So who are you?'" Marty mimicked. "You think this is a showgirl you're talking to? This is my niece."

"Since when you got a niece?"

"Since last night," said Marty. "A Radcliffe graduate. You ever hear of Radcliffe, Joey?"

"Hey, please, don't make fun of me in front of two such lovely young women," said Joey, looking not at the singer, but only at Diana. "I know Radcliffe. We get Radcliffe girls in here every night with their fancy guys looking around for the criminal element."

"That's what I'm looking for myself," said Diana. "The criminal element."

Marty seemed about to get annoyed with this comment, but stopped himself. "Yeah, that's right, but keep it down," he said to Diana. "The criminal element. Jesus. We spend years trying to get respectable, Joey, and now my Radcliffe niece is here looking for the criminal element."

Under the brighter light of the hotel bar they took her to a few minutes later, Joey Marino was far more attractive than she'd first thought. The black eyes were enormous, the bones of his face dramatic enough for any matinee idol; under the green lamp shade that directed the light over their table, he seemed more like a man on a stage or on a movie set than a stranger just met.

"Okay if I call you 'Diana'?" he asked, looking from Diana to Marty.

"Sure, Joey," she said.

"I mean, if I'm coming on with this 'Miss Mann' this and 'Miss Mann' that, I feel too much like hired help, if you know what I mean. But I guess that's what I am. I mean help—and I was hired." Diana watched as he drank his whiskey in one eager gulp, then licked his lips like a young boy, shivering at the pleasure the liquor brought his body. "Are you a married lady?" he asked.

"No." She was about to tell him about David Stern but had no idea how to mention her lover. Diana hadn't even told Marty about David's existence, for fear he would doubt her motivation for bringing the arms to Palestine.

"You don't look married, Diana," he said. "You're not drinking?" He lifted a finger for the waiter, and when he'd caught the man's attention, he pointed down to his empty whiskey glass. Marty Bernstein frowned at this refill.

It had been Marty's idea that they go out for a drink to get to know each other. All he had told Joey so far was that they would be helping his niece with a "project" that she would explain to him. But because this project was of a sensitive nature, he preferred that Joey leave the singer behind.

As the waiter approached with a second drink for Joey, Marty raised his hand. "He doesn't want that, buddy."

"What do you mean, he don't want it? He just said he wanted it, didn't he?" said the waiter. Joey looked up at the waiter in astonishment. It was perfectly all right for Marty to contradict Joey, but for a *waiter* to contradict *Marty*—that was an unbearable affront.

Joey stood up, his hands shaking at his sides. "What're you, crazy?" he said to the waiter. Without thinking, he'd knocked over the man's tray, sending the glass shattering to the floor.

"Hey, look what you done, you jerk," said the waiter, still not understanding what sort of people had wandered up to his station. He started to bend down to pick up the tray, but even as he did so, Joey hit with his right fist into the man's left ear. The waiter fell down, his hands landing on the broken bits of glass from the whiskey he'd been carrying to Joey.

"Leave him alone," said Diana, because she could see that it was not yet over. Joey bent down and reached for the man's hair, pulling him up at the scalp till the waiter was once again looking directly into Joey's black eyes.

"Who are you calling a jerk?" said Joey.

"I'm sorry, sir," said the waiter.

"I got a lesson for you, jerk," said Joey. "When this man"—he pulled the man's head around so that he would be looking at Marty—"when this man says he doesn't want something, you listen to him. Do you understand?"

"Yes, sir."

"And when you call somebody a jerk, you better think twice," said Joey. "Because if they're not a jerk, they may just kill you the next time. Do you understand what I'm telling you, or do you want another lesson?"

"I understand, sir."

Joey let go of the man's hair. The waiter gasped at the release and hurriedly backed away. "Where you going, pal?" said Joey. "Clean up this mess."

The waiter stopped in his tracks. "I'm sorry," he said. He turned around and got back down on the floor to pick up his tray and the broken glass. Diana, who could not stand another moment of the man's humiliation, got out of her chair and got down on the floor next to the waiter and started to help him pick up the glass.

"What're you doing, sweetheart?" said Marty. "You're going to cut yourself."

"This is the man who's supposed to help *me*?" said Diana.

"You want I should stop her, Marty?" said Joey.

"No, of course not," said Marty. "You let her do what she wants. Unless she's going to hurt herself. Otherwise, she's my niece and you let her do what she wants."

"Sure, Marty," said Joey, sitting down again. He picked up his empty whiskey glass and looked at it. "Could I have a ginger ale, Marty?"

"Sure," said Marty. "Have anything you want unless it's liquor. We got important things to discuss, and I want you to be all here, okay?"

But it was difficult to discuss anything once the waiter was sent off and Diana returned to the table. The manager of the hotel bar had finally recognized Marty Bernstein, and every waiter in the place now tried to get close enough to their table to see the famous gangster without getting close enough to disturb him. Diana wanted to explode at her uncle for allowing Joey to behave the way he had, but she held herself back: these were the kind of people who could help her.

"I want to explain it to her, Marty," said Joey. "I don't think she understands."

"You won't be able to explain it," said Marty, but he spread his hands wide, as if to allow Joey all the room he needed.

"You can't let people insult you like that," he began.

"You're crazy," said Diana. "What insult? The man was doing his job. You wanted a whiskey, and he brought it over, and then Marty said you didn't want it, and so naturally he questioned that—"

"No," said Joey. "He can't question Marty Bernstein."

"I'm sure he didn't know it was Marty."

"But now," said Joey triumphantly, "he knows."

"So what? This is all so idiotic—"

"Hey, don't call it idiotic, miss," said Joey. "I work for Marty, and when somebody insults him, contradicts him, doesn't show him respect, I got to react. That's part of my job. We don't have problems in New York, because people respect us. We're trying to get along with everybody, cops, bookies, bar owners, and we get along fine, our business is clean, and this is all because of the fact that we get respect."

"What business?"

"Our business," said Joey. "You know. All kinds. What Marty does. Bars, gambling, like that."

"I don't see," said Diana, "what picking on a poor little man like that waiter does for your respect, Mr. Marino. I was here, and I was able to lose all respect I had for you the moment you first hit him."

"I told you," said Marty. "You can't explain it."

"Hey, Marty," said Joey. "This lady is lucky she's your niece. I really wish you'd tell her that too."

"What is that supposed to mean, Mr. Marino?" said Diana. "That otherwise you'd belt me one?"

"You want I should answer that, Marty?"

"No, Joey," said Marty, and then he turned to his niece and shook his head. "Louie was like that. He could be like a diplomat and at the same time he could just say whatever the hell was on his mind, no matter what the consequences. I thought you wanted to get something accomplished with Joey."

"I want to get something accomplished, Uncle Marty," said Diana. "But I don't want to do it with him."

"You're not going to do it without him."

"Listen," said Diana, leaning forward as if the motion would somehow isolate Joey from the conversation. "I understand that you're trying to help me, and you don't want me to get into any trouble. But I really think I can handle things very well by myself. This man is going to be nothing but trouble, I can see that. He's a hothead. I don't need that. You want me to talk to people, great. I'll go anywhere, I'll talk to anyone, no problem. Just let me do it alone."

"No," said Marty.

"Hey, listen, Marty," said Joey. "If the girl doesn't think it's love at first sight between the two of us, maybe there's somebody else you want to go along with her."

"No," said Marty. "It's got to be you."

"Why does it got to be me? And what's this all about anyway?" said Joey, his voice whining up the scale like a little boy's. "I really don't know what I did that I should get insulted like that, I really don't. She's practically calling me an idiot, did you hear her?"

"Look," said Diana. "Maybe you're not an idiot, but you're not the person I need to go along with to help raise guns and money for the Jewish cause in Palestine."

"The what?" said Joey, smiling now, as if the entire conversation thus far had been part of an elaborate joke.

"You heard her," said Marty. "I'm sending you to Las Vegas, both of you, to see some old friends who might want to help get guns to the Jews over there."

"Marty, they're hoods over there in Vegas—why should they want to help this girl for something like that?"

"Because she's my niece, because she's Louie Bernstein's daughter, and because you're going to go with her and remind everybody of those facts."

"You don't mean the kind of reminder that you give over the telephone? You mean like I should make my point very clear?"

"I don't want a war, Joey," said Marty. "I just want my brother's daughter treated the proper way, you know? When a beautiful woman goes out to a place like that, there's a lot of mugs who can forget themselves. You're going to make sure nobody does."

Diana started to protest again, to point out that as a journalist in Palestine there was no one but herself to look out for her, but they were interrupted by the waiter bringing a ginger ale for Joey, and a moment later, one of Marty's employees hurried up to their table to whisper something in his boss's ear.

"You want to make some money for Palestine?" said Marty to Diana. "Number three in the third, Firebird."

"What's that?" said Diana.

"A horse," said Joey glumly. "And I'm supposed to be dumb."

"Tomorrow, the number three horse is Firebird," said Marty quietly. "And I understand he's going to win."

"How can you be sure?" said Diana.

"This is the girl who wants to go to Las Vegas to talk to the big guys all by herself?" said Joey.

"Wait, I just want to understand," said Diana. "I'm not saying it's right or wrong. If you know it's a sure thing, I'm not going to ask you how, all right? I just want to know how can you be *sure*?"

"Because jockeys," said Joey, "find it kind of tough to ride horses with their legs broken."

"You broke someone's leg?"

"What he means," said Marty, "is that someone must have insisted that Firebird win a race. And the other jockeys understand that it would be a good idea to let that happen tomorrow, because otherwise someone, not Joey, not us—someone else—would be very angry."

"So it's a sure thing," said Diana. "Firebird, number three in the third."

"Nothing's ever sure in a horse race," said Marty. "But this is about as sure as it gets."

"Would you excuse me?" said Diana, standing up quickly, smiling happily. She walked over to where their demoralized waiter sulked, waiting for further peremptory commands. "Hey," she said. "That's Marty Bernstein over there, and he says to tell you that the horse tomorrow is Firebird. Number three in the third race."

Joey couldn't hear her from where they sat, but he and Marty both guessed what she was telling their waiter. "I was going to give him the tip," said Joey.

"Do yourself a favor, Joey," said Marty. "Don't get soft in the head on me."

"You think it would've been wrong?"

"To give the bastard the tip on Firebird? That would've been fine. I'm talking about something else. I'm talking about my niece. She doesn't scare, she's beautiful to look at, and she believes in truth and justice and all the rest of that. Don't go falling in love with her, Joey. She'll turn you to mush."

"There is no way in the world—" began Joey, incensed at the idea that he could fall for someone so insulting, but he stopped himself as Diana approached the table.

"Our waiter thanks you for that tip," said Diana to Marty. "And I want to apologize for what I said before about Mr. Marino—Joey. You made it clear to me under what conditions you'd help me, Uncle Marty, and I accept those conditions."

Diana stuck out her hand across the table to Joey, thinking all the while of David Stern, of how he would approve of her clear thinking. "Friends?" she said.

Joey Marino took her hand. "Yeah," he said, smiling his handsome smile, looking directly into her eyes so that she and Marty would both know that he was unafraid of her, that there was no chance that this Radcliffe girl would bewitch *him*. "You want to be friends, it's fine with me."

"So when do we leave for Las Vegas?" said Diana.

"Tomorrow," said Marty Bernstein. "I'll just need a few hours on the telephone." He shook his head at his lovely niece and then turned in his seat to his favorite employee. "If you think you're through shaking," said Marty, "you can let go of my niece's hand."

"I'm through," said Joey, letting go of Diana. The redness of his handsome face gave Diana one of the most flattering moments of her life.

FOUR

Diana never slept more than six hours at a stretch, and found it difficult to sleep at all on an airplane, whether it was flying over water or land, through calm skies or wild weather. With delays at Chicago, thunderstorms throughout the Midwest, and the incredible spectacle of Joey Marino not once waking for the first fourteen hours of their trip, Diana was in a foul mood. She wondered what kind of man could sleep so long, unless he was a fool; and she worried about his temper, his ignorance, his lack of understanding, until he finally emerged from his sleeping berth, very pale in the face, and asked her how much longer they had to go.

"Three or four hours," said Diana.

"I can't sleep any more," said Joey, sitting down next to her with a sigh of resignation. A steward walked up to them, asking Diana for the fifth time in as many hours if he could get her anything: their DC-6 was flying with only twenty-odd passengers, though it was built to carry fifty.

"Perhaps you'd like to come up front and visit the pilots," said the steward, hanging over the two of them with a beatific smile.

"No, thanks," said Diana. "Maybe you'd like to?" she began to say to Joey, but he was already shaking his head violently, his eyes looking firmly at the newspaper held over his lap.

"You don't happen to have a sleeping pill?" said Joey as the steward walked off. Diana laughed out loud, a short, indignant expulsion of breath. "A sleeping pill? Is that all you do—sleep? You've already slept through one entire day—"

"Forget it," said Joey, interrupting her. "I slept enough."

"I was under the impression that you had a great deal to tell me about the people we're going to be meeting with," said Diana. "Marty seemed to think it important that I know all about them, so I don't make any faux pas, but I guess you were just so tired at the prospect of sitting next to me all those hours that you just couldn't get out of your berth."

"Is it raining?"

"No, I don't think so," said Diana, looking at him quizzically. "What are you reading so intensely?"

"Didn't you feel *that*?" said Joey, still not looking at her. The plane had shuddered slightly as it went through a bit of turbulence, but certainly nothing to be alarmed about. "Just my luck we'll be flying into a storm."

"It's not going to be raining in Nevada," said Diana.

"Maybe not *in*, but it could be raining *over it*," said Joey, and it was then that she noticed how tightly his hands clenched the newspapers in his lap. If his face had the pale look of fatigue, it was not an illusion caused by oversleep, but by the simple fact that he had not slept. He was terrified.

"Hey, it's okay," said Diana. "You've been sleeping. You're not used to the turbulence. It's normal. There's nothing wrong. Believe me, I know. I fly all the time."

"There. Did you feel that?" said Joey. "That thing, like we start to go down and then up in the same second?"

"Sure," said Diana. "That's normal. I promise you it's nothing to be worried about."

"I'm not worried," said Joey hurriedly. "It's just that I'm not used to flying. I hate flying. I been out here a hundred times, and I love the train. I love the meals, the scenery, the people, the chug-chug-chug. I hate flying."

"I thought it would make more sense to fly this time, because of the hurry."

"You don't have to apologize. Marty says fly, we fly. And I wasn't worried before. I mean, if we're going to go down, I'll be the only one on board who won't scream out. Screaming doesn't do a thing. I just wanted to know if we were going to crash or if it was my imagination."

"It was your imagination."

"Sure, good," said Joey. "Look, I don't want to give you the wrong idea about me. I'm supposed to look after you and all that, and you think I'm a little scared of airplanes, it doesn't make me look too good. I don't want you to worry about me. It's the truth that I'm not worried now, but I don't always look too good on planes. Maybe it's got to do with the war. I was in the Philippines. There's plenty of guys who could tell you that I'm not afraid of things, of anything. It's just that being up in the air, this high, it's out of my control, you know what I'm saying? I don't like the feeling, and even if I'm not scared, I don't mind admitting that I'll be happy to be back on the ground where I'm in charge of do I stand up or do I fall down."

"Anything interesting in the paper?"

"What?"

"Joey, look at me," said Diana, and she could see the superhuman effort it took him to move his head away from the newspapers to turn to her. It was as if he held the fate of the airplane's steady progress through the air in the careful way he moved and breathed. "Forget about being in the air. It's out of our hands, right? You said it yourself. Have you eaten anything at all?"

"Oh, no," said Joey, as if the idea was horrifying.

"Perhaps you'd feel a little better if you had something in your stomach?"

"I'd feel better if I knew that none of this would get back to Marty," he said.

"Of course."

"Do you know that once, in the Philippines, all by myself I charged a sniper's hut, without cover, and only a revolver in my hand? I killed four Japs with the one gun. I got a medal. Jesus, I think it was better when I was lying down. Maybe I ought to go back to the sleeping berth."

"Tell me what's in the paper," she tried again. It occurred to her that he might be younger than her own twenty-five years, but she refrained from asking this at such an embarrassing time. "Anything about the UN?"

Now that he was looking at her, he seemed incapable of turning his eyes back to the newspaper. But for the first time since they'd begun talking, she thought he seemed a bit more relaxed and happy, as if he were about to reveal some new strength.

"Nothing about Palestine," he said, "but 'Site Plan Accord Cheers Committee.'"

"What?"

"That's the headline over the story. About getting the UN over to the East River. You want to hear the story?"

"Not especially. I think I've read it."

"So have I," he said, and now he seemed to have genuinely forgotten his fear. He was smiling happily now. Speaking at a steady pace, he said, "Quote: 'The United Nations General Assembly's Committee on Headquarters, approving President Truman's offer of an interest-free construction loan of sixty-five million dollars, voted unanimously yesterday to erect the proposed glass-and-marble structure in midtown Manhattan as a dramatic symbol of permanency.' That's the end of the quote. New York *Times*, November 14, 1947."

"So that's what you've been doing," said Diana with relish, taking the newspaper from his lap. "I thought you were sleeping, while all the time you were memorizing this story."

"I don't memorize," he said. "I mean, not the way you think."

"I don't understand."

"It's true I was looking through those papers, to take my mind off . . . well, being in the air, but I didn't try to remember that story. Not particularly. By tomorrow I'll forget it, unless I make an effort to remember it now. But even without an effort, I remember everything in all those papers that I looked at."

"That's not possible."

"Only because you don't think I'm too bright. No college, and no officer—even though I could've gone to officer school, but I turned them down—and no gentleman from Harvard. But I got this memory. I'm not saying I'm a genius, but I can do something that almost no genius can. It's called total recall."

"I know what it's called," said Diana, looking through the papers on her lap. There were half a dozen issues of the New York *Times*, all of them rumpled and disordered. She came across an item about a scientist of whom she'd never heard. "All right," she said. "Who is Linus Pauling?"

Joey Marino thought for a minute. "Yeah," he said. "Just a second.

Okay. Page 30. Saturday's paper, November 15. Linus Carl Pauling. From Pasadena, California. He won the Royal Society's Davy Medal."

"I don't believe that you can do this."

"Don't you want to know what he won the award for?" Joey shook his head. "You see, you almost had me when you said Linus Pauling instead of Linus Carl Pauling. I mean, it's not a story that I would've seen, much less remembered, if it wasn't for all those hours up in the berth trying to get sleepy. Anyway, he won the award for distinguished contributions to the theory of valency and for their applications to systems of biological importance—whatever that means."

"Does Marty know you can do this?"

"Sure. He relies on me for special information. Stuff in the paper that he never got the chance to think about, I cough back to him once a week. Not like this science stuff. But on the same page, one column over to the left, you see a little headline?"

"'Seven Held as Bookmakers'?"

"Yeah," said Joey. "That's an item for Marty, so I'll remember that for sure. You want to see?" Diana nodded, still scarcely believing him. For a moment she thought he might be able to somehow read the words in front of her, so she cupped her hand over the small print as he quoted: "'Seven men employed as clerks by the Metropolitan Life Insurance Company in its building at Madison Avenue and Twenty-fourth Street were arrested there yesterday by detectives under Deputy Inspector John Ferretti of the Fourth Division on charges of bookmaking. The arrests came after a—'"

"Wait a minute," said Diana. "Stop."

"Did I make a mistake?"

"No. I want to see something. There's an advertisement on the page—"

"Two. For Macy's and RCA Victor."

"Yes. Well, in the RCA Victor advertisement they list records for sale. What's the record by Robert Merrill?"

"Let me think," he said. She watched his eyes blink; though they didn't turn from where they had been looking at her, it seemed as if they were scanning a page brought out of memory and placed before him. "''In the Gloaming." "Drink to Me Only with Thine Eyes." Robert Merrill, baritone, with orchestra. Seventy-nine cents.'"

"Yes," said Diana.

"I remember the Macy's advertisement too."

"I'm beginning to believe it."

"*'Macy's is the friendliest place I've ever worked!* That's what Marion Burger thinks of Macy's—and she's had several other jobs. *I've worked full-time ever since I graduated from Erasmus High a year ago. I like the girls in the Candy Department—it's fun meeting new people all the time—and I like the atmosphere in Macy's.'*"

"I believe you," said Diana. "You have an incredible gift."

"It's great with cards."

"Cards? You mean playing cards? Well, I can see that. But what about medicine, law, business? I mean, with a mind like that—"

"Don't start, baby. I already got a Jewish mother."

"I don't like to be called 'baby.' And if I'm offering you a compliment, I don't see why you get so upset."

"I'm not upset, okay?"

"And why 'Jewish'? Why couldn't an Italian mother be as demanding and supportive—"

"Hey, I said 'Jewish' mother because my mother is Jewish."

"*Your* mother?"

"Mrs. Marino, right. She's Jewish. What the hell was that? Didn't you feel the plane move?"

"Of course I felt the plane move—we're flying, Joey."

It wasn't until they were finally on the ground three hours later that Joey explained about his mother, and shrugged off his photographic memory as something that gave him more trouble from mother, teachers, and Marty than it was worth. A dour-faced Sicilian, who spoke to Joey in that language, picked them up in a brand-new Packard convertible, and Diana was assigned the wind-blown backseat. As they drove the two-lane highway into town, Joey kept turning in his seat to shout at her—pointing out sagebrush, an abandoned brothel, an ancient cowboy roadhouse. But Diana understood that he was less interested in pointing out the scenery than he was in reestablishing his sense of balance. He had been frightened on the plane, and she had not only not ridiculed him but also had tried to help him over his fear. Joey Marino was now, with his booming voice, his expansive courtesy, his eagerness to please, trying to pay her back, at the same time attempting to erase what he felt must be a cowardly impression he'd given her up in the air.

Even with Joey's commentary along the desert road, Diana could see little through the wind and the glare of the Nevada afternoon sun. The Sicilian drove at a maniacal pace, and as he passed old trucks and older cars on the narrow road, Diana shut her eyes against the threat of oncoming traffic and a head-on collision. After the very long flight, the fresh dry air was not as pleasant as she would have imagined: the dust and the wind were irritating, and the November heat was surprisingly intense. Once again she had a sense of her distance from David Stern in Jerusalem, both a physical distance and an emotional distance. She wondered if he thought about her, even if only for a moment. Perhaps he thought about her when he thought about the guns she had promised to get for him, though it was likely that he had little faith in her promise and therefore didn't think of her at all.

Joey and Diana were given adjacent suites at the Flamingo Hotel. The hotel was a famous gambling palace built by the recently murdered Bugsy Siegel in an attempt to make the rough-and-tumble town of Las Vegas into a city of gentlemen and ladies in elegant evening wear, gambling through the night and into the dawn. Every amenity was provided: the best food, the best accommodations, the best entertainment. In the months since his murder in June, the hotel had become even more famous. Hollywood stars rubbed shoulders with visiting South American playboys and the dissolute scions of Northeastern banking families. The men in jeans and cowboy hats looked at this apparition of Italian marble in the midst of their desert with wonder. Already it was known that no brawling, drunken advances to strange ladies, or even general roughhousing and cursing were tolerated by the men who ran the hotel and its casino; and these men, though dressed in elegant business suits, weren't the sort of "dudes" who used to pass through the area and take snapshots of the sunset. They were men who wore guns under their jackets and carried the police and the city's officials in one or another of their big-money pockets.

Even Diana was impressed by the opulence of the hotel. For one thing, it was air-conditioned, that postwar wonder gradually becoming an institution in movie houses and department stores. For another, there was champagne waiting in a bucket of ice, along with a maid ready to unpack her suitcase and draw her bath. A pageboy brought up a message from the desk before she could get into the tub: an invitation to dinner at one of the hotel's private rooms. As the invitation was from Kalman Meyers, she hastily penciled in her ac-

74

ceptance of the invitation for herself and Joey and gave it to the pageboy along with a quarter.

"Oh, no, thank you, Miss Bernstein," said the boy, giving her back the coin.

"My name is Mann, not Bernstein," said Diana, but the boy had already turned around and was making for the door.

"I can't take tips from you, no matter what you call yourself," said the boy. He wasn't happy about this, but he was respectful, as if she were part of some privileged family that he longed to serve.

As Joey Marino elaborated later that day, he was part of that family too. "I mean, my father wasn't the King, like they called your father, but he was part of them. He knew Louie Bernstein, he knew Kalman Meyers, he knew Lucky, he knew Bugsy, he knew Chuck Marandino. My mother, the Jewish mother, right? She wasn't from the Jewish gangsters, so it must have been a real shock for the families, hers and my father's, when they got hitched. But I don't know much about it. My father was murdered when I was a little boy. All I remember about him was how he smelled. He smelled like soap. And he was always kissing. For a man, he kissed and hugged all the time, he was really an emotional guy."

Joey's father had first worked for Louie Bernstein as a bodyguard, and later on as a bootlegger and loan shark. But these "professions," Joey insisted, shouldn't be looked on as necessarily brutal or bad. In one, he supplied liquor like any salesman, and in the other, he lent money at great risk.

"And what if their clients didn't repay the loan on time?" said Diana.

"We rip off their fingernails, slowly," said Joey. They were in a small lounge off the main lobby of the hotel, having drinks before the dinner with Kalman Meyers. Small as the lounge was, there was no one there to share it with them. Everyone else, it seemed, was gambling. The clatter of the nearby slot machines was a constant reminder of why they were there, how rich and powerful were the men who had congregated around this fledgling metropolis of gambling. "What do you think a bank does if you don't pay them back? They don't kill you, they break you. What our guys did," continued Joey, "was stop the whole break-the-knee-caps routine. That wasn't necessary. That was old-time. In your father's time and mine, they started to take over businesses instead of kill the welchers. The garment business was a place your father got started with, and then my father, and Marty after him. Just businessmen who were respected because they were tough."

"And carried guns."

"Sure," said Joey. "They had to protect themselves." But he was half-joking now. He took another sip of Scotch, then went on to explain about how he saw the life of his father. In 1925, the year that Louie Bernstein and his wife died in an automobile accident that was set in motion by an assassin's bullets, Joey's father was funneling bootlegging money into New York City's garment center. Loans were given to legitimate businessmen who were eager to gamble on the high-flying prosperity of the times. When their gambles didn't pay off, they found themselves inheriting silent partners who "excused" their unpaid loans in return for sizable percentages of the businesses. "This wasn't my father's thing, you understand," said Joey. "He was strictly Louie's guy. And even after Louie died, Marty was just a kid himself really, I mean he was twenty, twenty-one, but my father accepted the fact that Marty was the boss. It's like the royal family in this business."

Joey's father didn't outlive Diana's by too many years. Following the repeal of Prohibition in 1933, well-heeled gangsters scrambled for a piece of the legal liquor market. Marty Bernstein's organization was well-placed for entry into this new legitimate field, financed by their bootlegging and gambling fortunes, and much of this money was channeled through their legitimate garment-center interests in concert with men like Kalman Meyers. But unfortunately for these gentlemanly gangsters in search of a more "honest" trade, a war over the control of New York and New Jersey's gambling empires had broken out between rival gangs. One of the first casualties was Joey's father.

"My mother showed me his picture in the paper," said Joey. "Not then. Years later, when I was old enough to hear her side of it. You know, it called him a 'gangster' right there under the picture? It was a good picture, but not the way I remember him. It's funny I don't remember more. When he died, I was already almost eight and playing with cap guns."

"But if he died in 1933 and you weren't even eight. . .?"

"I was almost eight."

"I was just trying to figure out how old you are."

"I know you are," said Joey, blushing. "Well, I'm twenty-four. Almost."

"No you're not. If fourteen years ago you were eight—which you weren't—you'd be . . . twenty-two." Diana shook her head in wonder. "You look much older."

"I'm not twenty-two, I'm twenty-three. I mean, I will be next month. I'm closer to twenty-three than twenty-two, so if somebody asks, I say twenty-three."

"You told me twenty-four."

"I didn't want you to feel old."

"Thanks," said Diana, laughing out loud. "I'm an old lady of twenty-five. That's positively ancient."

"I like older women."

"I am *not* an older woman, and you have no business thinking about me in that way anyway—this is business, right?"

"Sure," said Joey. "But don't think of me as a kid. I saw plenty in the world before I was sixteen. It aged me."

"I can see that," said Diana, still laughing.

"Don't make fun of me," said Joey, and the words came out with such sinister force that she was brought back to the moment in the New York bar when he'd humiliated the waiter who hadn't at first recognized Marty Bernstein. But he was not angry at her. In the minutes before their dinner, he told her about how Marty had taken care of his mother and himself after the death of his father. This had not been simply a matter of money. Marty had taken an interest in Joey's schoolwork, prowess on the ball field, career plans. Joey and his mother were sent down at Marty's expense to Miami and Havana for winter vacations, where Kalman Meyers and Louie Bernstein had established gambling empires.

"Marty never wanted me to get into trouble in school," he said. "So I tried to stay clear of trouble. It wasn't like he was another father to me, or a rich uncle or something. He was my real father's employer, and he was always very straight and proper. My father died in the line of business, and Marty felt responsible. But he never pretended with me. I'm not his son, and he never made me do the things he'd have made a son of his do."

"What would a son of Marty Bernstein's do?"

"Be a lawyer. That's what Marty *suggests* I do, but he won't *tell* me, he says. Because I'm not a son. And my Jewish mother, she's worse. Because of my memory and all that, they think it would be a snap, law school. They don't know what a headache you get trying to read and remember all that. I bet it's easier when you read the way ordinary people do."

"How did you get involved in Marty's business?" said Diana.

"What do you mean? I was born into the business," said Joey, smiling. But then he paused, narrowed his eyes, and pulled his head back. "Oh. You're thinking that your uncle probably didn't want me to work for him, is that it?"

"Maybe he wouldn't—especially when you're so young."

"I joined the Marines when I was eighteen," said Joey. "That was only a tough decision because I was already working for Marty for three years. You know it's not Murder, Incorporated anymore. Those days are over. This is gambling, liquor, hotels, entertainment, unions—very legitimate. So don't go thinking we're all animals in this business. I may even do that law-school thing someday, if I can forget about college somehow. But that's only because a lawyer is good for our organization, a lawyer who's one of us too, if you know what I mean. We trust each other. You know another business where they'd feed and clothe and look after a mother and child after their husband and father got shot? These are good people, and you better remember that, because it's time to go meet them."

"When's your birthday?"

"What?" She could see him trying to think fast. "February. February eighth."

"Okay—then you're not going to be twenty-three next month. You're going to be twenty-two in February. You're twenty-one, aren't you?"

"I am not ever again going to talk with you about the subject of ages, is that clear?" said Joey. "And please remember what I said about these people. Kalman Meyers is an important man. He has dinner with bankers. He's very distinguished, and he'll know right away if you're looking down your nose at him. You got that?"

Joey led her to the private dining room, where Kalman Meyers had prepared a gathering of six dozen Jewish community leaders and one Italian sympathetic to Jewish causes. Kalman was very tall and very thin, and unlike the others assembled there, very informally dressed in a rumpled open-necked shirt.

"Louie's daughter," he said, speaking with the untrammeled energy of the Lower East Side of New York. "Come here."

"Mr. Meyers, it's a pleasure to meet you," said Diana, but the tall man wasn't listening. He embraced her and then held her at arm's length, and then he embraced her again.

"Louie's daughter," said Kalman to a dark and handsome man of about fifty-five as he pushed Diana toward him.

"She don't look like him," said the man, who was Chuck Marandino, Kalman Meyers' associate for thirty years.

"It's Louie's daughter," said Kalman Meyers again, and Chuck Marandino embraced her too. Between Kalman and Joey, Diana was introduced to the others in the room: three of them were "with the gambling," two were "hotel businessmen," and one was just in from Los Angeles, where he was a "union worker."

Joey turned to Diana and reminded her to keep her talk simple, as Marty had advised. Kalman told her to sit wherever she wanted, as he himself sat down at the head of the table. "Maybe she wants to sit there, Kalman," said Chuck Marandino.

"In my seat?" said the old gangster. "Even my seat, she wants it, she gets it."

"This is fine right here," said Diana, sitting at Kalman's right hand. Joey sat next to Diana, and the others all took seats at the same time. The waiters were freshly shaved older men who smelled of cologne and didn't seem the least intimidated by the diners: most of them were frequent dinner guests at one room or another in the great hotel, and all were big tippers and hearty eaters.

"So Marty? He's healthy?" said Kalman to Joey.

"You spoke to him, right?" said Joey.

"Sure I spoke. Why do you think we're eating here?"

"Then you know he's healthy," said Joey.

"What kind of talk is that to talk to Kalman Meyers?" said Chuck Marandino.

"You're right," said Joey. "I shouldn't say nothing. This meeting is just about Diana here, and how we're all going to help her. It shouldn't have nothing to do with Pittsburgh—even Marty said so."

"He's talking about Pittsburgh!" said Chuck Marandino, dropping his spoon and slamming his fist to the table.

"Chuckie," said Kalman. "We're all friends here."

"Please, I don't understand what everyone is getting upset about," said Diana. "I've never even been to Pittsburgh. I don't know why Joey brought up Pittsburgh, and I'm sure he's sorry he did, and so we can go on with what I came here to discuss."

"I'll tell you about Pittsburgh," said Kalman Meyers. "Your Uncle Marty thought he owns Pittsburgh. Some people here, at this table, had different ideas."

"How can anyone own Pittsburgh? Pittsburgh is a city," said Diana.

Joey put his hand on hers to quiet her. "This is just a little chat about gambling rights, Diana," he said. "But Kalman is right. We're all friends. I was wrong to speak disrespectfully before. I apologize. I spoke in anger."

"What have you got to be angry about?" said Kalman. "I do everything for this boy. I open doors for him, I speak to everyone I know, I say nice things. You work, you eat, you got good clothes, that's not only Marty all these years doing this, is it?"

"Marty was there first," said Joey.

"Yeah," said Kalman. "I like that. Loyalty." He was looking at Chuck Marandino now with a smile. "Marty and I reached a compromise about Pittsburgh."

"What compromise?"

"He gave me the control, I give him some of the money."

"How much?" said Joey, incredulous at the news.

"Ten percent," said Chuck Marandino.

Joey was starting to get up now, but Diana restrained him. The waiters took away their largely uneaten first course, oblivious of the sense of violence in the room. Most of the others at the table were quietly observing Kalman Meyers, looking at him the way veteran theatergoers watch a Broadway star lead into a climactic moment.

"How the hell did you ever get Marty to agree to that?"

"It was his idea," said Kalman slowly. "Or partly his idea. Eat your soup, it's going to get cold." He lifted a spoonful of consommé to his own lips. "Most of the time, my boy, our interests can lie along the same road, and that's good. That's much better than fighting, isn't it?"

"Look, either somebody tells me what happened with Marty or I get up and go call him right now myself."

"Marty found Louie's daughter, and Louie's daughter needed some help," said Kalman. "I knew this the night it happened, the night you dropped in on your uncle for the first time," he said, turning to Diana. "Marty called me, woke me, to tell me that Louie's daughter came to see him and he thought I'd want to know. That's how much Marty loves me, see?"

"I know that Marty loves you," said Joey.

"I called him a day later, and he tells me about this girl, this very nice and very pretty girl and what kind of help she's looking for, and I'm thinking, maybe I can do something here for the King, and for Marty, and for myself too, right?"

"What has this got to do with Pittsburgh?" said Joey impatiently.

One of the "hotel businessmen" spoke up, a slight, dapperly dressed man in his early forties: "The biggest son-of-a-bitch illegal exporter of arms to Egypt is in Pittsburgh."

"But it's not illegal to export arms to Egypt," said Diana. "That's the whole problem. There probably will be an arms embargo to the Middle East if partition comes through, but meanwhile the Jews in Palestine can't import arms, but all the Arab countries around Palestine can; and those arms end up being used by Arab guerrillas in Palestine."

"Keep it simple," said Joey.

"I'm telling you the guy's an illegal exporter, honey," said the "hotel businessman." "What I mean is, he doesn't look for permits, he's not interested in duties, taxes, that stuff. He just gets the stuff out to the Port of New York, and somehow it gets stuffed on board the boat to Egypt under the barrels of junk that's going there legally. The guy will be set up to ship illegal, legal, or any way, no matter what happens with the feds."

"So that's what I gave Marty for his part of Pittsburgh," said Kalman Meyers.

"I don't understand," said Diana.

"Marty said it was all right?" said Joey. "No strings?"

"You're here, the both of you. I want to see if I can help—we can discuss—Chuckie here knows the Port of New York better than anybody. There's plenty we can do at the Port, even with a phone call from Vegas, we can do plenty."

"I don't understand," said Diana. She turned to Joey. "What did they do, Marty and him? What was the deal they made for me?"

"You want I should spell it out, Kalman?" said Joey.

"You don't understand, honey?" said Kalman. "I told your uncle it could be helpful to what you want—Palestine, I'm talking about—if this Pittsburgh arms dealer wasn't in business anymore. So he said fine. I mean about the ten percent."

"Wait, wait," said Diana. "I'm not really all that slow in the head usually, but I don't see how you could make a deal like that, over the phone, in a matter of days."

"A matter of hours," said Chuck Marandino with a smile. He pointed to his boss. "Kalman Meyers. Just a phone call."

"A phone call to do what?" said Diana.

"To put him out of business, my dear," said Kalman Meyers.

"But that's what I'm asking," she insisted. "How did you get him to go out of business—just like that?"

Kalman Meyers looked directly down the center of the dining table, his eyes focused on nothing in the room. The silence lasted for only a few moments, but it was an awkward silence that needed to be broken, and Joey Marino broke it first.

"He died, Diana," he said. "The arms dealer just died."

"Oh," she said, and she tried to smile up at Kalman Meyers' face, but her lips wouldn't move, and her eyes found a point in the center of her soup bowl from which they couldn't turn. She had come to America to get help for Eretz-Israel, for the Holy Land, and she had remembered where she had come from, who her true father had been, because that man had been a man of violence, and his friends could help her. But she had never imagined that help could come this quickly, and in this form. A man had been murdered, a man she didn't know, in a city she had never visited. She had come from Palestine, and her uncle had mentioned her desire to help, and a man named Kalman Meyers, famous in every corner of America, had ordered the death of a man, and he was now dead, and it was her fault, as much her fault as if she had pulled the trigger.

"Are you sorry for him?" said Kalman Meyers slowly. He turned sharply, and Diana raised her eyes to meet his look. "He was getting guns to Arab guerrillas. You're trying to get guns to Jews fighting the guerrillas. We're talking about guns, not soda pop. You know what guns are used for. Now I'm asking you a question: Are you sorry that this son-of-a-bitch had an accident and is now dead and gone?"

Diana wanted to explain that she hadn't asked for anyone to be killed, but had hoped that someone would know where and how to buy guns, how to smuggle them safely out of the country and into Palestine, and that would be fine. Somehow, she had been used to settle a gangster dispute over gambling territories. The man in Pittsburgh had been murdered as much for that as for the future Jewish state. But she could feel the force of her lover, David Stern, with his lost pistol and desperate eyes, and she understood that she was in some way part of a war, of a war that took lives, and though she hated the fact that murder had been done, she knew she had to express her approval or these men would never be of help to her and her people. "I'm not sorry," said Diana. "If there are no more arms going out of Pittsburgh to the Arabs, then I'm not sorry at all."

Kalman Meyers shook his head from side to side, a smile slowly coming on his face. "Just like Louie," he said. "He always needed a very good reason to shoot somebody. Even if they were after him, he needed to explain why he did it. Even if they were going to shoot him down, he had to explain himself, why he shot back." Kalman cleared his throat and wiped his dry eyes, as if forcibly dragging himself back to the present. He looked at Louie Bernstein's daughter.

"Okay, sweetheart," he said. "You know what kind of people we are. What can we do for the King's daughter?"

FIVE

Joey Marino was much relieved to discover that they would be returning to New York not by air, but by train. Kalman Meyers had arranged for meetings between Diana and various of his "colleagues" in Denver, Kansas City, St. Louis, and Chicago. Joey called it the "gangster fund-raiser," but she could tell that he was anything but blasé about meeting the famous racketeers on their own territories— saddled by a girl who talked too much and by a need to ask for help rather than make a demand. Still, in the whirlwind eight days of cross-country travel, Joey and Diana grew used to the welcome prepared for them by Kalman Meyers and Marty Bernstein's phone calls: this was Louie Bernstein's daughter, and she was to be helped in any way possible. Murder was being inflicted upon Jews without arms, and no legal recourse was open to them, and the King's daughter was appealing to his old friends to provide an illegal recourse. One old Sicilian mobster gave her ten thousand dollars in twenty-dollar bills on her first night in Denver, unable to say anything more than that it was for Louie. In Kansas City a group of young gambling-club owners held an all-night crap game for Palestinian Jews; too young to have known Louie Bernstein, they were still in awe of his name. In St. Louis one young gangster had been with the U.S. Army at the liberation of Auschwitz. He swore to Diana that he would be personally responsible for one planeload of rifles. In Chicago there were promises of money and arms from four rival gangs, each one anxious to know which gang had pledged the most. By the time they arrived in New York City on the eve of the United Nations' General Assembly vote on the raging partition debate, Diana was carrying eighteen thousand dollars in cash and had been pledged nearly seven hundred thousand dollars. More important, she had been promised guns: from Los Angeles to New York, dozens of gangsters were looking to buy surplus Army rifles and machine guns—or steal them. Bosses of half a dozen East Coast ports were being approached about the ways to get contraband out to sea; teamsters and stevedores were being recruited to aid in hijacking and smuggling; ship captains were being tempted with magnificent bribes for carrying heavy crates that would be marked "Industrial Equipment" and would have to be sneaked through the British customs control at Haifa.

"Joey, I want to thank you for coming along with me—" Diana began to say as she followed their porter to the taxi stand.

"Skip it," said Joey. "I'm not going nowhere. We're still traveling together, till Marty says so, okay?"

"I'm just going to the Waldorf. If I can't be safe at the Waldorf—"

Once again Joey interrupted her. "You're carrying cash, right? You're talking to gangsters, right? There's money, there's mobsters, there's people six thousand miles away who'd be happy if you were dead, okay? I'm sticking with you till Marty tells me to blow." The handsome young man turned his anger on the porter. "You—easy with those bags—they ain't coconuts you're carrying."

"Okay, Joey," she said. "I'm happy to have you along for the ride. But once I'm at the Waldorf—"

"In your room," said Joey. "Just like in all the cities we been. We check you in, get you safe and sound, and then I call Marty, and when he tells me to blow, I blow, right?"

Diana waited for Joey to overtip the porter, bark at the cabdriver, and settle back in his seat, taking care to avoid bodily contact with her in the close confines of the car, before speaking. "Why do you say 'ain't'?" she said.

The driver pulled out of the cab line and into the chaotic midday traffic. She had expected his reaction to be violent, as violent as his attraction for her. But Joey simply clasped his hands together and turned his black eyes on her with an attempt at indifference. "I've about had it up to here with you," he said. "'Ain't' is language, just like 'isn't,' just like 'are not.' I'm not stupid, I ain't stupid, I say it when I say it when I feel like it, okay?"

"I'm not criticizing, Joey. I know you know how to say the right words, I was just wondering why you sometimes do and you sometimes don't—I was just wondering."

"They *ain't* coconuts," said Joey. "That's right when you're talking to the guy who carries your bags, okay? When I'm talking to someone like you with her nose in the air, I speak a little differently. Of all the stuck-up broads I've ever met—"

"Don't call me a broad."

"Yeah, you're right. Marty would be mad."

"That's not the reason. It doesn't suit me, and it doesn't suit you saying it. You've got a lot more class than that."

She could see the surprise on his face, and at first she thought that he'd taken her words as a compliment; but the surprise wasn't for her words, but for the feeling growing in him that was impossible to stop. Joey unclasped his hands, and he was so slow that she could see the diamond ring on his left hand flash as he moved clumsily her way, as if fighting through turbulent water. Diana had ample time to stop him, but she couldn't speak until he had embraced her. Joey put his arms about her neck and pulled her face to his, and Diana allowed this, as if by granting this boy a kiss she would be doing a good deed. She knew that his infatuation for her had been building throughout their trip, and that she had done little to put a stop to it. She had been occasionally annoyed with his attentions, with the way he looked at her as she moved toward his table in a restaurant, seeming to follow every step she took with the devotion of a teenager for his first girlfriend; and she'd been afraid that this much infatuation could lead to problems in their working together. But more than any occasional annoyance, Diana knew that she had been profoundly bothered by the sexual hunger coming from him. Like it or not, she had responded to this hunger, had been flattered by it, had been excited by it. Her lover was far away in Palestine, and she felt terribly guilty that this under-educated, underage gangster could excite in her anything other than contempt.

But now she allowed the boy his kiss, and she had shut her eyes, and immediately an image of David Stern passed before her: blond, unbendingly determined, passionate. And she kissed Joey Marino, and through the boy's lips she felt the concern, the desire, the overwhelming desire to possess her that she never felt from her lover, and the shock of it was delicious, and terrifying. Even in a half-moment, David's image dissipated to nothing, and she was opening her eyes to the handsome young man and pushing him away with fury.

"You don't fool me," said Joey, the anger returning to his eyes. And he held her wrists in his hands and kept his eyes open on hers, kissing her warily, as if she were a snake about to strike, a flower whose very center was poison. But this time she didn't respond. Her lips were shut, her eyes dead.

"Let go of me," she said quietly, and Joey did as she had asked.

"You kissed me, or I'm crazy," he said.

"I kissed you, but it was a mistake."

"No, the mistake was when you stopped," he said. Joey retreated to the far corner of the cab, sulking. "I never understood these games. It's always been very simple for me. I don't enjoy pretending. Maybe it's because I'm not high society."

"I wasn't pretending. I never meant to suggest—"

"Stop it," said Joey. "I get the message. No, is that right? The message is no, no, no."

"You and I have a business relationship," said Diana.

"Sure. You're Marty Bernstein's niece, and I'm his prize flunky. That's how close we are, right? That's the whole thing, isn't it? Ain't it?"

The cab turned suddenly right, sending Joey along the seat cushions close to Diana. "Hey, you," said Joey to the driver, "you trying to put someone into the hospital?"

"What are you," said the driver, "from out of town?"

"Joey," said Diana, "I like you very much, and I appreciate all you've done for me, and I think you're intelligent, extremely attractive, but as I've told you before, I am very much involved with a man in Palestine, with David—"

"This is New York," said Joey.

"And this is the Waldorf," said the driver, who had overheard Joey and now rushed out to help the Waldorf's porter with the bags.

"This has got nothing to do with any guy in Palestine, Diana," said Joey. "Just look at me, and stop thinking about over there, and just think about now, right now, okay?"

He had taken hold of her chin now, and his touch was gentle but insistent, and she looked at him as carefully as he had asked her to do so, and she slowly shook her head. "It's not like that between us," she said. "I'm much older than you—"

"Stop that crap, will you?" said Joey. "You're older, there's a guy in Palestine, so what? Tell me about us, not about a lot of garbage that's got nothing to do with anything."

"Joey," said Diana, "I don't know what else to tell you. I like you, I trust you, I want us to be friends, but we're different people, committed to different things."

"Hey," said the driver, placing his head next to Diana's open window. "If you want to keep talking in there, I'll put on the meter and go for lunch."

"This guy's crazy," said Joey, but Diana squeezed his hands and smiled at him like he was an upset little boy. "I could kill him."

"We should really check in and call Marty, don't you think?"

The doorman helped her out of the cab, and Joey slapped two bills into the driver's hand with force, and hurried after her. "You think I'm in love with you or something, maybe that's what's bothering you. No. Listen, Diana. I like you, right? We get along, right? All I'm trying to do is be natural with you, do what feels nice. I don't want seeing you every day to just end like that, now that we're back in New York. I'm not on my knees or something, asking you to wear my ring."

"I want to see you too," she said. "Of course. We know each other very well, and now we're friends."

"Friends who kiss once in a while," said Joey, and as they crossed the elegant lobby, he turned her around and threw her against his chest and kissed her as if she were a rag doll. This time Diana reacted in the way she had been trained; she slapped Joey Marino across the face. "That's okay," he said. "It don't hurt. At least you're looking at me like I'm alive."

Diana didn't answer. She was angry, and getting angrier at the way he was trying to get beneath her skin. Leaving him in the center of the lobby, she tried to walk calmly to the reception desk. He was just a boy, she reminded herself. A bad, wild boy who wanted his way. It was silly to concern herself with anything to do with Joey Marino when the United Nations was about to vote on the fate of Eretz-

Israel, when her lover awaited her help and her love in beleaguered Jerusalem.

As she began to sign the hotel registration form, she could feel a man standing behind her and watching intently. "Okay, Joey," she said. "You've got me to the hotel, I'm checked in, thank you very much."

"Pardon me, Miss Mann," said an unfamiliar voice, British-accented and assertive. Diana turned around, red-faced and anxious. No one knew she was here except for Marty and David; and David's voice was British-accented, and she knew in an instant that this man brought nothing but bad news. "You are Diana Mann?" he said.

"Yes, what is it? Is anything wrong?"

He was dressed, not in the ubiquitous khaki of Palestine but in a simple gray suit, but Diana was sure that this stocky young man with the shock of sun-bleached hair was not only from Eretz-Israel but was a member of the Haganah. "I am a friend of David's. May I accompany you to your room?"

"Yes. Of course. How is he? If something is wrong, you must please tell me."

"When we're alone," said the man from Palestine.

An assistant manager had come up to them from behind the desk, waving a key. "I'll take you up, Miss Mann. It's good to see you again."

"No, that's all right. You don't have to come up," said Diana. She took the key from the startled assistant manager's hand.

"It's no trouble at all, Miss Mann," said the man, but Diana had already turned her back to him and was urging the Haganah man to the elevators. Somehow the bellboy had gotten to the suite before them. Even in her anxious state she noticed that the boy had brought up Joey's bags as well as her own. As he fussed over the window shades, turned on lights, and rearranged the luggage on its rack, Diana found a bill in her purse.

"Okay," she said, giving him the tip. "You can go now." Diana followed the boy to the door and shut it after him. "All right now," she said. "Please tell me."

The man approached her, attempting a smile of encouragement. "Look, my name is Arye Grinberg. I know David very well."

"Is he dead, just tell me—is he dead?"

"No, Miss Mann," said Arye, and he put his right arm about her shoulders, gesturing to the couch in front of the fireplace. "Let's sit down, all right?" As they did so, Joey Marino emerged silently from the suite's adjacent bedroom, a snub-nosed revolver held carefully in both hands.

"Don't move," said Joey. "Either of you."

"Joey, put that gun down," said Diana.

"Shut up, Diana," said Joey. "This is a hair trigger. I cough, and your friend is going to be floating over Park Avenue." He took a step closer, and Diana could see that he was serious, not simply jealous or raging. "All right, mister. Very slowly, and I mean slowly, take your hand off of her shoulders. *Slowly*. And bring your hand into your lap, and clasp your hands together. Like you're praying. Do it."

Diana felt Arye's arm ease off her shoulder and watched out of the corner of her eye—she didn't want to break Joey's concentration and lead to an accident—as the man's hand moved to his lap.

"Joey, this man is a friend of mine and I want you to put that gun down this instant."

"Diana, please," said Joey, his eyes only on Arye. "You didn't say anything about a friend meeting you here, right? How do I know he's a friend? Maybe he's kidnapped your mother and you're afraid to talk in front of him."

"Don't be an idiot," said Diana.

"You, mister, what's your name?" Joey took a step closer to the couch. "Diana, ease over to the end of the couch and stand up. Go ahead. Okay, mister, I'm waiting."

"My name is Arye Grinberg."

"How do you know Diana? From where?"

"I met Miss Mann only a few minutes ago. She and I have a mutual friend."

"What mutual friend?"

"That is of no concern to you, sir," said Arye. "It is only relevant that he told me where Miss Mann would be staying, and I learned through the hotel what date she was expected back. And I was here to meet her and give her a message."

"Joey, put down that gun," said Diana. She had crossed over to the corner of the large room, standing well out of Joey's reach. "Arye's telling you the truth."

"You never met this guy before today?"

"No."

"Then how do we know who he really is?" said Joey.

"Because he knows my friend—he knows David."

"David," said Joey. "I see. He says he knows David." Joey paused, and stopped himself from turning a withering look on Diana. "What if David's in trouble, and he's not his friend? What if he's here because David's been caught by the Brits and has told them all about you?"

"That's ridiculous," said Diana, and without thinking, she took a step closer to Joey, a clumsy step that hit against the leg of a chair, and Joey's head turned toward the origin of the sound. It was only for a moment: a moment in which Joey, alert and wary, turned to Diana and then began to turn back; a moment in which his hand remained firmly on his snub-nosed revolver, pointed at Arye Grinberg. But a moment was enough for the man from Palestine. Even as Joey's eyes began to turn to Diana, he was out of his seat on the couch, his right hand open for a blow under Joey's chin, his left hand clawing at the revolver's cylinder, so that even if Joey hadn't hesitated, he would have been unable to fire the gun in the half-second before it was torn out of his hand.

The blow under Joey's chin forced his head back, his eyes to the ceiling, as Arye twisted the gun out of his hand, taking care to retain it; at the same moment, he had stomped onto the instep of Joey's left foot. Joey Marino had been a street fighter since his early teens. Even through the haze of pain that surrounded him as he allowed the man to trip him to the floor, he was astounded at the ease with which he'd been disarmed and beaten. He looked up into the barrel of his own gun.

"You'd better be who you say you are, mister," said Joey, "Because otherwise you're going to have to kill me, and even if you do that little thing, someone is going to find you and twist some piano wire round your neck."

Diana got down on a knee next to Joey, trying to help him. But the pain was mostly in his foot now, and secondary in magnitude to his humiliation.

"That was no hair trigger," said Arye.

"You nearly broke my finger off," said Joey.

"I had a choice. Either try to get my hand between the hammer and the barrel and then twist—the hammer couldn't hit the firing pin then, and I'd have probably broken your trigger finger—or just try to take hold of the cylinder. That's always easier. I try to do what's easier. I'm afraid I'm going to have to ask you to get up. Just don't put too much weight on your left foot. It's not broken. The instep's very tender, so it hurts, but I didn't break anything."

"Please," said Diana. "This is all a terrible mistake. Joey is my friend, he's very sorry, he's supposed to be helping me—"

"Protecting you, yes," said Arye. "I know all about Joey Marino. We've already spoken with your uncle, Miss Mann."

"What do you mean, 'spoken'?" said Joey. "If you even touched Marty Bernstein—"

"Mr. Bernstein was nothing but a gentleman, and so we acted like gentlemen with him," said Arye. Joey had gotten to his feet, and Arye gestured for him to turn around and face the wall. "Hands on the wall, spread your legs," said Arye, and as Joey complied, Arye frisked him with one hand.

"I want to know about David," said Diana.

"I'm sorry. In a moment." Arye turned Joey around and gestured for him to take a chair. Joey sat down heavily, and Arye placed the revolver in his pocket. "I'll give it back to you when you're more at ease," he said.

"Look, I'm sorry about all this," said Diana. "But if you don't tell me what's going on with David, *I'm* going to reach for that gun."

"Sit down," said Arye, pointing her toward the couch. Diana did as she was told, hunching forward, her hands on her knees, as if her state of seated readiness would prompt his message all the sooner. "David's in prison," said Arye. "The Brits are going to give him about ten days. Then they're going to hang him."

Diana stopped interrupting. Arye preferred to speak without interruption. He was used to commanding in the field, and able to explain a situation, a plan of attack, anticipating and answering questions as part of his talk. Now he spoke rapidly, with little inflection. He had already tried to prepare her for a shock. Now there was no point in holding back what she wanted to know.

In the short time that Diana had been in the United States, there had been three separate violent incidents along the Tel Aviv–Jerusalem road. Arab guerrillas from Syria and Iraq were coming across the border to Palestine in increasing numbers; many of them were quartered with Arab civilians in the little villages overlooking the dangerously low road that led up to Jerusalem. Separate guerrilla bands had struck at a Jewish bus, at a convoy of four trucks loaded with food for Jerusalem, and at a Jewish interurban taxi; four Jews had been murdered in the incidents. The bus and taxi were shot up and afterward caught fire and left black hulks in the ditch alongside the road. The trucks were looted by Arab villagers, and were eventually reclaimed. None of the Jews in any of the incidents had been armed, and the Haganah command had decided to send as many armed men and women into the daily buses and taxis and trucks between Jerusalem and Tel Aviv as possible; otherwise a panic would set in. Tel Aviv was self-sufficient, surrounded by solidly Jewish territory; but Jerusalem could be cut off from the rest of the Jews of the country without the use of the road. The British were supposed to maintain the safety of the road for Arabs and Jews alike. But in the tense days before the partition vote, the only action the British were taking on the Jerusalem road was in searching Jewish young men for guns. Four days before—only five days before the partition vote—the British checkpoints along the road multiplied, and David Stern was caught with a gun strapped under his seat at the back of the morning bus to Tel Aviv. He already had a bruise under his eye when a Haganah man—a lawyer—was able to see him for a moment at the Latrun detention center. Since then he had been transferred to the infamous Central Prison in Jerusalem, where Meir Feinstein and Moshe Barazanni had blown themselves up with a shared hand grenade rather than let the British execute them ignominiously.

"Have you seen him?"

"No."

"Has he been definitely sentenced? Can't he appeal? Why ten days? Did they have any proof that it was his gun under the seat?"

"Miss Mann, you don't understand. Under the Emergency Regulations there is no appeal. David Stern was tried before a military court. There's no jury of peers, no legal precedent, just the Emergency Regulations. The court's made up of British officers, usually without any legal training."

"A kangaroo court," said Joey Marino. "I know all about courts like that, and how to deal with them."

"I'm not sure I understand," said Diana. "To the best of your knowledge, David's already been tried, sentenced, and cannot appeal the sentence through any legal means?"

"Yes."

"And the sentence is death?"

"Yes."

"They kill you for having a gun strapped under a seat?" said Joey. He could feel Diana's love for the doomed man grow moment by moment; David Stern was on his way to martyrdom, and if Diana had loved him before, she would love him better now.

"But that's impossible," said Diana. "You people can't allow him to die just like that. There must be some way. The newspapers, not just in Palestine, but here. I'll write an article, I'll expose it, I'll take out a full-page advertisement. In London too. The English can't be in favor of this. It's that maniac Foreign Secretary Bevin. The British invented the jury, for God's sake. The people who invented the jury system aren't going to stand by and let someone be hanged because he had a gun under his seat—a gun to be used only if they were attacked by Arabs. Well, tell me—what are you going to do?"

"Me?" said Arye Grinberg. "Well, if it's all right with you, I'm going to take over your job. I've explained to your uncle that you have a sick friend you would want to visit in Jerusalem, but that it would be difficult for you to go unless I could take over your duties here. I am an ordnance expert. With Marty Bernstein's cooperation, I'm sure I'll be better suited than you are to supervise the kinds of weapons we want to smuggle out of the country and into Palestine."

"I'm talking about David," said Diana. "What are you going to do about David?"

"We would like you to visit him for us," said Arye.

"All right," said Diana at once. Her heart began to pound violently. She would be afraid, but must not show the fear. They would ask her to do something dangerous, and she must not allow anyone to see that she was a coward.

"They don't allow visitors," said Joey Marino.

"What?" said Diana, as if Joey's intrusion into their dialogue threatened to break apart her false front of courage.

"They don't allow visitors before hanging," said Joey. His eyes had the intense glare they took on when he was calling forth information he understood imperfectly. "Meir Feinstein and Moshe Barazanni were in the newspapers here. I remember the names. The article was too long ago to remember precisely, but I remember the reason they blew themselves up. They were planning to kill some Brits. That was the idea. They weren't just suicidal." He turned to Arye Grinberg, trying to get him to see that his courage and his sense of justice were as remarkable as his memory. "It really affected me, what I read.

They had this grenade, smuggled in somehow, and they were going to explode it just when the Brits were going to execute them—the idea was to take the Brits with them. But there was this rabbi there. He was there to oversee the execution, to pray for them, I guess. So they killed themselves before the execution, before the rabbi could be put into their cell. That must have been a hell of a thing, pulling the pin on a grenade and just leaving it in your hand. Anyway, I'm saying all this—I have this memory, so I know what I'm saying—in Palestine, you can't see a condemned man now. No lawyer, rabbi, not even a wife can get into the cell before a hanging."

"You're right," said Arye. "Ordinarily he would be allowed no visitors. We're hoping that Miss Mann will be allowed, due to the influence of her family. You know the Financial Secretary in Palestine. He's one of only three men in the country that reports directly to the High Commissioner. We suggest that he be informed that David Stern is your fiancé and that your recent trip to the United States was to inform your family of your plans to marry. All pressure must be exerted on his behalf, and it is not inconceivable that such pressure can lead to a reduction in sentence. But at the very least you'll be allowed to visit him. That is what we really want."

"I don't understand something," said Diana. "'We' is the Haganah, of course. I know that David is important, but it seems that you're going to a great deal of trouble to get me to see him. So far as I know, he's not very high up in the Haganah command. Very high-up officers don't usually ride shotgun on buses."

"I don't know what you're asking, Miss Mann."

"You haven't told me what you want," she said. "Please."

"We want you to carry a bit of wire into the prison," he said.

"Wire. What sort of wire?"

"Killing wire. For garroting. For David to kill his guard and get out of his cell."

"That's ridiculous," said Joey. "You're asking her to kill herself. I been to prisons—visiting—they search women just the same as men. They keep you five feet away from anyone you're going to see. It's a crazy risk. A wire's not so hard to spot. She can't do it."

"A wire is difficult to spot," said Arye Grinberg. "And we understand what we're asking, and why."

"This isn't for David, is it?"

"Not only for David. They have someone else, the Brits. In solitary. He's in charge of our illegal-arms industry. We're making small machine pistols, not very accurate, but better than some you can buy and then have to smuggle in. And he's the inventor of an excellent land mine we're starting to produce in secret. He's irreplaceable. We have to get him out. You have to get the wire to David, and then David will get him out. They'll both be free. But there's no one else that we can get into the prison. It has to be you, Miss Mann. We appreciate what you've begun to do here, but you have to go back and do this thing for us, or else we'll lose the chief of our armaments industry. And of course, David Stern will be dead."

Joey so forgot himself in his concern for Diana that he had gotten to his feet and crossed the room to her. Arye allowed this, because he had anticipated it; and the hotheaded young man was part of the deal he had made with Marty Bernstein. Diana's uncle had made it clear that he would continue to cooperate with the Haganah after Diana went back to Palestine only if Joey Marino could accompany her.

"You can't do this, Diana," said Joey Marino. "Marty won't let you do this, and I won't let you." He took hold of her hands and pressed them. Diana knew that he could sense her fear, even if Arye couldn't. "Look, it's terrible about your friend, but even if he was your fiancé, there'd be no reason for you to go and try a crazy stunt like that. You can get your family to call their British connections and all that, but anything else is suicidal. This guy doesn't care about David anyway. He's only using you and using David to save some guy you've never even seen. There's no shame in your not going, do you understand? There's nothing wrong with saying you can't do it, you won't do it. Tell him you won't do it. Go on. You don't want to go back there and get yourself killed. Go on, tell him."

Diana turned her green eyes on the man from Palestine. "How soon can I leave?" she said.

"Tonight," he said.

"Well, I'm going too," said Joey Marino. Forgetting about the gun the man had taken from him, forgetting about how easily Arye had wrestled him to the floor in pain, he came at him now, red-faced with anger. "Do you hear me, mister? I'm going too."

"Fine," said Arye Grinberg. "Perhaps with a little training you might be helpful to our cause." Joey stared at the man in shock. He hadn't expected such an easy acceptance. And as the man handed him back his snub-nosed revolver, Joey Marino wondered just how far he'd been manipulated, just how much he would come to regret the decision he'd made that day.

SIX

Diana and Joey missed the celebrations.

The United Nations General Assembly voted thirty-three to thirteen in favor of the resolution to partition Palestine. There were ten abstentions. The United States and the Soviet Union both voted in favor of the resolution. Cuba voted against it, as did Greece, perhaps because of the great number of its citizens dispersed in the Arab world. All the other states that had voted against the partition plan were Muslim or Asian. And although the partition plan hammered out by the United Nations did not fulfill the dreams of the Jewish people—Jerusalem was to be administered as an international city, and the Jewish portion of the divided Palestine was not only far smaller than what had been agitated for by Zionist leaders, but had a tortuous, nearly indefensible border—the world-wide reaction among Jews and their supporters was ecstatic.

Diana and Joey's TWA flight had been delayed for eight hours at Gander, and delayed once again at Shannon, in Ireland. It was there that they got the news, from a smiling Irish waitress. "The Jews have done it," she said to them. "Got the British out, and God bless."

"What do you mean?" said Diana. "Are you sure? Is the vote in?"

"They'll be celebrating in Dublin tonight," said the waitress. "And not just the Jews."

Later they learned about the spontaneous exultation in New York on that Saturday night. Crowds danced the *hora* in the street, the blue-and-white flag of the soon-to-be state hung from Lower East Side tenements and Fifth Avenue town houses, synagogues filled up for prayers of thanksgiving and more temporal merrymaking. As the news flashed out to the rest of the United States and to Europe and the Middle East, the sense of joy spread. If the Jewish state was possible, anything was possible. There could be peace. There could be an end to anti-Semitism. The horrors of the Second World War and its holocaust of blameless victims could begin to be atoned for. The nations of the world wouldn't allow a wholesale massacre of the Jews three years after the liberation of Auschwitz.

At Orly airfield, outside Paris, Diana's plane picked up three American correspondents, one of them Jewish, and all of them ecstatic about the chance to cover the events in Jerusalem right after the United Nations success.

"They're dancing in the streets," Diana was told by the men from Paris, who had already picked up the stories flooding in from Palestine on the wire services. Their DC-4 was three-quarters empty, and the few passengers on board were as eager to hear news as Diana. The Paris correspondents regaled all of them with what they'd been able to gather so far:

The Jews of Jerusalem were celebrating into the early-morning hours. Strangers hugged and kissed, passed around bottles of vodka and beer, listened to the ancient sounds of the shofar blowing from one corner of the city to the other in honor of the future independence. "Hatikavah," the Jewish national anthem of hope, burst out through the night. British soldiers tossed aside caution and joined, to a large extent, in the impromptu celebration. At Ciampino Airport, outside Rome, there was another lengthy delay on the already interminably long flight. Here a rumor was picked up of trouble at Lydda airfield in Palestine; another of a series of blunt declarations from the Arab League member nations—Egypt, Iraq, Saudia Arabia, Syria, Yemen, Lebanon, and Transjordan—calling for the destruction of the Jewish state.

"There won't be any trouble while we got the Tommies there," said one Englishman to Diana shortly after their plane took off from Rome. Joey had forced himself to remain in his chair, having already spent most of the last twenty-four hours in his sleeping berth trying to fight back his fear of air travel. As this Englishman was big and blue-eyed, with a handsome gap-toothed smile, and was standing conversationally in the aisle next to where he and Diana sat—as if he had dismissed Joey's presence as insignificant—Joey had something to concentrate on other than the roiling in his stomach and the taste of terror at the back of his tongue. "It's afterwards I'm afraid of a bloodbath," continued the Englishman. "The Arabs aren't about to mess with a hundred thousand British troops. But a hundred thousand Jews, that's something else."

"There are six hundred thousand Jews in Palestine," said Joey, feeling the fear fade away from the back of his tongue.

"Well, yes," said the Englishman, looking away from Diana reluctantly. "But they're not British troops, then, are they?"

"You think the British are going to keep order, then?" said Diana as pleasantly as she could. Her share in the joyous news was much diminished by the knowledge of David Stern's imprisonment. She wondered if the guards had told their Jewish inmates of the news; she hoped that the sounds of the shofar, of the singing crowds, had managed to penetrate the prison walls.

"Of course they shall," said the Englishman. "I wouldn't be running about doing business there if I didn't think so."

"We're with the Irgun," said Joey Marino suddenly.

"I beg your pardon?" said the Englishman.

Joey repeated the absurd phrase, and for once Diana didn't mind his belligerence. "Irgun, you know," said Joey, affecting a British accent. "The Brits are giving us all amnesty because they're so thrilled with the partition plan."

"Now, see here, my good man, a joke is a joke—"

"You're a joke, you limey bastard. Now, take a walk before I take out the rest of your teeth."

"Rude, that's most rude," said the Englishman. His smile was gone, but as he looked into Joey's cold black eyes, he knew a fist fight on board the TWA plane to Palestine was out of the question. This was a boy such as he had often seen in the war, one who didn't care what happened to him. Such a boy could kill him. The young woman was certainly pretty, but nobody was pretty enough to warrant standing up to this young madman.

"I say, quite," said Joey. "But we Irgun boys are rude indeed. We were rude enough to kill 127 of your brave Tommies between now and the end of the war. And if you don't go away, I'm going to personally make it 128."

As the businessman departed, Diana remarked that she could imagine Joey in the Irgun.

"Your David Stern," said Joey. "He wouldn't be in the Irgun?"

"No. He's against the Irgun philosophy," said Diana. "He calls them gangsters."

"Does he?" said Joey, grinning widely. "Now, he of all people shouldn't have anything against gangsters. Look at the guns we're going to be getting for his Haganah."

"I don't think of you and Marty as gangsters," said Diana. "Not exactly. It's like what you explained. About the gambling. The whole operation is more like business now."

"Businessmen didn't shoot the bastard in Pittsburgh who was shipping arms to the Arabs," said Joey. "And no businessman is going to get your David out of that prison, either."

"No," said Diana, answering so quietly and sadly that Joey felt rebuked. He was about to apologize when the plane shuddered.

"What was that?" he said.

"Oh, Joey, it's nothing," she said. "How can you be such a wild man, and at the same time worry about an airplane ride?"

"I am not worried about an airplane ride," he said. "I'd sit outside on the wing if you asked me to. I'm not afraid of anything. I just like to know when we're going to crash. Just a point of information, that's all."

"Sure," she said, sorry she'd insulted him. In the blur of events prior to their takeoff from New York, she hadn't had a chance to think too much about the fact that Joey was coming along with her to Jerusalem. If she had thought of it at all, it was as one of Marty Bernstein's conditions to Arye Grinberg. Remembering how terrified he'd been on their first flight together to Las Vegas, she knew what a sacrifice it must have been for him to sign on for a thirty-three-hour flight—that is, thirty-three hours under the best of conditions. With all the delays, they'd be lucky to arrive at Lydda airfield sixty hours after they'd taken off from New York. And even if he'd been a lover of airplanes and endless flights, it would have still been a remarkable sacrifice to make—to insist on making—the trip to a country that would probably soon break out in violence.

"I'll tell you something else," said Joey. "I'm getting used to flying. It's not so bad."

Diana put her hand over his where it clutched the armrest. "I haven't thanked you for coming along with me."

100

"I didn't think you were so anxious to have me come at all."

"I didn't think it was fair to drag you into this. This isn't Las Vegas we're going to," said Diana. "I don't know how long we're going to be here, and I don't know where you're going to find a place to clean your silk shirts."

"Hey, I was a Marine," said Joey.

"You were a baby during the war."

"I joined when I was sixteen. Just a little lie. Everyone was doing it. I signed up with a kid six months younger than me. I was seventeen when I got out of boot camp. Saw the Philippines. So I know something about all this. We lived on nothing but mud and guts, so I don't need silk shirts every day."

Diana reminded herself again that she was talking to a boy, not a man. Joey was vain, not with a man's vanity, but with a boyish insistence on his own perfection. "I'm sure you'll be better able to handle yourself once we land than I will," said Diana. "I only meant to say that I had a very specific reason to go, and you didn't."

"You're wrong."

"I'm going to get David out of prison."

"So am I," said Joey.

"You won't have anything to do with it," said Diana, snapping out the words. "I have to go into that prison, and I have to go there alone."

"Maybe."

"Not 'maybe,' Joey. Definitely. I have to do it. You're not going to ruin it, all right?"

"I wasn't planning to ruin it. I was planning to make it work. I am not a complete imbecile. I understand that you're in love with this man, and you want to help him in any way you can, and you think that I'm so madly in love with you that I'm practically *unstable*. That's not true. I like you, you know that. But I have experience where you don't. And if I want to help with the prison thing, you're going to have to let me."

"I'm not going to have to do anything," said Diana. "Marty wanted you on this trip, and I've already told you that I'm glad for the company, and I'm glad that you care enough to want to come. But this prison thing. Listen. I'll be lucky if I can visit alone. You can't come with me. And I don't want you to jeopardize my chance to see him—"

"Maybe there'll be an amnesty," said Joey, interrupting her. "Maybe the British will just let everyone go in honor of partition."

While refueling in Greece, they learned of Arab riots in Damascus, Amman, and Beirut. At Farouk Airport, outside Cairo, the last stop before Lydda, they learned that three Jews had been murdered in an ambush outside Tel Aviv. Diana took each little bit of news as another personal blow. Arabs had ransacked an American embassy in Syria; Jewish homes had been burned in Iraq; King Ibn-Saud of Saudi Arabia pledged to die leading his troops in battle against the Jews. There would be no amnesty, of course. The British weren't anxious to make up with the underground groups that had hounded them out of Palestine. She understood better than Joey why the English business-man on board their flight was so complacent. The Jews could celebrate for their brief moment, but the British were betting that the moment wouldn't last. Their troops could begin to pull out of Palestine, but the Jews themselves would beg them to come back.

The seven Arab League nations had five regular armies, forty-five million people, huge oil revenues; their territory was two hundred times larger than that of Palestine, their area thirty times more populous. British policy believed that the 600,000 Jews of Palestine could barely hold out against the 1,200,000 Arabs living in their midst. They were certain to be overwhelmed by the Arab League, and when the powerful armies of Iraq, Egypt, and Transjordan were fighting over the bones, the British would return to take control over this tiny strategic area of the world, and it would have the world's blessing to do so.

They landed in rain at Lydda. It was Monday, December 1, shortly before noon, and there were riots in Jerusalem, Jaffa, and some minor disturbances in Haifa. "I forgot to tell you," said Joey as they were coming down, the rain making a terrifying racket. "That horse Fire-bird, it came in at twenty-two to one. Marty had twenty G's on it, laid out all over the place." The plane's wheels lightly touched the runway, then bounced up and down, and finally settled into a bumpy rush that seemed to last forever. "That's four hundred and forty thousand dollars," said Joey between his shut teeth. "Marty says it's from him to the Jews. He wanted me to tell you, because he thought you'd make too much of a fuss."

"I don't understand. What's he going to do with all that money? Use it to buy guns?"

"No, that's something else, the guns. This is just money for whatever they need over here. I got it with me."

"With you? Where?"

Joey patted his attaché case. "C-notes and bearer bonds, very negotiable." Cautiously he turned his head to the window. "Thank God, we're not going to crash."

"You are carrying four hundred and forty thousand dollars in cash and securities in that case? Right there?" Joey nodded, and Diana shook her head. "What does Marty want you to do with it here? Give it to the Jewish National Fund?"

"He's left it up to you. You can give the whole thing to Ben-Gurion, or we can use it to bribe prison guards or customs officials. It's yours, Diana. Yours to spend to help out the Jews, that's what Marty said."

There was tight security at customs. Marty had procured Joey a press card at Diana's suggestion, and insisted that the young man leave his revolver at home. Now the paltry protection of the press card didn't seem like a great thing; the customs man who opened a case of nearly half a million dollars would have more than a few questions to ask the two of them. And she had no great faith in Joey's temper under fire.

"Miss Diana Mann?" said the cockney-accented customs clerk, flipping idly through her passport. "Right this way, please."

"We're together," said Joey Marino.

"What's your name?" he asked, and Joey told him. "I don't have your name down here."

"Down where, pal? What's this, a laundry list?" said Joey, turning around an official-looking memorandum from the office of the Financial Secretary.

"He's always joking," said Diana pleasantly to the customs clerk. "In New York they call him Joey-the-Joker."

"Reporter too?" said the clerk, looking idly at Joey's press credentials and passport. "Well, okay. But tell the truth here, will you? We're not monsters. We're just doing a job. Just like your cops-and-robbers movies, right, Yank?"

"My name's not Yank," said Joey, brushing past the clerk. A moment later they were met by a tall yellow-toothed Englishman with jerky movements; he stuck out his hand for a shake so clumsily that for a moment Joey thought he was about to try to slap his face.

"Miss Mann, I'm Charley Rudd," he said, exhibiting an identity card. "The Secretary's sent me. Financial Secretary? Right? You did expect?"

Charley Rudd was much more than Diana had expected. When she had telephoned her parents in Los Angeles, they were angry with her for returning to Palestine at all, even before she mentioned that she was going back to get an interview in a prison by means of deceit. She had told them that David Stern was a close friend but that for purposes of entry to the prison she had agreed to say that he was her fiancé. She asked her parents to pull every string with their family in London to get her in to visit David.

"I don't like it," her father had said. "I think you're becoming too emotionally involved in this whole Zionist cause. The British don't go around throwing people in jail for nothing, darling."

"You're not in love with this man?" her mother had asked.

"If you can help me, and choose to do that, I'll always be grateful," Diana had said. "If you can help and won't, I'll never forgive you." Her parents hadn't liked the tone of that ultimatum, and told her so; moreover, they had questions about her meeting with Marty Bernstein, about what she'd been doing in Las Vegas, about why she hadn't had a chance to visit them upon her return to the States. "Please help me get to this man," Diana had said. "Please." Her parents were not used to the plaintive voice. Embarrassed, they had said they would think about what could be done to get her in to see the man in prison. "Thank you," she'd said. Without knowing why, she stopped them from hanging up. "I just want you to know that he really isn't my fiancé but that I am in love with him and that he's very important to me. This is not for a newspaper story. This is for me, to see him. Just once."

"I'm afraid we're going to be going in convoy," said Charley Rudd cheerfully. "Slow things up a bit, but I suppose it's better than getting shot, right?"

"Who's arranged this service?" said Diana tentatively. Rudd's driver was loading their luggage into the trunk of a dusty Bentley.

"The Secretary, of course, Miss Mann," said Charley Rudd. "But pardon me, if you don't know, then you haven't been informed. You shall be granted your request to visit your unfortunate fiancé at noon, the day after tomorrow, if that time is convenient."

"Yes, that's convenient," said Diana. She opened the Bentley's passenger door herself, so suddenly did she find it necessary to sit.

Joey followed, sitting opposite her in the large rear compartment of the car. He placed his attaché case under his legs and smiled deliberately at her. "Well, how nice," he said, using his fingers to keep his smile in place, urging her to do likewise for Rudd's benefit.

But Diana couldn't smile. She had already steeled herself to accept the fact that she could never see David again. If Rudd had told her that the death sentence had already been carried out, she could have understood this with less confusion, even if her grief would have been unbearable.

Now she would have to do what the Haganah had asked.

She would see David, she would try to touch him one last time, and perhaps he would even acknowledge her sacrifice with some fleeting glimpse of love. But then in a moment, or in an hour, he would be dead anyway, and so would she. Diana sat in the car, her eyes open to nothing, understanding that she had undertaken something from which there could be no pulling back. She would go to the prison, she would try to set in motion a series of events that would lead not only to David's death but also to her own; and there was nothing she could do about this.

"It's going to be great, baby," said Joey, slapping her knee. "It stopped raining, see? That's always a good sign." He turned to the yellow-toothed Charley Rudd. "She's worried about her fiancé," he said.

"Terrible business," said the Englishman. "I'm thoroughly opposed to the entire policy of the administration—but then again, I'm not capable of rectifying a thing."

"Diana," said Joey. "If you've gotten a chance to see David, maybe that means they're softening. Maybe it means they'll release him."

The car pulled softly away from the terminal, passing an armored personnel carrier. Diana forced herself to listen to the talk in the car. She understood that she was afraid, that for all her love for David, her fear was greater than this love; and this shamed her. There was no guarantee that she would die in trying to help David's cause; the only sure thing was her cowardice, and this she resolved to vanquish. Even if they would be the last moments of her life, she wanted David to understand that she was worthy of his love.

"What are we waiting for, the tanks?" said Joey.

The car had stopped behind an open Army jeep, and both vehicles were now being waved off the road by a policeman. A moment later a clumsy Eged bus, armored with steel plates, waddled up the hill behind them to the main road. It drove at no more than five miles an hour, and looked as pockmarked as if it had been the single stationary target in a camp of sharpshooters. Charley Rudd explained that there was a mail carrier in their own convoy, and one armored police car that would take up the rear.

"What about that bus?" said Joey.

"That's a private bus. A Jewish bus," said Charley Rudd.

"Yeah?" said Joey, not understanding.

"They won't get any protection," said Diana. "They're on their own."

"That's not absolutely true, Miss Mann," said Charley Rudd, his face turning as red as his name. "There are checkpoints along the highway. There are patrols. This country still has a significant British presence in it, and is not totally without laws."

"The laws exist, Mr. Rudd," said Diana. "But that bus, and all the Jewish trucks going back and forth to Jerusalem, should have some form of British military escort. Like we will."

"They're too slow, Miss Mann. They take hours. We can't police everything in the country constantly," he said. The mail-carrier jeep arrived, and behind it the armored car. In each of the jeeps was a pair of soldiers with machine guns. The armored car at their rear had a gunner in its turret and a man with a Bren gun sticking out through the steel plates at the rear. Almost immediately after the armored car arrived, they set off, the jeep in front, the armored car at the rear. "This doesn't afford us much protection either," said Charley. "We'd be no use against mines. Our driver could be picked off by a sniper, the men in the jeeps are sitting ducks. Even the armored car could be taken, with a bit of planning."

"Taken by who?" said Joey.

"Terrorists," said Charley Rudd.

"Arab or Jewish?" said Joey.

Rudd hesitated for a moment, but then he said, "The Arabs wouldn't hit us on this road. There'd be no point, right?"

In place of the rain, a noontime haze sat over the highway to Jerusalem, and as they climbed the first hill, passing the Jewish bus, Joey saw the first Arab village come to life under a sudden burst of sunshine.

Rudd seemed to be struggling with his words, the way he struggled with his awkward limbs. He tugged on a yellow incisor tooth as if it might be loose; he scratched at his hairy wrist and adjusted his banker's tie. "Look here, my good man," he said. "The truth is that I'm completely on your side, if it is your side. Perhaps I should say on the side of the Jews. It's disgraceful how the government has totally abnegated its responsibility towards the Jews at this time, disgraceful. It's horrible to say so, but the Mandate's giving precious little help to the Jewish buses and trucks going on up to Jerusalem, because it would just as soon let them get blown to bits. But you needn't quote me. And you must remember that not all Englishmen like their country's foreign policy, and that it's thanks to your country that there's such awful feeling about the immigration. I don't blame the Jews for wanting to throw bombs when we English won't let in your 250,000 refugees in Europe into their own country—what I feel is their own country. But don't forget that America let in less than five thousand Jews last year. Less than five thousand was all they would take, for all their talk about humanity."

The rainfall must have been light, for as Joey observed, the land sucked up the moisture almost at once; as the haze continued to break apart into a brilliant wintry sun, the eroded land reminded him of the country outside Mexico City, where he had gone to deliver a package for Marty shortly after the war. Arab peasants who looked at them from the edge of the road were no more or less foreign to him than the peasants of Mexico; their dark eyes looked at the convoy without interest, without expectation, as if they were insubstantial. Perhaps a figment of the imagination against their timeless landscape.

"Who got me the permission to visit David Stern?"

"I don't know, Miss Mann. I'm not official. I work with the Financial Secretary, of course, but not for him or the government. I suspect they sent me rather than someone else because they know my politics."

"But the Financial Secretary was told about the permission—"

"So far as I know, this had very little to do with the Secretary. It happened in London. Your family knows the Secretary here, and I believe you've dined with him—ergo, here I am to deliver the message and see you to your hotel safely. I am a private citizen, a banker in fact, doing a favor for the Secretary at his request."

They passed a small herd of goats, the driver in the first car honking to alert the goatherd. "Good place for an ambush," said Joey, looking up at the low hills about them. He loosened his silk tie, though he was not at all warm, and wished for the comfort of his revolver nestled against his chest.

"This is not such a good place," said Charley Rudd. "Not with Bab El Wad coming up."

"What's Bab El Wad?" said Joey.

Diana explained: "It's the entrance to the valley. It's where every car on the road becomes an easy target from the hills above. It makes this place we're going through feel as safe as midtown Manhattan."

"What valley? I thought we just keep climbing up?" said Joey.

"We do keep climbing," said Diana. "But you'll understand Bab El Wad when we get there." After Charley Rudd's little outburst against his own government, Diana had relaxed a bit. Her fear didn't vanish, but the biblical landscape around her, and Joey's wide-eyed first-time look at it, allowed her to think in terms of miracles. Perhaps David would live, and she would live, and the Jews of Eretz-Israel would live too. If more British were like this eagerly sympathetic banker in the car with them, David would never have been arrested in the first place; his armed presence on the defenseless bus would have been legal and proper in the eyes of the government, instead of an abomination to be punished by death. The colors of the familiar landscape reappeared as the sunshine continued to intensify: the sand turned from brown to yellow, the stones turned from black to white. Even the sense of abandonment, the air of desolation that surrounded the poor untilled soil, seemed to lift into a more hopeful frame, even as the road wound higher and higher toward the Judean hills and Jerusalem. She told Joey how the road ran from sea level to 2,500 feet above it, and that the modern paved highway followed the path that had been used by caravans and pilgrims for four thousand years and more.

"Why would people use a road for four thousand years that was always so easy to get ambushed on?" he said.

"There was no choice," she said. "There was no other way to get up to Jerusalem." The convoy picked up a little speed going down through the Valley of Ayalon, but there was no time to tell Joey the story of how Joshua had been graced by the sun's standing still for an hour in this very place, because Rudd had begun to talk again, insistently.

"You must convince all the Jews you know in Jerusalem that under no circumstances must they leave it, no matter how bad it gets," he said. "This whole issue of internationalizing is crazy. There is only one Chosen People, and that is the Jewish people, and we cannot hope for redemption if they are removed from the City of Zion." Rudd pushed back a lock of his lank hair and smiled at them gamely, as if to demonstrate that he was not crazed, simply a bit religious, and he hoped that was all right with them. "I fully accept the right of the Jews to live in Tel Aviv and Haifa, and think their settlements in Galilee and the Negev are remarkable," he continued. "But if the

Arabs force the Jews out of Jerusalem, it might not mean the end of the Jewish state, but it might mean the end of a chance for redemption for a thousand years. Are you at all religious?"

"Not very," said Diana. Joey shook his head.

"No matter," said the Englishman. "Religious or not, you're still part of the Chosen People, part of the Design. You're here, aren't you, and you're going to Jerusalem, and that is all part of His Design."

Joey was about to correct him about the fact of his Jewishness; he felt he was at least as much Catholic as he was Jewish, particularly since his last name was Marino, and was therefore perceived by the world as an Italian Catholic, like his father before him. Diana's mention of the fact that the Jewish religion regarded him as completely Jewish, not even in need of conversion—simply because he was the son of a Jewish mother, and Judaism based one's Jewishness along matriarchal lines—seemed irrelevant to him. But Charley Rudd's earnest, gawky mannerisms were now revealed as the outward manifestations of a full-blown fanatic, keeping his feelings to himself. Now these feelings came out, unstoppable; and Charley was smooth, or as smooth as passions learned by rote could ever be.

They passed Latrun, the British fort and prison—"concentration camp" was how Diana had always heard it described by David—that commanded nearly ten miles of roadway from its secure position on the high ground. But Joey had only a glimpse of barbed wire and the nearby red-tiled roofs of the Trappist monastery before Charley Rudd diverted his attention by taking hold of his hands:

"'As the mountains are round about Jerusalem, so the Lord is round about his people from henceforth even for ever.' Psalms, of course. And from Galatians: 'Jerusalem which above is free, which is the mother of us all.' That is not just the mother of the Jews, you see, but of us all. And if we let Jerusalem sink back into the hands of the Arabs, we lose our home, our hearth, our center. It is not your obligation alone, but mine as well, since I understand and believe. The Jews must stay in Jerusalem, regardless of what suffering they must endure."

Barren pines lined both sides of the narrow road as the convoy slowed and then stopped. The first jeep had heard the sound of an approaching truck barreling down the narrow gorge, and because the way was so narrow, decided to wait till it had come down and passed them. But it was more than just a truck: the pale blue buses of the

Jewish Eged line came first out of the gorge, driving at reckless speed. Neither bus was armored, and the windshield and windows of each were shattered and stained with blood. The second bus in the line was listing heavily on its left side, where its tires had been shot out, and its wheels turned on ruined rims. The truck came third in the line, an ancient orange-painted flatbed, laden not with produce but with the wounded and the dead.

"This is Bab El Wad," said Diana.

The buses pulled off the road, and the truck continued on, honking its horn continuously. Joey was restrained from getting out of the car by Charley Rudd. The ambulance corps had already come up behind them from Latrun, and with it, two personnel carriers. "They're safe now," said Charley, "and I doubt there's going to be anyone on the road so soon after an attack. Let's go on up."

They could hear the cries and screams from the buses and truck long after they'd entered the gorge. Bab El Wad was indeed an entrance to a valley, though the valley was the roadway, and all about it were the steep hills and sheer walls of rocks and trees that girded this path through the mountains of Judea. The road to Jerusalem wound on, always climbing, a twisting, difficult road under the best of conditions; accidents were frequent as cars collided around blind curves, or roads washed away under a winter's rainstorm. Coming around a curve, the sun would suddenly appear blindingly; the road would dip for a moment, then climb so precipitously that the gear box trembled. There was flooding in the winter; in the summer, the roadway buckled, and was often covered with slippery patches of sand. It was twenty miles of climbing curves from Bab El Wad to Jerusalem, twenty miles in which one climbed two thousand feet above the level of the sea. Driving a little path of straight road was comforting, but only a little; even here, Arab irregulars could be waiting behind the rocks, in the spare trees with the sun at their backs, always high above them. Charley Rudd had told them that it would be all right, that the Arabs wouldn't want to attack a British convoy, and Diana believed him. But still, the sounds of the wounded and dying Jews echoed through Diana. If they would not be attacked, it didn't lessen the chance of others being murdered along this same path. If this road was safe for her now, it might not be safe the next time, and she agreed with Charley Rudd that this road must never be abandoned. Jerusalem had to survive, and as they traveled up to the

Holy City in the wake of the latest atrocity on the road, she didn't quite see how it would be able to.

They passed a burnt-out shell of a jeep, poised at the edge of a cliff, and a hundred yards farther on, a shot-up truck's skeleton—its wheels, engine, lights already scavenged by its attackers. Joey reached out to take hold of Diana's hands, sensing her fear, and understanding it. It would be stupid to disregard the ominous nature of this place. Every sand pit, every pile of rocks and debris, every half-ruined one-story stone hut seemed to hide men with guns and bombs and hate. If the Arabs were to make good their pledge to drive the Jews into the sea, this road to Jerusalem was as good a place as any to begin. For as Charley Rudd himself had said, the land of Israel without Jerusalem was like a body without its soul. And a country without its soul would not be able to live.

They approached a checkpoint manned by British and Arab members of the Palestine police. An Arab villager dressed in a white-and-brown robe that dragged in the dust was speaking to a British policeman, apparently trying to sell him the goat he had on a string. When they drove through the checkpoint, the villager turned his head and Joey caught his eyes, and this time the eyes looked at him, as if they were memorizing his face. Joey was visible now, and this Arab was not a peasant, and the man's face blew up big as it rushed forward and pressed itself against the passenger compartment's window, the fierce mustache, the thick stubble of beard caught in a blaze of reflected light.

Joey tore at Diana's hand violently, throwing her to the floor of the car and diving on top of her. He shouted "Drive!" but this was unnecessary, as they were already in motion, even as the Arab's gun blew a hole through his own robe, shattered the Bentley's passenger window, and pumped two bullets into Charley Rudd's brain.

SEVEN

The Arab wounded two policemen before he was shot down and killed. Charley Rudd died instantly. Diana wouldn't ride in the Bentley for the rest of the trip, calmly telling Joey that if there was no other way, she would wait for an interurban taxi to get to the checkpoint. She didn't cry, and when she tried to throw up, she was unable to do even this.

"As you can see, I'm not so brave," she told Joey, her eyes narrow against the sun. There was blood on Joey's suit jacket, and when this bothered Diana, he tore it off and threw it away.

"This isn't a country for suits anyway," he said.

They rode the rest of the way in the personnel carrier, a cramped, very hot vehicle pierced by beams of light through its gun ports. The rear gunner was very nervous. He kept explaining that the Arab was probably an isolated assassin, that there was no chance that he was part of a bigger group that would be waiting to attack them. "But I'm ready to use this on the buggers, don't you think I won't . . . filthy bastards . . . cowards is what they are . . . don't care if they get shot themselves."

His fear wasn't infectious. Watching the gunner hang on to his Bren gun for dear life, even Diana began to calm down. "He was killed for being sympathetic, do you understand? The ones who are sympathetic get killed."

"He had no escape route," said Joey. "That was a kamikaze hit—it didn't make sense. Who in the hell would take Charley Rudd seriously? He was nice, but he was crackers."

"It's worse if you're an Arab," said Diana. "I mean, an Arab that isn't preaching extermination of the Jews. They get shot by the Mufti's men or by some religious fanatic from Syria." Diana suddenly shut up as the personnel carrier ground to a halt at the crest of a hill. They waited for the jeep to drive down the valley and up the next rise before the mail carrier joined it, and then finally they continued, the gunner in the turret and the rear gunner straining for signs of life in the bald hills glimmering in the winter sun.

There were four constables in the carrier, sitting calmly in the confined space, each with a tommy gun in his lap. None of these men was surprised at the murder of Charley Rudd, though all of them were incensed by it.

"It's not like us, you understand," said one of them. "They don't have a regard for human life, if you see what I mean. If someone says 'go,' they go. It doesn't matter if they get their heads blown off, as long as they do it for Allah."

"There's fanatics in every country, soldier," said Joey. "I seen guys in my army who were looking to die for glory, and they'd be upset everytime the shooting died that they were still alive."

"You don't understand this country," said Diana, so suddenly angry that Joey knew she was once again thinking about David. "Charley Rudd was an Englishman who favored the Jews and had some influence, therefore he was killed, murdered in cold blood. That is the way this country works. You don't find the Jews doing that."

"What's that, lady?" said a previously calm constable, his face puffing up with anger. "What about the Irgun? What about that Begin boy that nobody can catch? What about the soldiers not even wet behind the ears that get shot behind their backs? That's not Arab shooting, that's Jews."

Joey would've felt obligated to intervene at that moment—even with a tommy gun in his lap, the Britisher had no right to talk to Diana like that—but one of the constables caught sight of yet another wreck on the road, this one of a private car.

"It's not the Jews doing that, is it, Tommy?" said Diana.

"Don't call me 'Tommy,'" said the constable.

"She can call you anything she wants, fat-boy," said Joey. "And you don't get up, you're in the army, or the police force, or whatever the hell it is. Have a little discipline. If you want to break my face, I'll give you a chance out of that uniform. I'll meet you anywhere you want, as long as it's a public place, and you don't come with a gun and five friends. Did you hear me, fat-boy?"

"I heard you, Yank," said the constable. He was fingering his tommy gun, as if wondering whether to take it off his lap and slap one of his hands into the handsome American's face.

"Well, what's the place?" said Joey.

"Leave it be, Yank," said another constable. "We got enough blood in this country without any of yours."

"You guys are brave when you come in groups," said Joey. "I'm talking to fat-boy, who insulted this lady. Does fat-boy want to meet me for a drink tonight? I haven't slept in three days, he has a good chance of living."

"Stop it, Joey," said Diana. "You're crazy, you really are nuts. These people are here to help us get to Jerusalem, and you're antagonizing them, like a little boy." She began to cry now, whether for the dead Charley Rudd, the imprisoned David Stern, or simple tears of vexation, Joey couldn't tell. The crying quieted both Joey and the Englishman. They had all passed through enough blood and misery for one day. Joey patted Diana's hand, apologized, smiled at the fat constable, and apologized to him too.

"You a reporter, Yank?" he asked Joey.

"No. I'm a gangster from New York," said Joey.

"You Yanks. Always joking."

"Joey Marino," said Joey, sticking out his hand to the fat constable. The man took it and introduced himself as Elliot Crawfield. "We can still have a beer without the fight," Joey suggested brightly.

"I'd like that," said Crawfield.

"I'm buying," said Joey.

"I'd like that even better." The constable wrote down the name and address of a bar that he'd be going to that evening and that Joey said he would try to visit if he had the time.

They passed the Arab villages that looked down at the defenseless road from their naturally fortified heights: Kastel, sitting atop the ruins of two thousand years of castles and fortresses that had guarded

114

Jerusalem by dominating this road; Abu Gosh, where King David had camped for two decades before entering the Holy City; Kolonia, where Titus had stationed his legionnaires during the siege of Jerusalem nineteen hundred years before. The turns and curves and bumps in the badly sprung vehicle were an inglorious way to enter the city, but as they climbed higher and higher and finally reached the sign in English—"YOU ARE ENTERING JERUSALEM,"—Joey had a curious reaction that had nothing to do with an end to the possibility of violence. He felt as if he was trying to remember something that he had somehow forgotten.

"Where are we?" he said to Diana, looking through the gun ports at an undistinguished collection of one- and two-story buildings of dilapidated stone.

"Just a suburb, or the outskirts . . . I don't know . . . I'm a bit disoriented." But she recognized the Jaffa Road, and when they were finally able to get out of the carrier at yet another checkpoint, Joey had his first view of the Old City's walls.

There were streets leading to it blocked off by barbed wire and guards; there was a platoon of blue-bereted Life Guards marching distractedly toward their checkpoint; there was the always eager clamoring for attention of beggars and merchants; the insistent demands of the police for passports and press credentials; the cacophony of wheezing buses and squalling babies and men made mad by the last war, railing at the world. But the walls loomed up in the distance, and visible beyond them were the somehow familiar spires and domes and steeples of the religious buildings sheltered within them. Joey blinked at the sight, struggling at the sensation that he had seen all this before. His memory, unlike the memory of most men, did not play tricks on him. If he had seen this place before, in a book, in a magazine, he should be able to to dredge up the image more clearly, and with it, the time and the place he had seen it, the number of the page on which it had appeared.

But it was not like that.

This was not something he'd seen in a book. Looking toward Jaffa Gate, he remembered the way the sun lifted up from the east in the morning, illuminating the Temple Mount with a golden haze. He had never seen the Temple Mount, never heard the words, but now they came to him, and he was sure of the memory, as sure as he was of anything he had been able to impress upon his brain.

"The Temple Mount is where the Mosque of Omar is, right?"

"What?" said Diana. "Joey, give the man your passport."

"And it was the site of the original Temple, the Temple of the Jews that was destroyed by the Romans in the year A.D. 70."

"This is not the time to show off how you've memorized a guidebook. The sooner we get through these police procedures, the sooner we'll be able to get a bath and change of clothes and know what we're going to do."

"I've been here before," he said.

"Of course you haven't," said Diana, as if she were reprimanding a little boy. Then she shook her head, smiling broadly. "I see. You have that feeling. Like you've seen all this—"

"I do—"

"Joey," she said. "Everyone has that feeling."

"Not like this."

"Everyone who comes here and sees the wall of the Old City reacts the same way. It's a storybook picture, and we've all seen that storybook somewhere."

"No," said Joey. But then he stopped trying to convince her. Perhaps there was a memory from his childhood he couldn't quite make clear; perhaps his father had shown him a book of the holy sites, or his mother had spun out a tale so concrete with images that they had somehow taken shape in his mind, waiting for this moment. It made no difference. He liked the scent of the dry air, the sense of permanence and continuity emanating from the walls that seemed to run on into a horizon that included space and time. He had come to this place to be close with Diana, but already he had another reason to be here: to understand the tremendous feelings of love that were sweeping through him now, not love for a woman, but love for a city that had never meant a thing to him before.

They passed through the checkpoint and were transferred to a police car without armored plates. Nearby, an explosion went off— perhaps a bomb, a firecracker, or an accident with a car—and their police escort urged them not to worry: this was merely the expected reaction to the end of the Mandate, the police would soon have everything under control. Three armored cars with turrets guarded the intersection of King George Street and Ben Yehuda Street, but their car was able to pass by them without ceremony. They skirted a gathering crowd of mourners, mostly Moroccan Jews, descending en masse to the scene of the murder of a shopkeeper that morning. A narrow and steep street, Queen Melisande's way, was momentarily full of a crowd of Arab boys carrying sticks, but the boys took off as one of the policemen in the car opened his door and held out his gun. Then they were able to proceed to the courtyard of the headquarters of the Palestine police, where two officers took their depositions about the murder of Charley Rudd.

"Say," said Joey Marino as good-naturedly as he could manage, "is there any way that I can get hold of a gun—legally, I mean?"

"A gun?" said the police officer. "Absolutely not. You're a reporter, not a gunman."

"Yeah, but this town looks a little bit like the Wild West."

"I wouldn't worry too much, Mr. Marino. We should have things under control in a day or so. Until then, you might feel more comfortable inside, if the sight of crowds disturb you."

"Yeah, I really quiver inside every time I see one of those Arab kids with a stick in his hand," said Joey. "Luckily, there are so many big brave Englishmen around with tommy guns that I don't have to worry too much." Obviously, thought Joey, he would have to buy a gun on the street, at whatever the going rate was.

Diana started to apologize for Joey's ill manners, but stopped herself. She was tired of picking up after Joey's messes, and turned her smile on the police officer not to make up for Joey, but to ingratiate herself with the man.

"I was very grateful to learn that the government would be allowing me to visit my fiancé, officer," she said. "I don't know if this is the proper department to speak of it, but since poor Mr. Rudd is dead, I don't know who to turn to."

The police officer explained that she would be allowed to visit David Stern, and would find out about the exact time and procedures after she and Joey presented their press credentials at the Public Information Office.

"And as for you, Mr. Marino," said the police officer, "don't think your press card gives you impunity to be rude. This is still a bit of His Majesty's empire you're standing on, and if I give the word, we'll have you thrown out like the trash you look like." He turned to Diana. "If you'll pardon me, Miss Mann . . ."

Another police car took them along crowded and tense King George Street, where the news of an anti-Jewish riot swelling up for the second time in two days in the Commercial Center had infuriated the entire Jewish population of the city. Turning into King David Street, they could see the tension in the eyes of the soldiers—young recruits from the Warwickshire Regiment—standing beside the road-block that guarded the famous King David Hotel. The sandbags and barbed wire and armored cars emphasized the fact that half the hotel had been taken over by the British government. No one had forgotten the Irgun's bombing of the hotel's south wing in July 1946. The cavalier attitude of the British who had refused to heed the Irgun's warning to evacuate their headquarters, believing that no one could have penetrated their defenses, had ultimately led to the tragic loss of eighty lives. Symbolically, the David Building had been rebuilt and made as impregnable as possible; a cavalier attitude had been changed to one of the righteous terror, of caution with cause. Their police escort turned them over to a constable whose task was to escort them through the restrictive maze, bureaucratic and security-intense, that led from the entrance to the fifth floor of the building, where the Public Information Office was located.

Here, Joey and Diana were issued local press passes and were given a short lecture on streets to avoid even in daylight hours. But Joey found himself distracted once again, unable to listen to the information officer's advice about the prevalence of petty thievery, random violence, nonpolitical criminal acts that were accelerating as criminals began to take greater advantage of the local turmoil, and the knowledge that the government would not be around to prosecute them much longer. From the fifth-floor office there was a view of the Old City that drew him to the dirty window and kept him there, as if he was forced to search for something in the confusion of spires and domes that would explain his sense of having been there before. He could see the Mosque of Omar, its golden dome beating back the winter sun with force. On the horizon, beyond the city's eastern walls, he could see the Mount of Olives and Mount Scopus, but didn't know their names or what they were. Still his eyes caressed the heights and slopes, and turned to the mountains of Moab in the distance, and felt the landscape touch his heart. Within the walls, he could see the smaller Mosque of el-Aqsa near the more famous Mosque of Omar, though he knew neither of these names, but only that they stood on the site of the ancient Temple of the Jews. He could see the clock tower of St. Savior, and the much newer Church of the Holy Redeemer's belfry, but these structures didn't seem to have a place in his memory, though the vistas over which they towered seemed familiar, like a childhood schoolhouse visited as an adult. He turned and saw an incongruous windmill, built by Sir Moses Montefiore in the nineteenth century to help poor Jews grind their grain; but Joey didn't know this, but felt as if the ground on which it stood seemed to be radiating a message of longing to him.

"Beautiful, isn't it, Mr. Marino?" said the information officer. "But you must be very careful. Down there's Yemin Moshe, full of Jewish snipers these days. They may not be shooting at you, but what if they miss?" He laughed at his own joke, and Joey turned about to find Diana staring at him impatiently.

"Looks familiar too, does it?" she said.

"Never mind," said Joey. "Are we through here?"

"I'm waiting to find out about visiting the prison." The information officer was on the phone, and at Diana's words, he smiled up at her.

"No problem there," he reassured her. He listened to the voice on the other end of the line, all the while smiling cheerily. When he hung up, he shook his head in wonderment. "I am the bearer of good news, wonderful news, Miss Mann. There has been a reduction in sentence."

"What do you mean? How is that possible?"

"In a world where it's possible to sentence someone to death for carrying a revolver in self-defense, it's certainly possible to reduce the sentence, what?" Diana found herself taking a chair, unable to fully appreciate the reality of yet another Englishman who for all his starched mannerisms was sympathetic and friendly. All she could concentrate on was the possibility that David might not die, that he might once again hold her in his arms, fill her with love and desire.

"If the sentence is reduced, that means he's not going to be killed, isn't it? Tell me, please just tell me, and I'm sorry if I'm shouting, but tell me."

"Of course," said the Englishman. "He is to be sent to Kenya. To be imprisoned for twenty-eight years."

The information officer had arranged rooms for them in the Salvia Hotel, but Diana wouldn't hear of this. She had the key to David Stern's apartment, and fully intended to stay there. Joey invited himself to stay there as well, and Diana was glad of this; if he hadn't been so eager to force himself on her, she would have had to ask him to stay anyway. She felt as if her cowardly nature had broken out in full bloom. The fact that David could live had brought her a measure of joy, but only for a moment. Reason had prevailed as she and Joey rode through the city in a Jewish cab, taking a roundabout route that tried to skirt roadblocks, checkpoints, riots, Arab neighborhoods, and streets made impassable by bombings and fires. They reached David's apartment in Nahalat Shivah in twenty minutes, four times as long as a direct route from the King David Hotel would have been just a few weeks ago.

"Why Kenya?" Joey had asked in the cab, and she couldn't give a very good explanation for why the British had placed hundreds of Jews from Palestine into prison camps in Africa, other than that it was too far to visit, and much too far to allow the prisoners any direct affair in the politics of their country. Twenty-eight years had no reality for her, any more than the idea that she and David would be parted forever had had a reality. Diana had always been able to get what she wanted and needed, within reason, and try as she might, she couldn't imagine a world where David would be taken away from her, hanged by the neck until he was dead, or placed in an African hole until he died of old age or disease. She wanted David, she had made love to David, she had sacrificed for David; nothing but David hearty and hale and free in their bed would satisfy her. And reason told her this was impossible. Reason told her that if she would see David, it would be for one last painful time.

For some reason unknown to Diana, the visit to the prison was postponed for two days. She was certain that in that time the Haganah would contact her, tell her what she must do for Eretz-Israel. And she would do it. She would pretend that she was brave, and she would do it, and hope that her cowardice wouldn't ruin the plans of men smarter and braver than herself. She hoped selfishly that what she would do would be admirable in David's eyes.

Nahalat Shivah was in the center of Jerusalem, quite close to Jaffa Road, and not more than a twenty-minute walk to the Old City. But in its state of disrepair, its dark alleys and filthy courtyards with stunted trees and stone outhouses, it shocked Joey, like a slum that had no right to be, a bizarre twisting of Jerusalem's beautiful stones and vines and olive trees into something dim and dank and inhospitable.

120

David's apartment was on the third floor of a drafty stone house whose courtyard gave way to the main alleyway of the neighborhood. Across this alley was a Hasidic synagogue, and as Joey and Diana struggled with their suitcases, from where the taxi had dropped them, to the entrance to this courtyard, a young man with side curls, dressed in the eighteenth-century black gown of his Polish forebears, stared at them as if they had just landed from Mars or some yet more distant planet.

"May I be of assistance?" he said in Yiddish-accented English.

"Thank you, no," said Diana. "I know the way." She turned her back to the young man, surprised that he had spoken to them at all, as the Hasidic community was noted for its insularity. She felt her heart race as she walked through the courtyard, and tried to blink back the tears as the shock of the familiar hit her: the lines of laundry with its preponderance of wet khaki, the black cats that belonged to old Mrs. Kalman scavenging for food, the chatter of Hungarian coming from the third-floor balcony in the building next to David's where they were sure the lingerers over Rosa Sussman's Turkish coffee could hear them make love. Five separate buildings ringed the courtyard on this side of the alley, and each was filled with the sort of individualists that Jerusalemites took for granted. There was one building filled with Orthodox Jews from the Ukraine, a collection of four families who had emigrated together after the First World War, and had grown populous on five tiny child-filled floors. There were freethinkers in the other buildings, atheists, anarchists; there were right- and left-wing Zionists, an English Christian Zionist couple and their family of red-headed children.

In David's building were a musician who played piano, flute, and oboe and taught bad English on the side; an ascetic Viennese who was one-quarter Jewish and had come to teach at the Bezalel art school after the war that had destroyed his faith in Austrian culture; a fiery Histadrut—the Jewish labor organization—official had never-ending meetings on the fourth floor, above them; a Berlin-born sociologist from the Hebrew University had a tiny book-filled flat on the ground floor—he used to wait up for David to try to snare him into some German conversation, though David Stern had grown up to despise the sound of his own native tongue.

"Is that where we go to the bathroom?" asked Joey about the stone outhouse in the corner of the courtyard. Diana explained that only one of the five buildings around the courtyard was without indoor plumbing; thankfully theirs had plenty of water, hot and cold. The question had brought her back to earth, but only momentarily, for she remembered asking David the same question, and his response: "Don't worry, princess. We have all the Hollywood luxuries waiting for you."

They climbed well-worn stone steps along the outside of the building that fronted the courtyard; at the second-floor level Joey noticed what looked like a tiny restaurant in the adjacent building—four tables jammed together, with two others sharing a small patio. Diana said that she had often eaten there with David; there were no set hours, and it was simple to wake the Italian Jewish woman who supported herself with this home-set restaurant. Similarly, Mrs. Sussman's third-floor flat was a café of sorts, even if the loud philosophers who frequented her balcony were usually drinking for free.

The door to the flat was locked, and Diana took this as a good sign. If his apartment had been ransacked by the British, they would have been hardly likely to lock the door after they had done so.

Diana fumbled with the key, finally dropping it to the stone flooring. Joey put down his suitcases and attaché case and hurried to retrieve it. Once again, she was crying, unable to face the apartment. Joey put the key in the lock and turned it, and threw open the door. "Come on," he said. "We need a wash and a nap, right?"

But Diana wasn't listening. She left her share of the bags and walked through the open doorway. A window had been left open in this tiny front parlor, and the single rubber plant she had last watered a month before stood, tired but alive, in the pretty pot David had brought her from Jaffa. Behind the parlor was the kitchen, and here the window was closed, and there were coffee grounds in the sink, and a smell of decay coming from the empty oil can they used for garbage.

"David," she said, and Joey heard her, and the sound of her love for this stranger was both maddening and exhilarating. He wanted her to love him, but he appreciated the power of her love for this unknown man. In his conceit, he imagined that she could love him that way someday, and perhaps even more. And he could imagine nothing finer than being loved with such dedication, such single-minded passion by a woman like Diana Mann. He watched her walk about the kitchen, touching the edge of the sink with the heels of her hands. She wandered into the adjacent pantry that they had used as a dining room, and there she sat heavily at one of the two chairs around the rickety bridge table, looking across its surface as if the man she wanted was about to materialize in the other chair.

Diana didn't see David sitting there. She was tired, suddenly as tired as if she hadn't slept for a moment on the endless flight from America, as if she had been running uphill in the rarefied Jerusalem air, as if she had been fighting and thrashing about in an endless struggle that was nonetheless finally going to cease.

"Are you okay, Diana?" said Joey, but she didn't hear this, and he went to the tap and let some water pour into a cup, and she didn't hear this either, but before he could bring her the drink, she sat bolt upright in the chair and turned her attention to the closed door to the bedroom. She was sure that she'd heard a sound—a sigh, a whine perhaps, a breath of life in this flat without her lover.

She opened the door to the bedroom and saw at once the unmade bed, with its stiff linen sheets and parti-colored cotton blanket. When David had sat up half the night at the room's tiny desk working on a Haganah code or writing a pamphlet for distribution in England or America, she would sit up in the ancient wing chair, wrapped in the blanket, feeling his fluid settle in her body, feeling the warmth of his flesh as if she were touching him at that moment from across the room.

She sat down at the edge of the bed, looking up at the cracked window where the rain and the wind had leavened the heat of their pleasure with a draft from the outside world. Slowly she took off her shoes and pulled herself across the bed's surface, resting her head against the headboard, pulling the bright cotton blanket over her shivering form.

"We got company," said Joey.

Diana threw off the blanket and started to swing her legs off the bed. The young Hasidic man who had asked them if they'd needed assistance stood next to Joey in the doorway to the bedroom, and there was no shame in his eyes at looking at a woman in her bed.

"I have a message for Miss Mann," said the young man. He no longer spoke with a Yiddish accent, and Diana supposed that his side curls were false and that under his gown he carried a gun.

"I am Diana Mann."

"You are to go to the Church of the Holy Redeemer in the Old City tomorrow at ten. Walk all the way to the top—it will take about fifteen minutes. Stand facing the east and observe the sights. A man will come to you and tell you what you need to know."

"Are you from David? Have you seen him?"

The young man smiled and shook his head. He spoke once again with a Yiddish accent. "*Oy vey*—I have nothing to do with anything . . . I am a student and *das is alles.*"

"But I am still to see David the day after tomorrow—that's all set up—you still need me to see him?"

"I am a simple student, and I should not be alone with such a beautiful young woman. Not a moment longer," he said in Yiddish-accented English. But then he hesitated, and his eyes revealed the depth of his unease. Once again he spoke without the accent, and Diana wondered if he might have been South African, or if he was another German Jew, like David, who spoke every language with the same rootless accent, the product of half a dozen lives lived around the world. "Miss Mann, there is really nothing I am permitted to tell you, but perhaps you can tell me something. The guns. Are we going to get guns?"

Diana looked at the young man in the other-worldly costume, and remembered how desperately David had looked at her on that terrible November day when he'd had to leave his gun behind for the British.

"We don't know this guy," said Joey.

"We'll get you what you need," said Diana.

"Please tell me," said the young man. "What. When. We have nothing here. We're training with sticks instead of rifles. We throw oranges instead of grenades. The situation is desperate. There is going to be hand-to-hand fighting in every neighborhood. The Old City is in terrible danger, and we're all of us sharing the same few guns." He took off his hat absentmindedly, and Diana could now see the false curls had been attached to the crew-cut head of a boy of no more than seventeen. "If we could get hold of them—or at least know we're going to get hold of them. Only a few. A hundred guns would make such a difference, Miss Mann. With a hundred guns we could do anything."

"You'll get them," said Diana.

"Are they on the way?"

Diana didn't actually know the answer to this, but she supposed it would be all right to say that they were. She imagined Arye Grinberg wasn't dragging his heels in New York with the weapons and money she and Joey had called forth from Las Vegas to New York. "They are on the way. Much more than a hundred. Thousands of them."

"My brother was killed last month, you see," he said "He was on guard duty in the Negev. With a Lee-Enfield rifle. It was one of three the kibbutz had been able to buy from a British soldier, and all of them were defective. My brother worked on his. He had to file the firing pin, he told me. I saw him the day before he died. But the rifle was no good. It jammed after the first shot. We never even got his body back. I don't know what those bastards wanted with his body, but we never even had a chance to bury him."

"You'll have your guns," said Joey. "They'll be in Haifa in three weeks."

"You don't know that, Joey."

"Approximately," he said.

"And in Haifa," said the young Haganah man. "What are you going to do about getting them through customs?"

"No problem," said Joey.

"Thank God," said the young man, putting his hat back on his head. He turned to face them from the doorway. "If you can bring us what we need, and in time, you will be saving us. If you can get those guns to us, it can mean the difference of whether we become a state or whether we simply die trying." The young man smiled weakly, as if to exhibit that he believed their words, that he was sure that all would be well.

When he had gone, Joey sat down next to Diana on the bed and took her hands. "You better get some sleep," he said. "I'm taking a little money from your big score, if that's okay?"

"What score?" she said, already drifting away from his words, feeling David's presence in the familiar shapes and colors about her. He quickly extracted a wad of bills from the attaché case and secreted the case under a pile of soiled linen.

"Not a very good place for hiding this much loot, but I'm leaving it in good hands," said Joey. Diana hardly knew what he was talking about, beginning to remember the enormous gift of cash from Marty Bernstein, the result of his bet for her in a fixed horse race. But she quickly let go of this memory, settling into the too-soft bed as if it were the embrace of a dream. She would not think about prisons, about guns, about war. There would not be a terror of anticipation, waiting to see David the day after tomorrow, wondering if they had hurt him, if they had marred his beautiful face. She would not think about the Haganah boy's brother, dead because he had no decent gun, nor would she worry about the future of the Jewish state. There was only the bed, and this blanket, and though David hadn't slept there in weeks, she imagined she could smell the sweat that collected in the small of his back, that she licked under his chin; she could feel the welling of tears in the corners of his eyes when he remembered the past hell he had lived through, witnessing the murder of the Jews of Europe, the murder of all those he had ever loved.

Joey tucked the blanket under her chin, and she looked up at him briefly, as if she didn't know who he was. "If you take two seconds, you can be clean as a whistle and get out of those airplane clothes," he was saying, but to Diana it was as if he were speaking a foreign language. "Never mind, just sleep, and stay put. I've got to go out."

Joey wrote her a note: "Went to meet Elliot Crawfield, the constable I almost punched on the way to Jerusalem. Back late. Don't leave. I've got the key. Joey Marino."

Quickly Joey opened his large suitcase, looking for his alpaca sweater, a present from his mother on his last birthday. There, in the balled-up right sleeve, he found his switchblade, and under it, folded in the white-on-white shirt he'd bought in Havana, he found his brass knuckles. Without realizing it, he was shaking his head as he slipped this into his pocket; he hadn't used "knuckle dusters" since before the war. But without a revolver on hand, this was certainly better than nothing. With two thousand dollars and a new "friend" in Elliot Crawfield, and as much liquor as Joey could pour down the constable's throat he was sure he could buy a gun that evening.

He took one last look at the sleeping Diana, her lips twisted into a smile, and then shut the bedroom door. Selecting a cashmere sports jacket to go over his slightly bulging right pocket, he smiled at his eager reflection in the ornate oriental mirror near the front doorway. He was going off to war, he thought, and he felt the excitement in his veins like an elixir, like a lustful promise.

EIGHT

Joey walked into the crowds on Jaffa Road, looking for a barber. There were three hours to get through before he would show up in the bar whose address Crawfield had given him, and he knew no more restful way to spend an hour than getting a shave, shampoo, and haircut. Without Diana next to him, and perhaps without the running commentary of the Englishmen who'd been shepherding them about, he felt less of the tension that the street had given forth earlier in the day. Perhaps it was the two weapons in his pockets that were comforting, or more simply, it was the way any sophisticated city had of dealing with a crisis: swallowing it whole.

Most of the shops had signs in three languages, Hebrew on the left, Arabic on the right, with the central and biggest sign reserved for English. Joey selected a barber shop that had only two languages on its sign, Hebrew and English, but managed to find himself sitting in the barber's chair with an Arab holding the shaving knife over his throat.

"Thick beard," said the Arab, stropping the razor.

"Haven't shaved in three days," said Joey. "Very tender skin, so be careful."

"I shave babies," said the Arab, which Joey hoped was either a bizarre joke or a confusion with the English tongue.

"Lots of commotion here today," said Joey affably.

"You English?" said the Arab, holding the knife to his throat.

"I'm on your side, pal," said Joey.

"I wouldn't cut your throat if you are Menachem Begin," said the Arab. He shaved under Joey's chin with quick expert strokes. "You are American, yes?"

"Yes"

"Newspaper?"

"Sure," said Joey, so used to the lie that he had half-begun to fancy himself a journalist. And as long as he was in Palestine—a war correspondent. "We cover the world, right?"

"What you say?"

"About what?"

"About all this here?" said the Arab barber pleasantly. He held Joey's nose and shaved above his upper lip with short scraping motions. "You should ask me, and I will tell you the truth because I am not afraid." He looked at Joey as if he were examining his worth as a newspaperman, and Joey tried hard to look like a globe-trotting reporter eager for a scoop. "They killed my brother," said the Arab.

"Who did?"

"The Mufti's men," said the Arab, but he whispered this even though the only other man in the shop was another barber sleeping in his empty chair. The Mufti, Haj Amin al-Husseini, though nominally a religious leader of Jerusalem, was actively trying to gather all future Arab political power in Palestine into his own hands. Having been a leader of Palestinian nationalism since the anti-Jewish riots of 1920, he had returned from a fruitless collaboration with the Nazis in Germany—hoping for their aid in the destruction of Palestinian Jewry—and now, from Cairo, was calling for riots, strikes, and armed insurrection against the Zionists. The Mufti's "soldiers" were badly trained Arabs from the poorest classes, often illiterate, ignorant of the volatile political situation about them; they acted on orders, the way that gangsters acted on orders. And the Mufti's men were not simply trying to pave the way for Arab rule of Jerusalem or of Palestine; they were attempting to endure the leadership of the Mufti above any other Arab leader.

"What do you mean?" said Joey. "What did your brother do?"

"He taught philosophy," said the barber. "Not like me. Very smart. He studied in Beirut and one year in Paris. He knew many Jews here, and he played music with them. The violin. I didn't like, but he was good, they say he was very good with the violin."

"But why did the Mufti's men kill him?"

"He made a talk. Lecture. A speaking before some people, Arabs and Jews, talking about peace. He wasn't looking to be anybody. My brother didn't want to be a mayor. But the Mufti doesn't care. And I'm not afraid of saying it. The Mufti isn't just against the Jews, he is against the Arabs. We could live in peace with the Jews, with the United Nations, with the British. But the Mufti kills everyone who doesn't say with him. My brother didn't say with him, so he is dead. You will write this, yes?"

"Sure," said Joey.

"I don't care about governments," said the Arab barber. "I care more about my brother, my family. There is many governments, but only one brother, and he is dead."

Joey left the barber confused. The enemy wasn't clear-cut. The British weren't as anti-Semitic as their government's policy, and the Arabs weren't as anti-Zionist as the widely circulated tirades of their leaders would have indicated. Joey brought to mind something he had read on the plane, given to him by Diana; he had read it, but not fully understood it, and now he brought forth the words and went over them as he walked the Jaffa Road.

King Faisal hadn't found it against Arab interests to enter into an agreement with Chaim Weizmann at the end of the First World War, an agreement which accepted the ideals of Zionism. Other Arab leaders of this time, including his father, Hussein, the Sheikh of the Hedjaz (later Saudia Arabia), actively urged their fellow Arabs to welcome the Jews. Among the Arab bourgeoisie there were many contacts and friendships with the Jewish world, and almost none of the enmity that the world seemed to take for granted when Arab riots against the Jews broke out in 1920, and again, with worse violence, in the 1936–1939 period. But according to Diana, these riots were inspired by complex political machinations once again outside the scope of the Arab-Jewish question of coexistence. The British had used, then removed the Mufti for their own purposes; the Mufti had first used the British, then their enemy the Germans, for his own purposes. These purposes were essentially the same—to control this strategic bit of land. Now the British Foreign Office—unsupported to a large extent by the British people—were still looking for control. Just as they had cynically allowed the Mufti's rioting gangs to wreak a certain amount of havoc in the late thirties to threaten Jewish immigration and soften Jewish demands for a national homeland, they were prepared to tolerate similar manifestations of Arab anger at the coming partition of Palestine. But as in the late thirties, it was the British and not the Arabs who benefited from the Mufti's rioting gangs—so much so that the Mufti had fled into Hitler's arms as a staunch ally against both the Jewish people and the British government—and these gangs weren't nationalist volunteers, but were mostly mercenaries, many of them from Syria and Iraq. There was talk that even the razing of the Jewish Commercial Center, a few blocks from where Joey now walked, was begun and largely completed by mercenary gangs. Ordinary Palestinian Arabs felt themselves in a vise: the actions of their leaders didn't mirror their own desires, but it was by these actions that the rest of the world, including their Jewish neighbors, was going to be forced to judge them.

Diana had insisted to Joey that the fact that the Jews had been without a state of their own had cost them six million lives in the holocaust, and that like it or not, the state of Israel, a Jewish homeland, was going to be born. The Arabs of Palestine would have to accept the fact of living as a minority in a Jewish state, or if this was insupportable, choose to leave to any of the seven Arab states that surrounded them. Beyond all the angry rhetoric imposed upon the Arabs of Palestine by their leaders, there was an eagerness to be let alone, to be left in peace. There was little doubt in Joey's mind that the man who had just shaved his face and throat had no desire to fight for a fabricated nationalism. He was an Arab, and he was proud of his heritage, but in the thirteen centuries that Arabs had lived in Palestine, they had never formed a national identity that separated them from other Arabs in other British- or French-created nations. In fact, the Arabs of Palestine were usually a minority in the crossroads country, as were the Jews, but with the great difference that the Jews had built their four-thousand-year-old history around the uniqueness of their homeland. While the Turks ruled their great empire, of which Palestine was a small part, the Arabs there never dreamed of throwing off some imperial yoke. They lived on their land, they prayed to their god, they loved their families. It was the Jews in their midst who never forgot the promise of Eretz-Israel, whose very existence in the far-flung diaspora was unified by the promise of a return to this land. Arab nationalism developed in the twentieth century, but it was a force directed at liberating their people from foreign rule, not at creating nation-states where these rulers had drawn imperial lines.

130

The same Arabs who had lived under imperial Turkish rule and British rule could live within a democratic Jewish state.

But it would be hard for these Arabs to ignore the slogans, the shouts, the shootings. The British-backed Arab landowners, many of them who had never lived in Palestine at all, would continue to incite the mobs. And if the mobs wouldn't riot, then the imported mercenary army would riot on command. All the years of Jewish friendship, the earnest promises extended to the Arab community for cultural, political, and economic freedom, would be worthless against the fact of terror. If the choice was to hate the Jews or be branded a traitor; if the choice was to boycott the friends of a lifetime or be shot in the back by one of the Mufti's gunmen; if the choice was accepting a new political world of Arab strength or being crushed in the preaching of peace—the choice for most would be obvious.

As Joey walked the streets of Jerusalem, he knew what the choice would be, what choice had already been made. The Arabs in their tarbooshes, worn with robes or Western suits, were setting themselves apart from the Jews on the sidewalk, from the English crossing the road, from the entire world of the West. They had no hate in their eyes, no enmity; there was a weary inevitability instead. There was movement, and it was of one culture pulling back from another. There was sadness for the streets that would never be the same again, for the promises that would be broken, the lives that had been intertwined that would be snapped apart with violence.

This street would not be administered by the United Nations, Joey knew. It would be a street in Jerusalem ruled by Arabs, or a street in a Jerusalem ruled by Jews. And the war to decide who would rule had begun the moment the Jewish Commercial Center was put on fire, the moment the first sniper lying on some sheltered roof had selected his victim and pulled the trigger. Near the bar where Joey was to meet the constable Elliot Crawfield had been an old synagogue nestled in a stand of pines. The civil government had posted a sign outside the structure, in the three languages of the Mandate, Hebrew, English, and Arabic, and in each language it said the same thing: "Quiet! SYNAGOGUE!" But the sign's exhortation was hardly noticeable anymore, for its letters had been shot through with scores of bullets, and the synagogue behind it had been burned to the ground two days before. Whether this had been done by the Mufti's mercenaries, or by drunken British soldiers, or by a mob of Palestinian Arab nationalists was irrelevant. What mattered was that violence had been done, that violence was in the air, and that violence—not good intentions, not justice, not the vote in the United Nations— would win the day.

"Hey, Yank, it's you!" said Elliot Crawfield when Joey walked into the surprisingly large bar shortly before seven o'clock. There was a grill, and Joey could see the remnants of shepherd's pie on the sloppy counter.

"Joey," said Joey, jerking his thumb at his chest. "You're not too drunk to get that straight, right?"

"Joey-the-Yank-from-New-York," said Crawfield. He was still in his constable's uniform, but his collar was undone, his lank brown hair was falling into his eyes, and he stank from beer. Crawfield was genuinely happy to see Joey. He had few friends among the constables, and this bar was almost exclusively full of Army men from unfamiliar regiments, most of whom were already drunk.

Hardly glancing at the barman, Joey hissed out his order: "A beer and some shepherd's pie," he said, and he flinched as Crawfield put his heavy arms about him like a long-lost friend.

"Great that you came, Yank," said the constable. "Let me buy you a drink."

Joey took the man's hands off his body, looking him in the eyes. "It's good to see you, Crawfield. But we Yanks don't like to be touched, okay?"

"What?" said Crawfield, not quite understanding.

The barman slapped down Joey's pint. "The pie's coming," he said. "That's fifty mils for the beer."

"You take dollars?"

"I'll take whatever I can get."

Joey gave the man a single dollar and told him to keep it. As fifty mils was about twenty cents, the barman placed an English shilling on the bar. "This is your change. The rest will pay for the pie."

"I said keep it, pal," said Joey. And he placed another dollar on the bar. "And that's to keep my friend here in beer."

"You smell nice," said Elliot Crawfield.

"I've been to the barber," said Joey.

"How's your beautiful wife?"

"She's not my wife," said Joey. "She's fine, she's resting."

"She's very beautiful."

"Yes." Joey drank his beer, feeling the shock of the wet against his parched throat. The pie was terrible, but he was hungry, and as he ate, he watched Crawfield guzzle down another beer. He wanted two things from this man: a gun and a way to break out of the Central Prison. Looking at the man's pathetic, lonely figure as he gratefully drank the drink that had been bought for him, Joey wished there was some other man he could use in his stead.

"Hey, copper, you're not supposed to drink with your snout," said a high-pitched voice from behind Joey's head. As there were no other police officers standing at the bar, he knew that the insult was directed at Crawfield, but did not as yet turn around. Crawfield didn't turn either, perhaps because he hadn't heard.

"Now I got to buy you one, Yank," said Crawfield. "Fair's fair, isn't it?" He looked in his pocket for change.

"Searching for your balls, fat-arse?" said the high-pitched voice, this time laughing at his own witticism. Crawfield still didn't turn, and Joey felt his anger begin to grow out of control.

"You don't have to buy me one, Elliot," said Joey, putting his arm around the fat man's shoulders. "I owe you. You took me to Jerusalem, didn't you?"

"I was on duty—"

"If you don't want a drink from the Yank, fat-arse, I'll take it," said the high-pitched voice, and now Joey finally turned around, his hand caressing the brass knuckles in the pocket of his sports jacket. The man was big, as tall as Joey, but broad and ugly, with a flat nose and cauliflower ears. He was a sergeant, and his eyes had already measured Joey and found him weak. "I said, Yank," he said, "if fat-arse doesn't want your American charity, here's one poor bloke who's only too glad."

"My name's not Yank," said Joey. "And my friend's name isn't fat-arse."

The barman put another pint of beer in front of Joey, who had turned his back to the sergeant. Now another voice erupted from behind him, and this one was low and sarcastic, its northern English accent difficult for Joey to comprehend. "Maybe he's a schoolteacher," said the low voice. "Teaching us names."

"He don't look like a schoolteacher," said the high-pitched sergeant's voice. "He looks like a guy named Yank."

"Standing next to a guy named fat-arse."

"Maybe he likes it with fat-arse, slim-arse, anyways they can get it, as long as it's up an arse."

Crawfield's face was red now, and he moved closer to Joey at the bar and whispered, "This place isn't so good for food. We ought to go over to this place in Talbieh."

"Aren't you a constable?" said Joey, speaking in his ordinary voice. Slowly he turned his back to the bar so that he could have a look at the army sergeant's friend.

"You see something you like, Yank?" said the sergeant. The friend was a corporal, and he was short and stocky, with wispy black hair over a greasy scalp.

"Maybe he doesn't like the way we're talking to his friend," said the corporal.

"He thought he was a copper, so that nothing could happen to him. But he don't understand that a copper don't mean nothing to us. We're not law-abiding civilians, are we?"

"It's okay, Yank," said Crawfield, trying to turn Joey away from the two Army men. "The military police will be passing through, and if there's any trouble, they'll handle it."

"What do you want, Elliot?" said Joey. "Would you like to go?"

"Yes, that would be fine. I know a real nice place—"

"We have to go," said Joey to the sergeant. "But we can't until you apologize."

Elliot Crawfield was suddenly a lot less drunk. "That's really okay, Yank. It's just words. Let's just go."

The sergeant reached out an index finger and poked Crawfield in the chest. "Your friend doesn't want to go, so don't hurry."

"Don't push me, mate," said Crawfield, pushing aside the man's hand. "You push me, and I'll break your head."

The sergeant had talked long enough, and Crawfield was the sort who needed only a drop of blood trickling from his nose to collapse from fright. He hit the fat man with a right jab that managed to miss the nose and hit Crawfield squarely in the mouth. Crawfield fell back against the bar in pain. "You hit me," he said, as if this were somehow unbelievable. "I'm a constable, and you can't get away with this." Not much of this was able to be heard by anyone in the bar, for a considerable commotion had broken out almost simultaneously with the sergeant's right-handed punch.

Joey Marino had brought his right hand out of the pocket of his cashmere sports jacket, the brass knuckles slipped over his fist, and slammed the heavy metal into the sergeant's jaw.

Joey heard the crack with no regrets. There was no point in using brass knuckles if you didn't want to hurt someone, and Joey had wanted to hurt the sergeant, and was satisfied that he had broken the man's jawbone.

But not so satisfied that he paused for self-congratulation.

The sergeant's scream was loud and genuine. He fell back and clutched his face as if it were in danger of falling off. There was so much pain and regret in that scream that for a second the corporal didn't think of hitting back at his friend's attacker, but only of what kind of punch could have caused such a reaction. And in that second Joey Marino struck again.

This time the brass knuckles landed on the side of the man's head. There was no crack of bones, but the scream was as loud, and as painful. The corporal wanted to speak, but couldn't; he wanted to fight, but was momentarily paralyzed by fear. But this fear was replaced immediately by pain, unbearable pain that was somehow not yet localized: his entire body was in agony, throbbing not from some central place in his head but from every nerve ending. Head, limbs, solar plexus, all rioted at the pain that had started up from the shock of brass knuckles bouncing off his brain.

There was about to be a crowd. A two-second fight always brought a crowd in a bar, a crowd that smelled blood and victory, that lusted for a winner and a loser and a chance to drink to someone's health with a glass of beer. Crawfield was pushing himself off the bar, amazed at the destruction wrought by Joey Marino: the two Army men were on the floor, the bigger one holding on to his broken jaw with tears running down his cheeks; the stocky corporal rolled over onto his side, rubbing his eyes as if he couldn't quite see. Joey's brass knuckles were back in his pocket, only partially because he didn't want the crowd about him to see how he'd hurt their fellow soldiers; primarily, he needed to exchange the brass knuckles for his switchblade, and this he had done with so much speed that it seemed as if the knife had always been there in his hand.

"Apologize," he said to the sergeant with the broken jaw. Joey had opened the knife, and pulled the big man's head by the hair so that his throat was flush against the point of the blade. The sergeant didn't seem to understand what Joey was saying, even though Joey had gone down on one knee and enunciated the word very clearly in the man's ear. As the little crowd gathered around, Joey remembered a time in Brooklyn in a waterfront bar when he had slashed open a man's cheek with the same knife, waiting for him to make a promise: that he would never try to extort money from Marty Bernstein's dockworkers again.

135

There had been a crowd around him in Brooklyn too, a crowd waiting to see if the longshoreman—in the pay of a rival Brooklyn gang—would make that promise, and Joey hadn't hesitated to help him along by slicing through the soft skin of his cheek. He didn't try to justify the act by thinking about the good that Marty Bernstein had done for him or his family; or by running through the times that the rival gang had beaten or killed dockworkers under Marty's protection. Joey was twenty then; he was not quite twenty-two now. He was not acting out of some carefully reasoned ethical code, but out of instinct. Raised in a world that had murdered his father, that had thrived on sudden, irreversible acts of violence, he had long since learned to fight in only one way, and that was without thought. Once the decision to fight was reached, there was only one way to go, and that was to try to damage the man you were fighting until he no longer represented a threat. "Apologize," said Joey again, aware of the men crowded around them, none of whom uttered a sound.

"It's okay, Yank," said Crawfield. "He doesn't have to apologize. We can just go. I'm sure he's sorry."

The corporal stirred on Joey's left. If he was armed, he could shoot, and Joey turned on him with the knife and motioned for him to slide over to his friend on the floor. "I'm going to kill your friend, asshole," said Joey. "And then I'm going to kill you, unless he apologizes."

"Go on," said the corporal, not to Joey, but to the sergeant. "The Yank's going to slice right through you."

The sergeant's lips parted slightly, and a breath of air hissed out. The broken jaw made it impossible for him to fully open his mouth, and even the lightly parted lips were askew in pain. "Sorry," he said, the word distorted, but Joey heard and got to his feet, still waving the switchblade before him.

"Get out of my way," he said to no one in particular, but a path through the crowd quickly appeared, and he walked slowly to the front door, with Crawfield in his wake. "You got a car, Elliot?"

"No, Yank."

"You live in a barracks or your own place?"

"I got a flat, a nice flat," said the constable. It had gotten very cold, and the wind whipped at them in the dark alley. Joey wanted Crawfield sober and grateful, and so he put his arm about the fat man's shoulders and said, "We sure showed those bastards, hey, Elliot?"

"It was you, not me."

136

"Are you kidding? You threw the first punch. I might have been scared, but what the hell, once you started slugging, I figured, why not? You're a good man to have in a tight spot, Constable."

Crawfield shook his head wonderingly at this false report of his bravery, but buttressed by Joey's strong arm, he almost believed what he had been told. They couldn't find a taxi, and Joey was eager to get as far from the bar as possible; he wasn't sure how many people other than the two who had been hit knew that he had used brass knuckles. Some people have been lynched for much less than that. He marched Crawfield quickly, following the map he'd memorized of Jerusalem, trying to walk so fast that the streets would follow the same twists and curves that they did on paper. The constable lived in Talbieh, in its pretty north section where Jews and Arabs lived in proximity without as yet breaking each other's heads. It was an unusual place for a constable, especially a single man, but as Joey was soon told, Crawfield had been married, and his wife had died in childbirth at the Hadassah Hospital during the second year of the war.

"The baby died too," said Crawfield tearfully as he let Joey into his ground floor apartment, its windows covered by a series of palm trees and one great pepper tree illuminated by Jerusalem's ghostly winter moon. "It's why I never went back to England. There was nothing for me there, nothing. The people here aren't so bad, really they're not. If only they wouldn't hate us so much. I'm not bloody Bevin, am I, Yank?"

"Where's your gun, Elliot?"

"I don't carry it off-duty. Not usually. Some do because of the troubles, but I don't like to. It's heavy."

"Where is it? I want to see it."

"Why do you want to see my gun?"

Joey tried to look hurt, but Crawfield had momentarily turned away, his eyes downcast. The apartment was fussily neat, with a framed needlepoint representation of a Shropshire cottage that the departed Mrs. Crawfield must have labored over under her husband's tender regard. "Look, Elliot, maybe you don't realize this, but I just saved your bloody life."

This wasn't quite true. Crawfield might have gotten pushed around, perhaps as much as a black eye. But no drunken soldiers were planning to do much more than tease and torment the fat constable. "I know that," said Elliot. "Don't think I don't know that."

"You certainly don't act that way," said Joey. "You don't seem to like me very much, or trust me either. Here I am in your flat, you haven't even offered me a nip of whiskey—that's what you English call it, isn't it, a nip?"

"I'm sorry. What would you like—would you like a whiskey?"

"I want to see your gun, not your bloody whiskey, your gun," said Joey. He walked over to a little tea table, where a starched tea cozy sat, waiting for the departed wife's gentle touch, and willed himself to be calm. Joey knew that his anger was out of proportion to his needs, that he was partially angry with himself at having to manipulate this man.

"I'll show you the gun, Yank," said Crawfield. "I don't know why you want to see it, but if you want, I'll show it to you." He brought it out of a bureau drawer in its stiff leather holster, and extracted it, a standard police-issue gun, too big and bulky for Joey's taste, but a gun nonetheless.

Joey took it from Crawfield and pointed it at his face. "Do you trust me, Elliot?"

"Yes, but don't do that."

"I want you to trust me," said Joey. He put the gun down and sat on Crawfield's favorite armchair. "It's important for you to trust me, Elliot, because I'm going to have to trust you." The simple thing would have been to kill him, take his uniform and gun, and use it in some plan to get David Stern out of prison. But Joey told himself that Crawfield could be useful alive, insisting on this in his mind to forgive himself his reluctance to murder the man. "Do you love your mother?"

"Of course I do," said Crawfield.

"She's pretty healthy for a woman of her age," said Joey.

"How do you know? She is healthy. Like her mom, eighty and going strong, and my mother's not even sixty."

"If anything happens to me, Elliot—anything—your mother is going to be killed."

"What?" Crawfield didn't like the sound of this, and the waves of nausea sweeping through him were momentarily beaten back by an urge for clarity. "What's my mother to you?"

"What's your mother's name, Elliot?"

"Helen."

"Of course it is. Helen Crawfield. And her address?"

"What do you want with her address?"

"I have been told her address, you big idiot. I just want to make sure we are talking about the same Helen Crawfield. Don't you want to help your mother? I can help her stay alive."

"Who wants to hurt my old mom? Nobody's gonna hurt my old mom!"

Crawfield had become suddenly bold, but still didn't comprehend that Joey was his enemy. But in his half-drunken desire to know what possible danger was befalling the only living person in the world that he cared for, he thrust himself at Joey. The young hoodlum was ready for him, sending his fist into the fleshy region just below the breastbone—the solar plexus—and driving the man's chin into his raised knee.

Crawfield collapsed into the chair just vacated by Joey, the pain sweeping away the drunkenness, the unknown fear to his mother exaggerated by the violence that had descended upon him from nowhere. "Nobody's going to hurt your mother, Elliot," said Joey. "I thought you trusted me. I saved your life in the bar. I could have killed you a moment ago, and I could kill you now. I want you to trust me, you big idiot. Now, tell me—I want to know if they have the right address. What is it?"

Crawfield gave Joey the address, a fourth-floor flat in the East End, in an old tenement owned by a Jewish lady his mother had known for fifty years. "Yeah," said Joey. "That's the address they've got. They're going to kill her. Look at me, Elliot. If you can help me stay alive, they won't kill her."

"What do you have to do with my mother?" he pleaded. "Please, Yank, I don't understand." He tried to sit up, but the pain from the blow to his solar plexus left him doubled up, his head raised awkwardly to look at Joey Marino.

"You see this?" said Joey, taking out the brass knuckles from his pocket. It was obvious that Crawfield hadn't seen these during the fight, because now he looked at them with horror.

"You didn't hit them with that?"

"Yes."

"You could've killed them with that," said Crawfield. Now he sat up, ignoring the pain. Joey held out the switchblade as if it were the second piece of evidence in a trial to prove his status as a gangster. "Look at this, Elliot. I'm not a newspaper reporter, I'm a hoodlum. A gangster. I kill people."

"I don't believe you," he said, but it was obvious that Elliot

Crawfield did believe Joey, and that the fear was mixed with loathing, and that he was so confused he wished he were lying blind drunk in some pit rather than in the comfortable parlor decorated by his poor wife. "What do you want with my mother? I don't believe anything you said."

Joey lifted Crawfield's gun from where he'd placed it on the floor and shoved the barrel against the man's mouth. "No," said Joey. "Open your mouth, that's it." Joey pressed the gun barrel into the man's mouth, pushing hard until the fat man had wrapped his lips around an inch of steel. Finally Joey had placed the fear where he wanted it, and that was directly against this man's heart. No longer was he thinking about mother, wife, Joey, brass knuckles, drunkenness. Crawfield's fear was as big and as breakable as a bubble. Joey had his attention. "I won't kill you, Elliot. I just want you to listen," he said. "Your mother is safe. Nothing will happen to her unless I die. And you must see to it that I don't die. You don't have to nod. Just look at me. You're going to help me because I saved your life, and because if you don't, men that you can't stop are going to find your mother in London and beat her to death. It will be your fault if that happens, Elliot. Because it's so easy for you to help me."

Joey slowly took the gun from the constable's mouth and replaced it in the holster. Crawfield looked at him, his mouth still open. "What do you want from me?"

"Give me a uniform and a gun."

"I only have this gun."

"The hell you do," said Joey Marino. He had never known a cop who didn't have more than the police pistol issued him. New York cops carried guns strapped to their ankles and behind their backs, besides their heavy service revolvers. He was angry that Crawfield was still showing resistance to him because he needed him to be totally and dependably on his side.

"It's not a police gun," said Crawfield. "It's a Colt."

"Well let's see—get it."

Police in the United States usually liked the .38 special or .45-caliber revolver. In Europe, police who carried guns preferred the .25-caliber automatics. Palestine was a special place for a British-trained constable, because in England the police didn't carry guns at all. So Crawfield's offer of a .45-caliber Colt semi-automatic was particularly appealing to Joey: he had a feeling that the big softhearted man would carry just such a monster-killer under his shirt.

"What do you want with a gun and a uniform? My uniform won't fit you."

"Better that it's large than small," said Joey, removing the magazine from the Colt, looking through the rear sight, hefting the weapon in his hand. "Look, this isn't all bad news, Elliot. I think you're a nice guy and you deserve a break."

"Take the gun. I can report it stolen. I'll forget I ever met you or had a drink—"

"Shut up, Elliot," said Joey. "This is out of our hands now. You and I both know that. It's not my decision. I have a job to do, and you were selected to help, and if you don't, it's not me who's going to pull the trigger on your mother, but some mug over in London."

"You never heard of my mother till tonight."

"Don't call me a liar, Elliot. I might shoot you."

"You won't shoot me. You need me. And I gave you that address that you never had because I'm an idiot. I could arrest you tomorrow and tell my mother to go to the country—"

"They'd kill her in the country. And she'd have already lost her son Elliot by then. You can count on that." Joey took out the wad of one-hundred-dollar bills in his pocket and peeled off the top two. "This is for your gun and your uniform."

"I don't want your money."

"And I've got a thousand for your mother. That's three hundred pounds, Elliot."

"It's two hundred and fifty pounds."

"All right. We'll send her twelve hundred dollars, okay? Tomorrow morning at nine o'clock we'll meet at the bank and we'll send her twelve hundred American dollars that you won in a poker game with your friend Joey Marino."

"I can't take the money," said Crawfield, but Joey could see that he was already figuring what his mother would do with that much unexpected cash, how much joy it would bring her in bankrupt England. "Come on, it's not a terrible thing I'm asking you to do. It's to help someone."

"You're trying to bribe me."

"It's not really a bribe, Elliot. It's a gift. If you don't help me, I'll kill you, and someone will kill your mother. So you can't call this a bribe. It's more like a gift, just because you deserve it."

"Why did you do that tonight in the bar?"

"The fight, you mean?" said Joey.

141

"Yes. You didn't have to get into that fight to get me up here. We could have just gone drinking, like pals."

"I told you," said Joey. "I like you. You're a nice guy, and they insulted you, and you're my friend. That's all it's about."

"But you'd kill me?"

"I'd really hate to," said Joey Marino. "Not just because you and I could probably become friends, Elliot, but because I really need you."

"My mother's very poor. I send her money already, but it's not enough. It's expensive over there, back home, and things she likes she hasn't had since before the war—she loves chocolate."

"So does my mother," said Joey.

"Do you get good chocolate over in America, Yank?"

"Sure, Hershey's—I'll send you some when I go back."

"I heard of that," said Crawfield. "Hershey's . . ." He went into the adjacent little kitchen and came back with a bottle of Scotch. "So I'm taking a bribe," he said. "There's worse things happening in this country every day of the week."

They drank the bottle, and Joey showed Elliot how to put on the brass knuckles, and Elliot showed Joey how even drunk as he was he could break down and clean the Colt with his eyes shut. He stopped asking Joey what more he'd have to do for him besides giving him the gun and the uniform. Joey said that he was sure Elliot would be able to do it bravely and well.

"But is it dangerous?"

"A little," said Joey.

"And against the law?"

"Elliot," said Joey, "we're going to help bring a pair of lovers together, one of whom is the woman you thought was my wife."

"She was very beautiful."

"Yes. And we're doing this all for love," said Joey.

142

NINE

Diana woke to the sound of rain. She knew at once that she was in David's bed, in the city of Jerusalem, but had not woken with any illusion that David had slept with her, that her body had luxuriated in his touch, that the pillow and the sheets and the length of her heavy dark hair were redolent of the fragrance of sex. Rain had always had a romantic appeal for her, perhaps because of the ceaseless sun of a Beverly Hills childhood. Waking in David's arms in a November rain, as Jerusalem had begun to descend into its bleak winter, had been a recurrent dream of hers while she and Joey had slept in a half-dozen different beds in different cities on their gun-seeking tour of America's gangland. But it was a dream, and not even a memory; David wouldn't ordinarily sleep through the night with her body's weight pressed against his. He tended to sleep alone, in a rigid little space, the product of the concentration camp's restricted room. It was impossible to touch him without waking him, and angering him in the process. But it was possible to wake before him, with the rain falling hard enough to shut out the world, and to watch his beautiful face rest from the anxieties of consciousness.

"Okay baby, up and at 'em," said Joey's voice from across the dark room. Diana was annoyed at the tone: he wasn't simply familiar, but commanding. The handsome boy had a tyrannical streak. She could imagine him in charge of his own network of hoodlums, his own family of attentively obedient children. His wife would be more than just obedient. She'd be blond and little and eager for his regard, a pat on the head from her lord and master. "I said get up, we've got a date in an hour and a half."

"What time is it?"

"You're up," said Joey, smiling at her response. He crossed the room and opened the weather-beaten wood shutters that did little to shut out the rain and wind coming through the cracked window. But a bit more of the morning's gray light filled the room. "I'm afraid you're not going to have time for a bath," he said. "It's your fault. You slept about a hundred hours."

Diana sat up in bed, looking at the bright-eyed Joey. She was suddenly very conscious of her filthy and rumpled airplane clothes, and Joey's always immaculate appearance annoyed her by its invidious comparison to her own.

"You look like you've had a bath, you swine."

"Come on, up, up, up," said Joey, throwing off the covers.

"What if I was naked?"

"I'd die of embarrassment," said Joey.

"Am I insane, or do I smell coffee coming from the next room?"

"You're not insane."

"Did you find coffee? Coffee is rationed! Joey, you're wonderful, I take it all back." Diana got out of bed, her head heavy from sixteen hours of sleep. Joey took hold of her arm to steady her. "Where did you sleep?"

"On the couch," said Joey.

"Is that a vicuña sweater?" she said, touching the gangster's sinfully soft cardigan.

"Don't kid me about my clothes," said Joey. "I wasn't born with a silver spoon in my mouth like some people I know."

"I didn't say a word about it. I like it. You dress very elegantly. I wasn't criticizing you, even if you do look like a walking recruitment poster for a life of crime in Havana."

"My life of crime hasn't been all bad," said Joey. Diana was surprised to see that the edge that usually accompanied his defending his occupation, clothing, speech, or education was missing that morning. He was happy about something. There was an air of triumph about him that disconcerted her. She wanted to know what the boy had up his sleeve, because she was afraid of his impulsiveness. While she had slept off the fatigue of the overlong air flight, Joey had been free to do anything. Like a big sister or a mother in charge of a rascally little boy, she needed to know at once what he'd been up to, because she had a feeling she'd find out when it was too late to patch up whatever transgressions he'd committed.

But she had no time to question him further, as Joey hurried her out of the bedroom in her stocking feet and into the kitchen, from which the smells of coffee had indeed originated.

"Mrs. Sussman, what are you doing here?" said Diana.

Somehow Joey had managed to procure not only coffee but also the proprietress of the third-floor café in the adjacent building.

"He pays me too much money, American dollars. I have eggs, cheese, hard rolls, and it costs you more than if you bought in a restaurant."

"We're ready to eat, Mrs. Sussman," said Joey.

"You don't have to yell at me."

"I didn't pay for a speech," said Joey. "I paid for breakfast. We can do this again; it all depends on you."

"Listen to him," said Mrs. Sussman to Diana. Then, as if she remembered that Diana was somehow allied with this attractive young American, she added, "I wonder what Mr. Stern would say about all this special breakfast service. Mr. Stern isn't so fancy, I don't think."

"We are both friends of Mr. Stern," said Diana severely. "Mr. Marino and I are both here because of Mr. Stern, and for no other reason."

"Okay, okay, I didn't say nothing," said Mrs. Sussman. When she'd finished their omelets she slammed down their plates on the little bridge table in the pantry and advised them to finish everything she'd prepared. "Other people are hungry in this country, and it's going to get worse." But finally she left, and Diana and Joey relished the freshness of the eggs, which came from a nearby kibbutz, and the richness of the coffee, and the sweetness of the rolls. It was a little too comfortable for Diana, who remembered the hasty breakfasts and dinners with David Stern on this same table, with her lover's attention usually elsewhere, on some task for the Haganah, or some past from which Diana was excluded. The food and the coffee awakened her too. She had not simply rested, she had retreated from the problems, the terrors at hand, and now with sugar and caffeine racing through her blood, they had returned. David Stern was in prison. She was to help get him out. That very morning she would receive the instructions that could bring him to freedom or send both herself and David to their deaths.

"You could at least say thank you for arranging this meal," said Joey. Diana looked up at him, and again caught the unmistakable sense of his unusual measure of self-satisfaction. He wasn't hurt at her inattention; he seemed to be playing with her.

"Thank you," she said. "Now, suppose you tell me where you've been while I was asleep."

"No time, Diana," he said, and now his smile was as arch as an actor's villian, hamming for the audience. "I was involved with far too many things to tell you about, see? If you're nice, I'll tell you later."

"Joey, I want to know right now."

"Miss Mann, there are some things that even you can't get just by asking," said Joey Marino. "Now, hurry up and change your clothes. We've got a date at ten o'clock, and it's going to take at least forty-five minutes to get there."

"Joey, did you do anything that can get David in any kind of trouble?"

"No. Now, hurry up, baby, come on. You can't be late for the Haganah," he said. Diana could see that he was not about to be budged, that her influence on him had somehow dwindled while she slept. She quickly got out of her chair and walked into the bedroom to change. Joey poured himself another cup of coffee, congratulating himself on how well he'd handled Crawfield an hour before, while Diana still slept. The constable had been bleary-eyed and irascible, so hung-over that his eyes could barely focus on Joey when he'd shown up at the neat Talbieh flat before eight.

"I've thought it over," Crawfield had said. "And I can't do it. It's against the law, and I don't break the law. Last night I was drunk. So don't say anything or I'm going to have to arrest you."

Crawfield had not yet dressed that morning, and in his tatty robe and shabby slippers he was particularly pathetic to Joey, who had to instantly decide whether or not to kill him after all. Instead, he pushed past the constable into the apartment, closed the door, and kicked into the man's shin with his alligator shoes. Crawfield had

146

gone down, looking up at him like a half-dead fish drowning in air. The constable was remembering the night before, when he had been drunk, and was believing that the nightmare had actually happened. This time he didn't scream, and the effort to hold back his pain from exploding into sound exhausted him. Joey got to one knee and took hold of the man's right hand. "I could break your fingers one at a time, do you understand?" he said. "There's nothing you or your police force can do to stop that, not this second. You're in my power. Of course, if we go to the bank and you find another copper and start shouting for help, and pull out your gun . . . well, it would be messy. I would kill you, of course, and someone would kill me. And then your mother wouldn't get her three hundred pounds, and she'd be killed herself, like I promised you. Now, this is the last time I am going to say this. Then I will start breaking your fingers, and if that doesn't work, I will kill you. Okay. Are you ready to come to the bank with me?"

Crawfield had been ready. Joey, while waiting for Diana, did not think proudly of the way he'd intimidated the constable, but of the more subtle way he'd been able to befriend him in the very awkward hour they spent together. Joey had complimented him on how he'd managed to hold his liquor the night before, on how his hung-over condition was barely noticeable. He'd asked him questions about his wife, whose name turned out to be Violet, and Joey admitted that was a name that anyone could love. Crawfield had spoken with admiration of the staff of the Hadassah Medical Center who had taken charge of him after his wife had died. In the midst of his suffering, he couldn't help but be shocked by the gentle way he'd been treated by doctors and nurses. He had not been used to such treatment, and years later, it had remained with him, even in conversation with an American gangster who had threatened his life and that of his mother.

In the bank, Joey had felt no threat coming from the constable. He had already been beaten. It would have been a simple thing for Elliot Crawfield to draw his gun and shout for help in his uniform. But Joey could see that the man was distracted: he was thinking of Violet, and of his mother, and of the possibility that Joey had planted in his mind that perhaps what he was doing was not cowardly, but rather somehow a repayment to the Jewish doctors and nurses who had comforted him after the death of his wife. Joey had tried to emphasize this connection, not by extolling the virtues of the Haganah or the perfidy of the British Foreign Minister, but by calling forth the very real virtues of the English Mandate in Palestine. The young gangster showed the constable that he believed that there were good Englishmen and bad Englishmen, and that he was giving Crawfield a great compliment by enlisting him in the Jewish cause. As Joey arranged the transfer of American dollars to Crawfield's mother's account in England, he reminded the constable that such easy transfers of money were possible from Palestine only because of the British banking system. If Palestine was never a member of the Commonwealth, it still had been allowed participation in the sterling bloc of finance and trade; Jewish citrus farmers had an all-important open market in England. Drawing on his photographic memory, Joey listed other British deeds, from the Balfour Declaration's legitimization of Zionist aspirations for a Jewish homeland, to the thirty years of protection that the British Navy had given the Jewish settlers.

"The Navy doesn't let the refugees land," Crawfield had said. Joey pointed out that they didn't let the Nazis land either. He gave Crawfield the bank receipt that would show the transfer of money, and didn't bother to point out that a transaction in a public place had taken place that he would find very difficult to explain to his superiors on the police force. Crawfield already knew this, in the same way that he knew he had been intimidated, bribed, and manipulated. But he was trying hard to believe that what he was doing was all right, that the money going to his mother would not cover the tracks of some monstrous deed. And when they left the bank, Crawfield standing as tall and proud as he could in his uniform, Joey had taken his hand and looked him in the eye and thanked him.

"It's you giving me the present, Yank."

"It's you who's going to be there to help, the way you already have," Joey had said.

"You're not going to kill someone with my gun?" said Elliot Crawfield. "Not wearing my uniform and killing someone in cold blood?"

"No," said Joey. "With you to help me out, I don't think anyone will be hurt, see? You're the kind of guy who knows how to keep things going smooth and easy."

"What things?" Crawfield had asked, still not knowing what Joey wanted of him, but Joey explained that he would be told in good time, and that he didn't have to worry about a thing.

"I got confidence in you, Elliot," he had said. "You and me, we're going to do fine."

When Diana was through dressing, she came out of the bedroom and looked at Joey Marino with anything but confidence. "About bloody time," said Joey.

"Are you attempting an English accent?" said Diana.

"Trying to be less conspicuous," said Joey, patting the gun he had placed under his belt, out of sight behind his rich vicuña sweater.

"You sound like a Dead End Kid imitating Noël Coward."

"I know what I sound like," said Joey. "And I know what I can do, all right? You don't think much of me, but I've been here less than a day, and I've done plenty, I've done more than you'd believe."

"I'd believe it if you'd tell me," said Diana. She waited for his superior smile, and it came slowly, then all in a rush, lifting his sensuous lips. "All right, we'd better go," she said.

The Haganah boy dressed in Hasidic clothes hadn't told Joey that he couldn't come to the meeting at the Church of the Holy Redeemer, but Diana told Joey in the cab to the Old City that he would have to wait for her outside the church.

"No," he said. "Where you go, I go. I'm not quoting the Bible. I'm repeating Marty Bernstein's explicit orders."

Diana didn't fight him. Going through the police checkpoint at Jaffa Gate, she was reminded of the power of the British. David had been picked off a bus at a British checkpoint, and now was their prisoner. She had never completely believed the widely circulated stories of how some British guards treated their inmates—the beatings, the always manacled hands and feet, the stripping away of clothes and bedding on a cold night, the humiliation of having to scrub out a cell on your hands and knees, using your own toothbrush—but now that she was getting closer to seeing David, the fearfully pushed-back images of her lover's face, reacting to some horror outside her experience, began to reach her. So she was glad of Joey's presence. Diana didn't know that he was carrying a gun as they walked through the police checkpoint, flashing their press credentials and American passports; she didn't know that he had nearly killed two British Army men the night before and had successfully beaten and bribed a veteran member of the Palestine police into doing his will. But as they entered the Old City through Jaffa Gate, Diana was aware of his vigilance, his anger, his desire. He clutched at her arm, and she allowed this, and as they entered David Street, he pulled her through the crowds as if she and they were both in league against his power.

"We go straight till after the big bazaar," she said.

"It's all a big bazaar," said Joey, snarling at a boy with strings of beads in their path. "And I know where we are, I saw the map."

"Yes, your memory," said Diana, remembering walking this narrow, congested street with her lover. The rain had recently stopped, as it had stopped then, and the stalls and the street peddlers and the sellers of coffee and water and wine all blared forth their cacophony of welcome.

"Take a walk, Jack," said Joey to a peddler with Swiss watches on a flimsy string barring their way.

"Very fine, very rich," said the peddler. "You are American? I very much like Americans." He hadn't moved, and when Diana tried to pass him, he stepped in her path.

Joey pushed the man so hard, he fell into the side of a stall, knocking down a row of camel-leather bags. Diana pulled Joey quickly forward, afraid of a fight, a crowd, the intervention of the police. "That's not what we need," she said.

"We got a date, right?" said Joey. "We can go left at Muristan, if we can find a sign—just to get away from this crowd." Diana caught sight of a blue-eyed Arab boy, his light eyes shocking in a swarthy face, helping his father—or grandfather—prepare couscous. The narrow street had occasional steps, taking them down a slow decline, until they had passed into the outskirts of the spice market. Here the path was covered by stone arches lit by wan sunlight, flickering electric bulbs, and oil burning in brass lamps. The crowd surged forward and back, moving along like a snake, its body united in spite of its parts. The smells were foreign to Joey, and unpleasant; even the fruits and vegetables looked like misshapen versions of America's produce. An old man pushed a wooden barrow their way, urging it up low steps with indecipherable curses, ignoring pedestrians, peddlers, and even the red-faced policeman who spoke to him sharply in Arabic, apparently telling him to watch his step. It was only as he passed them that Joey could see that one of the man's eyes was blinded by glaucoma, the other eye nearly completely clouded as well. The barrow was filled with chick-peas, and Joey wondered what force impelled this old man up the incline in this cold and inhospitable street; what would be his reward for such difficult work? He took a handful of chick-peas and shouted to the old man his thanks, at the same time dropping a dollar bill into the frayed jacket he wore over his robes.

"We're a little early. Perhaps we should kill some time in one of these shops," said Diana.

"Let's get there first," said Joey. "I want to see the outside of that church before I'm satisfied."

"I know where we are," said Diana. "I've been here before, remember?"

"I don't want to go into any shop. The smells are making me crazy."

"I thought it was where I go, you go, right?" said Diana.

"Right," said Joey, "but this morning I'm in charge of where you go, see?" But Diana didn't hear this. At that moment, one of the numerous hand trucks, pushed by overzealous teenagers, was speeding down the incline right for an oblivious Joey's back, and she grabbed him instinctively, pulling at his waist, so that the hurtling vehicle missed him by inches.

"Jesus," said Joey. "They don't fool around, those little bastards." He watched as the Arab boy who'd been alternately pushing and riding the four-wheeled vehicle now jumped off, and deliberately landed on the dead rubber tire that trailed it on a thick rope. This was the brake, apparently. Stomping on the flaccid rubber and pulling at its rope helped slow the onrushing hand truck; but nothing could have stopped it from ramming into Joey's broad back. Watching the Arab boy follow it down into the quickly parting crowd, Joey realized that Diana had probably saved him from a broken back, or worse. "Hey, thanks," he said. "Could have killed me." He smiled that maddeningly vain smile and glanced at his watch. "You want to go shopping, babe, we go shopping, okay?"

"I've asked you a hundred times not to call me 'babe.'"

"Okay, okay—no more babe. We've got fifteen minutes. You want a camel-leather bag? You want a bedouin necklace?"

"I want to know why you're carrying a gun," said Diana. She spoke the words as unemotionally as she could. Ever since she had woken to his air of supreme confidence, she had been afraid to know what trouble he'd caused; now, on the way to a meeting with the Haganah, with the city filled with soldiers and police, with checkpoints everywhere, he carried a gun.

"To protect the two of us," said Joey.

"We don't need protection. We're not going to rob a bank."

"I don't rob banks, baby," said Joey. "I'm a little more sophisticated than you think."

"I don't think you're sophisticated at all, Joey," she said. She pulled him closer, and stood with her back to a vegetable stall, busy with old women shoppers arguing over the price of peas and beans. "Any policeman can search you, legally. I found your gun just by touching you accidentally."

"I need a gun, all right?"

"No, it's not all right. I can't afford to get stopped by the police. Neither of us can afford to get thrown into prison right now. I have to meet this Haganah man, and tomorrow I'm supposed to see David, and this . . . this gun can ruin everything."

He could see how suddenly upset she was, and he took hold of her abruptly, even though he was convinced that she was wrong. "Look, I won't jeopardize anything. I swear it. If a cop comes for me, I'll take off. I won't take the gun with me when I'm with you like this, all right? I'll do whatever you want."

"Then take me to the church and wait for me outside," said Diana.

"I can't do that."

"Then get rid of that gun," said Diana. "I can't risk getting alone with you in some place like a church, and if the police find the gun on you, then I'll never see David again. Can't you understand that? I'll never see David again."

Joey agreed to what he considered an unreasonable demand only because she had just pulled him out of the path of that speeding hand truck. He knew what value a gun possessed. There was always a risk that a cop could try to grab you on some kind of gun charge; but this was far less important than letting someone shoot at you, without having some way to answer in kind. They walked into Muristan Street, and Diana asked him where he had bought it. "I'm really impressed," she said sarcastically. "I thought it would take a gangster at least a week to find his foreign equivalents."

"I didn't buy this from a gangster," said Joey. "And one day, real soon, you're going to be thanking me."

But Diana had no gratitude in her heart at that moment. She was shutting Joey out of her concerns, believing that he would do as he said, wait for her outside the church. He said something to her as she hurried up the steps to go inside, a caution perhaps, but Diana was listening only for the man from the Haganah, the man who would tell her what she must do for David.

The bell tower was one hundred and fifty feet tall, and reached by a winding staircase of nearly two hundred stone steps. As Diana passed through the door to the bell tower, she heard an onrushing of feet coming her way. It was suddenly very cold, as if a wind had blown into the stairwell from above. Two large women, chattering in German, hurried down the steps, one after the other. They were very much out of breath. One of them laughed at Diana and huffed and puffed for her benefit. She pointed up and said something in German that escaped Diana, though she had studied the language for a year. Diana had to press against the wall for the women to pass her in single file, and then she began to climb in earnest, going from a relatively dark landing to an increasingly light and windy region. The steps wound very tightly about the turret; she was turning completely around every half-dozen steps, and becoming dizzy. Suddenly she found herself at a landing where two more tourists were busy with chattering out their exhaustion, this time in French. The landing was open all around, with windows cut into the stone, and it was from here that the wind and the gray light came twisting into the stairwell. One of the tourists urged Diana up the steps, assuring her that the view was the best in the Old City.

Diana hardly stopped to catch her breath. She had gotten used to the twists of the stairwell, and was careful and quick on the smooth stone of the steps. The next landing came quickly, and she walked past this at once, certain that the Haganah man was waiting for her, eager to unburden himself of his message. Because she hurried, she grew dizzier. Near the end of the climb, the landings were farther apart, and the lack of windows in the stone created regions of perfect darkness to walk through. Idly she wondered if this was where the Haganah man would surprise her, pressing her against the cold stone in the dark so that she would be unable to see his face. But a few moments later she left the dark and came out to the observation landing, letting the cold wind buffet her gladly, to relieve the dizziness and the apprehension.

The boy from the Haganah had told her to face the east, and that a man would come to her and tell her what she needed to know. But Diana couldn't stand still. It was too cold, and the view too magnificent all about her. Besides, there were no other tourists at the top of the bell tower; no other tourists, and no man from the Haganah.

To the east she could see the Mount of Olives, working its way out of the mist. Farther down the mountain, the light had broken out into bands of color, from a pale red to a periwinkle bit of sky framing the cupolas of the Church of Mary Magdalene. To the west, the wet air had evaporated into fresh white light, the dry light of the city. The Tower of David stood tall and proud in this light, as if ignoring the presence of the British Army in its ancient stronghold. In a matter of months it would be a central point of the conflict between Arab and Jew, Diana knew, as it had been a point of conflict for a dozen conquerors since the time of Herod. Beyond the tower where the Old City wall ended was the New City, sometimes called Jewish Jerusalem, and her eyes were drawn to the red stone of the King David Hotel, another central point of British command. Everything in the city seemed to revolve around David: David Stern, King David, David Street, the Citadel of David, the King David Hotel, the City of David.

"You're supposed to be facing east," said a mild voice behind her. She turned and saw a tall man with a broken nose, dressed in khaki and a green sweater.

"I know you," she said. "We've met."

"Yes, Miss Mann." He had been wearing the same sweater then, the same khaki clothes that the future leaders of the Jewish state wore as a uniform of austerity. "Waiting for David to come to the synagogue. You were very brave."

"I was crazy," she said. "I don't remember much—I just remember you didn't bother me with questions." It had been in the underground chapel of that synagogue that she had promised David that she would get him guns, guns to keep Jerusalem alive.

"Now I hope you won't ask me too many questions, Miss Mann," said the Haganah man.

"Just tell me what I have to do."

"Well . . ." said the man, and Diana could read death in his eyes, in the hesitation to speak.

"Did anything happen to David?"

"Please, not too many questions," he said. She noticed that the man's brown eyes were flecked with gold and that his white, even teeth were marked with spaces where he had lost a lower canine tooth and an upper incisor. He had a level-eyed, healthy face, the calm exterior of a teacher of physical education, sure of his body; the lost

154

teeth weren't the result of disease, but of a blow, a beating. "I don't know about David," he said. "All we know is that the man we wanted is already dead."

"What man you wanted? You want David, don't you?"

"David is one of my closest friends, Miss Mann. But the man we wanted was more important to us, because of his expertise with arms. We were willing to risk very much to get him out of prison. We were willing to risk even David. Now that he is dead—"

Diana didn't want to interrupt, and didn't want to ask too many questions. But she hadn't been told how David was, and she needed to know that instant if her lover was alive.

"If he's dead, just tell me. I want to know about David, not about the other man."

"David was alive yesterday," said the Haganah man. "That's all I know."

"I don't think so," said Diana. She turned about in exasperation, looking at but not absorbing the kaleidoscope of shapes and colors in the brightening morning: the green domes of the Russian cathedral, the castlelike shape of the Augusta Victoria Hospital, the black dome of the Ethiopian church, the red wall of the Petra Hotel, the crenellated spire of the Italian Hospital. "Something's happened to David, and you must tell me what it is."

"You can see David tomorrow," said the Haganah man. "That hasn't changed. You have our blessing."

"What do you mean, I have your blessing? I thought you wanted me to take something to him, some wire, some device. Aren't you going to help me get him out?"

"No," he said. "Not anymore."

For a moment Diana couldn't speak. She had come six thousand miles on a moment's notice to help these people get a man out of prison—help them together with her lover—and now that this task was no longer possible, she was being cast aside. "You can't do that," she said.

"Miss Mann, David is safer in prison than he would be trying to get out."

"David is needed outside," she said.

"Of course he is, but so are the people who might die in trying to help him."

"I can't believe he's any less important than the man who was just killed. It's because of David that you're getting arms, isn't it? Isn't that worth something?"

"It's because of you that we might get some arms while they can still be useful," said the Haganah man evenly. She could see quite clearly that his anger was rising to the surface, struggling with a disappointment in David Stern's choice of lover. "David had nothing to do with procuring arms for the future Jewish state. If you feel that your involvement with us is based solely on trying to help David Stern, we are very much surprised."

"I only meant that I should be treated . . . David . . . that *we* deserve to be helped," said Diana.

"Each case is treated individually. David is helpful, but he is not essential. The risk is not worth the goal in his case. We would love to see him free. I would love to see him free. But I would not risk my life to do this now, not when I am needed in the defense of Jerusalem." He paused for a moment, looking toward the Mount of Olives, where the last shreds of mist were turning the color of salmon, streaked with ethereal lines of vermilion. "David would want one thing from you now, Miss Mann, and one thing only. That is to help us. To continue to help us. To get us more weapons, to get them past American customs and past British customs. That is what David would want."

"Yes," said Diana. "Of course, you're right." But she had turned her back to the man and begun to walk down the steps.

He came after her at once, and touched his hand to her shoulder. "You will see him tomorrow, of course?"

"Yes."

"Will you tell him that Kazi tells him to be strong?"

"Is that your name?"

"It is a name that I use and that he will know," said the man from the Haganah. "Tell him that I said to be strong, and that soon he will be free, in a free Eretz-Israel."

Diana nodded, and the man told her that he would prefer to go first down the stairs, and that he would be quickly out of her way. She let him pass, and leaned against the cold wall listening to his steps grow indistinct and then finally vanish into the sound of the wind. Then she began to walk down, holding the wall with the palms of her hand, feeling the rush to get to the ground grow moment by moment. There were tears in her eyes as she hurried through the dark, as she caught her breath at the bright landings, as she imagined a life without

David. Kazi had known something about David, perhaps that he'd been in trouble in the prison, that his beautiful face had been marked or broken, that he'd lost a tooth, an eye, a hand. David would never live in Kenya, not the David she knew. He would be not only fearless but also foolhardy; not only arrogant to the guards but also insulting. As she grew dizzier coming down the steps, she saw his role clearly in the Haganah: the man who had nothing to lose. Of course he had been the perfect prisoner to help their arms expert escape. The man who had escaped from the death camps, who had outlived the holocaust, who had witnessed the destruction of his family, had no personal fear, no sense of dread as to what would happen to himself. He only cared for the cause. Whether he lived or died for Diana was not part of his consciousness. He wanted to live for Eretz-Israel. That was enough for him. He would sacrifice himself eagerly, because he was a man without personal ties. In Kenya he would try to escape regardless of the risk, because he was of no use to anybody so removed from the struggle of Palestine. If Diana couldn't help him now, he would go to Kenya, and he would try to escape and he would die.

Joey was in the church, not in front of it as he had promised. He told her that he saw the Haganah guy come and go, and she didn't trouble to ask him how he knew who the man was and why he wasn't outside the way he was supposed to be. She was very dizzy, and her eyes were red, and he took her down the steps of the church and into the windswept street. "You got a problem, babe?"

"I can't ask you to help me, Joey," she said, shaking her head. "You really can't, it's too dangerous. They won't help me, and I have to get him out. I won't let you. I'm sorry, but I have to do this myself."

Joey wasn't sure what she was trying to stop herself from asking him, but still the vain smile came to his lips, and he put his strong arm about her shoulders and looked into her lovely green eyes. "Whatever you say, babe," he said.

TEN

David Stern woke to the sound of the key in the lock of his barred cell door. His hands had been freed sometime during the night, but his legs were still manacled, and as he tensed, the chains made their heavy jangle.

"Stern, are you all right?" said the guard, a hulking Welshman with a pockmarked face that seemed to be permanently saddened by his choice of occupation. The prisoner didn't answer until he had tasted water from the cup brought to him by the guard, and then he said, "No."

"I have to get you cleaned up," said the guard.

"Why don't you clean me the way they cleaned Zilenko?" said David. He took another sip of the water and sat up on the filthy mattress, which lay on the cold stone floor.

"I wasn't there, Stern," said the Welshman. "I don't know what happened."

"You want to know?" said David Stern.

"Of course. But drink a little, and have some cereal. You don't look well."

"I don't look well?" said David, and he laughed at this, laughed so hard that the cup fell over, and for half a moment he wondered if he had the strength to drag the guard's head into the iron bars of the cell, and make a run for it. But he had little strength. Not after going to Zilenko's aid in the shower room, not after the repeated blows to his stomach with the ubiquitous police batons that the guards wielded so expertly, so proudly.

"Stern, you know I am very sorry if you are uncomfortable," said the Welshman with gravity.

"Sure," said David. He took a spoonful of the cold oatmeal, chewing it quickly because there was a big portion this morning. For some reason, they were feeding him, cleaning him, perhaps even clothing him. Abe Zilenko had been attacked in the shower room only four days before. Zilenko, who was not quite five inches taller than five feet, who was frail as a skeleton, never having fully recovered from the Russian slave-labor camps, who was afraid of the dark, of streetcars, of barbed wire, of trains, of planes, of sticks, of guns—this terrified little man had been held under the cold water of the shower for three hours, beaten with sticks and wires, kicked and slapped and abused. A braver man would have cracked. "He wasn't brave," said David to the Welshman. "Zilenko wasn't brave."

"But he never told them."

"That's because he was so scared he couldn't move his lips," said David. Greedily he swallowed the oatmeal, his appetite coming back to life with the taste of food. All the Haganah men in the prison knew of Zilenko, of his secrets, of his importance. Zilenko was a genius, or at least a genius in constructing mines and grenades and automatic weapons from the miserable industrial parts available to the Haganah. He knew where the laboratory was, built under the kibbutz field of sunflowers; he knew where the underground factory was; he knew the names of the British officers who had sold them weapons and information. But he told them nothing, and now he was dead.

"You were crazy to try to help him," said the guard.

"We should all be so crazy," said David Stern.

"Every friend of mine among the guards thinks it terrible. I swear to you. It was a mistake, and a disgrace."

"It was a mistake to kill him," said David. "They wanted him alive. They wanted him to talk." He had been passing from the exercise yard to his cell when he heard the sounds of a beating: the thud of the baton on the back, the openhanded slap to the face, the punch to the distended, ill stomach. He knew it was Zilenko. No one else was being tortured. There were no screams, and there were no encouraging words from the guards in the shower room, perhaps touched by embarrassment in the midst of their inhuman actions. The shower was turned on, and David had turned politely to his guard and said, "Excuse me," and stepped sideways into the shower room.

In that moment he had seen Zilenko for the last time: naked, his skinny legs chained together at the ankles, his weakling's arms handcuffed behind his back, his pale lips blue from the cold, the blood washing away from mouth and ears under the shower. He was held up by one guard, whose uniform had become soaked in the process, and the mark of distaste on this guard's face was the first target of David's rage. David was able to land three blows: a kick to the side of the knee of the guard who held Zilenko, a punch to the neck of the guard with the swinging baton, a blow with his elbow at the chest of the guard who tried to grab him from the rear.

Then they were all over him, and he was too weak, too full of the image of the tortured Zilenko, too aware of the sentence of death hanging over his head, too tired of a decade of brutality and murder to count the guards who pummeled him, to remember their faces. It was all the same face to David Stern, the same German face, Russian face, Polish face that had warred against his people, that had destroyed the Jews of Europe and now threatened to cheat this last remnant of their natural homeland.

"They say he was trying to escape," said the Welshman.

"Who says?"

"The official report. Do you remember any of the guards that attacked you? Do you want to make a formal complaint of brutality? I'll do it for you, Stern. I'm not afraid. I don't give a damn. They don't have a right to beat a man like that."

"I'm all right," said David. "It's good practice for Kenya."

"Maybe you won't go," said the Welshman. "They changed their minds about hanging you, they can change their minds about sending you out of the country." He pulled David's thin blanket closer; the prisoner was shivering, without realizing it. Ever since the attack in the shower, he had been in this cell, on quarter rations, without clothes. Two nights before, a soldier had spoken to him through the bars: "They ought to hang you, you murdering bastard, the way they murdered my brother. Do you hear me? The way they murdered my brother!"

160

"You don't like the way we treat you here?" David had said through swollen lips. "Then get the hell out of my country."

The guard had swung at him through the bars with his baton, but David was too far away to touch. Another guard had grabbed the attacking guard from behind and screamed at him, "What are you, a Nazi? You're supposed to be an Englishman!" He was so mad at the first guard that for a minute David's cold heart had felt touched by decency. There was always an urge to discover something noble about the men who caged you, as if to prove that there was something about yourself deserving of being imprisoned, something about the men who had the power of life and death over you that made them worthy of this unequal strength. But David had stifled this impulse. One wasn't more noble; it was simply that one was a bit less inhuman than the other. He loathed them both, as he loathed all the guards in this prison, as he loathed all guards and all prisons everywhere.

"I liked Zilenko," said the Welshman. "He used to talk to me. Did you know that?"

"No," said David. "Maybe he was afraid you'd beat him if he didn't." The guard looked pained at this suggestion. David drove his point home: "If you're trying to show me how different you are from the fascists who run this place, open my cell door and give me a gun and let me the hell out of here."

"Come on," said the guard. "I've got to get you cleaned up." Gently he helped David to his feet in the tiny cell, taking care that the man's blanket didn't fall to reveal his nakedness. David did little to help. The swelling in his lips had gone down, but the aches in his legs and arms were almost as strong as yesterday. His ankles hurt where the manacles chafed him, and when he pointed this out to the guard, the man said that he hadn't been told that he could remove them.

"Just follow orders, then," said David. "If they tell you to drown me in the shower, do that too. It won't be your fault, either."

The guard hesitated, wanting very much to show his concern. He felt in his pocket for a key, and then all of a sudden got to his knees and unlocked the manacles. "Your ankles are pretty cut up," he said. "Wash them well."

"What are you, a doctor?" said David. But even David was softened by the look of rejection that the big Welshman gave him then.

"Hey, you're right. I'll wash the wounds well. Gangrene is something I wish only on Nazis."

"I wasn't authorized to do this," said the Welshman for the second time. There was something else he seemed anxious to say. "You know Zilenko, he once told me that he didn't hold it against me. You can believe it or not. But he said that he didn't hold it against me, and that someday, after the Mandate was through, we could even be friends."

"Hey," said David. "Thanks for doing this."

"You're going to be all right. I'm going to clean you up and get you some fresh clothes, and you'll have full rations, and no one's going to bother you in the shower room."

"Why?" said David, finally awake to the special attention. He wondered, without fear, if this was some way of softening him before interrogation. Perhaps they would show him how comfortable he could be if he learned to cooperate. But that made no sense. He had nothing to tell them, except names; and even the British knew he would sooner die than incriminate a fellow member of the Haganah.

"I'm not supposed to tell you that either," said the Welshman. David leaned on him heavily as the man took him from the cell and brought him to the shower room. "Go ahead, go in."

"Tell me," said David.

"You have a visitor coming."

David held his breath. Now that he was out from under the sentence of death, he could be visited again. Someone would come for him, someone with strength and courage and a knife strapped to his ankle. He would get out of here. He would live, and live in Jerusalem, and be alive at the declaration of the creation of the new Jewish state. "I thought I wasn't allowed visitors."

"Look, the regulations are crazy," said the Welshman. "We never hung anybody for carrying a weapon. Only the Irgun boys get sent to Kenya. It's because of this United Nations. Everything's changed today, and everything changes every day of the week. Something's changed today, and you've got a visitor and you're getting cleaned up. My advice is to please listen to whoever is speaking to you. Not every guard is like me. The streets are wild out there, and some of the boys in here are scared. So don't act crazy. See your visitor, and find out about your legal rights, if you have any. Okay?" He urged David into the shower, where the blood had long since washed away. David showered, refused the chance to shave under the guard's supervision, and dressed quickly in clean blue-striped prison garb. He was given his own black shoes and socks and then brought back along the main corridor of the prison, to the office of the captain of the guards. Here the Welshman knocked once, very politely for his huge size, and smiled weakly at David.

Inside, the captain's voice boomed out, "Yes!" and the Welshman opened the door for David to enter.

The captain was standing behind his desk, his customary glare firmly in place. A woman with black hair was sitting facing him, and for half a moment David had the extraordinary impression that this black head of hair belonged to Diana Mann. But he knew that this was impossible, because she was in the United States of America.

"Prisoner Stern," the captain was saying, "you will tell me please the name of your fiancée."

David looked at the captain in amazement. He could feel the presence of the big Welshman behind him like a friendly dog, eager to be loved. A fiancée. He had no fiancée. He had a wife, and she was dead, murdered by the Nazis. The black-haired woman turned around, and the green eyes reached for his newly bearded face, and her pale skin went still paler and she was out of the chair, coming at him in a half-crouch, too weak to stand for his embrace.

"David," she said, holding him, and she could feel the pain in his body, she could feel the shock shaking in his weakened frame. "David, what have they done to you? David, darling, David."

"Prisoner Stern," repeated the captain, looking at this display of heterosexual love with aversion. "You have not answered my question."

But he had first to answer her question, not the question of what had they done to him, but the question of her embrace. This young woman had never ceased questioning him, not since their first meeting, and the question had always been the same: Can you love me, will you love me, do you love me at all? And certainly there was a part of him that was made soft by her touch, by her yearning desire, by the character that had crossed oceans for him, that had broken laws, had risked the ties of family for a lover she had created over his own insignificant frame. But he had closed himself to love. Love was something that had existed before the war, before the death camps. To feel love now was impossible, because his wife was dead; to feel love now was a treason that he could never commit. Still, David held her, answered the pressure of her embrace with his own. She had worn scent, a necklace of pearls, a cashmere sweater, and all this luxury was simultaneously repellent and attractive to him. He wanted to push her away for her prettiness, her cleanliness, her sweet-smelling breath; but he wanted to swallow her whole too, he wanted to eat of the fruit of the vine, he wanted to bathe in a scented bath, he wanted to go to some mindless region where memory was dead, and there was only this softness, this sensuality, this woman. Then he would make love to her. He would answer her then. Yes, he would say, in this place that would be no-place, in this land that had no people, in this country without a past. Yes, I would love you then.

"What are you doing here?" he said by way of greeting. His words were sharp, not intentionally, but sharp nonetheless. He remembered how sensitive she was to a rebuke, how eager she was for his praise, and he forced his tired face to smile. "I am happy to see you."

Diana pulled away from him. They hadn't kissed. His beard was blond, shot full of red, and not filled in. His blue eyes were bloodshot, and over his right eyebrow was a bruise. David's lips were swollen, as if they'd been stung by a bee, but the fact of his suffering came not from these little marks, but from the way he held his head: he seemed tentative to Diana, tentative in the way of a marionette. David was stiff with pain. He held himself erect, waiting for a chance to be moved. If there would be help for him, it couldn't come from David himself; he would have to be pulled out of there. Once again she heard the captain speak, demanding that David name his fiancée. It would be simple to do as Joey had told her. There was an absolute need for her anger to find an outlet, and this martinet captain seemed made to order for her needs.

"Her name is Diana Mann," said David, understanding that she had come to this prison under the pretext of being his fiancée. But how had she known he was in prison? And how could she have left her vital work in the United States just to visit him? "And we would like some privacy."

"You would like some privacy," said the captain, without sarcasm, but with obvious distaste. He wasn't prepared for the rich American girl, who was probably Jewish as well, to turn on him in anger.

"What have you done to him, you bastard?" she said, remembering Joey's urging to use profanity, to incite the beast in the heart of propriety.

"I beg your pardon—" he began to say, but he was begging noth-

164

ing, his face already red with anger and indignation. But Diana would not let him speak.

"Shut up when I'm talking to you, you animal," she said. "This is Diana Mann you're talking to, not a prisoner in your concentration camp. Do you realize who I am, do you have any idea how much trouble I am going to cause you?"

David, who knew Diana better than anyone else in the little room, that is, better than the captain and the Welshman, whose friendly aura was now marred by intense embarrassment, could sense that this was not Diana speaking from any natural source of violence. She was acting. This was clear to him, and his body stiffened yet further, and he felt the familiar pain in his left knee; he had to beat back indifference, because if Diana was acting, there had to be a reason, and the only reason that made sense was the chance for freedom.

"Now, see here, Miss Mann," said the captain, and now he had actually taken a step back from behind the desk, as if beginning to circumnavigate this stolid fortress of forms and permissions and orders, just so that he might confront this hellion two inches from her face.

"I said shut up, and you'd sure as hell better, buster," said Diana. "This is my fiancé, and I don't recognize him. He's lost twenty pounds, he's got bruises on his face, his lips are swollen, he's been tortured, and goddamn it, you're the one who's going to be held responsible. Do you understand? Do you think you're dealing with little people who can't answer you in kind? You're going to be sorry you were ever born. I have an appointment with the Attorney General, I'm going to see the High Commissioner, my uncle in London is going to meet with the Prime Minister, so don't talk to me. You're a little man, and you're going to be destroyed, *destroyed*."

Diana's fury did little to dampen the spirits of the captain. He had done nothing wrong. Orders had been followed. There was no torture of this man that he had authorized. She could rant and rave to the Prime Minister's office, for all he cared; she would still not be tolerated in *his* office a moment longer.

"Show her out, Ames," said the captain to the Welshman.

"I'm not leaving," said Diana, waiting for Joey Marino. She did not run through her mind the plan that Joey had sketched for her, but only the fact that in a moment he would come through the door, and at that point events would come so quickly that there would be no chance for fear, no chance for thought. She had last seen Joey sitting in a jeep of the Palestine police, wearing not only the too-large uniform, pinned in a dozen places, but also a too-large pith helmet. Constable Elliot Crawfield had been at the wheel, his knuckles white, his eyes masked behind dark glasses. They were parked two blocks from the Central Prison. Diana had passed them at a brisk walk, feeling Joey's eyes on her back. All she could focus on as she approached the prison were the great concrete blocks set up around it to prevent tanks from storming into this center of British power. They had been nicknamed "Rommel's Teeth" when that German general had threatened the Middle East. Diana wondered why the concrete blocks were still standing. The Haganah had no tanks, and would get none until the British had left Palestine and lifted their blockade.

"I'm sorry, miss," said the big Welshman. He extended his hand as if he had asked her to dance, but Diana didn't even glance at him.

"I want an explanation, Captain. I'm waiting for an explanation." She sat down in the chair across from where the captain now stood. David caught Ames's eyes and held them. The choice of the Welshman for a guard at this moment had been lucky. He would hesitate because he didn't want to hurt, and he didn't understand why people like David Stern were in prison to begin with.

"There is no explanation," said the captain. "You have the unmitigated gall to accuse me of crimes that haven't been committed, and to threaten me with your powerful connections—"

"It's not a threat, you bastard, it's a promise."

"I won't stand for this. This is impossible. Ames, do as I say. I want this female escorted out of this prison at once. At once."

Joey had had a moment's displeasure earlier that day when he had first told Crawfield where they were going. The constable hadn't rebelled. Instead, he sat down and began to laugh. Joey couldn't threaten a man who was hysterical, and surely Crawfield was that. When he had calmed down enough to explain why the prison was impregnable, Joey relaxed. Now that he had become reasonable, he could be convinced. "What do you think of my British accent, Elliot, ey, what?" Joey had said.

"Your accent, Yank?" said Crawfield, at a loss for words. "It sounds a little posh."

"Is that good or bad, old fellow?"

"It's good if you're talking to someone who don't know," said the constable. Joey explained that his plan left Crawfield totally in the clear. He would drive up to the prison with Joey, get out of the jeep, and simply say nothing until they were in the captain's office. Joey would have both guns, but Crawfield's holster would be closed, and later he would be able to say that the gangster had forced him at gunpoint.

"What jeep?" Crawfield had asked.

"Can't you do anything without my help?" said Joey. Crawfield was due to go on duty at noon at the Citadel, and could think of no reason to requisition a vehicle until Joey suggested that they hijack one. "Wait," the constable had begged. "I can say I've got a toothache. I need a jeep to get to my dentist. He's in the hills, in this new suburb. Everyone knows about my tooth trouble."

"Fine. And I can simply hijack your jeep at a traffic light and keep you my prisoner until I no longer need you."

"But that doesn't explain how we're going to be able to take this man out of a prison cell."

"There's an old saying we've got in America, Elliot," said Joey. "If you don't got the key, get the warden."

Crawfield wasn't sure that Diana would have to meet with David in the presence of the captain. There were other offices that might have been suitable in the prison, but the constable did know that the captain's office had been used for a visit by someone of influence.

"Blimey, that's her," said Joey. "Real important."

"Don't say 'Blimey,' Yank," said Crawfield. "It's not like you." Then the constable returned to the worries at hand: there would be guards everywhere, first questioning them as to their reason for visiting the prison and then demanding to see release forms for the prisoner—if they ever got as far as the main gate with David Stern.

"I have a feeling you're going to enjoy this, Elliot," Joey had said. "Just remember to look really angry most of the time. When you're angry, they're going to think you're right."

"What if he's not in the captain's office?"

"We take the captain to the cell," said Joey. "He'll be happy to show us the way. I've got a special touch with wardens." When it was finally time to go, Joey played his last card with Crawfield. If the man wanted to turn him in, this would be the time to do it. "I want you to know that whatever happens, I appreciate your helping, Elliot. We haven't known each other too long, but I feel like we've been friends for a long while. I feel like I can trust you."

"You really don't think I'd try to turn you in," said Elliot.

"No," said Joey. He certainly understood that the possibility was there, but at least he'd have the pleasure of shooting him before he could be arrested.

"You know we can stop right now," said the constable one last time. "Your girlfriend will visit her friend, and nothing will happen, and she'll come out and we can take her home. And nobody will have been killed."

"Drive," said Joey.

"All right," said the constable. He turned briefly to Joey and nodded his head emphatically. "All right."

He jerked the jeep forward and drove to the police booth that guarded the way to the prison. Crawfield started to slow down, but Joey stepped on his foot on the accelerator pedal so that the car pulled past the booth before finally stopping with an exasperated screeching of the brake. "What did you do that for?" said the constable as a police officer hurried up to them from the booth.

"Be angry, Elliot. We're in a hurry." Joey turned around to face the approaching constable. "Sorry. We're in a rush—orders . . ."

"Wait," said the police officer, coming around to Elliot's side. "Where's the fire?"

"Fire my arse," said Crawfield. "You got to check every copper coming through on his job?"

"Oh, it's you, Crawfield?" said the police officer, but the constable had already started to move forward, riding on the fabricated anger that seemed to have worked like a charm. He pulled directly in front of the building, where no one was permitted to park, and a guard hurried up to them to remind them of that fact.

"Jesus," said Crawfield. "Everyone's a little Hitler today. We're picking up a prisoner, special rush, and we're parking here. If you don't like it, eat the bleeding jeep."

Joey jumped out of his seat, nearly colliding with the guard. "You watch the car, pal," he said, trying out his English accent. "I'm putting you in charge of it."

"See here," said the guard. "This really is irregular. The captain—"

"Screw the captain," said Joey. "This is bigger than the captain." Crawfield caught up with him as they entered the prison, with its guard at a desk before a steel grille. Joey could feel the constable's giddiness and knew that the man was beyond fear now. He was like a first-time actor, intoxicated with the crowd's laughter and applause early in the play, rushing forward to the climax with a swaggering assurance.

"Where's Stern?" said Crawfield to the guard at the grille.

"I beg your pardon?" said the guard.

"Stern. He's supposed to be ready for transfer. David Stern. We've got the transport waiting, and we're in a hurry," said Joey.

"I have nothing here about a transfer for any prisoner," said the guard, looking down at his clipboard.

"Shit on the wheels of justice," said Joey. He brought his fist down on the desk. "I knew there'd be a bloody tie-up. Open up, we have to see the captain."

"What are your names, please?" said the guard, picking up the phone on his desk. Crawfield slammed down his identification card and turned in exasperation to Joey.

"We're never going to make it at this rate," he said.

"Just a moment," said the guard, with a kindly look at the impatient duo. Joey's hand moved quickly, producing the open knife and holding it up to the guard's neck in such a friendly, easy motion that for a half-moment the guard had no idea that a knife was held to his throat. He almost smiled at Joey's friendly look, but the smile froze on his face.

"Put the phone down," said Joey, still using the English accent.

"Better do it, mate," said Crawfield. "The guy's crazy." The guard started to turn his head away from the blade, but Joey's knife moved with him.

"There's nobody now," said Joey. The guard that had been on the other side of the grille had passed deeper into the prison a minute before. Slowly the phone receiver was placed back on its hook. "Stand slowly," said Joey.

"You're not police."

"I am," said Crawfield lamely, trying to look as if he were Joey's prisoner. "He has my gun."

Joey removed the guard's gun and shoved it in his belt. "Open it," he said, and the guard unlocked the gate to the prison.

"You can't do this," said the guard. "I don't have the keys to the cells."

"Walk to the captain's office," said Joey. "If you want to die, try something funny. If you want to live, act natural."

"I can't act natural, I've left my post," said the guard.

"Fast," said Joey.

The guard started to slide open the grille, and then, following the motion exerted to move the heavy steel, he whirled about and threw himself at Joey.

The guard managed to impale himself on Joey's knife, between the third and fourth ribs on his left side. Perhaps it was a combination of the guard's determination to fall on the imposter and Joey's will not to be moved; perhaps Joey drove the knife into the guard's body as much as the man had driven himself onto the knife; perhaps the guard knew he had as much chance to survive Joey's blade as Joey knew he had to silence him. There was no thinking on Joey's part, no weighing of the possibility of getting the knife out of harm's way and trying to wrestle the man to the floor without setting off the alarms. There was simply the attack, and the knife had penetrated the flesh, and Joey had twisted it out of the body in a brutal motion he had learned in Brooklyn and again in boot camp. And it was only in the second of release, when the knife was free in his bloody hand, that Joey realized that Crawfield's hand was firmly in place on the dead guard's mouth. It had been the constable who'd prevented the man from raising the alarm.

"Here," said Joey, giving Crawfield the dead guard's gun.

"Thank you," said Crawfield. But Joey had no time to listen or to express his own gratitude. If Crawfield didn't die in the next few minutes, he would have to join them as a fugitive; Joey had taken on a new responsibility. But he was able to shut this responsibility out of his mind. He dragged the corpse back to the little desk, leaving a trail of blood. Crawfield helped sit the body in the chair, and then Joey arranged the head and arms so that it would look from afar like a man sleeping with his head on the desk.

It was only when they had hurried away from the corpse and through the grille that the fact of murder finally penetrated Joey's consciousness. This comprehension didn't sadden him. It simply registered, and with it, the knowledge that he had raised the stakes in a game of his own devising, a game that no one, not Marty Bernstein, not Crawfield, not even Diana Mann, would fully appreciate. He was no longer simply a bodyguard to a rich young woman, an accomplice to the crime of having transported four hundred thousand dollars in cash and securities into Palestine. He had murdered a guard in a prison. He was in the process of freeing a convict from jail. As he turned toward the guard walking their way down the otherwise empty corridor, Joey was amazed at his own recklessness. Something more than love was propelling him, some affinity for danger, for violence itself, was feeding him. Perhaps it was to make up for never having been killed in the war, or more probably because the temper and violent behavior present in him since he was a little boy were still railing against the death of his father. The boy who couldn't help his father to live would now avenge his murder on every stranger that stood in his way.

"You," said Joey to the guard, who had his hand on his baton as he walked up to them, wondering at their police uniforms. "You'd better take us to the captain's office."

"Take you?" said the guard, not liking Joey's peremptory tone and not understanding why anyone needed to be taken to an office three yards away. Joey could see the man's eyes go to the gun in Crawfield's hand and the specks of blood along Joey's shirtfront. He raised his baton and stopped several feet from them.

"Shut up," said Joey, the knife in one hand, the heavy Colt in the other.

"Hey!" said the guard, swinging the baton and screaming: "Hey!"

Crawfield moved in on him swiftly, but the guard managed to hit the fat constable's head. Joey hit the guard with the Colt, swinging it into the bridge of the man's nose before he could raise the baton. From the corner of his eye he could see Crawfield stagger to the bars of a large, empty holding cell. The baton clattered to the ground and Joey raised his knee into the guard's groin. He shoved his gun into his belt and held the man's mouth shut with his free hand; the other hand held the knife to his throat. "You're going to tell me where the captain's office is," said Joey, and he released the man's mouth.

"Help!" he started to scream, but Joey clasped the mouth, and Crawfield came up to him, blood in his eyes from a scalp wound. Joey cut into the man's throat very softly, only enough to draw blood and terror. "I am going to kill you if you don't tell me where the captain's office is," he said.

Once again he took his hand off the man's mouth, and the man tried to scream, and this time Joey threw the man's head against the concrete wall, and he heard a crack, and the man collapsed. Crawfield was pointing to the door three yards away, marked with an administrative seal.

Joey stopped himself from asking Crawfield if he was all right. Instead he nodded, and they went for the door, and Crawfield threw it open. The big Welshman, Ames, had his hand on Diana's arm. David Stern, eyes alert, stood between the captain and his lover.

"Nobody breathe," said Joey Marino, and Diana found herself smiling, not from happiness, but from a light-headed sense of fantasy. She was watching a movie. Joey had dropped his English accent, and her handsome gangster was here to push all the bad guys around.

"What's the meaning of this?" said the captain, but Ames had already let go of Diana and started reaching for his baton. Like the other guards who had physical contact with the prisoners, he carried no firearm.

"Don't try it, asshole," said Joey, moving into the office and shutting the door. "Real quiet, or I shoot." He couldn't help staring at David Stern, even though the prisoner was the last thing in the room to need his attention. Crawfield took away Ames's baton, Diana moved close to David and gripped his hand, the captain started to go back behind his desk. "No," said Joey, and the captain stopped in his tracks.

"You'll never get out of here," said the captain.

"Do you have a family?" said Joey.

"What I have is my affair," said the captain. Joey pushed Ames into a chair, gesturing with the Colt.

"No one talks," said Joey. "Elliot, tie him up and gag him." The constable started to put his gun into his belt, but Joey stopped him. "Wait. Elliot. Give it to Stern."

"To the prisoner?" said Crawfield. It seemed for a moment that he had forgotten whose side he was playing on.

"Let me," said Diana. "He's weak." But Crawfield ignored her hand and gave the gun to David, whose eyes were steady and calm.

"We take the captain," said David, not asking, not suggesting, simply voicing what he knew was their only chance to get out of the prison. Joey was struck by the man's air of authority. As Crawfield tied up the big Welshman with the rope Joey had prepared, he could see Diana reach for David, dropping his hand to hold his waist, to touch his face.

"Captain, I've already killed today," said Joey, wondering how David and Diana would react to this news, "and I'd like nothing better than to blow away the back of your head. All you have to do is give me a chance." Yes, he admitted that the man was handsome, but not in the way that he would have thought. The man was blond, and old, and experienced. He would have imagined David Stern as dark, like himself, and young, like himself, even though Diana had long since told him that he and David were totally opposite. Already he was angry at the man's lack of gratitude, at the way he seemed to have taken center stage.

"He will take us out to the front," said David.

"It's arranged, Mr. Stern," said Joey flatly. "Just do as I say." Crawfield finished tying Ames, and Joey gave him the extra-large handkerchief he'd prepared for a gag. When the constable was through, Joey handed him his own police pistol, so that now all three men, besides the captain, were armed. At any moment Joey expected the alarm, the sound of men in the corridor, the metallic clicking of a hundred bolts, the loudspeaker blaring out the terms of surrender. It was all too easy. Not a shot had been fired. No guard had seen the dead man at the desk, the unconscious guard in the corridor outside. Even if only two minutes had passed, the roof should have fallen in by then. "You first, Diana."

"I should carry the gun, hidden in my bag, and David should walk between the captain and the constable, like a prisoner," she said. "David. Give me the gun."

"Let's go," said David, ignoring her suggestion. But Joey was struck by her words. It was what he had meant to do initially. It was only the sight of the prisoner, silent and strong, that had given him the notion to arm him. It was a pleasure to contradict him now.

"She's right," said Joey, looking directly at David. "We'll do as she says." David Stern looked at the man who had contradicted him, and for a moment Joey thought that he was about to refuse, that the man would simply ignore his rescuer. But then the pale blue eyes in the man's exhausted face seemed to grow brighter, as if the man himself was glowing with strength and wisdom. Without a word, he handed Diana the gun.

"Captain, take hold of the prisoner," said Joey.

"I will not submit to this charade," said the captain, and so Joey brought his gun flush against the man's right temple.

"If I kill you now, it will make it more difficult for us to get out of here, asshole," said Joey. "But if you answer me back one more time, I will kill you. Look at me, asshole. You know I will kill."

The captain looked at him then, and Joey did exhibit his best Brooklyn-killer glare, but the young man's concentration was not really on the Englishman, but on the prisoner; he could feel David Stern measuring his worth as he took charge of the captain, and it pleased him that Stern would see him so much in control.

"Elliot, take hold of David's arm. You, Captain, take hold of him on the left. Diana, walk with me behind," said Joey. "Think of your family, Captain. Think of the certain fact that you will be dead. The fact. Your only chance is if you do what I want, and what I want is to get out of here alive."

It had been four minutes since they had dragged the corpse of the guard at the grille back to his desk; three minutes since Joey had beaten the corridor guard into unconsciousness. He fully expected to see armed men in the corridor now, a barricade, machine guns, tear-gas canisters, bullhorns aimed their way. But there was nothing. Only the still figure of the guard, whose skull had probably been fractured, and who lay in a pool of blood, greeted them. Down the cool corridor came no sound from the prison cells, though as David certainly knew, it would have been impossible for the prisoners not to have heard the sounds of a beating from their nearby places. "Go," he said, and he watched the straight phalanx in front of him: Crawfield's thick figure, David's lean frame, walking with a jerky motion in his left knee, the captain's tall, erect walk, his shoes overloud on the concrete floor. Joey didn't look at Diana at his side, but he could feel her irregular heartbeat, as if it were pulsing in his own chest. She was fearful, and holding down this fear, insisting on a bravery that was not part of her natural equipment. Joey was without fear. He was perfectly willing to risk everything, like a gambler, in order to win big. Already he was imagining Marty Bernstein's face when he heard of this prison break. And his mother: she would be proud of him, and imagine him to be a Zionist, an altruist, a sympathizer of her people, conveniently forgetting that he was also a gangster, a killer. And as for this woman at his side, she would know, if she didn't know now, that what he was doing was far more than anyone else would have risked; even if he had set this madness in motion as much for himself as for her, she would never know that. Diana would regard the prison break as his present to her, his love gift, his proof of passion. For the moment she was busy with fear for herself, with concern for the torture undergone by David. In an hour, she would understand to whom she owed gratitude. As they approached the dead man at the desk, Joey Marino knew that he would soon have Diana Mann in love with him.

"Hawkins," said the captain, not in an alarming tone, but in despair. They walked sideways through the grille, the captain's hand still on David's arm.

"We're going into the jeep," said Joey. "All of us. Captain, all you say to anyone is, 'As you were.' Ignore questions. Just, 'As you were.'"

There were guards at ease near the jeep, at least a half-dozen of them. Out of range of the prisoners' hands, these guards carried firearms. A hundred yards away was the checkpoint, where a machine gun was ready, where an alarm could go off and alert an armed city to rise up and quash any attempt at rebellion. Joey didn't regard any of the relative ease of the break as a matter of luck. Nor did he dwell on the fact that Diana's visit had placed David in the captain's office, and therefore out of the more closely guarded section of the prison. Joey's gun was in his pocket, but his hand was wrapped about it, and he was wound up like a spring; he was at least as eager to unwind into action, into finality, as he was to get away. He felt godlike, because whatever would happen, he would be the prime mover. No one could surprise him, wound him, imprison him. He would win or he would die, and when he died, he would not die alone. And because he was so certain, Joey didn't flinch at the men around the jeep; he didn't worry that the captain might try to bolt; he didn't imagine that David would collapse and need the help of the guards; he had no fear that guards would come pouring out of the prison, having discovered the corpse and the unconscious body of their friend.

"See?" said Joey to the guard who had first questioned them about the parking of their jeep. "I told you it was all right for us to park."

"As you were," said the captain, though there was little reason for him to say anything. Stiffly looking into space, the captain was helped into the jeep by Crawfield.

"Come along, sir," said the constable. "Very good, sir."

David Stern sat between them in the back, and Joey took the wheel, Diana at his side on the front bench. Joey popped the clutch in first gear, not out of fright, but out of nonchalance. He wanted the guards to later remember his impudence and bravado.

"Slow down," said David Stern from the backseat.

They rushed on to the checkpoint, and at the last minute Joey braked the car. "As you were," said the captain to the guards, and Joey pulled forward at once, winding the engine too tightly for a second gear.

"You're going to attract attention if you drive this way," said David Stern.

"I've done okay so far, pal, right?" said Joey, taking a sharp right turn away from the city's central security zone and toward Mea Shearim, the neighborhood inhabited by Orthodox and ultra-Orthodox Jews. Quickly he turned left, and then right, into a street no wider than ten feet, lined with little vegetable stalls. Men in black caftans and fur hats engaged in spirited conversation as they strolled the street, hands behind their backs. Women in black shawls, their shaved heads covered in tightly woven cotton scarves, haggled over the inflated prices of the vegetables. The Arab villages that had so long supplied the city's population with produce were being forced to halt their trade with the city's Jews; guerrillas from Syria and Iraq were paid to enforce the ban, and therefore the produce that got to the city, whether from Jewish or Arab farms, had tripled in price in the days since the United Nations vote. Joey stopped the jeep at the end of the street in front of a ramshackle stall serviced by an ancient Jewish woman with badly fitted false teeth. She smiled at them gamely over her stunted cabbages and radishes.

"May I serve you?" she said in a tone that suggested she served no one but her God and herself. Joey got out of the jeep and approached her.

"Go away for thirty minutes," he said. He showed her the two twenty-dollar bills in his hand. She reached out quickly and brought them close to her eyes.

"How am I knowing this real?" she said.

"Trust," said Joey, smiling at her the way he smiled at all women. The old woman fingered the bills carefully, squinting at the beautiful woman in the jeep, at the man in drab prison garb, and at his keepers. "Also because I am not English," said Joey.

Quickly the woman spoke something in Yiddish. Joey couldn't answer, any more than he could understand her. "Please, my mother speaks that," he said. "We're in a hurry."

"You're not English," she said. "Maybe." She took the money and turned her back to them, and walked off from the stall. Up the street other stall-keepers and shoppers looked their way, but none approached them, though their eyes were full of menace. Two days before, the British had arrested a Haganah boy of seventeen, armed with a pistol concealed in his canteen. He had been "loitering" in the Yemin Moshe quarter, or rather guarding the entrance to a courtyard where Arab snipers had shot out the windows a day before. The British sergeant who had arrested him had two of his men strip him naked, and then, against the protests of one of his soldiers, left him without his gun and without his clothes in an Arab slum in East Jerusalem. The boy was beaten with sticks and bottles, hit with stones and bricks, slashed with knives; he was dead and terribly mutilated when the British retrieved the body. His mother and sister were not allowed to look at the body; the British officer in charge had insisted on a closed coffin once the father had identified the body. Joey knew this story, if David did not. But in any case, the captain was in no danger of bodily mutilation from the Orthodox Jews of Mea Shearim.

"Out of the jeep," said Joey to the captain. He had removed his gun from his pocket and aimed it deliberately at the captain's heart. "You come with him, Stern."

"You've escaped," said the captain. "I've done what you've asked."

"Shut up," said Joey, and he pushed the man before him into the stall, behind the vegetable stands, and out of sight of the people up the street. David Stern joined them, standing behind Joey patiently, waiting for instructions.

"You're not going to kill me, are you? If you're going to kill me, let me at least write a note to my mother."

"Screw your mother," said Joey Marino. "I'm not wasting a bullet on an asshole like you. Strip."

"What?"

"Strip off your clothes," said Joey. He turned about to David. "You too, please, Stern." The captain complied at once, relieved that the man had told him he would not die. Shoes, shirt, and trousers were removed efficiently and folded unconsciously. David waited, stripped down to his ragged undershorts and socks. The Englishman managed to retain his dignity, helped by the wax in his mustache and the garters that supported his long socks. "I said strip," said Joey to the captain. "Everything."

"Surely you don't mean that I am—"

Joey pointed the gun at the captain's head. "Move it," he said. To David he said, "You'd better get into his clothes. If you want his underwear in place of yours, feel free."

David didn't answer this. He kept his own underwear and hurriedly dressed in the captain's clothes, taking the man's wallet and glancing automatically at the papers inside.

"On your knees, Captain," said Joey when the man was naked. When the Englishman complied, Joey took out the rope he'd prepared in his pocket and tied the man's hands behind his back, tied his ankles together, and tied ankles and wrists together in a powerful knot. Then he stuffed half a cabbage into the man's mouth and wrapped a handkerchief over this and around his neck.

"Are you trying to kill him?" asked David mildly.

"No," said Joey. "If I was trying to kill him, he'd be dead, believe me."

"I haven't thanked you yet," said David as they hurried back into the jeep. Joey turned over the engine, jerked the car forward, and made a screeching U-turn that scattered pedestrians in anticipation of their approach.

"Forget it, pal," said Joey. "There ain't nothing I wouldn't do for a friend of Diana's, see?"

"He loves to talk like a gangster, darling," said Diana to David, turning her beautiful head about to face her lover from the front seat. "But it's all just an act. Inside, he's soft and sweet as a lamb." Diana put her arm about Joey's shoulders as he drove out of the street and into the alleys of Mea Shearim. Joey allowed the touch, though he was not soft as a lamb, and though her calling Stern "darling" felt like a slap to his face. The jeep and the British uniforms would be good for only a few more minutes, if that. There was no way out of Jerusalem for them, no way out of Palestine. All of them, even poor Elliot Crawfield, were fugitives. And as fugitives, all they had was each other.

ELEVEN

David Stern knew what he wanted.

Joey's plans ran in a hundred different directions: where to ditch the car, whether to set it on fire, where to change their clothes, how to get to the bus station where he had secreted the attaché case full of money. He hardly knew whether to turn right or left, whether to ask refuge of the Hasidim, whose neighborhood they were in, whether to ask David Stern for advice.

"You did it, Joey," Diana said. "You actually made it happen."

"You too, kid," he said. "And Crawfield. How're you holding up, Elliot, my pal?"

"I'm a dead man, Yank," said the constable.

And this was Joey's fault too, and his responsibility. Not only must he find a place to hide, he must find a way to help the constable he had made a party to the crime of murder. And all the while, his brain ran helplessly, trying to pay attention to his driving, to the sounds of pursuit, to the feeling of the knife in the guard's ribs, to the way he'd bounced the second guard's head off a concrete wall—all the while, he had to contend with Diana at his side. Yes, he had made it happen, yes, he had got her David Stern, yes, he had murdered, and yes, he had effectively burned his passport, become a homeless fugitive; but did that mean she would love him? He tried to think of what to do next, but the girl was close to him, and her happiness radiated past her fear, and what he needed was her arms about his neck, was her lips on his, was her dedication, her love.

"Where are we going, Joey?" said Diana. "Do you know?"

"Of course I know," he snapped, but this wasn't strictly true, though he'd memorized the map of Mea Shearim along with the rest of Jerusalem, but he drove too quickly, the population was too dense, his attention too scattered to dredge up the twisted grid of the quarter's streets.

"Of course, of course," said Diana, smiling as frivolously as she could. But her thoughts were anything but frivolous. Like Joey, she could hardly see straight. Thoughtlessly she'd become a fugitive, a participant in a prison break that had claimed at least one life. If Joey had murdered, it was her fault, and her name would be posted as an accessory as clearly as his name would be posted as the assassin. She could check into no hotel. The King David press office would be of no help to her. There was no way to call her parents that she could think of, no way to explain to them or to Marty what had happened to the shape of her life. She was not planning what they would have to do, all of them, she was only thinking of her culpability. Joey's life was as irrevocably changed as her own, and for this she owed him something. So she smiled at him, aware at the same time that the smile was wrong for the moment as long as David's eyes were on hers. Frivolous was all right for Joey, desperately wrong for David. Now she had to please them both. It was David she loved, of course, but she owed Joey David's life, she owed Joey what he had risked, what he had sacrificed for her. "I'll never think you don't know what you're doing again," she said to Joey. "Not after today."

"Let me off, Yank," said Crawfield.

"We're almost there, Elliot," said Joey.

"I'm going to give myself in."

"You're not," said Joey. "They'll hang you."

"Maybe I deserve it."

"For what? You didn't kill anybody. I forced you."

"No, you didn't. There was something I could have done. I'm a constable, after all is said and done. And my old mom's got that money."

"She's going to get a lot more where that came from," said Joey.

180

"You did a good thing. You helped save this man's life. Now, shut up and behave yourself, see?"

"I'm a constable," said Elliot Crawfield. "It's different for me. This isn't my cause. I'm an Englishman. I'm an English constable."

"You're not," said David. "You're a wanted man. You can stay with us, you can help us, and you might live. Or you can give yourself up, and you'll go to prison and die."

Crawfield was as conflicted as Joey and Diana. He found the change in his life impossible to comprehend. It seemed monstrously unfair that the events of a single day could outbalance a lifetime of loyalty. He wondered whether he could become a constable in the new Jewish state. He wondered whether he could ever return to England, to a dinner with his old mom. Death seemed one direction, either by suicide or by allowing himself to be captured or by simply giving himself up. Adventure seemed another direction, allowing himself to go along with the crazy American, becoming a fugitive who could one day be rewarded by the new country for helping to defend it against its enemies. But he couldn't fight against Englishmen. But of course he might not have to: the fight would be between the Arabs and the Jews. And all his officers seemed to think the Jews had no chance, not with seven Arab states armed to the teeth, prepared to march in and slaughter the Jews. How could he be a constable in a country of the dead?

Joey finally stopped the jeep, pulling up behind a cypress tree that bent over a tiny cemetery with ravaged old tombstones. They were on the outskirts of Mea Shearim, near the road to Romema, and though the cemetery was Jewish, the neighboring streets were the beginnings of an Arab neighborhood.

"Let's go," said Joey. He had stopped the hundred conflicts in his mind, and had made a decision. They were within a quarter-mile of the home of Mrs. Sussman's ultra-Orthodox brother in Mea Shearim. Joey had spoken to her for only ten minutes that morning, waking her from a deep sleep with a hundred dollars in his hand. The woman who had given them breakfast the day before was mercenary enough to want to help Joey and Diana with "no questions." He needed a place to stay for himself, Diana, and one or two other men, and he would pay one hundred dollars for the privilege. She would have to bring over their luggage for them, and wait for them to show up all that day; above all, no names must be used, secrecy was what they were paying for. Mrs. Sussman's curiosity was burning a hole through her as she took Joey's money. After all, she was David Stern's neighbor, and David Stern was in prison, and this was a time of violence and lawlessness. But she was able to hold herself back from asking about David. Instead she came out with "Are you Jewish?"

"No questions," Joey had said. "But I am on your side."

Now, getting out of the jeep, he had only to lead them through the cemetery, to the first alleyway on the right, then to the second courtyard on the left, then through this courtyard to the ground-floor café on the other side. There Mrs. Sussman would be waiting to take them to her brother's apartment, a small widower's flat on the second floor of a building overcrowded with a sect of Hasidic Jews who were also Zionist.

"Where are we going?" said David as mildly as he could. Of all of them, he knew precisely what he wanted, and all his flagging energy was directed to that point. David needed to sleep, to eat, to heal. He wasted no thought on what would become of them, of how the Haganah would welcome a New York gangster, an English constable, a Jewish princess from Los Angeles. He wanted only to place one foot after the other in a straight line to a bowl of soup and a bed, to a haven.

"There is a woman who will take us to a place," said Joey. "Just follow me."

"Take off your shirt," said David. "You too, constable." He had already taken off the captain's shirt, stripping away the marks of rank. All of them wore undershirts, flimsy protection against the Jerusalem winter, in spite of the sunny day; but this would attract less attention in Mea Shearim than the uniforms of prison and police.

"Yes, I was about to do that," said Joey.

"Leave the jeep running," said David. "Perhaps an Arab will come up and steal it."

"Sure," said Joey, hurrying back to the jeep and starting it up. No one had seen them as yet; at least no one had shown himself in this lonely spot. Joey tried to gain back the control that he felt was his due. To David he said, "Why don't you put your arm around Diana? Walk behind us, like you're not with us."

"It's not a good idea to walk with your arm around a woman in Mea Shearim," said David.

"Come on," said Joey, not answering this latest rebuke. The wind came out of the south, whipping through the cemetery stones, and as Joey looked back, he could see Diana warming her lover in the folds of her sweater. He hurried the constable along, and keeping his eyes alert, led them through the tombstones. Many of the stones had been desecrated: swastikas had been painted over Yiddish inscriptions, and gashes and bullet holes were common, as if this were some sort of proving ground for young Arab guerrillas. They could hear rifle fire coming from away to the north, probably from the Arab snipers in Sheik Jarrah. Somehow, this distant gunfire reassured Joey. Their crime was not the only one in Jerusalem that day; far from it. Arab snipers in Katamon were daily claiming Jewish victims in neighboring Rehaviah and Kiryat Shmuel. Haifa was in a state of near-anarchy, with English soldiers being shot in the back by Arab and Jewish terrorists, and the unarmed civilian population living in terror of the next bomb, the next bullet to crash through someone's wall. Mortars were being fired from the Arab quarter in the Old City into the Jewish quarter, and snipers were using the ancient fortification of the Old City walls from which to pour lead into the Jewish neighborhoods below them, especially Yemin Moshe. Banks were being robbed with greater and greater frequency, the police unable to investigate the crimes under the weight of more pressing obligations. Two British constables were shot during the robbery of the Jaffa–Tel Aviv train last Wednesday; on Thursday a British café was bombed by the Stern gang. Certainly the prison staff would be in an uproar, the fact of Diana's family's influence in getting her in to see her fiancé would make its way to the newspapers, the highly unusual story of an English constable turning against his fellows would make a sensation: but it would blow over. Perhaps a thousand other murders, assassinations, and deaths had taken place in the last four weeks in Palestine, and these were deaths among Arabs, Jews, and British. A murder had been committed, a prisoner had escaped, but these were but motes on the balance of justice and vengeance in December 1947 in the Holy Land.

On the other side of the cemetery they were noticed at once. A group of yeshivah students, boys of ten and eleven with lengthy side curls and black skullcaps, chattered about the apparitions coming from the cemetery: men in undershirts on this winter's day, and a woman wearing her own hair, uncovered, long and voluptuously blowing in the wind. Their teacher, a very tall man in a black overcoat and black fur hat, hovered over them; his pale eyes looked through the four fugitives without curiosity as they hurried into the alley that led deeper into the religious quarter.

"David can't go this fast," said Diana.

"Don't talk," said David quietly. "No English. And don't stare at the crowds." The alley led to a series of houses built around courtyards, similar to David's own neighborhood. But unlike David's neighborhood, where the mix of Jewish people was remarkable for its diversity, the untrained eye could see only one sort of Jew here—the ultra-Orthodox. Though even within this street there was a score of different sects, one following a rabbinical dynasty originating in a Polish town one hundred years before, another worshiping the memory of a Hungarian rabbi who'd died a martyr's death in the First World War, one fanatically opposed to the Zionist movement (because the Messiah hadn't arrived on earth to lead the Jews to the Old City), another just as fanatically opposed to waiting another minute for either Messiah, Arabs, or British to give them their land—all these black-garbed people, men's features hidden behind beards and hair and hats, women's modesty protected by wigs and head coverings and shapeless clothing, looked like members of the same tribe to Joey. Crawfield found the crowded alleyway vaguely menacing, as if these indistinctly realized people were the remnant of the persecuted Jews of Europe, the pictures of the gentle martyrs of the concentration camps come back to life; and they would recognize in him the face of the oppressor.

"In here," said Joey, and he turned into a courtyard where a lone Hasidic girl, very frail and pretty, her blond hair braided like a German fräulein's, pumped water out of the communal well. She stared at them with enormous frightened eyes.

"It's all right, sweetheart," said Joey, remembering at once that David Stern had just demanded silence, and for good reason. The British might invade the neighborhood later in the day, after—if—the jeep was discovered next to the cemetery, and they would question everyone about any strangers that might have been seen or heard. Hurrying the pace against Diana's plea, he made it across the courtyard, emerging next to a tiny café paces ahead of the constable. Joey's hand was on his gun, secure in his pocket. There was a sign on the café in Yiddish, a religious notice of some sort that was superimposed with majestic seals. A tiny window revealed the café's interior:

three tables set around a display of religious articles for sale. Joey couldn't imagine a group of Hasidim sitting around these tables chatting and smoking; and indeed, there was no one inside, not even a shopkeeper.

"What now, Yank?" said Crawfield, huddling close to Joey as he shivered against the cold.

"Mr. Marino," said Mrs. Sussman's irritatingly familiar but now very welcome voice. "Over here."

And there she was, standing up the street with a short little man in a black coat, with a black beard that spread out all over his chest. Joey turned about, waiting for Diana and David to catch up. Near Mrs. Sussman, three pale young men stood in shiny black suits, oblivious of the cold as they argued over some talmudic point, their thin frames swaying to an interior rhythm as they drove home their arguments. A woman hurried down the street carrying a baby swaddled in dark blue wool; a man passed her, his back bent under the weight of two enormous oil cans, his eyes never leaving the ground. Mrs. Sussman hurried their way, and her eyes turned in grateful astonishment to the sight of David Stern.

"David!" she said, reaching for his hands, starting to kiss his grizzly cheek.

"Menye!" hissed her brother, the name emerging as a powerful warning from the diminutive frame. He reminded her in Yiddish of her obligations to him, to the passerby on the street, to the appearance of modesty required of all Jewish women. Mrs. Sussman let go of David's hands.

"My brother's a *meshuggenah*, you know that?" she said. "But he's going to help us."

"The money?" he said to his sister, speaking in English so that the others would understand.

Joey took out a hundred-dollar bill. "This is for the first day, pal," he said. "Be nice and we'll stay longer."

The money was enough to feed everyone in the brother's apartment building, at black-market rates, for the rest of the month. He took the bill swiftly from Joey's hand and put it into his own pocket. "You are criminals, are you not?" he said in a nearly accentless English.

"Your bags are there," said Mrs. Sussman. "Let's hurry. Get you off the street. David. Thank God you're alive. You're out of there."

Mrs. Sussman's brother's name was Reb Meyer, the "Reb" an honorific title, not at all equivalent to the designation of "Rabbi." He spent his days in study, one of a dozen men who bent over the Talmud in a yeshivah adjacent to his apartment. Once he had been a watchmaker and a jeweler, but those days were long past. He had saved enough money to sustain his earthly frame; now his days were devoted to enriching his soul. At least, this was what he claimed. His sister had another theory:

"Once his wife died, he went straight downhill. Right to the fanatics. He always went to *shul* on *Shabbes*. But now he doesn't want to work for a living, just like the rest of them." His apartment was small, a room filled with religious books on a dozen shelves, furnished with a long table and backless benches, and a second room with two narrow beds.

"I am not staying here," said Reb Meyer as he showed them into the kitchen, with its separate dishes and utensils for meat and dairy. "My sister will come and see what you want. No one in the building will talk, because the rabbi has been told that you are working to build Eretz-Israel. My sister tells me this is true."

Joey saw his and Diana's suitcases neatly piled in the kitchen next to a cast-iron bathtub of small size. There was a kitchen tap with cold water, and a three-legged Primus stove to heat it. Crawfield asked if he could light the stove, and Reb Meyer cautioned there was little fuel left.

"Take a sweater from my suitcase," said Joey.

As Crawfield went over to the alligator case, Diana let some water run into a pot.

"I'm going to have to heat this," she said. "For David."

"Sure," said Joey. "We'll pay for the fuel, whatever it costs. Could you get us some more, Reb Meyer?"

"I'll get it," said Mrs. Sussman. "Kerosene is not easy this week. You have to know people. It will be expensive." Joey sighed and started to reach into his pocket for more money, but she stopped him. "No, you've paid me too much already. Before, I didn't know you were a friend of David's."

"You can move one of the beds into the other room," said Reb Meyer. "So the young woman can have privacy. Even though I am not to be here, it is important that the house not be defiled by the appearance of sin. Sin is of course an abomination, but the appearance of sin, even if no sin is taking place, is an evil as well, for it can lead others astray."

"All right, mister," said Joey. "We got the message, and you got the hundred bucks."

"I only wish to add that the Talmud teaches us the way the world is preserved. By three things: truth, judgment, and peace. We in this building understand the purpose of the Haganah, and that it is an army looking for peace, looking to live in the Holy Land, in a manner befitting the Jewish people."

"We're not in the Haganah," said Joey.

"Lying, says the Talmud, is the same as stealing in the eyes of God," said Reb Meyer, trying to remember the passage. "'Whoever equivocates in his speech is as though he worshiped idols.'"

"Yeah," said Joey. "And speech is silver, silence golden."

Diana placed the pot of water on the stove, and Crawfield lit it for her. He had squeezed into a black angora sweater with a high neck, and some of the shocked look had worn off his face. He now had a dull purpose to his eyes. The constable knew what he was doing, and was taking in all he saw as part of the terrible new outline of his existence.

"Do not tell people," said David to Reb Meyer, "that we are with the Haganah. They will assume that anyway, but do not advertise it. There are some Jews who hate the army of their own people, and God will forgive you if you avoid answering direct questions with equivocations that can save lives."

"'The Holy One, blessed be He,'" quoted Reb Meyer happily, "'hates the person who speaks one thing with his mouth and another with his heart.' That is from *Pesachim*. You can look it up."

His sister finally dragged him out of there. Joey thought that the old widower was tired of all his studying, and in spite of the appearance of moralistic hostility, was fascinated by his hundred-dollar-a-day borders.

"Well, I guess Elliot and I will leave you two alone," said Joey.

Diana poured the first pot of hot water into the small tub. "David must have a bath," she said.

"I have to get my hands on our money," said Joey. He took out a mohair suit from one of his cases, and looked about for shirt and tie.

"You can't leave here, Joey," said David. It was the first time the man had called him by his first name.

"I'm not going to watch you bathe, am I?"

"There's another room," said Diana.

"You can watch me bathe, you can close your eyes, you can go to the bedroom or the study. There's some food here—beans I think. Can you cook?"

"I can," said Crawfield.

"How nice," said David. "The point is, no one leaves."

Joey found the shirt he was looking for, a white-on-white Swiss cotton, and a Sulka tie. "I'm going to change," he said, and started to stalk angrily out of the kitchen, but stopped himself after the third step. "One thing," said Joey. "You're not in charge here."

"Joey," said Diana.

"Neither are you, babe," said Joey. "I'm the one who killed. I'm the one who organized. I'm the one who screwed up Elliot's life. I'm the one responsible for all this. I'm in charge." He looked directly into David's exhausted eyes. "Is that understood?" he said.

"You can put yourself in charge of anything you want," said David. "Just don't walk out that front door."

"If I want to walk the hell out of the front door, pal," said Joey, "that's my business. This is what I am telling you, mac. Is that clear?"

"If you walk out that front door in your rich American suit, not speaking a word of Yiddish, without a single friend in the quarter, with the jeep abandoned five minutes from here, you're going to get picked up by the Brits," said David. "And if you get picked up by the Brits, we're all going to be picked up by the Brits. Is that simple enough for you to understand, Joey?"

"If you weren't . . . " began Joey, but rather than completing the sentence he simply turned from David to glare at Diana, as if it were her fault that he couldn't take out brass knuckles or switchblade and brutalize the Haganah man. Not deigning to answer David, he stalked out and went to dress in the bedroom.

"I can make some soup," said the constable, looking through the cupboards.

"That would be good for David," said Diana.

"Is he going to go?" said David.

"I think so," said Diana, who understood perfectly Joey's anger. He needed not so much to be in charge as to exhibit his childish resentment at the reunion of lovers.

"The Yank can take care of himself," said Crawfield. "He's crazy, but he can take care of himself all right." He had already mixed up the meat and dairy dishes, but the esoteric nature of the laws of Kashrut seemed unimportant to Diana at that moment. She filled the tub and told David to get into it. "I'll just leave this on the stove," said the constable. "Can you mind that it doesn't boil over?"

Before Crawfield could leave them alone in the kitchen, they heard the front door slam. Diana wondered what he would do, where he would go in his gangster's suit. But David was past caring. He needed the bath, the soup, the rest. A moment after Crawfield left the kitchen, they heard the front door open and close once again, the constable following the lead of the gangster. But Diana had already helped strip away her lover's clothing.

"Darling, they hurt you," he heard her say, but he merely shook his head and thrust his foot into the too-hot water of the iron tub. "Your back. You're all bruised. Sweetheart. Let me. Come on, get in," she was saying, but David was listening to his body and not to the words of the woman who had saved him. The water was so hot that it sent a flush to his face. He felt his pores open, and the delicous sweat run out. The tub was very small, and he sat with his back against the very hot iron, his knees drawn up out of the water, his feet firmly planted in the soothing liquid.

"I thought I'd never see you again," said Diana, and he heard this in some part of his brain, but he remembered too his dead wife, Miriam, how she had scrubbed his back for him, using a thick-bristled German brush, singing to him in her sweet girlish voice—for she was really just a girl when they were married, only eighteen, and she was still a girl when the Nazis butchered her. "When that Haganah man walked into the Waldorf—do you know him, Grinberg, Arye Grinberg his name is. No, don't talk. Just enjoy. When he came in and I saw his face, I thought I was going to die. I thought you must be dead, and here he was to tell me that. And you're not dead. You're here, and it's too good to be true. Here, and I'm touching you. Does your back hurt? You've so many bruises. And sores. You're so filthy, darling. I'm going to rub and rub until you're clean as gold, good as new, sweet and soft like a baby."

"Diana," said David. "Check that the front door is locked."

"Of course," she said, and when she had let go of him, he sank a bit deeper into the water, letting the warmth into the heart of his muscles, letting the tension twist away to another part of his being. He could smell the soup simmering on the stove, the olive oil in the soap she had lathered into his skin; he could hear the chanting singsong of some nearby study group, boys learning the Talmud, even in the face of the whirlwind; he could taste the residue of fear that had backed up in his throat since he had first seen Diana hours before. David was free, and he relished this, forcing himself to concentrate on what was simple and positive and clear: the soapy water, the soup, the touch of his lover's hands. Soon there would be a mattress, a bed, darkness. There was no reason to think past this, to remember who he was, to think of all the lives he had left behind, of the parents and siblings and wife and the child growing in her womb, to wonder to what purpose he was left, a man of violence in the land of the Jews.

"We're all locked in," said Diana, returning to his back. She kissed him now, very softly at the back of his neck, and he felt the force of her love as he pitied her. "The constable must have been too embarrassed to stay here with us. He must have been reading my mind, darling." Later he would get her to explain who these people were, the Englishman, the American. He would have to find out about the guns they needed so desperately. In a day he would contact the Haganah and see where he could be useful, and what if anything could be done to get Diana back to the States. But the little flare-up with Joey, the fact of the two of them, Joey and Crawfield, wandering about the ultra-Orthodox neighborhood together, faded now from his mind. There was no energy left to worry about that. If they didn't return, he would worry. But there was time. There was an hour, there was more than an hour, and he would let this young woman love him, let her pull the pain out of his back, rub soap into his dirty hair and beard, reach down and clean his genitals.

"Hello," she said, touching his penis, and David thought this just like Diana, deliberately light-headed and girlish, instead of womanly and serene. But his penis began to grow hard. This surprised him, as he had felt no sexual urge. His greater urge was to satisfy hunger and fatigue, but there it was, proof of the biological imperative. Past all the fatigue, he began to want her. Through his shut eyes, sitting in the hot water, he began to remember the smoothness of her flesh, the safety of her embrace. Letting himself into her body was like entering a palace of youth and beauty, of riches and luxury. Wanting her completely was an insistence on sensuality, on the present, on the world that existed outside the pale of the holocaust.

She brought soup to his lips, and the beans were hard and tasteless, and the nourishment trickled down his beard. Carefully she scrubbed his hair, his beard, his ears, she took his fingers one at a time and cleaned them, massaging the heavy olive oil into his knuckles. The water cooled, minute by minute, as a thick layer of dirt floated about his naked form. But the clumsy, earnest manner with which his lover cosseted him was endearing. She was trying to baby him, but she was like a first-time mother who hardly knew where to stick a pin in a diaper, how hard to strike the child's tender form to elicit a burp of pleasure. Half-asleep, half-starved, half-erect, he was still in control of this woman. He would take pleasure, but he would give pleasure too. She would not have left him with an emotional debt. He had too many debts already, and with each year of life they escalated. The love his wife still offered him from the grave was always about him, impossible to return in full.

"You came to me," he whispered from the filthy water of the tub.

"Of course," said Diana. "I would do anything—"

He stopped her sentence in mid-flight. Squinting against the low level of light, he raised his head to where she hovered over him, and opened his mouth for her kiss. On her knees, Diana held his bearded cheeks, she placed her tongue between his teeth, she moved her chest in its cashmere wrap against his soapy body.

"Help me," he said, trying to rise, and she was glad of the chance, grabbing him at the elbows, placing her palms firmly against the small of his back, against the flat abdomen, pulling at his underarms with gentle force.

"I want to help you," she said, and when he had gotten out of the tub, standing on the cold stone floor in a shivery pool of water, she took off her sweater and rubbed its soft, fine surface along his chest and back and limbs.

"I'm cold," he said, knowing the pleasure he was giving her in allowing this chance to penetrate his privacy, his needs and desires. He hardly moved to help her, letting his back lean into a kitchen cabinet, conserving energy.

"I'll warm you, darling," she said, her voice so full of concern, so plaintive for what she imagined him to have suffered, that for a moment David felt like an observer outside his own body, watching two lovers come together, two lovers of equal passion, of mutual desire. She wrapped her sweater about his neck and reached for a rough towel to dry the rest of him, taking special care with his thick head of blond hair, with the wet caught in his chest hair, with the soap in his ears. "Come on," she said, taking his hand and pulling at it, as if to snap him out of a trance. When he moved, he left tracks on the cold stone, and he felt the cold currents of air blow through his famished body. "Get into the bed," she said, pulling away the quilt.

"Thank you," he said. "You came for me."

"Come on, get in," she said, keeping her eyes on his beautiful face, refusing to let tears come. David sat down heavily on the narrow bed, so that the springs protested at once, and he let out a tiny smile.

She picked up his ankles, swiveling about his muscular lower torso so that he lay naked across the bed, his eyes staring wide, waiting for her to come into his field of vision. Quickly she bent over his face, her green eyes luminous and huge as she moved in to kiss his lips and eyes and cheek. He could see the pleasure he was giving her simply by allowing her to love him. Her beauty gave him a start, as if he had misplaced the memory of her features, and after looking at her absently for an hour or more, would suddenly see her.

"You're lovely," he said.

"Let me cover you," she said, blushing with joy. Diana didn't feel it was gratitude that was moving him to speak; it was fatigue. With his guard down, with his earnest anger at the world displaced by weariness, he was exhibiting his true feelings. Beyond all the seriousness, all the memories of war, all the worries about the present danger to Eretz-Israel, David was capable of love. She pulled at the blanket on which he was lying, trying to get it around his naked body, but David took hold of her wrist and pulled her on top of him.

"Cover me with yourself," he said.

"I love you," she said, trying to make her body light, lighter than air, so as not to disturb his hungry frame. She wished she could take him away right then, somewhere beyond the boundaries and borders of governments, somewhere where summer reigned and tropical fruits full of sugar and starch fell out of the trees. She would fatten him up, let the sun tan his pale skin, let his body sleep for tranquil hours bathed by the clean breeze of the sea. She would regale him with peace, he who had only known war. He would forget his past life, the life of Europe in its madness, he would look forward only to life with her in a place where life meant joy and love and happiness.

"You came for me," said David. "You came for me and you got me out of that place." She could feel the weight of his body settle more comfortably beneath her, approaching the restfulness of sleep. But his eyes were open, and his chest rose and fell in an irregular, still-wary rhythm. She was amazed to feel his hands behind her back, couldn't imagine how he had the strength to lift them; he had found the catch to her brassiere and uncoupled it.

"I would come for you anywhere," she said, helping him with the brassiere. His mouth moved slowly to her collarbone, and she could hear him groan, either from pleasure or pain.

"I want you," he said.

"I'm glad." She wanted to contradict him, to ask him whether it would be better to sleep. She would have been content to watch him rest, lying in a tiny corner of the narrow bed. But he was offering her love now, and she could not postpone this offering. She needed his love desperately, and she knew it could vanish as quickly as a dream.

"You were brave," he said. "Like the first time I met you." He had not told her that he loved her, but this talk about her bravery was the highest form of praise he gave; she took it as much like a declaration of love as she could. He wanted to help her out of her skirt, but she rolled off his body and hurried out of her shoes and skirt and stockings and underwear. He watched quietly until she was naked and then he raised his head from the flat little pillow and brought his hand out over the edge of the bed and grabbed her hair at the scalp line.

Diana let out a little cry, not at the shock of pain but at the shock of being wanted. He was strong as he took hold of her slender waist, letting go of her hair, and helping her fall onto the narrow bed, their bodies caught between the blanket and quilt, his knee raised up between her thighs.

"Where's my gun?" he said.

"Forget your gun," said Diana, and she pushed him off his side and onto his back, taking hold of his penis in her fist. "Forget everything," she said. Already she could hear his breathing change. The irregularity of wariness was waning. She bent low and swallowed the head of his penis, feeling it swell up against her teeth, feeling desire race through the two of them. He took hold of her head lightly and pulled away from her mouth, and then brought his lips to hers. His hand scratched along her backbone and took hold of her buttocks, and then brought her body flush against his, so that her head nestled under his chin, her breasts stood up against his belly, her pubic hair rubbed against his penis.

"All right," he said. "I'll forget everything." But this wasn't true, at least not at that moment, for whenever he was beginning to make love with Diana, he was showered with memories: the first woman he'd made love with after his escape from the death camp had been strong and lusty. She'd laughed at the tears she brought to his eyes, thinking them tears of relief, when in fact they'd been of remorse and guilt. Surely he had begun to bury his wife the moment he'd penetrated that Polish peasant. And there were other memories: some of desire, like the Jewish woman he'd found in Tel Aviv with copper-colored hair; some of longing, like the image of Miriam, standing under the wedding canopy, her eyes wide with terror and joy. But there was a way out of these memories, and that was through concentrating on the moment.

And so he kissed Diana with an intensity that she could only interpret as the mark of love. He held her breasts with such gentleness and passion, he rubbed his beard along her belly with such a need for closeness, that only a leap of the imagination could have disbelieved in the man's passion for Diana Mann. But it was not so. Even as he kissed the inside of her thighs, even as he thrust his tongue into her vagina, his hands clawing up her backside, the heels of his hands along her limbs, his passion was fabricated and fought against the past. He was moaning at the pleasure he remembered, the pleasure he brought her, the pleasure that was rising inexorably in his own tired frame. And Diana heard this, and her joy was fighting against nothing, her passion was nothing fabricated but everything that was real to her in the world. She heard him, and she felt her body reach out to embrace, she felt her love like a palpable spirit, a dream that has somehow come to life in the shape of a wave, or a mountain, or a wall of fire.

David moved his tongue along her thighs, he kissed her belly, he placed his teeth gently around the nipple of her right breast. And then he entered her.

"Oh, darling," she said, and David felt how tired he was, how weak every cell in his body seemed to be. Every part of him cried out for rest and food, but still his penis was swollen with desire, still the impulse was to move toward release, a release that was as much emotional as physical.

"My God," he said, for he felt the memories fading, the peasant woman's laugh and garlicky breath and powerful legs pulling him

194

inside her, Miriam's face as he told her why they must flee the only country they had ever loved, the sound of a million panes of glass breaking as thugs rioted in the Jewish neighborhood of his hometown. "My God," he said again, and without memories he was a shell, a baby born into a man's body, a man without allegiances, without guilt, without shame. "But yes," he said, as if answering his own question. Yes, it was better this way, this way inside Diana, as he moved slowly higher and higher, climbing with a woman who loved him, finding his own pleasure along the route that was the way to her own.

"I love you," she said, and even this couldn't snap his happiness, even this phrase that had been uttered into his ear by wife, by whores, by sad-eyed mistresses who never wanted to let go of him, even these three maddeningly possessive words couldn't stop the urge within him. "I love you," she said again, and she felt the pain behind the ecstasy, she could taste the fall before she had gotten to the top, and so she held back, she waited, she waited until she could believe that he would never leave her, that somehow beyond the glow in his ecstatic smile there was permanence, there was a need for her that would outlast this moment, this day.

But then she could go no higher. He said her name, she felt his body quiver as if it had been hit by lightning, and she could not remember what she was waiting for: there was no moment other than this moment, no before, no after. She felt his penis inside her, and felt her muscles pull him in, muscles outside her control, outside any thought. There could be nothing closer than this, she understood, nothing better for her than this moment with the man she loved. Diana tried to keep the moment in sight, to watch it, as if from a distance, to move into it slowly, like a boat coming inexorably to the shore. But a frenzy took hold of her. She could see nothing, and all she could hear was the expulsion of breath from both their lungs. They moved not as one, but as two looking to become one, hammering at each other as if insisting to be enclosed within one skin. And for a moment they were one skin—one skin and one heart and one mind. There was release, and desperately Diana hung on to him, her nails biting into his back. She wanted to love him a minute from now precisely as she loved in the heart of climax. She wanted this, she demanded this, and she looked into his blue eyes and saw tears.

"Are you all right, darling?" she said, holding, kissing him, brushing the hair from his forehead, covering the two of them with the quilt, hoping that the tears were tears of joy.

But there was no answer from David. His eyes closed as he shivered next to her, moving into her body for warmth. He had beaten back the memories, he had found release, he had allowed love into his life for the moment, and now that moment was passed. The tears might have been tears of joy, they might have been tears of guilt, they might have been tears for his refusal to renew his life with love. But now the tears were gone. Now he was free, and Diana was with him, and as she held him in her arms, he slept.

TWELVE

Crawfield shouted with all his strength, "Yank, hey, Yank! Wait for me!"

Joey Marino's tall figure and bare head stood out in the midst of the street's Orthodox Jews, but Crawfield could see that a car was pulling up next to him, a taxi. He shouted again, and he ran, but the American got into the car, and the car tore off at high speed. The constable felt his life force drain away. Without Joey, he had no direction. He knew perfectly well he would be picked up on this street by his former colleagues. There was nothing he could say in his defense except that he was sorry, that he hadn't meant to hurt anyone or break any laws; perhaps he would mention that it seemed unfair to send a man to Kenya for twenty-eight years for carrying a weapon in self-defense. But no, he wouldn't even bother with that. He wasn't political. Joey had sent money to his old mom. Joey had helped him out in the bar. And he had helped Joey. It wasn't a defense. It was what he had done, and they would hang him for it.

"Get in," said Joey Marino.

Crawfield stared at the American's face, magically next to his in the taxi window. "Yank," he said. "You left. I saw the taxi drive away."

"Get in," repeated Joey. He opened the taxi door and pulled at the slow-witted constable. "I saw you," he explained. "I told the driver to come back for you."

"Thanks, Yank. I really appreciate it. I don't know what I would have done if you hadn't come back—"

"Shut up," said Joey. "Are you crazy or something? I just ruined your life, and you're thanking me for giving you a ride in a taxi?"

"Well, what are you getting so angry for, Yank?" said the constable. "I'm not *criticizing* you, I'm *thanking* you."

"Tahane Ha-Merkazi," said Joey to the driver, who was still waiting patiently for instructions. At these words from the American, the driver slammed the accelerator pedal to the floor with such sudden force that the car stalled, and he had to start it up again.

"What did you tell him, Yank? You don't speak Hebrew, do you? Jesus, I've been here half my life and I don't know five words in that crazy language."

"I don't speak Hebrew," said Joey. "I just memorized a few phrases from a book. That's the central station that I asked for, the bus station."

The driver roared down a narrow street, scattering pedestrians with his blasting horn. He turned right so close to a stand of vegetables that the constable was sure they'd skinned a dozen apples. "This guy drives like a maniac."

"Nobody said you had to come," said Joey.

"I didn't want to wait around there," said the constable. "I mean, what was I supposed to do there? They missed each other, those two, if you know what I mean."

"No, I can't figure it out," said Joey, patting his gun in its holster under his jacket. He blew out a furious breath of air. "Giving me orders, that son of a bitch."

"Not orders, really," said Crawfield pleasantly. "I think he was just trying to help us all out, him being used to this kind of thing. Maybe he's right, Yank. I mean, I don't know much, but I am a constable, and after all, where would we look for people like you, if it wasn't the bus stations and all that?"

"If you're afraid to go to the goddamned bus station," said Joey, "then get the hell out of here, all right?"

"I'm not afraid," said Crawfield mildly. "What more can happen to me? I don't really care if they shoot me, Yank."

Joey looked at him sharply, letting the full force of the constable's

198

predicament land squarely on his shoulders. "Hey," said Joey. "Sorry if I was rough on you."

"It's that kind of day, Yank," said the constable.

"I don't want you to think that it's the end of the world, because it's not, see?"

"If you say so, Yank. I don't really care that much. If you meant what you said, that you might see your way clear to helping my old mom out a bit more, that would be nice, I could appreciate that."

"How's ten grand?" said Joey, very free with Diana's money. "Think your mom could do with ten thousand dollars?"

"Yank," said Crawfield, "she could buy a shop with that, and fill it up, and be free and clear of everything. Ten thousand dollars. She won't mind that I can't go back to England, not with that much money."

"And I've got plans for you too, Elliot," said Joey. "There's plenty you can do, once we get you out of Palestine."

"I'm a constable, that's all I know."

"You play cards, pal?"

"A little bridge," said Crawfield. Joey laughed at this, but patted the fat man on the shoulder. He could imagine him in a dinner jacket in Las Vegas, a croupier with an English accent, a dealer, or a floor-walker. Marty could arrange it. The money would be very nice. The fussy man could have a neat little bungalow out in the desert, a new life with dry air and sunshine, and pretty girls from Los Angeles, eager to learn the dealer's name.

"Elliot, I promise you, your life can be wonderful," said Joey. "It's not the end of the world, it's just the end of your being an underpaid constable. I'm going to get you a job in a place where it's always sunny and warm and where you'll have lots of cash, and beautiful clothes—"

"Not a criminal, Yank," said the constable. "I couldn't do anything criminal." Joey smiled at him, liking the fat man very much at that moment. He assured him that there would be nothing criminal involved, except for a change of name and passport to make it simpler to get out of the country. "You really think it's possible," said Elliot Crawfield, shaking his head in wonder. He had already made up his mind that life was over for him, but this crazy American's talk held out a last straw of hope that tantalized. Perhaps he would live after all, and out in this unnamed sunny climate he would finally lose weight, grow prosperous, remarry, and start a family; if he was going to dream, he might as well dream in capital letters.

But the sight of a great crowd around the bus station settled over Crawfield's sunny dream like a wet cloud: there were perhaps two hundred people, mostly Jews, held back by barricades manned by a dozen policemen. They would know him at once, he thought, recognize his face or his big profile or his nervous walk.

"*Attah yachol le-chakeh?*" said Joey to the driver, pulling another phrase out of the hundred he'd memorized.

"*Bevakashah*," said the driver, with expansive hands.

"What did he say?" said Crawfield.

"I told him to wait. I don't know what he said, but I think he said yes," said Joey. He opened the door on Crawfield's side, leaning across the big man to do so. "Just get out, Elliot. Relax, and walk like you own the place. We're going to the lockers. There's something I left there. You can help me. Go," said Joey, and Crawfield climbed out of the car, and felt a chill spread from his chest to the tips of his fingers. The taxi made no move forward, and Joey smiled at the driver.

"How long are you gentlemen going to be?" said the driver, his accent a mix of French and German, but the syllables clipped and precise.

"Five minutes," said Joey. "You could have told me you spoke English."

"I wanted you to practice your Hebrew," said the driver. "We need Hebrew speakers in this country, my friend."

"Five minutes," said Joey, not liking the man's tone. He walked directly into the center of the crowd, the constable hurrying to keep up with him. "You got any idea what this is about?" said Joey. "They can't all be waiting for a bus."

"They're waiting for the dead," said Crawfield.

"This way," said Joey, who had spotted a constable walking their way through the crowd. He hurried Crawfield to a side entrance, and followed a circuitous route about the crowd to the banks of lockers. "What dead?" said Joey as he took a key out of his pocket and unlocked locker A-414. The attaché case was where he had left it the day before, and as he took it out and slammed the locker shut, a great crying, joyful and miserable, broke out from the nearby crowd.

"What is it?" said Joey.

"It's the convoy—the buses that made it from Tel Aviv," said the constable. Crawfield had heard that the crowds had grown since the partition vote, and he had never imagined them this large or this terrified. Even from where they stood at the edge of the crowd, they could see anxious relatives charge the two armor-plated buses that had made it through. Later they would learn that another bus, an eight-ton steel-plated behemoth, had been crippled, its tires shot out, its radiator cracked and useless, and its chassis bent out of shape by a land mine. Arab mercenaries had swooped down on the stalled bus from their heights, and turned it over on its side with dynamite. Everyone inside who wasn't shot was burned to death when an incendiary bomb was pushed through one of the steel shell's eye slits. The British forces, sworn to keep the road open and safe for all, were nowhere to be found, though the fighting was within earshot of a British police post.

The joyful cries were for the fact that the buses, any buses, had limped into Jerusalem. Given the unguarded state of the road, and the fact that the British were routinely stripping the Haganah escorts of their arms—and imprisoning them for their attempts at self-defense—the total loss of a convoy was to be expected. Ambulances from Hadassah Hospital waited, their doors open, expecting the wounded to be first off the airless steel-shuttered vehicles. But the relatives got in the way of the wounded, fighting each other to get onto the buses before the passengers had been allowed to get off. A man with a black beard and a stentorian voice spoke through a megaphone in Hebrew, urging the crowd to keep back. But as the first passengers were finally exposed to the light, their bloody bandages wrapped around heads and arms and legs, some walking, some carried, some shouting for friends in the crowd, some as silent as the dead, the crowd could not be restrained. Men and women charged up the bus steps, pushing at the exhausted, the wounded, the dead. What each wanted was a face, a living smiling face that would shout out a welcome, that would announce the fact of life. For as each passenger left the bus, wounded or unscathed, the chances that an as-yet-unseen loved one being still alive diminished. Each bus had been shot at, but most of the victims aboard came from other vehicles, jeeps and trucks that had wandered into mines or been hit by grenades or machine-gun fire. As Joey and Crawfield made their way back to the taxi, their eyes were drawn to the spectacle of the dead: corpses were being carried from the buses and laid out on the asphalt like fish on a saltwater dock. Members of the crowd averted their eyes from this spectacle of dead bodies. Only after the last passenger had walked out of the bus would relatives venture to turn their eyes to the cold ground, littered with bodies waiting to be claimed by some heartbroken friend.

"Say, Crawfield, what are you doing here?" said a hearty English voice, the voice of a police officer. "I like the duds, governor," he added, fingering the constable's sweater—borrowed from Joey.

"Take your bleeding hands off me," said Crawfield. He could feel Joey tensing at his side, but knew that this was no time for a confrontation. The man obviously knew nothing about the jailbreak, or if he did, that Elliot Crawfield had been one of the gang that freed David Stern.

"All that blood make you crazy?" said the police officer. "I'm just not used to seeing your fat body in such nice clothes. Bloody mess, this place. And I mean bloody. Flaming farce, if you ask me. Let the bleeding Arabs shoot the bloody Jews just because the bleeding Foreign Office wants some more oil wells. What about the law, is what I'm thinking."

"It's a bloody farce," agreed Crawfield.

"This your friend?" said the police officer, looking at Joey.

Crawfield hesitated for a moment, but Joey spoke quickly. "I'm a tourist," he said. "This man's showing me where the cabs are."

"A tourist?" said the police officer. "What kind of a bloody time is this for a flaming tourist to come to this bleeding town? You must be crazy."

"It's okay. I was a Marine," said Joey.

"The cabs are just around the corner," said the police officer.

"I'm going to show him," said Crawfield. "Maybe I'll share one with him."

"Why aren't you on duty today?" said the police officer.

"I had a toothache this morning," said Crawfield, pointing to his yellow teeth. "Too much chocolate. Be seeing you."

Their driver was standing outside the taxi, and as they approached, he swung open the rear door with comical civility.

"So you had a toothache," said Joey. "You're getting good, Elliot. You may have a future in this." He told the driver to take them back to Mea Shearim.

"He knows me, Yank," said Crawfield. "Everyone's going to know it was me at the prison, and he saw me."

"So he saw you, right? He saw you at the bus station. They're going to be worried you're in Haifa or Lydda or Jaffa. It's good that he saw you, see?" Joey sat back in his seat and smiled. He had a gun, he had money, he had his wits and his health. He would get Diana out of Palestine; he would get them all out of this miserable place, except for Stern, who wouldn't want to go.

Diana slowly pulled herself out from under David's sleeping body. The bed was so narrow that she found herself holding the floor with one hand, while extricating her pinned legs from her lover's embrace. But though the springs groaned and whined, David didn't wake. The weeks in prison had left him spent; even his hair-trigger tendency to wake at the slightest provocation was gone. She took a chance and brought her lips quietly to his damp forehead, his shut eyes, his bearded cheek.

Then there was a knocking at the front door, a violent insistent knocking.

Diana looked on the floor for clothes to cover her nakedness, not knowing whether to wake David; but in that instant, he was awake and rolling off the bed, pulling at the quilt as if for cover. "Dress," he said, and not looking at her, he hurried out of the bedroom in a half-crouch, going for the kitchen and his gun. Diana pulled on her sweater, damp from when she had used it to dry off her lover's bathwater. She found her skirt, and as she hurried barefoot out of the room, she heard the front door open and close, and then a sudden silence.

David, his gun in his hand, completely naked, was embracing the Haganah man Diana had met at the top of the Church of the Holy Redeemer. He had said that David would know his name as "Kazi," but neither man was using code names now. David introduced him as Carmi, and then, suddenly remembering he was naked, ran out of the room to get some clothes.

"How did you find us?" said Diana.

"We hide a lot of people in Mea Shearim among the Orthodox," said Carmi, exhibiting his two missing teeth. "The British don't like to look here. They feel a little too much out of place with all the men in black." Carmi pulled his lips together and blinked. "So you did it."

"Not by myself."

"You did it," said Carmi. "Your visit made it possible, and we have our David back. Just in time. We need him."

"You can't have him," said Diana, more than a little serious. Surely the Haganah man could see how exhausted her lover was. "I was hoping there would be a way to get him out of Jerusalem altogether. For a while."

"There is no way," said Carmi, his smile gone. "David's important to us here. Besides, he could never get out of the country now, even if he wanted to. There's the matter of a British policeman killed and another seriously wounded, not to talk about kidnapping, jailbreak, robbery—"

"But he needs rest," said Diana. "I insist on that."

"She insists," said David, coming into the study room. "Aren't these women remarkable?"

"Where are the others?" said Carmi. "I've heard there were two. One was the American who came with you, correct?"

"Yes. They went out."

"Not smart to go out right now," said Carmi. As if on cue, the front-door lock was audibly unlocked from outside. Both men went for their guns, and as the door opened, they leveled them at Joey and the constable.

"It's okay, Carmi," said David. "These are the men who saved my life."

Joey watched as the Haganah man slipped his gun back into his belt. In spite of himself, he was pleased—idiotically pleased—at David's words. "The men who saved my life." He was not certain that Diana had made love with Stern yet; after all, they might have been interrupted by this Haganah man. But it was not simply that possibility which pleased him. It was the fact of David Stern's praise.

"Yeah," said Joey. "He's right. We saved him for you. I figure you owe us a favor. Like some passports. We'll pay."

"Joey doesn't believe in any prefatory small talk," said Diana pleasantly. "What he meant to say was how surprised and pleased he was to see you here. It's nice to know that we have some friends out there."

"That's not what I meant," said Joey. "So don't go telling me what I meant. Where I come from, friends help you out of the slammer. Your friends," he said, turning to David, "didn't do nothing. It was me and Diana. And Elliot."

"Hello," said Constable Elliot Crawfield.

"English?" said Carmi. He had heard that an English constable had been involved in the jailbreak, but assumed that rumor to be false.

"An English copper," said Joey. "But he's given all that up, and we owe him plenty. Believe me, if it wasn't for Elliot here, none of us would have made it."

"But why?" said Carmi to the constable. "How did you ever get involved? Are you Jewish?"

"I just did it," said Crawfield, a bit testily. He smiled at Joey Marino. "He can explain it better than I can."

"All I want to explain is that we have to get out of here," said Joey. "Diana is very important to all of you, I understand that, and the man I work for is also important to all of you, if you want to get your arms into the country. And this man wants his niece safe, and right now she's in trouble."

"If you want to know why I did it," interrupted the constable without warning, "it's because the Yank is about the most crazy but decent man I've ever—"

A knocking on the door shut up Crawfield's praise. Hebrew words were loudly whispered, and Carmi took out his gun and rushed to the door. A young boy stood there, white-faced with terror. "Police," he said.

"How many?" said Carmi, as David readied his gun, backing off to the small windows that overlooked a courtyard.

"Three cars," said the boy, and suddenly there was a great eruption of noise, a cacophony of Yiddish, of pots and pans walloped into each other, of songs and screams and stamping feet.

"What the hell is going on?" said Joey, but seeing David start to smash out a window, he picked up one of the hard wooden benches and crashed it through the adjacent window.

"Land on your feet," said David tersely. "But try to do it in a crouch. I'll go first."

"You can't," said Diana. "It's two stories."

David used his gun to knock out the rest of the window, and Joey pulled up a bench for him to get up onto the window's level. "You go next, Diana. After me, through this window. Do you understand?" He put one foot through, not hesitating about the jump, but only about whether he had communicated what needed to be done to the others. "Use the other window," he said. "Go ahead, Joey. Show them."

Once again, in the midst of the cacophony, Joey found himself idiotically pleased by David's words: the Haganah man, Diana's intellectual lover, was singling him out: David Stern said that *he*, Joey Marino, should show *them*.

Joey picked up the attaché case, checked the lock on it, and tossed it out the window. Then he got up on another bench, put one foot carefully through the window space, and then, holding on to the sill, launched himself into space.

It was a very long way to jump.

In the moment that he was expecting to hit the crushed stone below, he felt nothing, only the continuing forward motion of his rush to earth; it was a terrifying half-second, like falling into a storybook's endless tunnel, and imagining terrors at the end, and as the end never came, the terrors grew and grew.

But then he hit, his toes lifting up at the last moment, his legs tensed, the shock going from the balls of his feet right through to his teeth, and a moment later, to his backside, as he slipped and slammed backward on the gravel.

Before he could feel where he was hurt, he heard a muffled cry of pain, and turned in the growing dark of late afternoon to see David Stern sitting on his backside and rubbing his left knee.

"You okay?" said Joey, standing up painfully and going to the man.

"Help me get away from the window," said David.

"Sure," said Joey. He picked up the man at his left elbow and pulled him toward the center of the courtyard, just as a body fell heavily to the earth in the spot that David had landed. It was Diana, and Joey let go of David's arm and hurried up to her.

"I'm okay," she said, getting to her feet and hurrying toward David. "Are you okay, darling?"

"What's all that noise?" said Joey, coming up to them. Stern was rubbing his left knee, and Diana was wrapping his arm about her neck for support. Another thud, and another cry of pain, this time from Carmi's young Haganah boy. Joey went for him, and helped him to his feet, stopping to pull his attaché case along with him.

"The people in the building," said David. "They're making it tough for the bastards."

"I hope Crawfield can get his fat behind through that window," said Joey. There was another crashing sound, and for a moment Joey thought it was Crawfield or Carmi come down to earth, but then realized it was coming from upstairs, from the apartment.

"Let's go," said David.

"What about the others?" said Joey.

"They'll catch up," said Diana. "He can't walk fast."

"Walk? Where the hell are we supposed to be walking?" said Joey, his gun in his right hand, the attaché case in the left. For a moment it seemed that the cacophony of voices had stilled, only to be replaced by a whistle, by three or four whistles. But then the voices started up again, even louder than before, and then over all of this a gunshot, the sound of death that seemed to clear the air.

Carmi jumped out of the window and landed lithely, like the parachutist he was trained to be, and hurried to them, his gun in his hand. "This way," he said.

"Crawfield," said Joey, and there were more gunshots then, and he caught the look in Carmi's face, and knew at once what had happened. "He was covering us," said Joey. "That stupid fat son of a bitch was covering us."

"Come on," said Diana, touching Joey's arm.

Carmi had already begun to hurry across to the other side of the courtyard. "Stupid bastard," said Joey, blinking away tears. He was last in line, following the boy from the Haganah, who followed Diana and David. He wanted to know who fired first, if Crawfield had taken any of them with him, or if he had just stood there, anxious to die, to get out of the world messed up for him by Joey Marino.

An ancient red truck was parked on the curb around the corner from where the British waited. The boy sat in the front next to Carmi, who drove, and David, Diana, and Joey got into the open back of the truck and covered themselves with a tarpaulin.

"Maybe he's alive," said Diana.

"No," said Joey. "He wanted to be a hero. It's not my fault."

Diana couldn't see Joey's face in the dark under the tarpaulin, and her fear as the truck started up and drove slowly away was making it difficult for her to understand the young man's pain. But she wanted to touch him, and she found his wrist and squeezed it, her fingers lightly brushing his gun as he pulled away from her offer of solace. "He wanted to be a hero," repeated Joey. "So he got what he wanted. I'll tell you something. I don't understand any of this. I don't know how you talked Marty into this. None of this is clear, none of this is clean. I'm just getting a lot of people killed, people who don't know any better. Jesus, that fat guy. He didn't know nothing about nothing.

I was going to get him a job dealing blackjack. He would've been beautiful with that accent. I could just see that guy in Las Vegas, dealing the cards, all red-faced from too much sun and booze. He'd have had a time."

"It would be better if we lie still now," said David.

"Sure," said Joey. He could feel Diana move slightly closer to her lover, and imagined that she was already forgetting poor Crawfield, already forgetting anything but David Stern. "Where the hell do you think we're going?" whispered Joey.

"Quiet, please," said David, trying to fight back his anger. The pain in his left knee was growing, and the touch of his lover's hand on his neck offered no comfort, only a reminder of obligations, constraints. The lovemaking was over; the desire was stilled. He had the fugitive's belief that nothing could get him back to a cell now, no force, no chance, no fate. He had a gun, he had the dark, he had the city. If they were stopped, he would force himself to ignore Diana, even if it meant her capture. Another night in a cell would kill him. He would rather die out in the streets.

They could all hear the truck's old engine whine mightily as it toiled uphill, every spring creaking, every part of its ramshackle chassis bounding up and down. When they turned, all three of them in the back slid across the flatbed, and slid back again as the wheels were turned straight once more. David tried to imagine the path Carmi was taking. Up and down meant little in Jerusalem, where one could climb and descend in almost every neighborhood. Street sounds were quiet, as people had rushed home to be out of the dangers of the dark. All of them could hear the occasional ominous crack of a rifle, sniper fire, but where the snipers were Jews firing into Arab quarters or Arabs firing into Jewish quarters, David couldn't guess.

Suddenly there was the sound of laborious downshifting, as if preparing for another descent. But there were voices now, Arabic voices uttering commands, and the sound of idling engines, the delicate knocking of a failing radiator, a big English voice:

"You, there, pull over to the right!"

David could see Joey's dark eyes shining in the space next to him. The bright lights of the checkpoint spilled over and under the tarpaulin, and he could see Diana's tense jawline, the beautiful black hair spread out like a dark wave, and he felt guilty that he could have imagined leaving her to her fate. No. He would not love her the way he had loved Miriam, but he didn't love life so much that he was willing to buy it for himself with the abandonment of this young woman. David brought his free hand across his body and took hold of her left hand and squeezed it. Diana turned to look at him, and he could see the love in them that he couldn't equal. Next to her he saw the American's gun ready, as his was ready, pointed up in the air, as if to beat back an attack from the sky.

The truck groaned over some rocky ground on the shoulder of the road, as the light lessened under the tarpaulin. But the booming voice followed them.

"Where are you boys going?"

"I'm not a boy," said Carmi. "I wish I were a boy, but after serving in the British Army, I don't let anyone call me anything but a man."

"Jewish Brigade?" said the booming voice, slightly more friendly. A sudden spattering of raindrops fell with thunderous force on the tarpaulin, nearly eliciting a scream from Diana. But when she realized that it was rain, her mouth shut tightly, and a smile formed. There wouldn't be a lengthy inquisition with the Jerusalem skies opening up on the policeman.

"No, I couldn't wait for the Brigade to be formed. I joined in 1940, right after I got to England."

"Bleeding rain," said the big voice. "Got a long trip?"

"Too long," said Carmi. "And my tires are shot to hell. You know what new tires for this moving junkpile cost?"

The rain was falling heavily now, so heavily that little streams and rivulets were forming on the tarpaulin surface next to their skins. David could see that the American had lowered his gun, his finger still on the trigger, but his vigilance relaxed.

"Too bloody much," said the big voice, hardly audible now through the tarpaulin and the rain.

"What?" yelled Carmi.

"Never mind," said the Englishman. "I'm getting out of this rain. You don't have anything in the back?"

"What?" said Carmi.

"In the back?"

"Rust and rainwater," said Carmi. They heard a smacking of baton on metal, the signal to go. Slowly the truck's starter motor began to turn; once, twice, and finally after a third time Carmi started the engine. The rain seemed to be coming down in sheets now, and the water found the little rips in the waterproof fabric, so that thin lines of rain now poured into hair and eyes and chests and feet. With great care, the tires spun against wet gravel, and even more slowly began to move off the shoulder onto the road. They stayed in second gear and went slowly downhill in the dark, the three of them united by the wet, the noise of the open heavens, the desperate sounds of the puny engine.

"We've left the city," said David, quite loudly now, so that all could hear through the rain.

"Does that mean we can talk?" said Joey.

"If you have to," said David. Joey could sense the man's turning closer to Diana, cuddling next to her for warmth.

"Where the hell do you think he's taking us?" said Joey. But there was no answer from David. He had placed his gun back in his belt and had shut his eyes against the dark, his senses against the cold and the damp, and fell asleep even as Joey spoke. "We're not going on the damn road to Tel Aviv. I've really had it for the day. I'm not going to get shot up by some Arab who wants this old truck for a souvenir."

"David's sleeping," said Diana.

"I bet he sleeps on planes too," said Joey.

"Joey," said Diana, putting her arm around him, so that each of the men was now in her embrace. "Why don't you sleep too? I'm sure you'll wake if the truck stops. Just get some rest. It's been a day we won't get over too fast."

"I can't sleep like this," said Joey, taking her arm off his shoulder. "It's not my idea of a good time, okay? If we're going to sleep, let's sleep. I can't sleep with you touching me. Don't you understand anything?"

She could barely discern his outline, hunched up away from where she and David lay. But as they drove through the rainstorm on the edge of a mountain, on the verge of a war, she could feel his anger and his love raging past all dangers. Joey wanted her, and she clung more tightly to David, the man she loved. Joey wanted her, and she shut her heart to the raw fact of his desire.

THIRTEEN

Their journey to the tiny Kibbutz Ha-Yad, one of several Jewish settlements in the hill country outside Hebron, would have ordinarily taken two hours. The roads were not straight, their surfaces poorly maintained, and the few gas stations were frequently without fuel or oil. But that night the rain made the trip last until the dawn. They had to crawl along the edge of a cliff at three miles an hour, rush through a sudden flood pouring from the wadi, stop and wait for the engine to cool and the visibility to grow from three inches to three feet. Never once did the truck get out of second gear. Two times they skidded off the road, the spongy brakes and locked wheels taking them once into a scraping sideways collision with a boulder, once within a hair of falling off the mountain into the valley below.

But toward dawn the rain stopped, and Joey threw off the miserably wet tarpaulin, heavy with rain, and stood up on the flatbed to try to stretch his aching limbs. Carmi stopped the truck to let the Haganah boy get a jerrican of gasoline from the back.

"Where are we?" said Joey. "Mars?"

The boy's eyes were bloodshot with fatigue, but smiling at the corners. He took the can from Joey and looked toward the rising sun. "The Judean hills," he said. Diana stirred, and woke to the sight of the lightening sky. She saw the strips of color she had only seen several times before in Jerusalem, toward dusk, when she'd first arrived there in the hot weather: a thick band of salmon, bordered by lines of mauve and vermilion, a wide expanse of periwinkle blue, and then finally a deep blue velvet, reaching up on the horizon, where stars were being extinguished in the rush to dawn.

"Good morning," said Diana softly to Joey, turning from him quickly to minister to the sleeping David. The truck started up a minute later, and though the air was cold, it was deliciously dry, and there was a scent of life coming from the dead soil.

"Like Nevada," said Joey by way of greeting to Diana. The landscape was not quite on the same grand scale as the Southwestern United States, but it had the same sense of permanence. No matter what manner of man wandered through these spaces, he could never change it. This land was ancient; it had been ancient in the time of Moses, and before Moses too. A car or truck or settlement could not mar the substance of this world of hills and stones and wadis; only the landscape was eternal, and no man, or object made by man, could long spoil it. "Remember Nevada?" said Joey.

"Sure I do," said Diana.

"Me too," said Joey. "It's where you started to get to me, babe." He was not speaking loudly, but the spectacle of her lover sleeping in her arms was not conducive to his declaration of love. "Not your fault, though," he said. "Nothing you did on purpose."

"Please, Joey," she said, looking directly at him with the green eyes that had long mesmerized him, speaking to him with that accent that had always seemed affected, rich, wellborn—everything he despised, everything he wanted to be. "David's not well. It was a hard night for all of us, but imagine what it was like for him, after the prison."

And then Joey saw what Diana had witnessed many times before: the sorry sight of her lover waking in fear. David's knees jerked up, his hands reached down to cover his genitals, his chin ducking to his chest, his whole body turned to the side. Every part of him was waiting for the blows to commence, every part of his being radiated fear and hate and violent revenge.

But then it was over, and he looked from Joey to Diana, getting up on one knee to look out at the dawn. "Did I say anything?" he said.

"No, you never cry out anymore, darling," said Diana.

"I'm still waking up in the concentration camp," he said to Joey. The older man's hands were shaking, and try as he might to slough off the moment of terror, Joey could see that it lingered in the blood, and that David found this evidence of weakness humiliating. "Not that waking up in this is much better. This shaking stops in a minute. I didn't scream?"

"No," said Diana.

"It's important that I don't cry out," said David, explaining to Joey. "I'm not much of a commando if I cry out in my sleep."

"You didn't say a word," said Joey. "I wake up noisier after a night hitting the bottle."

"We're in the hills," said David suddenly, looking about him. He stood up awkwardly, trying to mask the pain in his face with a twisted smile. "He got us out to the hills. That's fine. We're going to be all right."

Kibbutz Ha-Yad—literally, the "kibbutz of the hand"—did not specify whose hand they were honoring with this name. Some thought it referred to the biblical hand of God, others thought it referred to the communal idealization of the worker's manual labor, still others swore the name was insisted on by the man who had funded their water tower with a lifetime's savings as a watchmaker in Jerusalem and who was inordinately proud of his handiwork.

The kibbutz was new, one of a group of settlements built to safeguard the route from Jerusalem to the Negev. Though high in the mountains, and essentially disregarded by the British, it was not the safest place to be in December 1947. It was too new to have established a fearsome reputation like several of the other kibbutzim around Kfar Etzion, famous for its zealous fighters. The local Arab population was large, armed, and incited by tales of riches to try to infiltrate the kibbutz's primitive fortifications. A ragtag army of Syrian mercenaries was encamped in a village only a few kilometers away, and elements from this undisciplined troop regularly preyed on kibbutz members in the fields, or on trucks attempting to resupply them. They drove through a barbed-wire gate, watched by exhausted sentries from concrete towers, and were taken to a long low stone building where men and women in faded blue clothes were having their first meal of the day.

David knew many of them: Yakov, who had been born in Istanbul, waiting for a boat to Palestine, and who at the age of twenty-one had organized the first group of survivors from the Bergen-Belsen concentration camp to try to get into Eretz-Israel; Geula, a frail young woman born to German Jews in Tel Aviv, who had helped bring in illegal immigrants through Palestine's northern border; Yair, who was born in the bleak northern Urals in Russia, where his parents had been exiled for Zionist agitation, and had lost an eye defending a settlement from Arab attack in the Negev; Menachem, who had been decorated by the British Navy during the war, and later helped to land illegal immigrants on the shores of his country, blockaded by the same navy he had served. All were in the Haganah, and many of them had joined at sixteen, graduating from youth-group training to guerrilla tactics with as much ease of transition as a high-school student graduating to college.

All of them were full of news—deaths, imprisonments, terrorist actions—and desirous of news, particularly from Jerusalem. That David was alive and free was wonderful, of course, but as none of them had heard that he was in prison in the first place, their relief was not dramatic. No newspaper had reached them for two weeks. The roads were plagued with ambushes and attacks from the high country. They had little ammunition and hardly any rifles. One of their number had been publicly berated at dinner the night before for firing two useless shots at night prowlers when he'd been on guard duty: no one was to shoot unless the bullet had a clear target. A neighboring kibbutz had warded off an attack by an army of irregulars two days before, mostly by conserving their firepower until the Arabs had exhausted theirs.

"They come in the morning," said Geula, "only because they hate to fight as a group at night. And then they start shooting. They shoot at everything. It makes a lot of noise. Bullets everywhere, into the sky, the stones, the ground. They shoot at clouds, the sun. They shoot until their rifles are too hot to hold. If they decide to stay overnight, it becomes the Haganah's advantage. We'll send out a patrol and pick out their sentries from the dark. Sometimes they leave before nightfall because they're already out of ammunition. And all they've shot at is the air."

The other kibbutzniks at the table laughed at this, but it was not easy laughter. Not all Arabs were afraid to fight at night, nor did every band sent at them from Jordan or Syria fight without discipline. More and more the settlements about their own were cut off from

Jerusalem, from ammunition, medicine. food. They were isolated and felt the isolation like a constant weight on their souls. Here the Haganah had sent young men and women to be trained, here weapons had been secreted when Tel Aviv had been placed under martial law. But there were fewer young men now, and the weapons were in short supply, and new soldiers threw oranges instead of hand grenades, and drilled with sticks instead of automatic rifles. What news they received from Jerusalem was bleak: short supplies, riots, despair. And during the night they'd received word that the Wailing Wall, the holiest Jewish site in the Old City, had fallen into Arab hands.

"I don't understand," said Diana. "How can the British allow that? Do you mean there's no more access to the Wall?"

"The Wall is surrounded by Arab gunmen. There are no Jews praying there, unless they're dead Jews," said Menachem.

Carmi, who was exhausted from the harrowing drive through the mountains, interrupted him. "The war has already started. It's a scramble for position. The British won't let us bring Haganah troops into the Old City, but they are letting armed Syrians wander around the bazaars. We can't legally get any ammunition into the Jewish quarter, but the Arab Legionnaires are walking right across the Allenby Bridge in broad daylight, setting up positions all around the city. That's the reality, we all understand it, and we can't do anything about the British but wait for them to leave. But until then, we have to hold what we have, and if we can, take even more. Because once the British pull out, it won't be a little hit-and-run war of sniping and terror bombs. It will be a regular war, with fronts and lines of supply, and we had sure as hell better be ready for that war, because the entire Arab League is going to be on the other side."

Joey tried to follow the conversation, but his concentration wavered. He felt filthy and tired from the sleepless night in the truck, and worse than that, he felt ignored. Every so often the conversation skipped from English to Hebrew, leaving him behind. Names of friends fighting in the north, or the south, reminiscences of running illegal immigrants across the sea, tales of derring-do committed against various enemies, meant little to Joey. He wanted them to acknowledge his presence, to remark over the jailbreak he'd planned and perpetrated, to mention and mourn poor Crawfield. Diana didn't seem excluded from the proceedings, he thought. Sitting in front of her hard-boiled egg and watery coffee, she seemed a part of her lover. As the kibbutzniks questioned him, and called up old times they had shared, she needed no translation or explanation. She was content to keep her hand on his elbow, to see that he finished the food on his plate, to suggest that he get some rest after all.

"That's a very nice tie," said the girl named Geula in British-accented English. Joey was so tired that when she got up from her seat on the bench across from him, she seemed to float rather than walk around the long table to where he sat.

"My clothes are filthy," said Joey.

"We have clothes for you," said Geula. "Not so fine like yours, but better." She had gray eyes that seemed to flicker between sadness and violence. She wanted something from him. "Why do you carry that case?" she said.

"It's for her. Diana."

"You carry her case for her? Is it that heavy?"

"No. It belongs to her, but I am taking care of it. It's for the Jews here," said Joey. He knew that he sounded idiotic.

The girl touched the right lapel of his mohair suit jacket. "Let me show you where you can sleep," she said.

"All right," said Joey.

"I knew an American once. He was always wanting to take a shower," she said. Joey stood up, scraping the bench against the stone floor. There were about a dozen kibbutzniks there, some with rifles alongside their plates, and David and Diana and Carmi. The Haganah boy who had accompanied them was nowhere to be seen. Everyone turned to look at Joey now as he stood next to the frail young woman with a gun in her belt.

"I haven't introduced our hero," said Carmi.

"The man who saved my life," said David.

Joey was suddenly very embarrassed in the presence of the man with one eye, of the veterans of a hundred battles, of the men and women who had lived with austerity and deprivation all their lives. "I was just going to lie down," he said.

"Be careful with him, Geula," said David. "He's very delicate."

Joey's face turned a bit redder. He felt an urge to explain himself. This young woman wasn't interested in making love to him, she was simply showing him a bed. He wasn't delicate, but he wasn't a superman either. He had gone through rough times in the Marine Corps, but he hadn't lived a life of austerity. There was nothing altruistic about him; he was doing a job for his boss, Marty Bernstein, and whether or not he was in love with Marty's niece had nothing to do with anything.

"Finish your plate," said Geula sharply.

"What?" said Joey. He had been hungry, but he hadn't finished his meal of hard-boiled eggs. Automatically he picked up the half-egg left over and swallowed it. Diana was looking at him, and in her eyes was a kindness and concern that infuriated him; he didn't want her love to be mother love, or sister love. "Look," he said to Diana. "You'd better explain this to David. He'll know what to do with it."

"All right," said Diana, taking the case of money, Marty's gift to the Jews of Israel.

"But some of that's for Crawfield's old lady, okay?" said Joey. "His mother, I mean. His wife's dead, been dead for years."

"You've told me that already, Joey," said Diana. "I won't forget."

"Well, I better go," said Joey, turning around as the others continued to smile at him.

Geula took his arm with a fierce grip. "We go," she said, and marched him out of the dining hall. The sun had brought the bleak outlines of the settlement to life. There was a central watchtower, with a machine gun and sentry, and smaller towers all about the perimeter, which was delineated with barbed wire. There were none of the images that kibbutz life had always suggested to him—children with flowers in their hair, happy workers marching back from the fields with hoes on their backs, intellectuals arguing over some philosophical point while peeling potatoes. Kibbutz Ha-Yad resembled nothing so much as a prison camp. The structures within the barbed wire were squat, unpainted wood or concrete.

"Where are your fields?" said Joey.

"Outside," said Geula. "We can't get to them safely anymore. But we will again. Soon. Now all we have is our chickens. At least we can eat eggs until the chickens starve. In Jerusalem it's hard to get eggs. We don't leave things in our plates."

"Where are your children?" said Joey.

"What children?" she said.

"I thought that was part of it. The kibbutz ideal. There's a place for the children, everyone's raised together, so the mothers can go out in the fields—"

"And get shot?" said Geula. "This isn't that kind of kibbutz. There are no children. Maybe after, there will be. Maybe in a year everyone will marry and will plant flowers and we'll build a swimming pool and all you Americans will think we're living the good life. Here, there's no children, no fields. Only a chicken coop and forty members. You want to join, it's forty-one. We're all soldiers. We stay here and try to hold on, because it's the only thing that makes sense. If we leave, there aren't enough Jews in Judea. And Jews must always be in Judea, just as they must always be in Jerusalem."

Looking up at the central watchtower, Joey was blinded by the striking of sun on the sentry's weapon. The ground beneath his feet was barren and rocky, as inhospitable as the view of deserted hills and gullies through the barbed wire. She took him rapidly along an open aqueduct, through which rainwater ran, propelled by gravity into their water tower, which sat at the lowest point of the settlement.

"Not many Jews come to help from America," she said. "Especially the way you did."

"I'm not Jewish," said Joey. Geula looked at him sharply. She didn't like to be joked with. "I'm half-Jewish. My mother."

"So why do you say you're not Jewish, then? Are you ashamed?"

"Of course I'm not ashamed. It's just that I'm as proud of my father's family as I am of my mother's—and I wasn't raised to be especially Jewish or Italian or anything. I mean, the whole idea of separating people by religion seems crazy to me."

"Jews are not a religion. They are a people, a national group like any other," said Geula. "And thanks to your mother, the next time there's a Hitler in this world, your Jewish half will be just the same as my Jewish whole. Here's the laundry."

Joey followed her into a small concrete structure smelling of soap. Faded blue shirts were neatly folded in piles next to slightly darker workpants. A clothesline extended through an open window out to the bleak outside. A great bin of soiled clothing waited to be separated into a white wash, for underwear, and a dark wash, for the blue clothing that was a uniform in this settlement. Geula handed Joey a pile of socks, underwear, and a blue shirt and workpants. "You'd better get out of those clothes," she said.

"How do you know this will fit?" he said, taking the fresh-smelling, much-worn clothing.

"I looked you over carefully," said Geula.

"Is this somebody's clothing?" said Joey.

"Nobody owns anything here," said Geula. "Nobody owns a suit and a fancy tie." She had taken hold of his bright Sulka tie once again, and brought it up to her lips and eyes. "I can't imagine a world where people just walk into stores and buy ties and alligator shoes and cufflinks." She dropped the tie and looked at Joey with her gray eyes, measuring him. "Are you in love with that American girl?" she said.

"I don't see what that's got to do with anything," said Joey.

"Be careful of your gun," said Geula, and then she moved closer to him, her frail body desperately strong, and pushed him into a pile of clean unfolded laundry.

"Say," said Joey, not wanting to be the victim of some elaborate Haganah joke, but his protest was stifled by Geula's mouth. She straddled him on the clean laundry, holding down his shoulders with a wrestler's finesse, driving her tongue into his mouth as if claiming it for her own.

Joey was appalled.

Nothing like this had ever happened to him before.

Certainly there were girls who had been forward with him, night-club girls, bar girls, neighborhood girls seeing him pull up to the curb in a Packard. Many of these girls had been easy to seduce—a drink, a hand placed casually on her cheek, a first kiss while dancing that lingered. There was always something about a girl's desire that Joey could discern: the slight tension in the way she held her head, the awkward pauses in her small talk, the too-quick meeting of his eyes. And Joey knew how to deal with women who wanted him. He was a gentleman, up to a point, and after that point he threw himself at his women the way this Haganah girl threw herself at him. And soon there was no protest. They would simply acknowledge their mutual desire and consummate it.

But no girl, no woman, had ever attacked him like this. No one had ever indicated what she wanted with anything more than a smile, a tilt to the head, a slow exhalation of breath. This Haganah girl had indicated nothing. She had simply jumped him in the laundry room, her tongue sweeping through his mouth, her breasts rubbing at his chest through her kibbutz workshirt and his mohair suit.

"What are you doing?" said Joey finally when she took a breath of air.

"Hurry," she said. "We won't have this much privacy for long."

"What privacy?" said Joey. He looked at her openmouthed as she stripped off her workshirt and rolled off his body to get out of her pants.

"Well?" she said. "Don't you want to get out of those stupid clothes?"

"This is all just a little sudden," said Joey.

"We could be dead tomorrow," said Geula. "I like the way you look. What else do you want to know?"

Joey took off his tie and suit jacket. Geula had wanted something— he had sensed that from the start; she had wanted him. It was nice to be wanted. Living with Diana at hand had been a daily lesson in humility. She had wanted David, and she had David, and what he wanted counted for nothing.

He looked at Geula as she stripped off the rest of her clothes. "You're very lovely," he said.

"You don't have to say anything, just relax," she said. The Haganah girl helped him throw off his jacket, pull away his shirt. Joey felt that this was in some way a betrayal of Diana, but realized too that this was precisely what he wanted: to betray her. "Why did you ask me about the American girl?"

"You don't have to talk."

"Because I don't care about her at all, you understand," said Joey. He kicked off his shoes, and kissed her, even as she grabbed hold of his penis through the soft fabric of his pants. Diana didn't want him, he thought, but she was the exception. Everyone else wanted him, they always had, they always would. He was not a lovesick little boy chasing a femme fatale without hope of success. He was a lover, Romeo Marino, Playboy Joey, the handsomest kid on the block—and even this Haganah girl couldn't keep her hands off him. Joey stripped off the rest of his clothes and smiled at Geula. Her pubic hair was reddish blond, the color of the hair on her legs and under her arms. She was skinny, but he liked skinny girls, and now that her wants were the same as his own, he was no longer intimidated. He picked her up at the waist, raising her so that her lips would be at the level of his own, and then he kissed her, not simply thrusting with his tongue as she had done, but biting into her lips, her tongue. He raised his knee into her groin, and she let out a little moan of pleasure, and Joey was happy, not for the pleasure he was giving her, but for the affirmation of his own sexuality that she was giving him.

220

But Geula was not so quick to lie on her back and beg for pleasure. She had started this seduction, and she wanted to take as much as to give; just because his desire had risen was no reason to let this boy take control.

Joey started to topple her back onto the pile of laundry, but the Haganah girl slipped out of his grasp and took hold of his penis. "Oh, my God, what are you doing to me?" said Joey. Geula knew precisely what she was doing. Slowly she pulled him close to her, holding on to his swollen member, looking up at his handsome face as he forgot about all the reasons he wanted to make love, as he forgot about everything except his desire. Geula guided him gently to his knees, and then kissed him with a tenderness she remembered for a different handsome face, then held his cheeks with a sweetness she reserved only for her memories of the dead.

"Sweetheart," she said in Hebrew, and then she said, "You baby, you big darling baby," and Joey looked up at her quizzically, not knowing that she was using his body as a means to remember the past, as a way to call up a love that had died with the death of a Jewish hero three years before. She pushed him gently to the pile of laundry and ran her tongue along his chest, pausing to drive her teeth into his nipples, even as she held on to his penis in a grip that was as anxious for love as it was for violence.

Joey took hold of her neck and pulled her away from his chest and onto her side. He moved his lips over her chin and mouth and eyes, but did not kiss her. He was done kissing this one. She didn't want to be kissed. He brought his hand under her back and moved it on to her firm little backside, and then quickly he pulled his hand through her buttocks and then down, along the inside of her thighs.

"Yes," she said in Hebrew, which he understood, but then her words came in a rush, Hebrew words and a Hebrew name, Daniel, and he could see by her shut eyes that she was lost in an ecstasy that could have little to do with him. Her passion was real, and physical, and she needed his touch, she wanted his caress, she longed for the rough way he insisted on having her. But there was a specter floating in her brain, a love that was outside this room, and rather than let this kill his desire, Joey took hold of the dream behind her shut eyes and tried to inhabit it. Let her pull and bite and tease and kiss this dream; he would be there, and it would be good, it would be making love, even if the physical partners were separated by images, kept apart by

221

the knowledge that their lovers were denied them.

And so he stopped being angry at Diana Mann, stopped trying to push back the images of her beautiful face. He tried to push Geula over on her back, but she fought him, calling him Daniel, biting and scratching at his chest, laughing and loving him with an unreasonable intensity. She wanted him on his back, and Joey let this happen, let his powerful torso be turned about by the frail young woman, and let her shut-eyed face disappear as she straddled him. He had closed his eyes, but the passion in him was so great at that moment, it was like opening them to a sunburst. He shut his eyes, and she was on top of him, light and strong and wanting him inside her, and through the dark and the smell of soap and the sense of calm at the center of a madness, he could feel her hands take hold of him and place him inside her vagina.

She was very tight, and her muscles contracted about his penis, and it was essential that he keep his eyes shut against her beautiful face, because the face that was there had to belong to Diana, because no one could feel this way without love, no one could simply sub-stitute a wish for a reality and then feel this long, endless moment of suspended joy without a love that was real and tangible and alive. Geula was on top of him, and he was inside her, and she moved slowly, and slowly he parted his lips and her head moved forward sightlessly, finding his waiting mouth, and they kissed, both of them lost in their fantasies.

"Daniel," she was saying, but Joey said nothing, not because he was aware of Geula on top of him and was afraid of breaking her mood, but because he had nothing to say, didn't need to hear the name of the woman he loved when he felt himself inside her as surely as he did in any dream; and this was a dream, but better, because it was in the daylight, in the physical world, and his love ran straight through sleeping and waking, through consciousness and uncon-sciousness.

The Haganah girl kissed him, she kissed his neck, she ran her teeth along his chest, and all the while she moved: as violently as she kissed him, so gently did she move her pelvis, did she slowly draw his penis inside of her. Joey could taste blood in his mouth, could feel the nails and teeth breaking the surface of his skin, could feel the fury at what was not there taking itself out on his torso; but all the while, she was making love to him, and this love was gentle, this love was the fantasy that she insisted on, that they both insisted on, and it was in this terrible mixture of pleasure and pain, of illusion and reality, that Joey understood that he was lost.

"Oh, my God," he said, driven to speech, the ecstasy of the moment overwhelming. It was not that he understood that Geula was the woman with whom he was making love, or that the image of Diana straddling him was a twisted restructuring of a reality that he would never have. It was the knowledge of the love he was expending at that moment that made him feel like a man who had no way out, whose life was turned toward disaster. Feeling the pain all around him, not the pain of scratching and biting, but the pain of the world— the holocaust, the war, the sense of life on the verge of extinction— he could feel too the joy of lovemaking. He was moving inside this woman as if this mingling of flesh was the only answer to life's pain, and this mingling of flesh was an answer only if the flesh was his and Diana's. The world was outside, and it was bad, and he was inside, and it was good, and he was in love, and he moved with Geula, and together they moved to a region where the world didn't matter, where pain was extinguished, where everything was forgotten because consciousness was dead.

"Thanks," she said, much too soon after they'd come, and she got off him with his penis still hard, still wanting to remain inside, to stay sheltered from the world. But already she knew that he was not Daniel; she knew it in the first moment after she'd come. And he knew too who she was, and that she wasn't Diana, and that Diana was all he wanted, and that because he couldn't have her, life was unendurable, life was pain.

"No . . . thank *you*," said Joey politely. He tried to smile and think of something to say. But any compliment must needs be a lie, any endearment a sacrilege in the bed of clean laundry that had supported both their fantasies.

"Dress," she said, handing him his kibbutz clothes.

Not wanting to think about what had just happened, Joey thought ludicrously of his beautiful clothes, silk shirts and vicuña jackets, Italian-crafted alligator shoes, cashmere sweaters and lamb's-wool socks left for the British police in Reb Meyer's apartment in Mea Shearim. He dressed quickly in the farm collective's clothing, feeling their comfortably washed-out fabric next to his skin like a cloak of invisibility. Only his alligator shoes and belt, so inappropriate with his kibbutz outfit, marked him as an outsider. He placed his gun in his belt, and rolled up the mohair suit into a ball. Brass knuckles and switchblade he placed in the right and left pockets of his workpants, but his wallet, with all his money and identification papers, he kept in the inside pocket of his suit jacket, as useless in this place as any of his fancy clothes.

"I am glad it was your mother who was Jewish," she said to him when they had left the laundry. They turned down the hill to a concrete bunker where the men slept in shifts around the clock. "For myself, I think it a foolish law that we can accept as a Jew the child of a Jewish mother and a Gentile father, but that the same consideration is not extended to the child of a Jewish father and a Gentile mother. But others here don't feel the way I do. They would never offer you a chance to join us if it weren't for your mother's religion."

"Join what?" said Joey. "I don't join anything. I'm not staying here to shovel manure the rest of my life."

"I'm not talking about the kibbutz," said Geula. "I'm talking about the Haganah."

"Hey," said Joey. "That's crazy. I'm not staying here that long. I mean in this country. I've got a job, you see—and one thing I've got to do is get that American girl out of here safely. You don't mean that. I mean, you can't be serious."

Geula looked away from Joey, as if she were embarrassed for him. "You don't have to explain," she said. "Maybe it's not your fight. Maybe it's not worth getting killed over."

She showed him into the bunker, a narrow rectangle of concrete built half into the ground. Inside were mattresses in a line on the ground, five of them occupied, another fifteen or so vacant. Joey had to pick his way over the sleeping bodies, men and boys too exhausted to wake at his approach. Two of them had rifles at their sides. "Sleep anywhere," said Geula.

"I'm not afraid of getting killed," said Joey, as if he owed her an explanation. But her face wasn't reacting with approval or under-standing. They had just made love, and it was as if it had never happened. Joey watched her leave the bunker as he settled back, fully clothed on a mattress, separated by several feet from the other sleepers. He kept his gun in his belt. It was simple for him to sleep on his back, to will himself not to turn, and to be alert for any danger. He closed his eyes, and expecting to fall instantly asleep, was surprised by an image of Diana. She would know that he had been offered a chance to help her people and that he had declined. David was in the Haganah, and he, Joey, had declined their invitation. He opened his eyes and looked about the bunker, with its gun slits, its complement of guns and bodies. There was a smell of fear in the air, and he remembered how David Stern had woken up from his deep sleep in the truck.

It suddenly struck him: he was flat on his back in a bunker, six thousand miles from his home, surrounded by hostile Arabs, probably wanted for murder by the British, without his clothes, without the means to get back to New York and the comfortable existence he knew. And this was because of Diana Mann. Because he loved her. Because he was here to protect her, yes, but also to charm and beguile her; to make himself worthy in her eyes.

A sleeper near him stirred, groaned in his sleep, turned over so that Joey could see his freckly face. He was at most sixteen. One of the Jews the Nazis couldn't kill. It seemed incredible what Geula had told him, though he knew that it was true: Hitler would have sent his own half-Jewish body to the gas chambers. Joey, who had never lived as a Jew, whose family was a family of gangsters, who identified with no national group other than the United States, who cared for no religion other than personal power, found himself waxing sentimental over the plight of the Jews. He was not obsessed with the cause of the Jews in Palestine, yet he was prepared to help—because of the way David Stern had woken up remembering the concentration camp, because of the way Jerusalem had looked to him upon first sight.

So Joey slept in the bunker filled with heroes, and his heart no longer raced with a thousand queries. He was here, in the land of milk and honey, guns and bombs, in the ancient homeland of the Jews, and if he could help, he would. If they wanted him in their defense force, he would join it, and Diana would be proud, and David Stern would extend his hand in welcome.

Maybe she could learn to love him, he thought as he dropped off to sleep, his lips twisted into a smile. But he dreamed not of Diana, but of a city ringed by mountains, lit by a magical light, where men had built temples and worshiped their God. He dreamed of Jerusalem and slept deeply, and when he awoke it was dark and he brought his hands together to stop their trembling, reminding himself shamefully that he was afraid of nothing.

FOURTEEN

Joey and Diana quickly learned to hate hard-boiled eggs. There were few vegetables, no bread, and the occasional orange was doled out like a gift of heaven. David hardly noticed the diet of eggs. He gained weight, color returned to his pale complexion, rest brought a renewal of strength and purpose to his heart. Like the kibbutzniks, he wanted news, and he wanted action. After a week of waiting, news arrived, and with it the chance to return to the struggle in Jerusalem.

"Crawfield's dead," said David to Joey, his voice deliberately flat and unemotional. He didn't want the American to be upset. It was bad enough that Joey wandered around the kibbutz with those great sad eyes, eyes in love with Diana; it was worse that no matter what he tried to do with the kibbutznik-soldiers, he always came out feeling shoddy, secondhand, inauthentic. David knew the feeling. It was a feeling shared by the survivors of concentration and labor camps. They had not suffered enough, for they still lived. David knew the stories of the young men and women of Kibbutz Ha-Yad. It was not an accident that they had volunteered for a duty that might lead to death. Only those guilty for having survived would have been so quick to place themselves in the path of vastly superior Arab in-vaders.

"So," said Joey, his eyes dead. "I figured that the day we heard the shots. He wanted to be a hero, right?" He willed his hands to stop shaking.

"He was," said David. "I owe him my life, the same as I owe it to you."

"Okay," said Joey, trying to close the subject. He looked at the Hebrew-language newspaper in David's hand. "How did that get in?"

"By air," said David. The neighboring kibbutz had a makeshift airstrip, a delicate ribbon of smooth dirt carved out of a high, uneven plateau ten kilometers away. A Haganah training patrol had brought the paper, and the message for David, covering the silent miles in the dark. This was the darkest time of the year, with sunrise at 6:50 A.M. and sunset at 4:38 P.M., and throughout the dark hours, the tiny patrols of the Jewish forces trained and prepared for the greater conflict to come. David held the paper at arm's length. "They say he was killed in a crossfire between Jewish terrorists and English policemen. He's going to be given a medal. Posthumously, of course."

"Wait," said Joey, smiling in spite of himself. "He's going to get a medal? No black stain on the guy's record? I think that's great. I think that's fine. His mother will be proud of him."

"His mother with her new shop will be proud of him," said David, who knew of Crawfield's plans to make his mother's life easier. The attaché case of money would be delivered to the Jewish Agency, David had decided, and a way would be found to get Mrs. Crawfield ten thousand dollars through some fictitious insurance company.

"Does it mention Diana or anything else? The jailbreak?"

"Yes," said David, and Joey could see that the man was pleased with the news in the paper. "Apparently Diana Mann was abducted by her own fiancé, the convicted terrorist David Stern. The police are also looking into the possibility that an American journalist with false press credentials may have helped in the escape. That's you in trouble, not Diana. But it's not big news. I wouldn't worry."

A group of kibbutznik-soldiers passed them, marching double-time, singing a song. Joey had worked with them for the last week, trying to teach them some of what he had learned in the Marine Corps, and even more, some of the "combat" tricks he'd learned on the streets of New York. Their enthusiasm, combined with their physical energy, always managed to push his self-concern far from conscious thought. Simcha, who wore an eyepatch, legacy of his guerrilla days with the partisans in Bessarabia, and Kalmann, who had dreamed of being a soccer champion until his strength was drained away in Auschwitz, and Yael, whose parents were murdered by Arab terrorists in Jerusalem while she slept in a baby carriage ten feet away, were not unique here. Yair too wore an eyepatch, and Menachem had once dreamed of being a middleweight boxing champion, and Geula hadn't lost her parents to terrorists, but aunts and uncles and cousins to the Nazis. There were so many with numbers tattooed on their forearms like David, so many with old wounds that showed in a limp or a grimace, so many histories of pain that had led to this kibbutz on a mountain.

"I'm not worried for myself," said Joey. "It's Diana that I have to worry about. Getting her back."

"She's not leaving the country until it is a state, a Jewish state," said David. "And when that day comes, neither of you will be in any trouble with any legal authorities."

"If that day comes," said Joey.

"It will come," said David. He wished he could get through to Joey, make him understand how beautiful this place would be someday, like the kibbutzim David had seen in the north of the country shortly after he'd come to Palestine. Children seated at long wood tables out in the fields, doing their lessons under the guidance of a kibbutznik-teacher, while all their parents, mothers and fathers, worked nearby, singing songs of the "chalutzim," the pioneers. He would have liked to express to the young man the shock of seeing an irrigated field rise out of the desert with fiery flowers, or the joy at harvesttime at a settlement which a year before had been a malarial swamp. David was irreligious, but had taken a kind of fatalistic philosophy with him from the camps: there were some things which would come to pass, some things that no force on earth could stop. So much pain had no purpose in a divine plan, he thought; but with the same logic, he imagined that the psychic legacy of that collective suffering would be inescapably expressed. The land of swamps and thorns and deserts and rocky wasteland would be reclaimed by this energy, by this surviving life force. The land of David and Joshua and Isaiah would belong to their children, not by divine intervention, but by the ineluctable force of a people done with suffering. "Besides," said David, "Diana is going to be part of the ceremony tonight."

"How can she be part of the ceremony?" said Joey, momentarily pleased that Diana would see him take the oath of the Haganah.

"Because she's joining as well," said David.

Joey stifled the automatic protest rising in his throat. Of course she was joining. Here the girls joined together with the boys, just as early, just as eager, just as brave. Diana was certainly as likely a candidate for the Haganah as a half-Jewish gangster from New York. Marty Bernstein would be furious, of course, but Joey could only smile at what Marty must be thinking about everything that had happened with him and his niece in the last few weeks. There must be an official explanation for Diana's absence, and even if the explanation made no sense, even if she had not been charged with any crime, surely Marty Bernstein must understand by now that Diana was in Palestine for the duration of the conflict.

"I want to ask you something," said Joey. "Are you in love with her? With Diana?"

"I don't discuss love," said David. "All that you have to know is that she is my woman."

"*Woman*? What the hell does that mean? Do you want to marry her? Do you care about her? Does it make a difference to you if she lives or dies?"

"In Hebrew the word for 'woman' and 'wife' is the same," said David.

Joey looked impatiently at the sky, as if waiting for a biblical revelation. "So what?" he said. "Maybe you'll marry her and you won't give a damn about her. I'm just asking. I've got a right to ask. You said it yourself. I saved your life."

"Joey," said David. "I don't talk about things like love. Right now, even as we talk here, relatively safe and comfortable, there are twelve thousand immigrants, survivors, stateless people, my people, sitting in two overcrowded boats in the Mediterranean. They sailed from Bulgaria. Two underequipped, probably filthy, probably dangerous ships, the *Pan Crescent* and the *Pan York*. The British won't let them land here. They're Jews, and they can't land here, because the British say the communists have sneaked in some spies with them. Isn't that a good one? Communists on their way to Eretz-Israel to help overthrow the British Empire. Twelve thousand people who made it through the war, somehow, and who are right now sitting on that lousy choppy sea trying to get to the only place in the world they call home."

"That's too bad, see," said Joey. "But that's got nothing to do with what I asked you."

"I don't talk about love. I'm explaining why," said David. Perhaps it would be easier to just come right out and tell him, he thought, tell him that Diana was the sort of woman who loved a man like himself, and who could never love a boy like Joey. Joey was dangerous, and able, and handsome, but he was also a puppy, a lapdog; he had experience of the world, but not the depths of emotional experience that Diana wanted. David could have told him that whether or not he loved Diana, Diana belonged to him.

"And I'm telling you I have a right to know how you feel," said Joey. David could feel the violence rising up in the boy, as sure and firm as any sexual excitation. He wanted to tell him more news, how in the month that had just passed in Eretz-Israel four hundred and fifty people were killed and one thousand wounded; how the leader of the Arab Higher Committee had sworn that violence would grow throughout the country unless the British blocked partition; how the American embargo of arms to the Middle East, coupled with the British nonembargo to the Arab countries, was creating a disastrous balance of power for the Jews of Palestine; how former Nazis, Germans, Yugoslavs, and Arabs who had served with the Nazis were being recruited to destroy the Jewish state before it had a chance to be born. But there were far more immediate concerns to discuss with Joey, and he could see that the boy was adamant, and so David conceded, remembering how he felt with Diana when they were making love, and the world and memory was shut out of his heart.

"Of course I love her," said David.

"All right," said Joey. He looked as if he had been hit across the face. "See, that's all I wanted to know. I'm not her brother or father, but I work for her uncle, and I just wanted to make sure no one's taking advantage, because Marty Bernstein wouldn't like that."

"I know all about your Mr. Bernstein," said David. "And more than anyone else, I would do anything for that man. Not just for that money he's given us, but the arms, the organization, the power. Do you realize that he's about the only nonmember of the Haganah who could have found us here and gotten through a message to Diana?"

"What do you mean, he's found us? Marty knows where we are?" said Joey, looking around with incredulous eyes, as if half-expecting some New York gangster to slap him on the back.

"Maybe not the name of the kibbutz," said David. "But he knows you and Diana are fine, that you're going to Jerusalem."

"Jerusalem? I thought we were trying to get away from Jerusalem. How are we supposed to get there? What are we going for, anyway?"

David tried to answer Joey's questions, but he didn't have all the information the young gangster required. Arye Grinberg, the Haganah man left in New York to oversee the shipment of illegal arms from American gangsters to Palestine, had been Marty Bernstein's link to the Haganah, but David didn't know what pressure had been put on Arye, or how Arye had been able to locate them from six thousand miles away. What was most important to David was that Marty Bernstein's friends in London had arranged for a substantial bribe to be paid to a high customs official in Haifa, to allow a New York shipment of crates marked "Industrial Equipment" to pass without scrutiny through the British port authorities.

"What's that got to do with Jerusalem?" said Joey.

"Diana has to meet with the customs man there," said David.

"Diana? Why Diana? How does he even know who the hell Diana is?"

"I don't know," said David. "All I know is that she must be there tomorrow morning at nine o'clock, the Hotel Salvia, or there's no deal."

Joey started to object furiously. Whom would she be meeting, how did they know it wasn't a trap, how could they possibly get to Jerusalem that quickly?

"Do you know," said David, "if you're going to be taking your oath tonight, you had better learn to accept your orders without so much talking back."

"I didn't realize I had gotten an order."

"You're getting one now. You're coming with Diana and me to Jerusalem right after the ceremony."

"Only if I get to go with her to the Hotel Salvia," said Joey.

"All right."

"And just exactly what the hell are we all going to be doing in Jerusalem after that? With all of us fugitives. With all of us wanted by the British and no place for us to go."

David smiled. This was information he did have and could impart without compunction to the hotheaded young man. "We're going to the Old City," he said. "There everyone is wanted. We're going to the Old City to fight."

By five P.M. it was dark, with the stars blotted out by rain clouds. Joey had to leave behind his mohair suit, his alligator shoes, his Sulka tie, but in the pack on his back he carried half the cash and securities that had been in the attaché case since he'd left New York. David Stern carried the rest of the money in his pack. None of them carried identification papers, not Diana, who followed the fast-marching Yair, not Geula, who took up the rear of their little group. Only Yair and Geula carried rifles. Diana was without a weapon, while David and Joey had their puny little pistols against the overwhelming dark.

It was cold, and as soon as they left the comforting barbed-wire perimeter of the kibbutz, Diana felt the attack of fear. She forced herself to look at the back of Yair's legs as they moved steadily forward. All around her was silence, but the sort of silence wherein one could discover terror. She didn't want to be the one to hear a noise that was not there, see a glint of light that was the product of imagination. Diana concentrated instead on the steady pace of Yair's legs, thinking of how good it would be to be in David's arms again, out of the cold, away from danger. There was a ten-kilometer walk ahead of them, and that was six miles, mostly up and down narrow ridges unmarked on any map other than the one in Yair's memory. Geula had done the walk in an hour, with a heavy pack on her back; but six miles an hour was not a walk, it was a run, and they were all of them, for all the steady pace they were maintaining, not going faster than three miles an hour. So it would be two hours, without a word, waiting for the crack of a rifle, or the shout of a lookout, or the terrible ululating cry of a swarm of guerrillas.

Look at Yair's legs, she told herself, so that she would not think of the stories that had run about the mess hall: the women who had been raped repeatedly by a dozen Arab guerrillas, then sliced open with bayonets; the men whose genitals had been cut off and stuffed in their mouths while they still lived. But she looked at Yair's legs, never faltering, and realized that her own steady pace presented to David—who was behind her—a source of pride. That night she was to join the Haganah. She was an American, yes, an heiress who had lived in comfort all her life. But she had given David freedom, she had risked her life for his love, and what she had to do now was easy: simply

232

walk, follow Yair's legs, so no one would suspect that her fear was as big as the empty spaces about them.

But David could sense her fear. He was fearful himself. There was fear all about the mountains, fear that could bring murder down on them, and fear that could lead them all to heroic action. His fear was not like Diana's, however. He needed no force of will to keep him looking at Diana's back. There was the fear that he carried a great fate on his back, the fate of his people. So much money as he and Joey carried could be a decisive help at this point, during the war that was not declared, during the Mandate that offered no protection but only hindrances to self-protection. He had learned from the newspaper brought by the airplane that events conspired to prevent the Haganah from defending themselves. They needed weapons, but the embargo prevented them from being landed. They needed people, but the British were going to intern in Cyprus the twelve thousand refugees they had stopped from landing in Palestine. Only a day before, in Jersey City, New Jersey, a Palestine-bound ship was found to be loading 65,000 pounds of TNT, all of which was confiscated. He wondered if Arye Grinberg had been involved with that illegal shipment, if American public opinion would now turn against the Jews of Palestine for breaking the tranquillity of the New Jersey shore with an illegal act. But public opinion could not matter as much as concrete deeds at this moment. The Arab nations were being armed by the British. Riots in the Arab countries were slaughtering their poorly defended Jewish populations. Syria had announced that all her Zionist Jews must leave the country forever within the next ten days. The railroad between Jaffa and Tel Aviv was blown up. Forty-one Jews were killed in a terrorist action against the Haifa refinery. The Old City of Jerusalem was being stripped of its Jews, with the Jewish quarter blocked and besieged by Arabs. David's fear was not for the dark, not for any bullet that might find his heart while he walked the mountain path. His fear was for what he might not be able to accomplish. His money must get to where it could be used. And his strength and cunning must be allowed to live to help in the creation of the state.

If Joey had any fear during the walk to the neighboring kibbutz, it was that he might yet make a fool of himself over Diana. The night here had no terrors for him. It was cold, but he was wearing two heavy wool sweaters, knitted by American women and sent to Palestine as a form of aid. The silence was ominous, but he knew how silence could be broken, and what could happen in the event of an attack. He had learned in the Marines to be alert, but not overalert. Behind him Geula walked, saying nothing, but the comforting sound of her boots on the rocky path gave him pleasure.

At the halfway mark the wind shifted, blowing the scent of Turkish coffee in their faces. They halted, and Yair whispered to Geula, and Diana moved imperceptibly closer to David. Below where they walked along a steep ridge was the outer circle of an Arab encampment. Geula was the first to spot the fires. Strangely, Diana felt her heart relax. This mark of a real danger eased her fear. Now as they stepped quietly along the edge of the mountain path, she was listening for real sounds: an alarm, a sudden clatter, a rush to arms. But she heard none of these things, and was hardly aware of the speed with which they were now moving. A hand with a powerful grip took hold of her left shoulder from behind, and this didn't shock her either. She remained calm, waiting to understand what it meant. But then it was only the voice of her lover, and he spoke softly through the dark: "Can you see the watchtower?"

And there indeed, as a cloud shifted to light a patch of sky with stars, she could make out a ghostly shape—a boulder, a water tower, a pillar of salt. But then the moon rose over the horizon, slipping out from behind the rain clouds, and she could see the barbed-wire fence of a Jewish settlement, and the ghostly shape was the watchtower, and Yair was signaling to it with his flashlight. And they were safe.

A great grizzled bear of a man met them, and went straight for David, folding him into his arms like a rag doll. "We must rush," he said to David in English. "The plane will be here very soon."

The kibbutz in the dark was still noticeably different from Kibbutz Ha-Yad. There were clusters of buildings here, living quarters and stables and barns and warehouses. Geula had been inducted into the Haganah here when she was sixteen, and the induction had been done under cover of darkness in an abandoned barn on the edge of the kibbutz's property. Not everyone in the kibbutz had been a member of the Haganah then, and unlike Kibbutz Ha-Yad, the settlement had not been primarily established as a lonely outpost on a strategic road. This had been a working collective farm, with over two hundred members, more than fifty of them children under the age of twelve. Now all the children were gone, the farmwork had ceased, and the remaining members were all soldiers of the Haganah. There was no longer a reason to hide an induction ceremony from anyone. The large man who had first greeted David introduced himself as Uri and took them to the dining hall, which the members used as a place of meeting.

"You will sit there," he said to Joey, pointing to the head of a long wood table. He paused for a moment, looking at his watch, and then he turned to Diana. "And you too. We will do this at the same time."

Diana followed Joey to the end of the table, where a Bible and a handgun rested between two candles. A lovely young girl of no more than sixteen hurried to light the candles, and then almost at once the three electric lights that had illuminated the room were extinguished.

"There's only one seat here," said Joey, pausing behind it at the head of the table.

"Share it," said Uri. "You will share much more than a chair in the Haganah. If you are accepted." Joey sat first, and felt Diana sit to his left, her right leg comfortably close against his. The candlelight was soft, unthreatening, and it was still possible to discern the figures of David and Geula and Yair taking seats among a dozen-odd members of the kibbutz. He knew that this induction was supposed to be awe-inspiring, if not threatening, but the fact of the gun and the Bible between the melodramatically flickering candles was much less inspiring to him than the touch of Diana's body, than the fact of her scent.

Suddenly a blinding white light was turned on them, a projector apparently, and Uri's voice had become unkind.

"We are pressed for time and must quickly decide whether to trust you with the sacred task of the Haganah. You, Diana, will answer first. What is the sacred task of the Haganah?"

Diana knew the catechism, and repeated without thought: "The task of the Haganah is to protect the Jewish people in the Land of Israel from all attackers." But her words were heard with great clarity by Joey. He looked directly into the bright light, his pupils dilating, but his vision clear: once again he was seeing Jerusalem. As on the first day he had arrived in the Holy Land, he was reaching back through his remarkable memory and finding echoes and fragments of a past he was certain he had not imagined. With Diana at his side, he felt like a hero receiving a mission, a challenge to defend his people. He felt like a champion, the champion of the woman at his side, and of the people in this land.

"What is the Haganah?" he heard another man's voice say, and as he heard Diana speak out the answer, he felt his own lips move in the identical response, all the while growing more and more subject to the images he was taking from the light.

"The Haganah is the unified national, centralized, and graded military command of the Jewish people in Eretz-Israel."

"And whom does the Haganah serve?"

Joey felt the light, not as a blinding power, but as a source of strength. He felt as if it were not repelling him, but rather drawing him, and drawing him back to roots, to family, to love. This was his woman at his side, and these were his people, and he would go to Jerusalem and he would remember the past, he would allow it to be the foundation of his present.

"The Haganah serves the Jewish people in Eretz-Israel and the whole Zionist movement. The Haganah doesn't interfere with either the organization of the Zionist movement or the internal affairs of the Jewish community in Eretz-Israel."

Joey understood that a silence had filled the room and that he had become the focus of attention. He smiled, understanding that all would be well, that this was simply a formality, and then he and Diana would have joined the Haganah together, and be bound by this, as they were bound by so many other things.

"You are to answer the question," said Uri's harsh voice.

"I'm sorry. Could you say it again?"

There was a longer silence now, and then Uri barked: "Discipline. Describe the discipline expected of one in the Haganah."

"Strict military discipline," said Joey automatically, as if this were some sort of game that could go on simultaneously with his much more important concerns. The light remained steady and true, and he felt his penis rise, he felt the sexual power of the woman he loved grow over and beyond any other concern in the room. He felt that he and Diana sitting together must be reflecting the projected light; their own mutual glow must surely be as strong as any moon. "All Haganah members must be ready to obey all authorized orders. This discipline must come about from the conscience of every member and upon the rules of freedom, equality, and comradeship."

"Describe the rules of secrecy in the Haganah," said the voice behind the light. Joey's heart was pounding. He was going to Jerusalem. Diana would be his comrade. She would love him all her life.

"The weapons, actions, and plans of the Haganah are secret. The existence of the organization, the names of its members, its leadership are all secret. Whoever divulges the secrets of the Haganah is liable to pay with his or her life."

"What are the essential teachings of the Haganah?"

"Loyalty to the people, courage, independence, freedom, self-sacrifice," said Joey, his photographic memory running through the words as easily as if they were printed on a page he held in his hands. All the while he spoke, he felt Diana shivering at his side. The excitement he felt was a sexual excitement, an anticipation of love that was as certain as if he and she were naked in bed together, at the very point of union. But Diana's excitement was not at all sexual. She had no awareness of the mad rush of sensuality in Joey's brain. She was blinded by the light and saw no images there, and when she shivered it was for the same series of days that Joey so longed for: Jerusalem was in her mind, but not as a mystic culmination of a thousand wayward thoughts and dreams; Jerusalem was a city of dangers, and she was pledging herself to fight those dangers, and she feared for herself and for those she loved. "The Haganah teaches us the power to withstand suffering," continued Joey, "gives us respect for human life and all the values of civilization, Jewish and Gentile alike."

They were asked to rise, Joey and Diana, and the powerful light of the projector was extinguished, and first Diana held one hand on the gun, one hand on the Bible, and with Joey as her witness, she recited the oath of the Haganah, the candlelight dancing in her eyes.

She swore faithfulness to the Defense Organization and to its code of law; she accepted freely its authority, discipline, and call to duty. Her words were spoken softly, not because she had any reluctance to swear her allegiance, but because she was overcome by the approbation about her. She felt as if she were being wrapped in a thousand welcomes, as if the arms of the people in the room were going out to her and that David was proud and wanted her.

"My turn, babe," said Joey as he slipped his hand over hers onto the gun, and then Diana stepped back and Joey stood before the assembled Haganah men and women, one hand on the Bible, one hand on the gun, and quickly swore the oath of the Haganah. The candlelight carried no images, and he had stopped up his desire. Once again he knew that the woman at his side loved another man and that the dream of their union was only that and nothing more; if he wanted Diana, he would have to take Geula and let the magic of fantasy overcome him. But if his sexual excitement was gone, he was not through with excitement. Even if the images had stopped, he remembered them. He would be in Jerusalem. There he would understand what drew him, what made him weak with joy at the sight of the Holy City, what filled him with strength at the prospect of coming to its aid. Then the half-Jewish, half-Italian gangster from Brooklyn and New York concluded the oath: "I will dedicate all my strength, if necessary my life, for the defense of my people and my homeland, for the freedom of Israel and the redemption of Zion."

Someone had produced a few thimblefuls of whiskey, and everyone drank to life, and then there was no time for any more congratulations. Uri led them at a run to the far side of the kibbutz, where a line of trucks waited for the sound of a little Taylorcraft plane. They could hear the plane almost at the moment that they reached the first truck, and suddenly all the vehicles turned on their headlights, illuminating a makeshift runway that Joey would have found difficult to drive a car through. The plane dropped out of the sky like a bird hit by a bullet. It hit the ground and lifted off, then bounced along the dirt on flimsy little wheels.

"Oh, God," said Joey, with so much sudden fear in his voice that Diana burst out laughing.

"What is it?" said David, but his lover couldn't stop; there were tears running down her eyes, and she turned to Joey and pulled him close to her.

"Joey," she said, remembering how the impossibly reckless boy, afraid of nothing but airplanes, had been so embarrassed over his terror of flying. "Joey, you beautiful, crazy hoodlum," she said, not letting him go, and for a moment Joey accepted this embrace because it was about the two of them, them only, it excluded David, no one else knew about his fear of flying, no one else had the right and the desire to comfort him.

"What is it?" David repeated, a bit more sharply, and Diana still held Joey, but her laughter had eased to a foolish grin, and she turned her attention back to her lover.

"You won't believe this," said Diana. "But Joey Marino, the man who saved your life, the man with an icepick for a heart—he's afraid of flying."

238

It was during this speech that Joey pushed out of her embrace. He walked to the plane and stilled his heart. There could be no fear as strong as his hurt. That she could hold him with so little feeling, that she could talk to her lover with Joey in her arms, was more than infuriating. She seemed to be rubbing salt into an open wound.

"Joey," she called after him, a little laugh in her voice. "Joey, I hope I didn't insult you? Silly—what difference does it make if you get a little nervous up in the air?"

The flight was mercifully short. Almost as soon as the plane had braved the runway lit by the truck headlights and climbed into the moon-filled sky, it was ready to land. Joey kept his eyes shut, but sat away from them, where no one could see. He felt the currents of air lift the plane and lower it, push them forward and hold them back against the landscape of mountains that he refused to look at. The pilot was very cheerful, with a booming voice of self-congratulation that could be heard over the engine noise. He was telling David and Diana how when he used to fly little planes in the Andes he had to wait for the currents of air to lift his plane high enough to get over the peaks. "Not enough air, and what do you get?" he said. "Boom into the side of the mountain. *Boom!*"

Joey closed his eyes a little tighter, imagining the white towers that must be reflecting the moonlight as they sailed over the Holy City. The Taylorcraft dipped forward and went down quickly, so quickly that for a moment Joey was certain they were going to crash, and he thought he would open his eyes for one last moment to catch a glimpse of Diana, of life.

But he couldn't bring himself to open his eyes. The moment passed, and he knew that he wouldn't die that night, and he heard the plane's flaps beat back the air, even as he tried to beat back his feelings. They landed bumpily on the two-thousand-foot dirt runway built by the Haganah next to the Monastery of the Cross. At the last moment he felt Diana's hand take his and give it a squeeze, as if the encouragement he wanted from her was about flying in a plane.

"We made it, Joey," she said brightly. "We're back in Jerusalem." He didn't answer her. They were back, but it was with David, in a city where they were fugitives, in a country where nothing was promised as surely as death.

FIFTEEN

They slept in a Haganah "barracks," the living room of a retired doctor who was constantly urging the Haganah men and women who slept on his sofa and chairs and carpet to cover their heads at night. "That's where all the heat goes out," he said. "The head. Pneumonia kills just the same as the Arabs."

But that night there were no other guests in the doctor's apartment. The doctor distributed his wool caps to Diana, David, and Joey, explaining that they were not for the apartment, but for the cold nights outside. "Don't come back to me with your pneumonia," he warned them. "I'll know you weren't wearing your caps and I won't take care of you."

All night their sleep was disturbed by sniper fire. Every time Diana woke, she could see that both men were awake, turning restlessly in search of a few hours of sleep before the dawn. David rested on the sofa, Joey on two stuffed chairs pushed together, Diana equidistant from both men on a pile of cushions on the doctor's Persian carpet. They all knew the reasons for the sniper fire. In this period before the end of the Mandate, Jews and Arabs both jockeyed for position; each group wanted to control as much territory as possible the day the British sailed home. Snipers hoped to make life so dangerous and anxious for the men, women, and children of a neighborhood that only a handful would have the fortitude not to move out. The Jewish leadership, far more organized and representational of their people than their Arab counterparts, had made it a special point that no Jewish neighborhood, no Jewish farm, no Jewish house or apartment or rented room must be abandoned, regardless of the danger. In the neighborhoods closest to Arab-held heights, the Jews boarded up their windows, dragged their mattresses into inner hallways, trying to keep as many walls between themselves and the Arabs as possible. The doctor's apartment building had never yet been hit by sniper fire, and the sounds of bullets were distant sounds, but all three sleepers knew how deceptive sounds were in the vastness of a city, how many innocents had been killed by a bullet meant for someone else. David had promised them that they would all be safe the next day, that the Haganah would get them into the Old City, where they would be exposed to dangers they could look at directly. Diana wondered how David planned to get them into the Jewish quarter, to which the Arabs had blocked every convoy of food and supplies for the past week. She wondered how Joey and David would get along in the close confines of a quarter under siege.

"You'd better drink this," said the doctor, by way of waking Diana. She opened her eyes to the pale light of a drizzly winter morning. The old man, trained in Germany, born in Russia, and resident of Eretz-Israel for forty years, was holding out a tall glass of steaming milk mixed with honey. "The honey will stick to your insides," he said, very unscientifically. Joey and David were already up, standing at the window with their hot glasses, looking out through tired eyes at the dismal day. "This will heat you up, and if you keep your hat on, the heat will stay in. If you don't keep your hat on, don't come back to me to take care of your pneumonia."

Diana drank the hot drink, and it brought a smile to her lips. "It's very good, very warming," she said.

"You think it's compliments I want?" said the old doctor. "Not compliments, just kisses." And he took the young woman's chin in his capable hands and kissed her cheek softly. "Be careful," he said. "Life is precious, my dear. Now, drink up, and wear your hat. Drink it to the last drop, milk is rationed, you know. You're drinking with the privileged few."

They were on the street by eight o'clock, and in the rush of pedestrians, Diana felt anonymous, safe. She was without her American passport, her fine clothes, but in the simple clothing of the kibbutz, her hair disheveled from sleep, she felt part of the Jewish masses in West Jerusalem: underfed, anxious, eager to assert their rights at the slightest provocation.

David had gone off to a meeting in Rehavia, and promised to meet them at eleven at the Mamillah Cemetery, near Barclay's Bank. Joey walked well behind her, another splash of kibbutz blue in the sea of khaki and green. She walked into the Salvia Hotel at ten minutes to nine, prepared to meet the mysterious man who had required her presence to complete the illicit contract that would allow guns from America to get through British customs in Haifa.

"All right, sweetheart, we got you covered, so no funny stuff," said a voice vaguely familiar behind the put-on gangster accent. She turned around and saw her cousin Richard Mann, impeccably dressed for a society lunch in New York, holding out his arms for an embrace.

"I'm seeing things," said Diana, going to him.

"No, no, it's me," said Richard, pulling her into his arms. "It cost a lot of money, and who knows how many people had their arms and legs broken, but your Uncle Marty—"

"Wait, wait," said Diana. "Sit down. Come on, let's start from the beginning. What the hell are you doing in Palestine?"

"Just trying to learn the family business," said Richard.

"What family business?"

"Banking," he said, and he led her to the only table in the hotel restaurant with flowers on it, and hot coffee in a silver service, and French rolls, and English jam, and fresh butter. The food was too good to eat alone, and Diana stood up for a moment to look around for Joey Marino. He had taken a table too, in the corner of the restaurant, and when Diana looked his way, he turned around to catch her gaze, and she motioned for him broadly to join them.

"Don't say anything nasty about Marty Bernstein," said Diana. "Or this guy may shoot you."

"Mr. Marino, I presume," said Richard. He had stood up and put out his hand for Joey. Joey looked at the hand for a moment before taking hold of it and squeezing it hard enough to break Richard's fingers.

"Who are you?" said Joey.

"I'm Diana's cousin, actually," said Richard. "From the stuffy side of the family. Richard Mann."

242

"Nobody told us nothing about you," said Joey. "What about the customs guy—"

"Taken care of," said Richard. He put up his hands as if he were the host of a carefully arranged Waldorf breakfast. "But first things first. I insist on getting some food into you. You both look famished."

"It's the clothes," said Joey, trying not to apologize for his kibbutz clothing in light of the rich boy's elegant suit. "We don't usually dress like this."

"Joey is usually silk and cashmere all the way," said Diana, "except for the steel in his belt." For the first time in weeks, she actually remembered she was a journalist. One day she'd sit down and write this story: Clothes-horse gangster meets society boy from New York while Jerusalem is getting ready to go up in flames—and all that the fugitive gangster can worry about is the absence of his silk tie.

Richard had ordered breakfast, but even his money couldn't get them fresh eggs. The convoys to Jerusalem from Tel Aviv were not getting through, and none of them wanted to bother with powdered eggs, particularly the egg-ridden Joey and Diana. But butter was welcome, and jam, and decent coffee, and fresh oranges in abundance—two for each of them. "First of all, Marty says hello," said Richard.

"How did you get to Marty?" said Diana.

"He got to me."

"How did he know how to get to you?" said Diana.

Joey laughed at this question. "Hey, you're supposed to be a smart broad. And his niece. Marty can get to anybody. Anybody, and that means you, me, the President, the Prime Minister. Anybody."

"Well, actually, Mr. Marino—Joey—your Marty Bernstein can get to almost anybody. He thought we might be helpful in getting to some of those other people."

"What other people?"

"Like the Prime Minister of England," said Diana, anticipating Richard's answer.

Her cousin smiled at her and placed a cigarette in a gold-tipped cigarette holder.

"Not the Prime Minister, actually," said Richard. "But some rather influential . . . *stuffy*-influential people in England. Mr. Bernstein thought it might be a good idea to get to them through some of the family's banking interests rather than through some of his business associates."

"Sure," said Joey. "Marty figured some of those English hoods might have scared those guys half to death."

"Precisely," said Richard.

"But what are you doing here?" said Diana. "Are you saying that the customs deal through Haifa was taken care of? Who took care of it, and how?"

"My father helped," said Richard. He stopped Diana from interrupting. "Look, if you want to know the truth, he was glad to meet Marty Bernstein. Put a little excitement into his life. He's going to fly down to Las Vegas soon with some banker types, meet celebrities, shake hands with the infamous Kalman Meyers. But it was also you, Diana. Of course. Your family. Your adoptive family, but your family, the people who raised you."

"Okay," said Diana. "Sure, that sounds reasonable. My mother and father must have been thrilled to participate in the bribing of foreign customs officials with the help of America's most famous gangster, who is also my uncle."

"You're too hard on them, Diana," said Richard. "They've done a lot, more than you think." He reached into his pocket for two flat envelopes, and gave one to Joey, one to Diana. "I don't know what happened with that prison break, and who's wanted or why you can't get out of the country with your own passports, but here's a little present from your folks—and Marty."

They were two passports, for a married couple, Joseph and Louise Collins, born in New York City, resident in Zurich, and the passports were those rare and difficult ones to obtain, legally or illegally, for money or for power—from Switzerland. Richard started to explain the scheme that would take the two of them out of the country. When he had arrived at Lydda airfield, the little shuttle plane to Jerusalem had taken him and four others for ten dollars each from the airport into the city. For five hundred dollars the pilot would be happy to fly them straight to Haifa, over all the roadblocks and ambushes and Arab terrorists and British police. In Haifa an English pleasure craft, a yacht that had twice crossed the Atlantic and was as at home in Mediterranean waters as it was in the English Channel, would take them to Italy. From Italy they would fly with their Swiss passports directly to the United States.

"Think of the stories you could write for your newspaper," said Richard. "Once you're home, there will be no risk of prosecution for you, we can see to that. As for you, Joey, I'm sure your Mr. Bernstein will see to it that no harm befalls his favorite associate once you're back in New York wearing your beautiful clothes, driving your elegant car."

"Stop it," said Diana. She had sounded surprisingly angry even to Joey, so that he knew she must be sorely tempted by the offer. Even with David Stern ready to jump into the inferno of the Jewish quarter, she could imagine herself back home, safe. More easily, she repeated her words. "Stop it, Richard. This is all a lot of nonsense. The important thing is that you were able to arrange for that bribe. When will the weapons be arriving?"

"I don't know. Soon, I imagine, but I've been given no precise details. What if I was captured and tortured like in one of those war movies? I'd tell everything, wouldn't I?"

"Maybe," said Joey, looking directly into the rich boy's eyes. "But what are you doing here, then? Marty could have sent somebody else."

"I know what Diana looks like."

"Ever hear of the photograph? It's a new invention," said Joey.

"You were brave to come here, Richard," said Diana.

"Thank you," he said. "But I'm not brave, and you know it. I had to do something. Marty said he'd trust me to bring a suitcase to Geneva. And take something back to Palestine.

"I was very flattered. And my parents weren't angry. They were pleased with me. Things have changed back home, Diana. People feel the war that's coming to little Palestine. I'm not the only one who wants to do something. And I don't have the guts to do what you've done."

"We're not coming home," said Diana.

"I didn't think you would."

"Well, we're not, and that's all," she said. "You probably should get out of Jerusalem as soon as you can. It's not safe here, especially if you don't know your way around."

"I'm only here to deliver the message and the passports."

"They may still come in handy," said Joey. He was full of pride for Diana at that moment. There was no doubt in his mind that she was staying not simply for David, but for love of the future state. "It took guts to bring them in. They like to hang people in this country, and the prisons here don't carry champagne."

"When you come back, both of you, I'd like to buy you a few bottles," said Richard.

"You heard him, Joey," said Diana. "It's a promise. Dom Perignon. We're going to collect."

"Or we ask Marty to send over some of the boys," said Joey.

"Look, is there anything I can get for you before I go? I'm carrying a lot of cash."

"You're not carrying a gun by any chance?" said Diana. Joey smiled at her. She was talking his language now. "Or maybe a switchblade?"

"How about if you pay for this breakfast?" said Joey, smiling. David had taken the cash and securities with him that morning to the local headquarters of the Haganah. Joey had kept only a few hundred dollars for expenses, and three thousand dollars for emergency airfare out of the country. But without access to the much greater sums he was used to having in reserve, he felt strangely naked. There wasn't enough money in his pocket to risk at a racetrack, to bribe an official, to buy a wardrobe of English suits.

"What exactly are you going to be doing here?" said Richard. "Is there anything I can tell your folks back home?"

"No," said Joey, stepping in before Diana could answer. "Just that we're working for the right side."

"That we're well and happy and that we thank them for everything they've done," said Diana. "And the best way they can help is to tell everyone what's going on here, who the British are favoring, why getting arms into Palestine for the Jews is so crucial and how—"

"Forty-five hundred automatic rifles," said Richard. "That's the first shipment, with ammunition. That's what's coming through the port of Haifa, and if it's any help at all, the Jewish government is going to have to remember your Uncle Marty, because he's the one who's made it happen."

"Pardon me," said the waiter, his eyes strangely intense. "But are you Miss Mann?" Joey had his hand on his gun under the table. There was no reason that this man should know Diana's name.

"What's it to you what her name is, pal?" said Joey.

"Because, sir," said the waiter, "if she is Miss Mann, there is a gentleman waiting to give her a message from her aunt."

Diana stood up at once. "Aunt" was a code name for the Haganah, but with the spreading smile of goodwill on the waiter's face, it was obviously a code name known by many.

"What aunt?" said Richard Mann.

Joey stood up too. "We have to go," he said.

"I see," said Richard. He looked about at the unfinished breakfast with something approaching chagrin. "I certainly understand," he said, getting to his feet to once again shake Joey's hand. Diana kissed him quickly, and then, hesitating, she pulled him back into her arms for a lengthy embrace.

"Thank you for coming," she said. "It's important for me to know that you cared enough to risk coming, and that my parents are okay about all this. Grandmother would have been proud."

"I can stay, you know," he said. "I could find an apartment. They need volunteers." He seemed to be waiting for her to tell him what to do, to tell him if such a sacrifice would be worthy of her regard. But Diana couldn't think of answering for him. She was confused enough about her own motives for acting so heroically to the eyes of the world. "I mean, as long as I'm here."

"Richard, we have to go," said Diana. "Whatever you do to help will be good. What you've done so far has been wonderful. I can't tell you what to do. People are dying here every day. And maybe you can do more good back home. Just try to do something. And thanks. Thanks for coming."

Joey walked her out of the dining room so quickly that for a moment she felt like she was running away, deliberately turning her back on what was safe and easy and warm. But then she saw the face of the young Haganah man who was waiting for them: a fiercely bearded black-haired man in khaki clothing with a pistol stuck in his belt, without a jacket to cover up the presence of the firearm.

"Change of plans. You're not meeting in the cemetery. I'll take you to your commander," he said. The young man turned without a word, and they hurried after him, where an old Buick, its backseat windows replaced with corrugated cardboard, waited with its two right wheels on the curb. He drove fiercely, alternately stomping on brake pedal and accelerator. Diana asked him about the gun.

"I don't care who sees it," he said. "This is a war. It's a war now, not just in May. Now. We have new orders. Not to hand over weapons to the British upon demand. I show my gun, and if someone wants it, let him try to get it. I'll kill the son of a bitch." Beyond the wild words was a wound, obvious to Diana, a wound that he could assuage only with violence. Diana waited, and then it came: "Those bastards. Take our guns and give us over to the Arabs. Arabs walking around with gunbelts, plain as day. I'd like to see one of those Tommies try something with me. This is Jewish Jerusalem. If you're armed, you can show what you've got. Look at this."

He was making a left-hand turn at high speed, but as they screamed around the turn on underinflated tires, he tossed over a crumpled obituary sheet, one of the many that were tacked up all over Jerusalem, Tel Aviv, and Haifa, put in place by members of the Irgun and the Stern gang as well as the Haganah.

"We stand to attention before the memory of our comrade Dani Abramovitch, fallen in battle," began the notice, with its black print blurred around the edges, as if it was too soon snatched off the press, to make room for other notices, other deaths.

"Was he your friend?" said Diana. They were approaching a shantytown near the Jerusalem bus station that Diana recognized as a district of Yemenite Jews.

"They don't just kill, they mutilate," said the hotheaded driver. "The ears, the eyes, the balls—they're not human beings, not the British, not the Arabs. The British are even worse. They know what they're doing, and they don't give a damn."

Joey remembered Crawfield, and knew that there were British who were as decent as anyone. But he didn't interrupt the man's tirade. War made for great generalizations. Individuals were stripped of human characteristics, placed in one amorphous category of "enemy," like he had done with the "Japs." And Joey knew that a big hate, a simple hate, was good for a soldier. It took away the hesitation that one ordinarily felt before taking a life.

"The Old City is dying. The Jewish quarter is dying. The Wailing Wall is in Arab hands, so they can bring their soldiers to piss on it. Syrians, Iraqis, Transjordanians—they're all running into the city, guns in their belts, rifles on their backs, machine guns in their trucks—and that's fine with our brave English protectors. Just fine. Dani was going to be a doctor. A real student. Why did they have to do that to his body? He was dead, wasn't he? Why couldn't they leave his dead body in peace?"

They found David in a tiny shack with boarded-over windows breaking down his pistol. There were four other men in the single room of the house, taken over from a Yementine day laborer by the Haganah. Except for David, all the men wore the "uniform" of the

Haganah—corduroy slacks and khaki shirts, with dark sweaters wrapped about their waists. David was dressed in white, white pants and white shirt; like an ice-cream man, thought Joey.

"You're here," he said, as if he'd been waiting far too long.

"We came as soon as he got hold of us," said Diana. Joey felt himself wincing. She seemed so quick to apologize to her lover, always eager to please, never attempting to contradict or rebel.

"We were going to try to go in on the Number Two bus," said David. "It gets shot at all the time, but it at least gets through, and since the Brits turned over some Haganah boys two days ago to the Arabs, they haven't been searching the bus for weapons. They're afraid some Irgunist is going to shoot them in the back."

"Some Haganah boy," said their black-bearded driver, "is going to shoot them in the front."

"Only if he gets those orders," said one of the other Haganah men.

"The orders seem pretty clear to me," said the black-bearded young man. "If they try to take away your weapon, kill the bastards."

"No," said David. "The order is to resist, not to kill."

"I resist by killing. I shoot in the balls, just to make sure. You weren't here. You didn't see Dani's body."

"Why don't we just mutilate them altogether?" said David. "Sink to their level. Cut out their tongues and shoot their babies in front of their eyes. Put them in concentration camps like the Nazis. Why don't we go all the way?"

"I'm not a Nazi," said Dani's friend. "I was in a camp, just like you were in a camp, so don't try to call me a Nazi."

"Take it easy," said one of the others. "Both of you. You're both right. We're not going to mutilate or shoot in the back, but our orders are to resist, and that means resist to the death. That means, in Jerusalem, we carry our guns, and we stop pretending we don't exist. We exist, and when they try to search Jewish boys, they'll find out we exist."

"It's here," said another Haganah soldier, looking out the window. "Where are their clothes?"

Joey was handed a policeman's uniform, and without a word he began to strip off his kibbutznik's clothing in the crowded shanty. Diana was handed another uniform, all white like David's, and Joey realized that the lovers weren't parading as ice-cream vendors, but as doctor and nurse.

"Just change, Diana," said David. "There's no modesty among soldiers."

"It's okay," said Joey. "Anybody looks at the girl, I take care of later." It was said in a joking manner, which was a good thing, since everyone except Joey took a close look at the lovely American stripping down to her underclothes and hurriedly dressing in the nurse's whites. And more than just look, they had the time to comment in Hebrew and let out one or two whistles and comradely compliments to David Stern.

"Joey, you're driving," said David. And he opened the door and went out to a waiting ambulance, the driver getting out of the front seat with bloody hands.

"Too bad you're not a real doctor, my friend," said the driver.

The black-bearded Haganah soldier held on to the wounded man. "It's like we thought," he was able to say through his pain. "The British aren't doing a thing. The Arabs have taken over Jaffa Gate. The Number Two bus had to turn back. No Jews are getting into the Old City at all."

"Diana, in the back," said David, opening the rear of the ambulance.

"They're going to stop you anyway," said the black-bearded soldier. "You don't have papers. They'll shoot at an ambulance. They're animals."

"We're not worried," said David. "Let's go, Joey."

"Right," said Joey Marino. He wasn't worried. He had his gun, he had his switchblade and brass knuckles, he had the woman he loved in the back of the ambulance, and he felt as if no power on earth could stop him from penetrating the Old City walls. He heard the young soldier continue to warn David, but Diana's lover simply closed the ambulance door and told Joey to start it up and go.

The ambulance felt like a great truck to Joey as he tried to maneuver out of the alley behind the shanty. Not only was it badly sprung, but the alignment of the wheels seemed terribly off.

Diana came up to the partition behind where they sat. "It was my cousin who met us at the Salvia," she said. "He says forty-five hundred rifles are coming through the port of Haifa, any day."

"Automatic rifles?"

"Yes, and no problem with customs."

"Forty-five hundred automatic rifles," said David with such reverent happiness that for a moment it seemed to Joey as if the man had finally discovered how to express love. "My God, if this is true, Diana, you've done an incredible thing for us. For all of us. With forty-five hundred rifles we could open and secure the road to Jerusalem. With forty-five hundred rifles we could hold our own until the British are finally gone." David seemed to force himself out of his reverie of automatic rifles. "Put the siren on," he said, and when Joey hesitated, looking for the switch, David turned it on for him. "You turn left, and drive as fast as you can."

They heard the careening car before Joey saw it in his rearview mirror. He knew who it would be as he looked up and saw the dilapidated Buick passing them on the right at high speed.

"That's the guy—"

"I know who the hell it is," said David. "I'm just not sure what the hell he's doing." He directed Joey down a small street that led into the Jaffa Road. Cars and taxis made way for the speeding ambulance, but Joey couldn't catch up to the Buick. The ambulance wouldn't move that fast, and he was afraid to bring the accelerator all the way to the floor in such a badly aligned vehicle.

"Where the hell is he going?" said Joey.

"He's going where we're going, and he's going to get there first," said David. Out of the corner of his eye he could see that David's gun was out, ready to fire. A police vehicle turned into Jaffa Road, following them at first, then suddenly accelerating and pulling up next to them as cars continued to get out of their way. Joey could see the driver of the armored police car looking him over as he passed the ambulance, and screamed something up at him that Joey couldn't quite hear.

"He's making a way for you," said David. "Just stay after him." Neither of them could see the Buick, but they could hear the cacophony of horns, the gentle tinkling of crushing metal, the scream of brakes that preceded them, and as they neared the police headquarters close to where David had been kept in prison, they saw the big old car finally stopped, the center piece of a four-car collision.

Joey swung the ambulance around the mess of automobiles, but the police car was no longer leading him; it had stopped to let out an officer to sort out the confusion at the scene. As Joey slowed up at the next intersection, waiting for the cars to stop, he heard David let out a sharp breath of air.

"That maniac's not through," said David, and in the rearview mirror Joey could see the Buick backing up, scratching and banging into the already damaged cars that surrounded it.

Without realizing it, Joey slowed down, so that the entire spectacle played out in the tiny space of the rearview mirror: the Buick, battering its way free of the accident, sending one small car skidding into the glass-paned front of a shop; a police officer, no bigger than an insect, raising his baton and being struck sidewise by the careening Buick; a gunshot aimed at the Buick from the police car, but shattering the windshield of another car; the Buick skidding about, grazing the side of the police car, and righting itself with a squeal of tires; then suddenly the Buick increasing in size, blowing up like a balloon in the rearview mirror, accompanied by screaming brakes and the voice of the black-bearded Haganah man: "After me!" he shouted, and Joey turned his head, and David was screaming at him to move, and the Buick had passed them, and Joey brought the accelerator pedal to the floor, feeling the sure loss of control he so relished in a car, in a gun, in a woman.

There were other sirens now, other ambulances perhaps, or the noisy heralding of reinforcements from the police force. Joey held the wheel tightly, moving it left to keep straight as the bad alignment urged the car to the right-hand curb. He no longer slowed at intersections, as the Buick was paving their way with terror. With no siren other than the sound of its horn, it stopped the flow of traffic going into Jaffa Road. Joey willed himself to be calm, deliberately ignoring the rushing cars at the corners of his vision. He felt as if it were almost inevitable that they would crash, as if he were going down a precipice on roller skates and all his energy was concentrated on keeping his posture straight on the way to his doom. Cars skidded to a halt all about them, flying on locked wheels, leaning on their horns, adding their voices to the sounds of tortured machines. Suddenly the Buick's brake lights went on, and Joey automatically jammed on his brake, reaching for the throbbing gearshift as the big car turned almost sideways. It stopped within inches of crushing an old woman with a modest head covering crossing the Jaffa Road with a disregard to any source of danger.

"There's the roadblock," said David. "We should have loaded this thing with food."

At the entrance to the Jaffa Gate, previously manned by the British, was a motley crowd of Arabs brandishing automatic rifles behind a complicated barrier of wood and barbed wire and sandbags. Joey could see one or two blue caps and greatcoats of the Palestine police, but most of the crowd wore burnooses and heavy abayahs; some wore the distinctive red-and-white-checked kaffiyehs of the Arab Legion, a few wore Arab headdresses over ordinary Western suits, but the majority dressed in black robes, draped with gunbelts, their kaffiyehs immaculate. All about the armed crowd was a bigger crowd, Arabs waiting for a bus into West Jerusalem or a chance to observe something of the shifting of power from Englishmen to Arabs here at the entrance to the Old City.

"Now what?" said Joey.

"Just go," said David.

The Buick started up as the woman crossed the street, but this time the car drove slowly, approaching within a few hundred feet of the roadblock behind a line of cars and taxis, and then finally stopping as this line moved closer toward the Old City gate. Joey was right behind him, and stopped also. A police car came up behind them, and several police officers jumped out with drawn guns and ran for the stopped Buick. From his high seat in the ambulance Joey could quite clearly see the black-bearded zealot, still burning over the mutilation of his friend's corpse. He wasn't looking at them, nor did he turn around at the sound of the running police officers. He seemed to be counting to himself, waiting for an inner signal that would initiate his release from suffering.

"Get ready," said David.

"Ready for what?" said Joey.

"You know what he's going to do," said David. The policemen were close enough to shoot the young man through the car window, and in a moment would be close enough to tear open the car door. But it was too late for either action. The Buick lurched forward, the policemen jumped back, and only one of them fired, and that was a useless warning shot into the air.

Joey saw the Buick twist slowly about the short line of cars waiting at the roadblock and aim its long snout directly at the crowd of Arab barricaders. He had known all along, in some part of him, what the young man was going to do; but he had chosen not to think about it, because to Joey the idea of self-sacrifice was highly personal, his own final resource, and the idea of someone killing himself on his behalf was repugnant. He didn't want to carry that kind of debt, impossible to repay.

"Stay right behind," said David.

"I'm not stupid," said Joey.

"Tight behind," said David. And this was difficult to do, the Buick's eight cylinders taking the stopped car to killing speed in moments. No one among the Arabs had the time to quite believe what was happening, to take the seconds left him to drop to one knee, aim carefully at the black-bearded face behind the windshield, and squeeze the trigger. The Buick went unimpeded. No bullets hit any part of the car, the police officers unable to shoot at the target in the middle of such a crowd. Joey had only a glimpse of the impact, and so he saw none of the blood, nor the rag-doll spreading out of the bodies, unconscious or dead; but what he saw was horrifying, in the way a dream can horrify by its improbable twisting of nature. A woman, hit by the car, her head pulled back with her mouth open, went not under the car, but up and over it. Joey saw her flying. There was nothing in her eyes, no terror, no surprise, simply an absence of feeling, of life. She flew, and the car went on, crashing through the defenders of the barricade, trying to kill and confuse.

"Now," said David. "Go." Joey hadn't realized that he had slowed down, not for any other reason than to watch the man's death. He heard Diana's surprised sob, as if the sheer fact of the man's suicide was reaching her in a way that made no sense at all. But it was clear that the Buick had made it possible for the ambulance to pass. The barricade was in a shambles, the defenders had their guns trained on the stopped car, and as the ambulance passed through into the Old City, screaming around the turn to the border between the Jewish and the Armenian quarters, it was evident that no one would take the time to question them or slow them down.

David called out the turns, insisting that Joey not slow down. Just before Ararat Road, the ambulance hit a donkey cart, sending a load of sesame seed into the filthy ground. There was a checkpoint here too, but small, with two British soldiers standing idly in front of an old Arab flour mill. One of them put up his hand.

"Emergency!" screamed David, shaking his hand at the soldiers, and Joey would have run them down if they hadn't gotten out of the way. They crossed the road and screamed into an alley where Joey was forced to a crawl. "Faster," said David.

"We don't even fit on this street," said Joey.

"You want me to drive?" said David.

"No, just keep up the encouraging talk," said Joey. He didn't go over five miles an hour, and almost immediately his way was blocked by a procession of Armenian priests.

"I thought this was the Jewish quarter," said Joey.

"Pass them," said David. "Turn right. Blow your horn at them."

"Why did he do it?" said Diana.

"So we could get through," said Joey.

"We would have gotten through anyway," said David. "He was an idiot. He was a suicidal son of a bitch. I know the type. He should have been in the Irgun, not the Haganah."

"It's not your fault, darling," said Diana.

"I shouldn't have argued with him," said David.

Joey turned down another alleyway, this one so steep that the ambulance threatened to slip out of low gear. "You're wrong," said Joey. "Without him, we'd never have gotten through."

"I had a plan," said David. "It was an unnecessary death."

"Maybe he's not dead," said Diana.

"Let's hope to hell he's dead," said David. "Let's hope he had enough sense to make sure of that." When he looked at Joey, he was rubbing his eyes with the back of his hand, but Joey saw no tears. "You can turn off the siren," said David.

"Yes, sir," said Joey.

"He wanted to kill them for what they did to his friend," said David. "It had nothing to do with us. It made it easier for us, but it's not our fault. Turn."

A man in a white suit waited for them at the top of a cobblestoned street. He was very cold, and was beating his hands together as they pulled up. Joey moved over at David's direction, and the man took the wheel of the ambulance. "You got through," he said. "Did the British break the blockade?"

"Not the British," said David. The man dropped them off at the rear entrance to an ancient Ashkenazi synagogue. "Good luck," David told him. He hurried Joey and Diana ahead of him down smooth stone steps into a basement entrance.

"Can I ask you one question?" said Diana. "What was so important that they needed us here? What are we going to do?"

"Survive," said David. "Fight and survive. This is the center of the

Jewish world, right here, the center of the center. We can't give it up. We can't give it up without dying."

Joey heard this last phrase with a smile. That was what motivated David, what had motivated the black-bearded man, what fueled the spirit of the Haganah, of which he was a part. They would negate the legacy of the death camps, they would recreate the image of the Jew, they would seek bliss in dying gloriously. Even as David had criticized the young man who had driven his rage against the Jaffa Gate barricade, he had gloried in it. Joey was sure of this. David was longing for peace, and peace was a shout against the universe, was a last puny blow against the forces of evil before they overwhelmed you, before they ripped you away from life, before they stilled your consciousness and let you join the beloved dead that had left you behind.

SIXTEEN

It was simple to pick out the soldiers among the Jewish population of the Old City. About twenty-five hundred Jews remained in their ancient quarter, and many of these were elderly, Orthodox, often fanatically religious, given to fatalistic pronouncements, long beards, and an impulse to discuss the wonderful old days before the threat of violence. The Jewish soldiers in the quarter were very different. Most were young, as young as Joey, some in the middle of studying for exams at Hebrew University. They were usually beardless, dressed not in the traditional dress of Ashkenazi or Sephardi Jews, but in simple corduroy slacks and khaki shirts, wearing as many sweaters as they owned. There were about one hundred and fifty young Haganah men, and another fifty Haganah women. Perhaps another sixty men and women from the Irgun and the Stern gang patrolled the quarter. All these Jewish soldiers were sworn to protect the residents of the quarter from Arab attack, but not all of them acted in concert. Still, the soldiers had much in common: the cold, the damp nights spent in cramped spaces, the lonely watches, the sense of impending catastrophe. Eight days after they had come through the blockade at the Jaffa Gate in the ambulance, the British hadn't stopped the siege of the quarter. There was little kerosene, and therefore little heat, almost

257

no hot food; there was no fresh fruit or vegetables, and even though Hanukkah had passed with little celebration, everyone had had his fill of the traditional potato pancakes.

"We should have been here last year for Hanukkah," Diana told Joey on their ninth day in the Old City. "I can hardly imagine it the way they speak about it. Runners with torches coming into the city in relays, running through screaming crowds all the way from the tomb of the Maccabees. People dancing in the streets, singing songs, getting drunk."

"Eating potato pancakes," said Joey.

"You'd love these if they were better prepared," said Diana. They sat in the basement of the synagogue that had been their quarters since their arrival, sharing the dark space with a dozen others, men and women and several teenage boys. The pancakes were cold, prepared days before in the Haganah's own mess hall on the other side of the quarter.

"Anyway, Happy New Year," said Joey.

"Is it today?"

"I'm not sure," said Joey. "Not a sign of the ball going down in Times Square. But I think it's today, or tonight. Should I order champagne?"

"Please do."

"Oh, it's black tie tonight. Thought we'd catch a show, something light, have a midnight dinner on top of a skyscraper, then drive out to the beach to watch out for the dawn."

"Happy New Year, Joey," said Diana. She had a sudden sense of what the handsome young man had given up, sitting there with his cold potato pancakes, in his badly rumpled Haganah clothes. She didn't know if he was right about the date, but she could easily picture him back in New York, on New Year's Eve, or on any winter's day bright with a cloudless sky. On Fifth Avenue, broad shoulders and insouciant youth forcing his way through the shoppers and gawkers, proud of himself in his cashmere topcoat, Joey must have felt as much like a king as her gangster father had. "Joey, can you believe how far away we are from everything?"

"We can always go back, babe." He patted the Swiss passports that were in his breast pocket. "As Mr. and Mrs. Joseph Collins of Zurich."

"Joey, if you ever wanted to go back, I hope that you wouldn't stop yourself just because of me," said Diana. "Marty wouldn't want you to stay with me indefinitely. Your days as my bodyguard are long since passed."

"I know," said Joey. "I joined the same army you did, right? I'm not about to desert."

"It's not deserting if you go back to the States. This isn't like the American Army. You've done more than your share just by getting guns for the Haganah. And you're a hero by any standards for what you did for David."

"Diana," said Joey. "If you wanted to leave, I'd help you get out. I'd go with you, get you on a plane and into the country. And then I'd come back here. Are you listening to me? I would come back here and stay until the war is over, because this is a war, and I joined this Jewish army, and maybe I wasn't so motivated when I first got here, maybe it had something to do with you, but I don't walk out. I don't walk out on a war. I'm not sorry I'm here." He stood up and walked to the unlit three-legged kerosene stove. "Do you want a cigarette?"

"You know I don't smoke," said Diana.

"I'm polite. I can't help myself. You like it better when people aren't so damned polite, but it's my gangster manners, see? If I'm having one of my five daily Haganah rationed cigarettes, it's impossible for me not to offer one to you." Joey lit up his cigarette, an English Players—the brand whose tins were used by the Haganah munitions people to make homemade grenades. Besides the five cigarettes, Joey's rations consisted of four slices of bread spread with syrup, two potatoes, a bowl of soup, and a can of sardines. The potato pancakes were extra, holiday leftovers. "When the hell is your boyfriend going to be back?"

"I don't know."

"I should have gone with him."

"He didn't want you to. You're not a senior officer, are you?" said Diana.

Amos, one of their Haganah roommates, climbed down the stairs with two large oil cans, surprising them both. "Water," he said. "You want to help?"

Diana and Joey both hurried up the stairs. An Arab boy was selling oil cans filled with water. Another Arab boy held the reins of a huge camel and a donkey, heavily laden with the cans. Joey passed a can to Diana, and she asked for another one, saying she was strong enough to carry two. Going down the smooth stairs, she faltered, and Joey dropped his cans and took hold of her at the waist.

"Look what you're doing," said Amos, hurrying to stop up one of the cans that Joey had dropped. "Is that all you Americans ever think of?"

"Thanks, Joey, I'm okay," said Diana. "You can let go of my waist."

"I like your waist," said Joey. But he let go, and turned to Amos. "What we think of is none of your business."

"It's my business when you're spilling my water," said Amos. "Leave the girl alone."

Joey pushed the Haganah boy without thinking. It wasn't a punch, just an open-palmed push against his chest, but as Amos was carrying one of the heavy cans, he fell against the hard stone of the stairwell. But the young man didn't drop the can. His face turned red, and he slowly put the oil can down, and then he reached across and pulled the cigarette out of Joey's face and flicked it to the ground.

"Cut it out, both of you," said Diana.

Joey waited. If Amos was going to hit him, he had waited too long already. There didn't seem a way in the world that the Haganah boy could connect with Joey's face. Joey was electric with tension, aware of any and every movement in the young man.

"You don't push," said Amos.

"I push," Joey said. "If I want to push, asshole, I push."

Amos threw his punch then, a right aimed for the general direction of Joey's head, so sloppy a punch it seemed that he knew too that it would be blocked, that any energy put into it was wasted. And Joey did block the punch, throwing his left forearm stiffly to his left and moving into the young man with a right hook and a knee to the groin. Amos was flung against the stairwell wall, open mouthed with rage. But Joey wasn't through, and he wasn't reading the man's indignation any more than he was listening to Diana's shouting. Water was being rationed now, two gallons a day, but that wasn't his fault; no one could expect to treat him like that and get away with it. It was bad enough that he had to listen to David Stern. The Arabs had blown up the water pipes leading to the Jewish part of the city, and Joey had suggested a counteraction, blowing up the Arab water pipes, or shooting one of the rabble-rousers in East Jerusalem, or attacking one of the ubiquitous silver-colored Arab buses. But no, David was negotiating with the British. Not directly, of course, but unofficially, talk-

260

ing to a British civilian who would in turn talk to the representative of the Army. Perhaps the water would be turned on again a lot more quickly if another explosion went off in a British officers' club. Perhaps the interminable negotiations to open the Jaffa Gate to Jewish supplies would get some more results if a few pounds of TNT were stuck in the middle of the Arab barricades. "If I want to push, I push," said Joey, pushing Amos's chest, so that he was flat against the wall, unable to move.

Diana hit him finally, an easy blow to the back of his knees, so that Joey fell down, though not very painfully, letting go of Amos, and falling down the stairwell with an oil can of water in his arms.

"I'm sorry," said Diana.

"He's crazy," said Amos. "I don't care how many rifles he brings us, that man is crazy."

"Nice move, babe," said Joey, getting back on his feet.

"I'm sorry," said Diana, "but you weren't paying attention to me."

Amos picked up two oil cans and brought them down the stairs. "I'll pretend that didn't happen," he said. "We're supposed to save it for the Arabs. Right?"

"Right," said Joey, extending his hand. Amos took it, and Joey looked past him to where Diana was lowering another large can. He went up to her and smiled. "You did that okay," he said.

"I'm a natural at combat," said Diana.

"You're killing me," said Joey. "Slowly, but surely."

"Oh, Joey," said Diana. "I wish you wouldn't talk like that."

They ran up the stairs and brought down some more oil cans, and Amos paid the boys and shook his head as they hurried on down the street. "You don't see much of that anymore," he said. "They're getting afraid to come into the quarter, even to sell something. One of them says he can get me a Mauser. Old, but in good condition—for a hundred pounds sterling."

"That's not selling, that's robbery," said Joey. The Czech rifle could be bought new in Europe for twenty-five pounds. And most of the older ones bought on the black market were good only for getting grease on your hands and a jammed rifle on your shoulder after the first round. The boys stopped at the next house, a German doctor's immaculate little palace, where the overhanging balcony nearly touched the camel's modestly hunched head. The light snow that had magically fallen the night before had disappeared under the bright

261

winter sun; standing there in Jerusalem's clear light, it was hard to imagine that they had made footprints coming back from their night watch. Snow belonged to the outside world, not to this enclosed little city of shimmering stones. From the north, they could hear several muezzins, their cries overlapping one another as they called to the faithful, extolling Allah's power, looking for prayers.

"I'm going to try to beg a cigarette," said Amos.

"You sure you don't want the one you grabbed from my mouth?" said Joey, smiling. He reached into his pocket and took out his last two. "One for you, pal. No hard feelings, see?" Amos lit his, and Joey used the lit cigarette to light his own.

"Thanks," said Amos. "Now I'll do you a favor."

"What's that?"

"I'll take a walk." With a smile at Diana, David Stern's woman, he walked off toward the Haganah post on Ararat Road.

"You want to go back in?" said Joey.

"I don't like this, Joey. I don't like everyone to think we've got something going. David has enough on his mind without—"

"David should have you on his mind," said Joey. "If you were my girl, that's what would be on my mind, okay?" He turned away from her, taking a great drag on the cigarette, and choked on the rush of smoke. "I don't know why the hell I'm smoking. I wish they'd give me a steak instead of the cigarettes. I'm only smoking it because it's coming to me."

"Please don't talk that way about David. You know that he likes you, and how grateful he is—"

"All right, let's can that, okay?" said Joey. "Where the hell are all the people? It's at least an hour to dark, and nobody's on the street."

"It'll be dark in a few minutes," said Diana.

"Maybe they've all run home to see what's on television," said Joey. "Maybe there's a good fight on tonight. Joe Louis or something." He turned abruptly to look at her in the fading light. He wanted to kiss her, but stopped himself. Instead he took both her hands and pulled her close to him. Behind her a Sephardi Jew, dressed in loose-fitting clothes and an enormous black skullcap, hurried up the street, late for saying his prayers. "You know we don't fix all the fights. A lot of laymen, you know, people like your mother's family, they think all the fights are fixed by the hoods. It just ain't so. Marty once lost a bundle on a fight. And he was mad. Not at the money he lost. He was just sore he'd picked a bum, you know? Gangsters think they've got great picks all the time. They always got an opinion as to who's going to win."

"Who's going to win this one?" said Diana.

"Are you talking about the war, or about the way I feel about you?" said Joey. He put up his hands to apologize for his rash statement. "Hey, it's going to be all right. You know that. The guns are coming, right? All we've got to do is hang on until the British get the hell out and then we can land legal arms—and tanks and planes and everything else. If the gangsters gave so much money, imagine what everyone else is going to give once it's all legal."

"I'm not thinking about the spring," said Diana. "I'm thinking about right now. This week, the next few days . . ."

Joey had not let go of her hands, and now he pulled her closer to him, looking down into her green eyes. "I remember kissing you once, it seems a million years ago. Do you remember? In New York. I just did it, and I thought you liked it—"

"Stop it, Joey," said Diana. She pulled away from him and started to walk briskly along the street.

"Where are you going, babe?"

"I'm allowed to walk on my own, aren't I?" said Diana. She was angry now, not at Joey's boyish insistence, but at her own irrational response to it. There was no denying the fact that his attention flattered her, pleased her in a way that made little sense. She loved David, only David, she reminded herself; but there was something of Joey she was learning to love as well.

"Do you have a television set?" he said, catching up with her. The wind was coming down from Mount Zion, toward the Temple Mount, and Joey felt the chill of memories. Every time he raised his eyes to the place where once stood the Temple of the Jews, he was accosted by visions that he had never seen: visions of fire and destruction and sacrifice. "I bought a television set," he continued, keeping pace with her along the cobblestoned street. The street climbed to a point where they could see the top of the Old City Wall to their south. "It's an RCA Victor. Cost me a cool three hundred and seventy-five bucks. Diana, are you listening to me?"

"I'd like to be alone for a while."

"David's going to be back soon. We're supposed to wait for him. He said we might share a watch tonight."

"Joey," she said, turning to him as if she would finally find something to say that would settle his desire and give them both some peace. But his handsome face, waiting for her words, stopped up all thought. She didn't know what she wanted to say, because she didn't know what she wanted. "I'm sorry," she said, and as she started to turn away from him, he moved his hands to her cheeks and kept his eyes on hers, and didn't kiss her, because she had told him that she didn't want to be kissed, and he held her like that for long seconds in the waning light, and Diana couldn't summon the strength to move away from his touch.

"I wonder what shows they've got on television right now, back in the States," he said.

"You understand that I do like you very much, but—"

"I remember when I saw the Joe Louis–Billy Conn fight. I could've gone to the fight, but hell, I wanted to see what it looked like in there. I mean on my screen. You think there's going to be television in Palestine someday?"

She wasn't sure why she kissed him then. It had something to do with his own restraint, a restraint that was coupled with a bottomless desire. That he could talk so inanely and never once let go of her face, never for a moment stop looking into her eyes, made her believe in the possibility of a love that was bigger than life, bigger than the clash of armies. She moved her lips onto his and shut her eyes against his wide-open ones, and she felt the surge of joy rising in him, joy and hope that blocked out any other thought in his mind. Joey gave her all his attention. The kiss was his universe. He hadn't stopped to examine the meaning of it all, why she had initiated this mark of love. There was no thought of how long this moment would last, if she could possibly be even a little bit in love with him, if she had finally allowed herself to feel what Joey was certain was the natural inclination of her heart. There was only the bliss of the contact, the sense of being surrounded by her warmth, her wanting, her affection. There was only the kiss, and then, a moment later, like a thunderclap from some mad god, came the explosion.

Diana let go of him at once. The ground seemed to be swaying beneath her feet, and she was struck by a fear that was incapacitating, and infuriating, because she remembered that she must always hide this part of her. Joey, incredibly, remained looking at her, as if he hadn't heard the explosion. But of course he had, and when he turned

264

his eyes finally to the north, from where the mortar shell had been sent, his reaction was swift and sure.

"Come on," he said, pulling her down into a crouch and running with her at his side back to the synagogue's basement entrance. There was rifle fire, one or two isolated cracks from their quarter, and a great useless firing from the Muslim section to the north. But he wasn't afraid of a bullet, but of a shell. He had seen too many men blown to pieces by shrapnel to worry about a sniper's bullet reaching them from so far away. She was out of breath when they got to the stairs, and there was another explosion, this one striking a balcony across the narrow alleyway and blowing great chunks of stone into the air.

"What are they shooting at?" said Diana.

"That's got to be a three-inch mortar they're using," said Joey. "At least three inches. Where the hell are the British? I'd like to hear them tell us they couldn't find out who was firing a three-inch mortar from the top of the Muslim quarter."

The two Arab boys who had been selling oil cans filled with water from their mule and camel were running now, clearly terrified, pulling at their reluctant beasts as they ran toward Ararat Road.

"Boys!" said Diana. "You can come in here!" She was gesturing frantically, in case they understood no English, but they were not listening anyway. All they wanted was to get out of the quarter, and fast.

"Get inside," said Joey.

'All right," she said. There wasn't much they could do without rifles, or orders. Joey had his pistol, but weapons were still so short that they only had rifles in their hands when they were on duty.

There was another explosion as a big shell hit nearby, and Joey took her into the basement, reaching for the cigarettes that he didn't have, and then smiled at her. "Safe here."

"We should be out there," said Diana.

"We have to wait for orders," said Joey. "And David."

"How can they do that in broad daylight?" said Diana.

"You said it yourself," said Joey, going to her. "It's getting dark." He put his hands on her shoulders, feeling the fear that shivered through her frame. "They'll stop soon. We're safe in here. All this Jerusalem stone. Perfect place to defend against a siege." He kissed her forehead, and pulled back to see what effect this had on her. "You see what happens when we kiss?"

"I'm afraid, Joey."

"Afraid of kissing me?"

"No. Maybe that too," she said. "But I'm just afraid. I'm afraid all the time. I don't want to get hurt, and I'm afraid of anyone else getting hurt, and I feel so ashamed of myself, but I can't help it. They're shooting at us, and it's real."

Joey kissed her again, this time moving his lips onto hers, and he held her closely, and Diana listened intently for more explosions, but all she could hear was the sound of his heart pounding in his broad chest. Four days before, she had gone with David up the Mount of Olives, to the ancient Jewish cemetery. A Haganah soldier had been killed by sniper fire, and disregarding the angry mass of Arabs at the Jaffa Gate, they had been allowed by the blockaders to take their dead out of the Old City walls. But then, going up the slope among the tombstones, they were fired at from three sides, snipers above them and on both their flanks. They were unarmed, of course, having had to go through three separate British checkpoints. All they could do was lie flat. Some of the men in the procession took refuge behind the simple wood coffin. The shooting went on for ten minutes. No one was wounded by a bullet, but one girl broke her ankle in running for cover and falling hard into a pile of damaged tombstones. She remembered not only David's icy calm but also his absolute distancing from her own fear, as if it had been distasteful. She had steeled herself from crying out, from running down the slope in a hail of bullets, from bursting out into tears; but David had known she was afraid and had offered her no solace. Perhaps it had been a kindness for him not to criticize, but simply to shun the evidence of her terror. He probably hadn't known that her fear was as much for him as it had been for herself.

And so she held Joey now, battening on the source of strength he offered, a strength not in muscle or firepower, but a strength of sympathy. He was aware of her fear, and not judging her for it; all his attention was in offering her support.

"I can't give you what you want," she said.

"I know," said Joey. "You don't love me."

"It's not that I don't love you. I don't love you the way you want." He pressed his fingers to her lips, and then he kissed her again, not insisting, just wanting to touch her for however fleeting the moment might be. The sounds of the explosions had ended, and Joey wondered if one of the decent English soldiers on duty had gone further than his superiors would have wanted and actually prevented an Arab Legionnaire from trying to kill Jews.

They had stopped kissing, and had moved away from each other before David rushed down the stairs, red-faced with anger. He hardly noticed them, looking past where they stood, at sandbags piled in a corner.

"Get those outside," he ordered.

"What? The sandbags?" said Diana.

"Go ahead," said David, picking one up and starting to lug it up the stairs.

Diana hurried to do as she had been ordered, and Joey smiled at her. "The shooting's stopped," he said to her.

"I'm okay," she said, hurrying with a sandbag after David.

"Unfeeling son of a bitch," said Joey to himself. He picked up a sandbag and hurried up the stairs. David was fortifying the rear entrance of the synagogue. He wanted a street-level position to be manned, as well as the lookout on the roof.

"That was a three-inch mortar," said Joey.

"Maybe."

"I know what a three-inch mortar is," said Joey. "I went through the war too."

"What the hell difference does it make anyway?" said David. It was practically dark, and his voice carried down the empty alleyway. "What are you doing inside if there's shooting going on? Your purpose here is to maintain calm in the quarter, and your presence is supposed to do that."

"We were outside, but went in after the mortar shells hit," said Diana.

"That was the wrong thing to do. Both of you. You're both supposed to be soldiers. It's personally embarrassing to me if you don't act in an exemplary fashion. Bring some more sandbags. Let's go."

"Wait a minute," said Joey. "We don't have rifles. There's no one coming at us in the quarter. You don't see Arabs running through the streets, do you?"

"No?" said David. "Two Arab boys just threw grenades through the window of the synagogue at the end of the street. Right in the middle of afternoon prayers."

"Were they selling water?" said Diana.

"You saw them?" said David. "And you just let them go? What the hell is that pistol for, Joey? Just let them! They killed an old man in the middle of his prayers, and nobody stopped them, they're back in their own goddamn quarter, safe and free, and we did nothing."

He had his gun out in his hand, and he squatted down, very tired in front of a sandbag, looking out into the dark. "Who's on the roof now?" he said.

"Michal and Uri," said Diana.

Joey hurried to get more sandbags, and in his absence Diana touched David's shoulder. "They looked like poor children. Amos was here too, he stopped them actually. We thought we'd get the water while the getting was good."

"It's probably poisoned."

"We were going to go up to the roof and see if we could help. They have rifles there, and can see much more what's happening."

"I can tell you what's happening. The Arabs are winning. Not everywhere, but right here, right in the heart of everything that's made us come to Eretz-Israel, they're winning. The Jews are scared here, and they want to get out, and if they get out, this is no longer a Jewish quarter. The Wailing Wall won't ever be ours again, and every Jew in this country is going to feel like he gave up part of his soul. You know the song—Eretz-Israel without Jerusalem is like a body without a soul."

"I thought it was without the Torah."

"We changed the lyrics," said David.

Joey brought up two more sandbags, and sank down heavily behind them. He took his gun out and peered into the dark street. "See anything?"

"No," said David. "Of course not." He shrugged, and in the bad light Joey could see the man's self-deprecating smile. All the hardness drained from David's face, all the hate and anger, and as he spoke again, Joey could see how Diana had become infatuated with this man. "You can't see anything out there. It's stupid to sit here with a pistol, of course it is. If we want to help, we'd do better on the roof, just helping Michal and Uri stay alert."

"All right," said Diana, reaching for David's shoulder.

"I'm not angry at you, at either of you," said David.

"Everyone's a little anxious this time of year," said Joey. "New

268

Year's, I mean. But you gotta figure 1948 is going to be a heck of a lot better than forty-seven, right?"

David didn't hear a word Joey said, though he understood that the young man was speaking in consoling tones. But there was no way he could be consoled at that moment. The Haganah had gone to extraordinary lengths to get him into the Jewish quarter, simply because they hoped his presence would galvanize the other soldiers and that his wealth of experience would enable him to better deal with the frightened Jews of the quarter. But his presence had changed nothing. The siege of the quarter was complete, and the British were dragging their heels about breaking the blockade at Jaffa Gate. David had spoken to community leaders about the need for strength and fortitude, but too many of them were getting ready to leave, prepared to leave behind their houses and possessions in exchange for any dingy flat outside the walls of the Old City.

"Shall we go inside?" said Diana carefully. "You know it would be terrible if you were to get sick at a time like this."

"I won't get sick," said David. "I've lived through colder weather with less clothing and much less food." He said this so quietly that it was less an arrogant reminder of what he had suffered than it was an exhalation of sorrow. "Look, I have bad news," he said. "I'm afraid it's very bad news."

"What did the British say?"

"Forget that for a moment," said David. "Perhaps we should go inside. Is there any kerosene?"

"A little. We can use it if you'd like something hot," said Diana.

"We should wait for the others to come," said Joey. "It's crazy to waste the fuel on the three of us."

"It's not crazy if it's necessary," said Diana. She was talking in a harsh whisper that seemed less and less necessary as the number of minutes since the last rifle shot continued to lengthen. Joey felt his sympathy for David Stern retreat under the advance of Diana's blind concern. Her love for the man was so obsessive that it made Joey question the strength of her values, the qualities for which he had fallen in love with her. The way she took hold of David and tried to help warm him as they went back inside—he could imagine her fleeing Jerusalem if that was what David wanted; he could imagine her taking David Stern back to America to recuperate under the care of her family's influence and power.

"Joey's right, of course," said David. "I'm not a special case. Officers deserve no special privileges when their men are out in the cold with empty bellies."

"I can just make you some soup, darling," said Diana.

"No," said David. "We'll wait for the others." He sat down heavily on one of the mattresses, ignoring the fact that Diana was preparing to light the stove. Joey lit a candle and set it down on the floor between himself and David.

"Well, what did happen with the British?" said Joey, his back turned to Diana so he wouldn't have to watch her make her lover's soup.

"That's bad enough," said David. "But what's worse is what I heard on the way back. It's about Kibbutz Ha-Yad." Diana stopped her work at the stove and walked over to them, hearing the catch in David's voice.

"What is it?" she said. "What about the kibbutz?"

Joey knew at once. He knew that there had been destruction and death, and only waited to hear the names said out loud: Geula, with whom he'd made love; Yair, who would have grown to be a friend; Menachem and Yakov and Eli and Ari, and all the young men and women with whom he'd trained, waiting for the attack that had never come.

"They were wiped out," said David. "By an army. Maybe a thousand of them. Who knows how true the story I got is? But they had to have been a big army. You know how they fought, Joey. It couldn't have been a small group. They had to have overwhelmed them. They had to have come at them from all sides."

"But what army?" said Diana. "The British are turning their heads, letting in guerrillas with weapons, but not an army."

"An army," repeated David. "And there are armies penetrating into the north. The British control the coast, but all they're doing on the coast is making it impossible for Jewish D.P.'s to land. It's in the interior where the Arabs are able to operate. They walk across the border, and they are controlling big blocks of territory that are part of the Mandate, but the British are just not there anymore." David reached for his bottle of pep pills and opened them up with shaky hands.

"You should sleep instead of forcing yourself to stay awake," said Diana.

"I'm tired of sleeping," said David. "That's all we do here is sleep. We have to do something more decisive."

"Do you know how many died at the kibbutz?" said Diana.

"No, just that they were wiped out, no prisoners, all dead."

"Maybe someone was out on a march," said Joey.

"No, stop dreaming. All dead, all of them."

Joey tried to accept the fact, but couldn't. Even years after the fact, he found it hard to believe in the deaths of members of his platoon, even when he'd been there when they'd caught the fragments of metal that robbed them of so many years of life. Crawfield was dead, but he found that hard to believe. Geula was dead, all that intense love for some other hero was dead too, all that sexual frenzy and desire was dead; but he couldn't allow this fact to sit in his mind. Yair was dead, his strength and courage vanished, his memories rotting in his dead brain, but Joey could easily conjure up the man's face and smile, and though he understood the truth of David's words—they were all dead, gone from this earth—he stubbornly clung to his disbelief. It was a strange posture for a man who had not only experienced death in war but also killed men, and at close range, had seen the life pour out of their eyes. But this wasn't strange to Joey. He knew death, as he knew killing; but he could never be made to *believe* in its permanence. There was no proof that he would never see his father again, or Crawfield, or Geula. Still, this did little to temper his anger or his hurt.

"Don't tell me I'm dreaming," said Joey. "I loved those people the same as you. I want to do something the same as you. And until I see the body, there's always hope, right? Who told you? Maybe they're wrong. I just don't see why we have to sit in this hole here and cry about it. Maybe they're alive, some of them. Maybe, right? Maybe."

Amos returned to the basement a few moments later, followed by two of the teenage boys, Shlomo and Yoni, who shared their quarters. Amos had been crying, and beyond the tears was a frustration that fired the room. "Do you know?" he said.

"Know what?" said David, as if there were any number of things over which one could be crying that evening.

"My brother was caught trying to get through Jaffa Gate," said Amos, leaving his mouth open at the end of the sentence, as if he couldn't finish his words, as if they were twisting through his throat, tearing up his insides.

They all knew of his brother, a Haganah man who had a girlfriend among the female soldiers in the Old City. Amos had been predicting his arrival for weeks. Diana took hold of the young man's hands. "What happened?" she said.

"He's dead," said Amos quite calmly. "The British stopped it only after it was over. There was nothing to stop anymore, but they let the body through. That's how I know. I had to identify the body, and now we can't even bury it. We can't even bury my brother's body." He turned to Joey, as if remembering something about the American that pleased him. "You're crazy, aren't you, my friend? Maybe you can help me. Maybe you're crazy enough to help me, even if nobody else will."

Diana helped the young man to sit down, but a moment later he jumped up. It was against the Jewish mourning laws to sit on cushions, and the mattress to which Diana had guided him was entirely too comfortable for his grief. Amos ripped the collar of his shirt under his heavy sweater, he ran his fingers wildly through his hair. "I am in mourning," he said. "There is no funeral, but I am in mourning, and I will be in mourning until I have my revenge." A moment later, Amos stalked out, not answering David's question about where he was planning to go.

"They tore off the ears and nose," said one of the teenagers. "He's in the supply room with the other bodies we can't bury. I think we should burn them, I don't care what the rabbis say. We can't just leave the bodies in that room forever."

Joey hurried up the steps so fast that he hadn't time to say good-bye to Diana. He understood that this was partly due to fear of losing Amos and partly due to not wanting to have to defy David's order to stay. But the urge that hurried him out into the cold night was made up of much more than these things. He was still smarting under the fact of the destruction of Kibbutz Ha-Yad, still reacting to the mortar shells shot without fear of retribution into their quarter. Joey liked to feel powerful, and his time in the Old City had stripped away his sense of freedom, his proud feeling of being outside any ordinary restraints. Inside, under siege, his food rationed, his sleep schedule determined by his commander, his duties prescribed, his free time largely confined to a cold basement, Joey had become angrier and angrier, as if all the effects of the blockaded gate were directed particularly at him.

"Amos," he hissed into the dark, running after the man he had started to bully only a few hours before.

Slowly the young man turned around, his hand on a pistol, his dark hair pale in the moonlight. "It's you, Yank," said the Haganah young man, as if he had expected him all along.

"Don't call me Yank. The last guy who called me Yank got shot by the British. Call me anything you want, just don't call me Yank."

"You want to help me?" said Amos softly. "Or are you just here because of the girl?"

"I don't know if I want to help you," said Joey. "You said maybe I was crazy enough to help, and maybe I am, but I want to know what the hell it is you want to do."

Looking into Amos's face, Joey remembered the black-bearded zealot who had driven his ancient Buick into the mob at Jaffa Gate. Amos had the same urge that was part vengeance, part suicide; his anger would not be satisfied until it had consumed himself as well. "Hurry," said Amos, and the two of them sprinted, their hands on their guns, running on their toes for speed and silence. The houses they passed were dark, with little pinpoints of light hidden behind heavy curtains, and Joey knew that all about them, on roofs and on the top floors behind black windows, were Haganah men with their British Lee-Enfield rifles, and he was suddenly afraid that they might get shot by their own people.

The sense of fear woke him up. He had felt quite sharp before, but suddenly the adrenaline pumping through him brought a clarity of mind that he hadn't felt since he had taken David Stern out of prison. He understood now where he was running, and that was not in the direction of confrontation, but away from it. He could not spend another night in a room where David and Diana slept in each other's arms. Even if no sounds issued from the dark, even if he was too far away to see her arms cling to his body, even if there was no chance in the world that the two of them made love in a room filled with soldiers, Joey couldn't bear the thought of them together, a pair, a unit that excluded the rest of the world.

Amos guided him to the rear door of a very old house covered with iron bars and plastered with a score of mobilization notices urging Jewish males to register for military service. The Haganah man knocked on the door with his left fist, and then did this again, hitting out a rhythmic tattoo that Joey assumed was a code. There was a slight commotion on the other side of the door, but finally it swung open, the iron bars were lifted, and the two of them hurried inside, not even speaking to the old man who had ushered them inside. Joey had a glimpse of brightly colored wall hangings, carpets, and low oriental furniture, all muted by candlelight, before Amos could lead him to the rear staircase. They ran up four stories, and at the locked door at the top of the stairs, Amos beat out another signal on the door. This time a young man opened the door, a pistol in his hand and a look of surprise on his face.

"Ah, *shalom*," he said, expressing in Hebrew surprise at seeing them at their watch. A very pretty young girl at his rear lowered the rifle that had been aimed at the door. Amos answered in monosyllables, and then in English told Joey to follow him. They were on the roof, overlooking the dark quarter, with the nearby unlit Temple Mount and its golden-domed mosque little more than a sparkling shadow in the moonlight. Amos stepped quickly across the roof, and then continued to the adjacent rooftop, and to the next, walking across a series of half a dozen contiguous buildings until they reached a final balcony filled with ceramic pots and overlooking darkness.

"Now what?" said Joey.

"Now you tell me if you want to risk your life. Probably die. Maybe get cut up like the animals did to my brother."

"Tell me what you want to do, and I'll tell you," said Joey.

"I want to get rid of the blockade at Jaffa Gate," said Amos. "I want to be able to get convoys through, so the whole damned quarter doesn't run off like the British want. That's what I want."

"How?" said Joey, looking at the man's unblinking eyes in the near-dark.

Amos smiled. He spoke swiftly and matter-of-factly. "With a bomb," he said. "That's all we have to do is deliver it, in person. We bomb the bastards at Jaffa Gate."

"So now I know," said Joey, just as calm as Amos. "Okay. Suits me. We bomb the bastards at Jaffa Gate." In his mind's eye he could imagine Diana hearing about the explosion, waiting desperately for Joey to come back to her; and he was happy and content with the vision of her concern.

SEVENTEEN

It took four hours to get out of the Old City, and Joey, regardless of his photographic memory, would have found it impossible to retrace the labyrinthine path that Amos took. From the rooftops overlooking the dark alleyways of the Jewish quarter, they climbed over stone archways and balustrades; near the boundary of the Armenian quarter, they descended two floors below the ground, where an ancient synagogue was used by a congregation which had originated in Spain four and a half centuries before. Here a bookcase concealed the entrance to a tunnel that led them under the adjacent street and into a solid underground network of pipes, tunnels, and aqueducts. Sometimes they could stand, but most often had to crawl, Amos's flashlight leading them deeper and deeper into the cold and the damp and the dark. There was no talking. Every step they took was amplified by the stone and the silence. They were not afraid of the British here, or of the Arabs, but of the elemental dangers of nightmares: bats, scorpions, ghosts, monsters. Under the ground Joey was conscious of the weight of the earth above. He wanted to hurry, and found himself always at Amos's heels, the radiance from the flashlight pulling at the darkness two yards away, leaving his own body in the frightening limbo. He found himself out of breath, and realized that he was breathing too shallowly, afraid to pull in some black spirit in the underground air. Amos went up, finding steps and handgrips and ladders built into the stone; he went down, and this was far more frightening for Joey, as if every further descent was a descent to the grave.

Joey finally saw the flashlight discover a sign, a bright blue X painted on the stone. Here Amos stopped and snorted as Joey once again climbed onto his heels. There was a ladder made of wood, a new one, not the relic of a former century, and Amos picked this up and moved it along the low stone ceiling until he found an open space. He motioned for Joey to go first, and the American was only too eager to go up, with or without the light.

"*Le-at, le-at,*" hissed Amos in Hebrew, words that Joey understood: Go slowly, slowy. He forced himself to do as Amos had told him, and tried to relish each step that was bringing him closer to the ground, farther from death and decomposition. He could feel the air change about him, feel a lightness enter his spirit, feel as if chains were being pulled off his body. Then he heard the sound of shifting stone and the metallic click of a safety being pulled back, and through the dark, level with his face, he saw a gun barrel.

"*Herut,*" said Joey, the evening's password, the first syllable difficult to pronounce, so that the man asked him to repeat it. "Son of a bitch, '*herut,*' I said, didn't you hear me the first time?"

"You're the Yank, aren't you?" said the Haganah man softly. "The one who broke Stern out of the prison?"

"Don't call me Yank. I'm an American, you can call me that, but don't call me Yank. That's what the Japs called us, see? Joey Marino. Hell, I never want to go that way again."

"You have to be quiet, Yank," said the Haganah man, tensing as Amos came up the ladder. But the Haganah man and Amos knew each other, and instead of the password, there was a great silent embrace; somehow, the Haganah man had already heard of the death of Amos's brother.

They were still underground, but in the Armenian quarter, near the Zion Gate. The house above this secure little Haganah post was owned by an Armenian merchant sympathetic to the Jewish cause. Even though it was after dark, it was still well before the eleven P.M. curfew, and with a change of clothing and a reluctant depositing of their weapons—save for Joey's switchblade and brass knuckles—they were driven through Zion Gate's British checkpoint in the merchant's private car without incident.

"Too bad we can't get food into the quarter the same way we got out," said Joey.

"Are you hungry?" said Amos.

"Sure I'm hungry. I don't have any money, but I'm hungry as hell as a matter of fact." Amos smiled, and asked their driver to let them out of the car at the corner. They had arrived by a circuitous route around Mount Zion to the Montefiore neighborhood, and Amos said he knew of a little restaurant that would be open behind its black curtains. "And what are we going to do for money?" said Joey.

"I have meal tickets," said Amos. These unprofessional-looking chits were printed up by the Haganah to allow its soldiers to get meals at local restaurants; at some future date, when the state would be established, the Haganah promised to repay these meals-on-credit. But for those establishments which accepted the meal tickets, the food they dished out to the young men and women of the Haganah was not thought of as a difficult obligation, but as a glad opportunity. They wanted to feed these young warriors, the proud beginnings of an army that would one day be out in the open, in uniform, marching to the rhythm of the nation's independence.

Out of the car, they felt the great difference between the shut-in Old City and the wide-open new one. There was little activity on the streets, but cars did move, sounds drifted out of houses and restaurants, the voices of lovers whispered out into the night. They passed the Press Club, where a very noisy party was in progress, almost a celebration, and Amos remarked bitterly that for the journalists this would be a time of joy. "Imagine if I could bring them my brother's mutilated head," he said. "Imagine how happy it would make them. Think of the newspaper copies it would sell."

The restaurant he wanted to go to was on a relatively busy street, and he led Joey around a back alley, through an evil-smelling courtyard, and up to a kitchen door. He knocked, and they were enveloped by the delicious smells of a beef stew. The cook didn't know Amos, but the owner of the restaurant did; he too had heard of the death of Amos's brother.

"Mordecai isn't here yet," said the restaurant owner. "When he comes, I'll bring him right over to you."

There were six tables, close together around a tiny bar. Every table was occupied, mostly by young Jewish men; but there were English-speaking journalists at one table, and an American diplomat having a lonely meal at the otherwise deserted bar. Food was brought Amos and Joey at once: big bowls of stew, steaming fresh vegetables, cold sweet wine, and a large pot of coffee and chicory.

"Where does he get meat from, and vegetables?" said Joey.

"Who knows? The Arabs, I suppose. Even in the middle of a war, there are some people who can get anything," said Amos. Suddenly the young man put down his fork and tried to swallow the food in his mouth.

"Are you all right?" said Joey.

Amos finished swallowing, took a great draft of the wine, and then shook his head. "I shouldn't be eating at all," he said. For a moment it looked like he was going to burst into tears, but instead he laughed, a deep, hearty laugh that had nothing of the sepulcher about it, and yet Joey felt as if he were looking into the eyes of a corpse.

"Why not?" said Joey. "These aren't normal times. You want to do something for your brother, you should be strong."

"Don't worry about me," said Amos. "I'm strong, all right." He had stopped laughing and now watched as Joey wolfed down his food. "I'm going to have to depend on you, Yank."

"Sure," said Joey, no longer bothering to fight the name.

"You know, I was talking to my brother last week," said Amos. "I was sticking up for the Haganah policy, and he was telling me about why he was almost ready to join the Irgun. We had quite an argument, my brother and me. Seems sad now. He was coming to see me, I'm sure. That had something to do with it. He volunteered to get into the Old City, and I think that had something to do with me. I mean, I was the baby brother, and he wanted to look out for me."

"A lot of guys are trying to get into the Old City," said Joey. "It's not your fault, what happened to your brother. What you want to do, it can't only be because of your brother."

"He was right," said Amos.

"Right about what?" said Joey.

"About the Irgun," said Amos.

Mordecai joined them a little later. Joey could see the pistol in his waistband as clearly as he could see the furious energy in his frame. Joey was introduced as a relation of Amos's "aunt." Mordecai stared at Joey carefully, and Joey kept his eyes on the man evenly, not looking for a confrontation, but simply giving the man a chance to see that he was unafraid.

"I spent the last four hours with the Haganah idiots," said Mordecai. "The British made them an offer today: they'll offer protection to anyone who wants to leave the Jewish quarter, but no more Jews will be allowed to go in. They'll let a convoy through with food, if the convoy is searched, and then only under British control, and only through the Zion Gate. The Haganah is considering the offer. Everyone in the Old City is going to want to walk out of that place. We can't get guns in, and we can't get in reinforcements, and there's no way we can protect those people with some milk and bread."

"If they're offering food," said Joey, "why not say yes? Meanwhile we can keep trying to bring in guns and people the way we always have."

"No," said Mordecai and Amos almost in unison.

Mordecai cleared away the food in front of Joey as if it might interfere with the words he wanted to get across to the American. "We must strike. Hard. In real strength. With that, there is always the symbol of what we are doing, what we are showing. Not as beggars taking crumbs. But to make our point, show the British and the Arabs what Jerusalem means to us, and not just the new city, but the Old City. Not just the new settlements that we built up out of nothing in the last few decades, but the Old City, where we have always been, and always must be." Mordecai took his gun out of his belt and put it on the table. "I can do this now, in this part of the city, because I am a Jewish soldier, and I am not afraid to say it. We must not only get food into the Jewish quarter, but show that it is our right to bring food there, and weapons, and soldiers. You see what happens if we wait for the British. In the last two months they've jailed fifty Jews for carrying weapons. Not one Arab. Fifty against none. Now I wear my weapon, in my own city, and if they try to take it away, I will kill."

When they had all finished the pot of coffee, Mordecai took them out again through the kitchen exit and out into the courtyard. They walked quickly, climbing the steep streets leading up through the Montefiore neighborhood, twice coming upon Haganah patrols made up of one young man and one young woman, their faces shining with fellowship at the sound of their password. Mordecai had joined the Irgun after five years with the Haganah. He had known Amos's brother and had often argued with him about the Irgun's demands for stronger action than was agreeable to the Haganah. He had spoken with Amos a week before, shortly after Jaffa Gate had been blockaded, when he himself had been on duty in the Jewish quarter. There was one way to break the blockade, and it would have meaning for the fighters in the Old City, if it was done by a union of Irgun and Haganah men. Amos got word to Mordecai within a half-hour after he had seen his brother's corpse. "I am ready," he'd written, and wrote where he'd be that night.

"We are ready too," said Mordecai when they'd climbed past the famous windmill built by Sir Moses Montefiore for the poor Jews of the city ninety years before. A black Ford was waiting at the curb, with no driver in sight until Mordecai came into view. Then, as if by magic, a face appeared at the window, gun in hand.

"Friends?" said the driver.

"What else?" said Mordecai. They got into the small car, with Amos and Joey sharing the backseat. Their driver drove at a careful speed, trying to create as little noise and notice as possible. They went west, away from the British security zones, and into territory that was every day more and more the responsibility of the Haganah. Turning off a main road into a quieter suburban street, the car slowed down at a checkpoint manned by Jews. Joey found this somewhat miraculous, but what he was seeing was taking place all over the city. Solidly Arab neighborhoods were under the jurisdiction of soldiers from Transjordan or one of the Mufti's gangs; solidly Jewish neighborhoods were finally being allowed their Haganah checkpoints—even though these checkpoints were occasionally raided by British soldiers, who had the right to confiscate the weapons of the Jewish defenders and jail them without charge or trial. The British never did this to the Arab defenders, and indeed this uneven policy was what made the blockade of the Jaffa Gate possible: in an area where both Jews and Arabs lived, especially one of such strategic emotional importance, the British clearly favored the Arabs. A Jewish blockade of the Muslim quarter of the Old City would have been unthinkable at that time. The British would have broken it immediately with their superior force of arms. But the blockade of Jaffa Gate by the Arabs was allowed, and the British obligation as the mandatory power to protect the convoys of the Jews in the Old City was not being carried out.

"This is how we will end the blockade," said Mordecai, leading Joey and Amos into the back of a suburban automobile-repair shop. There were two barrels that might have once contained wine or beer, but now contained TNT and scrap metal. The fuses were primitive, and the wooden exterior of the bombs seemed to promise no threat, but Joey could easily imagine the destruction they would cause in a crowd. Mordecai spoke rapidly now, explaining about the police van that would arrive for them the day after tomorrow. He would drive, and Joey and Amos would light the fuses and push the bombs out the back of the van into the crowd. Joey heard him, and assimilated the words, but his mind had wandered suddenly, with urgent force, to Diana. It was almost as if she were calling to him, and he wondered if this was his fear surfacing, twisting around in a strange form so that he would not know his name. Yet he didn't feel frightened. "The timing will be essential. You cannot hesitate," said Mordecai. "You must get those bombs out and away, or we too will go up in flames."

That night, the night that Joey never returned to the basement of the synagogue in the Jewish quarter, Diana wasn't calling to him through some mysterious ether. She sat up on her mattress, her knees pulled up to her chin, and worried. Joey had impulsively followed Amos out into the night, but there was nothing for him out there, no way he could vent his rage on the murderers of Kibbutz Ha-Yad, on the mutilators of Amos's brother. All that the night offered was his own destruction. David had said as much before he had gone to sleep. "Joey is not stupid," he had said. "There will be nothing to do, and he will come back, with or without Amos."

She didn't think she'd be able to sleep, but she was, however fitfully, and when she was awakened at two A.M. to go to her watch on the roof, she thought for a moment there must be news of Joey. But there was none. His mattress was empty, and when she went up to the roof, wrapped in sweaters, she half-expected to see Joey waiting for her, smoking a cigarette in the dark night. But there was another boy there, younger even than Joey, and when he lit a match to light his cigarette, she could see the exhaustion in his eyes, the cold in his lips, and she hoped that Joey was still alive.

The late-night watch was strangely beautiful. She made herself comfortable, but not too comfortable so that she might fall asleep, against the sandbags, and sighted along the barrel of her Lee-Enfield rifle at the black line past Ararat Street where the Arabs were supposed to be watching. But she had never seen fire flash from that line, never seen a brilliant white kaffiyeh rise up from the black and scream out the ululating battle cry of the east. The line of black was an abstraction, as much an abstraction as the idea that she could fill her sights with a guerrilla and squeeze the trigger the way she'd been taught at Kibbutz Ha-Yad, and thereby send a bullet crashing into the chest of an enemy of her people. She was very afraid the first time she'd stood watch, but Joey had been at her side, fearless as always, not contemptuous of her fear, but glad of the chance to be supportive.

"Quiet tonight?" she asked her fellow watchman, Avi.

"Quiet and cold," he said. "Like the grave."

"Soon it will be dawn," she said, though this was an exaggeration. Joey had told her the same thing. Wait for the dawn, the first faint glow that promised an end to night, and that soon disappeared into blackness—the false dawn. But this was followed almost at once by sharp rays, a brighter luminescence, and with it the banishing of all the goblins of the night. But there were hours to wait for light now, and she let the cold air keep her alert, but at the same time allowed the night to send her the dreams she'd ordinarily receive in bed. The black line where the Arabs waited was as good as any black canvas for conjuring images, pretty visions backed by terror. Holding the rifle, feeling the winter air settle its chill into her bones, she could easily conjure Joey's handsome face as they walked in the desert air of Las Vegas, as he held her bags, ordered her drinks, demanded the chance to love her. All the while, behind the images, like the Arabs waiting in the dark, was the real Joey, somewhere in Jerusalem, full of violence and anger, full of a need for love that she couldn't give him.

"You haven't heard about Amos? The American?"

"I would have told you," said Avi. "What else do we have to talk about? Do you have pep pills?" Avi lit another cigarette. "So, what do you think? Will your David agree to the British demands? Are we going to get a food convoy this week?"

"I think he will," said Diana. "I certainly hope so." There was already so much blood, so much misery, and the greater war, the real war, was every day looming larger and more inevitable. She was so tired of being afraid, of drawing up her indignation to fuel her courage, of using her love for David as a shield against any other feelings. If there were no David, she would not be here with a rifle, but snug and warm in the Press Club at Yemin Moshe. If there were no David, she might be in Haifa with Joey Marino, overseeing the shipment of illegal arms; or better yet, in New York, sitting with Joey in a nightclub, looking for men with money and power to help the fledgling Jewish state. If there were no David, she allowed herself to dream from the roof of the old synagogue, she might actually fall in love with the young gangster from New York.

That would really be rather funny, she thought, letting the dream expand in the black air about her. Her adoptive parents would be shocked, but no more shocked than her natural mother's family had been when she'd run off with Louie Bernstein. There would be a certain justice in the King's daughter falling in love with a gangster. But he was not a gangster, not exactly. He was still a boy, a boy who had been a Marine, but who was like a child, an angry child with petulant lips. But what a lovely way he had of kissing. That delicious sense he gave her of being his entire universe. Of course he was young, and knew so little of her world. But what precisely was her world anyway? The world of journalism, where she had hardly managed to get a whole foot through the door? The world of money and privilege, in which she had no interest, no inclination to live? The world of political commitment, a commitment that he had picked up and made his own?

"Joey," she said out loud, softly, continuing to keep watch over the silent night. Avi turned his head to her and asked if she had said something. "No, no," she said. "Just daydreaming."

"A bad time of day to be daydreaming," said Avi, but he was not criticizing, the way David would have, he was simply making a joke, trying to make the night pass a little more quickly. And the night did pass. There were no sounds of sniper fire except ones so distant that they might have been the backfiring of a British Army truck outside the walls of the Old City. There was no sudden message from the group downstairs that Amos and Joey had returned, drunk on local wine, with their faces scratched from trying to make love to some Haganah girls in another part of the quarter. The dawn rose, striking with magic the mosques on the Temple Mount, clearing the ghosts, chasing the chill. She was suddenly very tired. Of course she had been dreaming. There was a David, her David, and he was the man she loved.

Downstairs she crawled onto her mattress, watching David sleep as the pale light drifted into the underground room. She fell into a deep sleep, a desperate sleep, as if she had manufactured a narcotic out of her fears, and only sleep would keep them from coming true. But Diana woke soon enough. She had slept perhaps an hour, and no natural force—no random sound, no fly in her ear—had jerked her from sleep with such power. It was as if she had been struck with an electrified wire. She sat upright and opened her mouth and tried to speak. About half a dozen people were in the room, but not David. His mattress was deserted, and her silently moving lips attracted no attention. She felt a wave of panic behind her throat, she felt fire behind her eyes, she felt as if a hundred pins were shooting through her body. "Joey," she said, and this time the name emerged as sound—whispered, from the back of her throat, with the full strength of her love.

"He's not here," said a voice behind her, David's voice, and then her lover's hands reached out and took hold of her shoulders.

"What did I say?" said Diana, reminding herself of the way David woke up, abashed at the possibility of having cried out in his sleep.

"You said his name. You said 'Joey,'" said David, and as she turned to face her lover, she could see that there was nothing of jealousy in his eyes, she could hear nothing of pain in his level tones.

Still, she felt urged to explain: "He's in trouble."

"Yes," said David.

"You don't understand. I felt as if he was calling me. It was like a dream, and he was in trouble, and I heard him calling me, and so I called his name."

"Well, in that case, you won't mind going to see him," said David. She had never before seen him look at her with such contempt. It was as if he were asking her a favor that he knew she would grant, and in so doing prove her disloyalty; but implicit in his steady gaze, his sharply enunciated words, was the sense that her disloyalty was not worth his conscious thought. She had betrayed him by dreaming of Joey, and it made no difference to him; it would make no difference to him if she had slept with the young gangster, had borne him eight children, had carried his machine gun in a violin case on the way to a massacre in Brooklyn.

"See him where? Is he hurt? What's wrong, David?" said Diana, conscious of the terror in her voice, but no longer caring to disguise her concern.

"Something is wrong," said David. "Your Joey, together with

Amos, has gotten out of the Old City, and tomorrow they're going to try to blow up the barricade at Jaffa Gate."

"They can't do that," said Diana.

"Of course they can't," said David, "but if they try, it can mean the end of our negotiations with the British. If Joey isn't stopped, we might all starve here before the British let any food through."

"Do you mean that you intended to give in to the British demands?" said Diana.

"I intend to negotiate a way to survive," said David. He told her more then, as she continued to wake from her paltry bit of sleep: how Joey and Amos had been spotted getting into the Armenian quarter, and how they had been seen talking with a member of the Irgun at a restaurant in West Jerusalem, and how that same member of the Irgun was the one agitating for a combined Haganah-Irgun attack on Jaffa Gate.

"That doesn't mean that Joey is going to want to join him, just because he's had a meal with him and Amos."

"You're not listening to me, Diana," said her lover. "Haganah intelligence has confirmed the fact that the operation is in place for tomorrow. If Joey and Amos are caught at the gate, it will be a political disaster for the Haganah. You must prevent that."

But she knew what she must prevent, what her dream of Joey had urged her to stop. Her young gangster from New York was urging himself on to his own death, and she must stand in the way of this, she must explain quite clearly why life was worth living, why there was love in the world, waiting for him.

"How am I supposed to stop him?" she said, and now suddenly David's mercurial expression changed from contemptuous to loving, confusing her with speed. He gently placed his hands on her face, and when he shook his head, there were tears in his eyes. Of course. The contempt hadn't been for her, but for Joey; the dark hatred had not been for her betrayal, but for Joey's crazy plunge into an adventure that could hurt the cause of the Jews in the Old City.

"I don't know, Diana," he said. "It's just that I know that he loves you." He let go of her and turned his back to where she sat on the mattress, and then he struggled to stand in the cold and damp basement room.

"I can speak to him," she said. "I'll tell him that you want to negotiate with the British and that he must come back at once. Back to the Old City." She stood up too and went over to her lover and put her hands on his waist. "I'll do what I can, darling."

"I know you will, Diana," said David. He turned around and took her in his arms, and when he kissed her, Diana didn't know anything: whether his love was feigned, whether she would run from the Old City to do his will, or whether she was simply following the ineluctable urgings of her heart.

EIGHTEEN

It was not difficult for a Jew to leave the Old City during daylight hours in the first days of the year 1948. The Jewish quarter was besieged precisely to get the Jews to leave; the British negotiations with David Stern hinged on their insistence that the Jewish population be allowed to leave, but not to enter. More than a dozen families were always clamoring to get out of the quarter, not because they were insincere in their devotion to the idea of a Jewish state but because they were simple people, without military training or experience, and they wanted to live. Much of David Stern's time in the Old City was spent in arguing with these families, insisting that they remain in the Jewish quarter, their bodily presence as important to the spirit and fate of the new state as the diehard kibbutzniks in the Negev. Still, many families defied the Haganah. They were not leaving Palestine, but only the Old City. They were certain they would return—the day that water ran through the pipes, that fresh milk and vegetables were available for their children, when bullets and bombs no longer punctuated the night sky as a matter of course.

Diana left with a family of Eastern European Jews, resident in the quarter since the early 1930's. She wore a modest shawl over her heavy sweaters, she pulled back her glossy hair into a bun and wrapped her head in an unattractive black cotton cloth. There were eight family members—a very old grandmother, her daughter and the daughter's gray-haired husband, and their five children, whose red cheeks from the cold looked strangely disconcerting in the thin, pallid faces.

"I'm not worried about getting out," Diana had said to David as she transformed herself from Haganah girl to Orthodox woman in front of his unblinking eyes. "I'm worried about getting back in."

"I don't want you to take any unnecessary risks," he'd said.

"You mean that a *necessary* risk is okay?" she'd said, but he hadn't liked her joke and shook his head as if he were her teacher, correcting her faulty logic.

"This isn't the time to be frivolous," he'd said. But she hadn't minded his concern, because it was clearly that—and she wanted concern from her lover as much as she wanted his regard.

But as she approached the heavily guarded gate, their little procession accompanied by three British constables, the load of household goods in the wheelbarrow she pushed growing momently heavier, she had a sudden pang of doubt: What was David's concern all about? After all, he had been quite eager to send her to stop Joey. Haganah intelligence had pinpointed the garage in Rehavia where he could be found. Certainly it would be guarded. The Irgun was notoriously trigger-happy. Was David worried that she might not live through the day, not be able to return to his arms, bring his children into the world? Or were his cares far more specific: Would she be able to stop Joey Marino?

They were through the gate very quickly, assailed by silence. She had expected worse, and had been prepared for it: insults, rocks, even a stray bullet from a distant sniper. But there was nothing like this. They walked with downcast eyes, their pathetic belongings like a pageant of defeat, their English escorts not so much their protectors as their witnesses; and what the police were witnessing was the precursor of a land crisscrossed with refugees.

When they had made it past the gate, into the Jaffa Road, past the Arabs queuing for buses, and into a mob of Jewish pedestrians, Diana asked the man of the family where they would go. He simply shrugged. "It is early in the day," he said. "There will be a place before dark."

She had to remind herself that she was not connected to the

sources of money and power that had always supported her. It would have been the natural thing for her to pull out a handful of dollars, to remove a ring from her finger, to write out a check for these people— one family among the endless families in need in this country—but she had no money, no checkbook, no jewelry. All she could do was wish them well, and kiss their children, and hurry off into the crowd, removing her cotton head covering, letting her thick hair out of its confining bun. It was impossible to find a Jewish taxi, and she let herself be pushed onto a bus, the crush of people warming her, the scent of their unwashed bodies reminding her that this part of the city was better off than the Old City, but still far from a paradise. Mail from overseas had nearly trickled to a halt, international phone calls were almost impossible to arrange, cables went undelivered, the judicial system had all but ceased to function. She thought how lovely it would be to have an hour of luxury, American-style luxury. She would bathe in scented water, she would dry her body with the softest of towels, she would curl up in a cashmere robe in front of a roaring fireplace, drinking aged brandy with the man she loved.

The man she loved, thought Diana, and she blamed the conflicting images of David and Joey that assailed her on her lack of sleep, and the sudden release of tension that was the delayed reaction to walking out of the Old City.

There was no seat for her until they had almost reached Rehavia, and when she finally had the chance to sit, she was afraid of the comfort, certain that she would fall asleep before her stop. And so she stood, taking in the images and the languages of the Jews from the East and the West, from North Africa and Germany, from Bulgaria and Hungary and Poland and India and the United States. She wondered how many of them carried arms now, how many had been inducted into the Haganah or the Irgun or had joined the Home Guard, or had contributed children like so many drops of their own blood to the border settlements that ringed the country. Diana felt the collective sense of foreboding, the easy camaraderie, the automatic good fellowship that came from the fact of war. No one in the bus had not experienced war, either directly or indirectly. The shadow of the Second World War, of the death camps, of the terror bombs, fell on all of them. Tension was growing in Jerusalem, surrounded as it was by hostile forces, separated from much of the rest of Jewish Palestine by inhospitable roads, by armies conflicting with each other as to who should have the honor of the Jews' destruction. Where before the Jews of the Orient looked askance at Jews from Europe, where fair-skinned Jews wondered at their relationship to dark-skinned Jews, where Jews chattering in Yiddish or Russian found the sounds of Arabic or Persian coming from the lips of their coreligionists difficult to bear, was now only a sense of union. They were all in the same boat, and its name was Palestine, and they had come from every corner of the earth to make it once again the home, the refuge, for all Jews, everywhere.

David understood this, of course, he had said as much to her many times, but she couldn't help feeling that so much of what David expressed was the result of unemotional logic: at times of war, diverse groups sharing common defense goals must needs grow closer. Joey might not understand or bother to think about the mechanics that powered the feelings of these people on her bus, but he would share with them their love, their hate, their rage. She remembered Marty's injunction to her when she had been ready to lecture gangsters on the political validity of the Jews' claim to Eretz-Israel. "Hey," Marty had said. "You're Jewish. They're killing Jews, right? So what else do you got to say, sweetheart?"

A fellow passenger nudged her gently and told her that they were coming to her stop. Diana thanked her in Hebrew, and walked stiffly off the bus into the brightening morning. She had memorized the address, of course. In the event of trouble with the police, she didn't want to have the address of a terrorist nest in her pocket. Now, for a half-moment, she couldn't bring the address to mind. It was as if some part of her was holding back, not wanting her to take the final steps to Joey Marino. She blinked, she pinched her cheeks, she thought about taking a pep pill that David had insisted she bring along to make up for her hour's sleep. But she knew the address was there, was certain that it would rise to the surface of consciousness as soon as she admitted to herself why she wanted to go there.

To answer Joey's call.

Yes, it was clear that he had wanted her, and she had woken with his name on her lips, and whether or not her heart was reserved for her lover, she must face the fact that she wanted to touch Joey, to raise her hands to his beautiful face, to hold his head against her chest, to ask him quietly, humbly, to please try to live. That was all, Joey. To please live, to do it not for Marty, not for himself, not for the Haganah or the Irgun, but for her own selfish pleasure.

A young man in green corduroys and a surplus United States Army jacket asked her if she was lost. There was a gun in a holster on his thick black belt, and he was very serious, carefully watching her face as if she might be a spy, and so Diana gave him the Haganah password, and her Hebrew accent was bad enough for him to recognize that English was her native tongue.

"You American?" he said, and she could see that this young man was an American too, and Joey's address popped into her head, and she asked him in English where she could find the street, and he told her carefully, asking her to repeat the directions after he'd finished giving them to her.

"So what's a nice girl like you doing in a place like this?" the American joked, his eyes acknowledging her beauty and searching for some interest in his countrywoman's face, six thousand miles from home.

"Oh," said Diana. "I guess I thought I'd do my bit."

"Not like you thought it would be?" he said, and Diana shook her head and slipped away from the young man before she could forget his careful, friendly directions. Certainly it wasn't like she thought it would be. It seemed a lifetime ago that she had come to Palestine, that she had met David Stern, that she had found Marty Bernstein, and Marty Bernstein had presented her with her very own bodyguard, champion, shadow.

The automobile-repair shop seemed exceptionally busy for the quiet suburban area where it was located. A dozen old cars were in various states of assembly, engine blocks were being wrested from the innards of antique wrecks by fiercely motivated mechanics, tires were being patched by boys no older than twelve years old with a speed that made no sense. Perhaps six or seven adult mechanics stopped what they were doing as the young woman made her tentative way into the courtyard of salvaged cars. One of the child tire repairers spoke first, in sharp Hebrew syllables. "What do you want, lady?" he said.

"I want the American," she said in her bad Hebrew, and it seemed as if every mechanic dropped his wrench simultaneously, and as if the man with the pistol behind her back had blown up like a genie out of one of the discarded bottles that littered the garage.

"Your name?" said the man with the pistol. "Don't turn. Just give me your name."

"Diana Mann," she said, looking straight ahead at the garage workers, wondering which of those cars would be used to carry bombs, or men with Molotov cocktails, or Joey and Amos with some shaky suicidal plan.

"Go sit in that car," said the voice behind her, and one of the child tire repairers swung open the door to a half-wrecked old Ford, and she walked briskly, feeling the fatigue in her knees, and sat down on the backseat, swinging her legs into the car before the child could slam the door on them.

It was stuffy and warm, and the shut windows muted the sounds of the men's tools and voices, and she thought for a moment that she could actually sleep, find the few minutes in which she would have to wait for Joey sufficient to reclaim her strength. But she couldn't bring herself to close her eyes. The children with their enormous dark eyes were diverted from their tasks by her presence. She hoped that they didn't think her an enemy. Carefully she smiled at them, trying to send them a mark of her love through the shut-up car, and it distressed her to see them turn from her gaze, as if she were a siren.

"I know you," said Joey Marino, his voice booming through the glass. He opened the opposite rear car door and swung himself inside in one easy movement. "I didn't shave," he said, touching his beautiful jaw as if to anticipate her reproach.

"And you're not dressed very well to receive a lady either," she said. Diana had turned to him so quickly that she could feel the hostile eyes of the garage workers on her, as if she might conceivably be a threat to the handsome young man.

"I told them you were my girl," said Joey. "Amos didn't say nothing. David sent you, right? Stern knows what we're up to and he sent you, is that the story?"

"That's part of the story," she said, and she took his hands in her own, and he turned his head slightly so that his dark eyes looked directly at her. "I thought you might want to see me."

"You thought . . ." said Joey, suddenly too annoyed to finish his sarcastic phrase. But he didn't pull his hands out of her grip, and though he had turned his head away from her for a moment, he turned back almost at once, and then Diana pulled on his hands, ever so slightly, toward her. "You thought . . ." repeated Joey, and now he did pull his hands away, but only so he could place them to her face, only so he could focus his love along the edge of his fingers, directly into the planes of her face.

"We should kiss, if I'm supposed to be your girl," said Diana.

"Not in front of all these people," said Joey. "Not until you tell me what it is that David Stern wants."

"I'll tell you," she said, placing her own hands on top of his, where they embraced her face, and then she hunched forward and brought her lips gently to his, and though he didn't respond, though his lips never opened, though no breath of air escaped, she felt a rush come from him, a great gusting of spirit as her lips brushed his and then moved quickly, chastely away.

"You're still trying to kill me," he said.

"You look so dissipated, Joey . . ."

"There was no hot water. Hey, come on, don't kid me. You know how I like to be neat."

"I like how you look," she said, raising a finger to the heavy stubble on his boyish face. "I wonder how you'll look when you're thirty. Thirty is so far away for you. Isn't that funny that you're not even close to thirty?"

"Let's go inside," he said.

"Yes," said Diana, so quickly and intensely that she worried Joey. Her desire was palpable through her bloodshot eyes; he was certain that she wanted him, as he had known once before that she had wanted to kiss him, to hold him in her arms and close her eyes to the world. But the world was still there. David Stern waited for her on the other side of the Old City walls. Nothing had changed that Joey could discern, except for the sense of wanting in her exhausted frame. He wanted her to love him, but it was important for him to know that this love was true, and not the product of pity or desperation. He opened his car door and hurried around to open her side, and when he offered his hand to help her out, he could feel her shaking. "I'm just a little tired, that's all," she said. "I had watch last night. I slept an hour."

"What was so important that Stern was able to find me?" said Joey. "What was so important that of all the men and women in the Haganah, he had to send you?"

She had placed her hand in the crook of his arm, like a debutante leaning on her beau, and Joey walked carefully about the obstacle-strewn yard, avoiding machine parts and tools as assiduously as if they were live land mines.

"Of all the men and women in the Haganah, I am the one who most wants you to live," she said.

Amos chose that moment to walk, stiffly erect, out of the auto-repair shop's little office. He snapped at Diana, "What does your boyfriend want?"

"It's not just what he wants," said Diana, looking up at Joey, as if he would protect her from further rude queries.

"If you're here," said Amos, "it's only about David Stern." He looked at Joey and added, "We should ask her to leave, and now."

"Are you through?" said Joey. "Or are you going to keep trying until I smack you one?"

"Yank," said Amos. "I don't want her here another minute."

"I don't give a damn what you want, pal," said Joey. "What I want is some time alone—you understand the word—with my girl." He held up his hands to Amos. "We go back a long way, and that's the truth, and the others all think she's my girl, and if it won't kill you, you can make believe it's true for half an hour of daylight. She's my girl. Right?"

"Just remember what the hell we're here for," said Amos.

"I've got a photographic memory," said Joey. "You're the one who's got to try to remember. This is my girl, and we want a half-hour."

Joey hurried Diana past him, through the office, and into a tiny back room that boasted a kerosene lamp, a sagging couch, and a pile of sloppily folded Army blankets. He shut the door behind them and bolted it with the door's flimsy dead bolt. Then he looked at Diana as if she had become his prisoner, his charge, and he hadn't the slightest idea what to do with her.

"So I'm your girl," she said, sitting down heavily on the old couch. Joey started to speak, to protest at her flippancy, but she was already shaking her head. "I really want to explain why I'm here," she said. "David asked me to come, that's true, but it's also true that I needed to come here, I needed to see you. Not for David, but for my-self."

"You can't stop me," said Joey.

"Once you said that if I wanted to go back, you'd get me back. You'd take me," she said. Diana was surprised that she had said this so quickly. This had been her last card, if all else had failed—logic, the warmth of their friendship, a call to his duty to the Haganah. And already she had blurted it out.

"You don't want to go back," said Joey, looking at her carefully from where he stood across the little room.

"How do you know what I want?" said Diana, and even to her her voice sounded shrill and full of panic. Perhaps she had played her last card first because what she truly wanted was to be gone from this place; to be safe, overseas, back in the United States, beyond the realm of terror and death. But even as the thought of safety penetrated her fatigue, she felt ashamed, unworthy. "I don't even know what I want."

"You don't want to go back, Diana," he said, moving slowly toward her and then dropping to a knee before where she sat on the couch. "I know you," he said. "The woman I know would never go back, not when she's needed."

"Joey, please don't do it," she said.

"Do what?"

"Don't play around," said Diana. "You know what I mean. You can't break that blockade. You're only going to damage the negotiations and prolong the siege."

"I don't know what you're talking about."

"I don't want you to get killed," she said, bursting into tears that seemed to have been building inside her since she had first dreamed of Joey during the night. "Can't you understand that, you big handsome baby?"

"Don't call me a baby," said Joey softly.

"I won't call you anything if you go out and get yourself killed just because you hate David."

"This has got nothing to do with David Stern," said Joey. He sat down on the couch, and he put his arm about her shoulders, and she rested her head on his chest. "Nothing to do with David Stern," he repeated. "I wish you could believe that I am somebody who gets ideas, who cares about what's happening here too. I'm not just an idiot who's crazy in love with you." His voice was harsh, but as her head rested on his chest, he wiped the tears from under her eyes with a gentle sweep of his index finger. She could feel the beating of his heart like some distant ocean's rhythm of life, calling to her, calling to them. But she was afraid, afraid of her own cowardice, doubting whether her love for Joey was real—simply a reaction to the difficult love offered her by David.

"Let me just tell you, Joey," she said, and what she wanted to tell him got lost in the fog of fatigue that hung about her: that she thought him not an idiot, but an intelligent man, with the gift of memory, of courage and strength that could take him anywhere he wanted to go; that she didn't think his love for her any more or less stupid than any love she had experienced or knew about; that the love he wanted her to feel for him seemed to be growing spontaneously, dangerously, without any regard for her love for David, her sense of duty. "I don't know what I'm saying, really," she said. "I do love David."

"Don't tell me about David."

"But I want you," she said. "I want you to live."

Then she felt the strong young man move, briskly and efficiently, as if she were a child and he was her father. Her head slipped from his chest to a coarse surface that she recognized later as an Army blanket folded over into a pillow, and then her shoes were pulled off, without ceremony, even as her legs were hoisted onto the surface of the couch. Joey covered her with two blankets, and she wanted to thank him, but her words got lost in the delicious anticipation of sleep. She would be with Joey, and there would be no task to accomplish, no argument to win. There would simply be a slipping away of con-sciousness, surrounded by warmth and by his presence.

Then she slept, dreamlessly, and when she woke, she was con-scious of a violence in the air, of a threat that lingered. "Joey," she said, opening her eyes to an empty room lit by the early-winter twilight.

He was gone, and all she could think of was that he had come and kissed her good-bye and that she would never see him again, never be able to tell him that she loved him. Diana stumbled from the couch, barefoot on the cold floor, pulling a blanket after her, and opened the connecting door to the garage's office, where Amos and an unfamiliar man were deep in conversation. They looked up at her with unfriendly eyes, but before she could ask them where Joey had gone, she saw him walking quickly into the office, his eyes bright with satisfaction. The young gangster from New York had managed not only a shave but also a complete change of clothing. In place of his kibbutz and Haganah workclothes, he wore a suit—badly tailored, and obviously years old, but a suit, with a silk tie and a cheap stickpin, and a handkerchief jauntily spread in his lapel pocket.

"Put your shoes on," said Joey.

"Yes," said Diana, "my shoes."

He had managed to hire a taxi, rent a rare suite at a Jewish hotel, buy the clothes and the champagne and the hot dinner with the sale of his diamond ring. Diana felt like a princess. Joey was gallant because he moved mountains for her, he made the impossible possible, he anticipated her desire and served it without deviating from his own sense of values.

"How could you sell that ring? Wasn't it a gift from Marty?"

"That's exactly why I could sell it. Can you imagine him smiling at the whole idea of it? The two of us drinking champagne while the bullets are racing through the air? Your uncle's got a romantic heart, you know. Otherwise he would've never helped you, he would have never even given you the time of day."

For a few brief minutes it was not impossible to imagine that the sale of the ring had accompanied a change of heart in the young man. Perhaps in his new clothes, in the suite rented to bring them a measure of peace in the tense city, Joey had decided to forgo his adventure. But she soon realized that this was not so. They drove to the hotel on the outskirts of Rehavia, and they climbed the stairs to their top-floor suite, and they lit candles behind the black curtains, and Joey poured champagne, and they drank the first glasses very quickly, for the warmth and the quieting of fears. Then Joey poured again and he said, "To the liberation of the Jewish quarter!" And Diana raised her glass to his, and they touched glasses, and Diana whispered hoarsely "*L'chaim*—to life"—and Joey smiled as if this was an unnecessary appendage to his own splendid toast.

"Of course *L'chaim*," he said. "I want to live." And he put down his glass and he pulled her into his arms, and Diana felt as if she were being pulled into an abyss. She wanted to stop him from offering his love, but realized she couldn't do this, because it was his love that she wanted. Yet she loved David, she was certain, and she wanted to voice this, she wanted to make sure that Joey would not be hurt by the fact of this love that was inviolable between herself and the austere figure who had changed her life since their first meeting. She had slept away fatigue, but if she was sharper now than when she had first seen Joey in the garage, she was also more alert to danger; and danger seemed everywhere. "I want you to try to forget," said Joey as he held her.

"Forget what?" she said.

"Diana," he said, his voice chiding her. She knew what he meant, of course. Forget David Stern, forget the mission he had sent her on, forget about whether Joey Marino would live or die. Forget everything but this moment, this space of fantasy carved out of terrible times.

"I slept, and when I woke, you weren't there," she said, as if this might explain everything. But Joey didn't answer. He lifted a glass of the bubbly wine to her lips, and he took pleasure as she drank, and then he raised a forkful of lukewarm meat from the meal that the hotelkeeper had prepared at great cost and left for them under a steel bell that reminded him of nothing so much as a bulletproof helmet. "Weren't the others angry with you, that I came, and I took up their space, and you went off to buy a suit—you look so nice in a suit— won't it be nice to be back in New York with a Sulka tie and cashmere socks and custom-made shirts of the softest silk?"

"Please, Diana," said Joey. "I can't stay here forever. You understand that?"

"Yes."

"You won't keep asking me to do what I can't?"

"No."

"Then, please," said Joey. "Let's just forget. Forget everything except the two of us, right here, right now." And he took a chance, because he could see in her eyes that she was wrestling with David's specter, with the responsibility she held to David as his lover and his soldier, with the responsibility she believed she had to protect Joey from his own angry compulsion. But as he kissed her he could see that it would be all right. There was a lifting away of questions and queries from her face. He could feel the veil of reason dissipate. What she wanted from him was more immediate, more encompassing than any struggle to understand her duty. There was no struggle, because her lips wanted his, and as he felt the force of her entire body shake in longing, he felt a glimmer of familiarity; once before, he had made love with this woman, through Geula's body, and so surely had he imagined Diana in his arms that time at Kibbutz Ha-Yad that as they held each other now it was as if he would make love with her for the second time.

But that memory faded soon to insignificance.

Geula had been quick and urgent, as if afraid to face the real lover in her arms. But Diana's urgency, while just as great, was held in check; she struggled to prolong the madness of their intimacy, because she was afraid that when it was over she would be left holding nothing, not even sure of a memory. She kissed him, and he felt the smile spread across her lips, and Diana felt the strength of his love like a stab of pain. It was sweet, but the sweetness was tempered by a sense of impermanence. The intensity of the feelings she was receiving were not able to last. They were like the last cries of a dying man, the last burst of strength from a man whose heart was on the verge of bursting. And so she tried to be slow. She tried to turn his love into a gentle flow of endearments rather than a mad torrent that must needs be followed by drought.

Diana wanted to trip him up with inanities that were nonetheless true. She wanted to thank him for the champagne, for the luxury of this private suite, for the trouble he had taken to dress for this, their most important "date." But there were no words that she could bring to the surface. Everything—all words, desires, fears—roiled beneath the surface of the physical impulse, the imperative to come together with Joey, to make love. And when he picked her up in his arms, like she had always imagined he would, and placed her gently on the soft double bed, and blew out all of the candles save one fat one sputtering in a glass, she was no longer conscious of any questions, any motives, any duties. She let Joey hover over her, like a god or a madman, like a friend or a brother or a lover. He took off her shoes as she stripped away his tie, he pulled inexpertly at her skirt as she ripped two buttons off his newly purchased rough cotton shirt. But none of this—which might have been cause for comedy if the night was later, or they were drunk on alcohol instead of desire—took away from their intensity of purpose. Diana was naked in his arms, and she could feel the shock rising through his powerful body, the shock of having what had been his obsession for too long finally in his power; but then this shock fell away too, as fear had fallen away, as logic had been banished. All was natural. This body was strange only for a moment, but then all at once it was familiar, and dear, and it belonged to him for the moment, and the moment was all, absolutely all.

"I love you," he said, and she heard this as if the words were limned in fire, and she gave no response, not able to whisper out the words, certain that there was no way she could speak them that would make any more sense to him than what she showed him with her embrace.

When he turned to her, she felt the smooth flesh of his young belly; she traced the muscles that girded his pelvis, his thighs, his knees, she buried her face in his broad chest, and raised herself on her own knees so that he could slip into her, so that they could bring their bodies together while she was over and above him, while she tried to keep him pinned to the bed, to the earth, to the world.

"Please, Diana," he said, and she was very surprised that he had spoken again, because she understood what he wanted, and didn't know why he needed the words spoken. But she could deny him nothing, not then, not with her spirit soaring, not with her heart glowing with a sense of love that was selfless, without any demands or judgments.

And so she spoke the words: "I love you," she said, and she raised her head slightly from his chest, feeling his swollen penis move slowly, slowly within her, feeling the tears at the corners of his eyes; and it was awful, and painful, and terrible to stand as much as it was good, and life-giving, and rushing with warmth, because beyond the tears and the approach to ecstasy was the fact of the world, and beyond the moment of orgasm would be the road to death, and she wanted Joey, she wanted him to live, she wanted his heart to expand in joy and fulfillment.

"I love you," he said again, and then he repeated these words until they became a litany, until they became a device to hold back the storm that was all about them, until the words meant nothing more than that they were coming together, they were becoming one moment of happiness that would be followed by an eternity of longing for what was so quickly spent.

They held each other for a long time after that, their bodies rigid, not with lust but with fear. No one wanted to speak first, and Joey, always eager to be the gentleman, knew of no way to walk out on a lady without hurting her as surely as if he would slap her face. Carefully, generously, Diana forced the tension out of her frame. She let her muscles go lax, she let her fingers lose their grip on his beautiful torso; she feigned sleep, breathing in a regular rhythm into his chest. She never learned whether he believed in her act, but she heard him say quite clearly, "I must go. Sleep, darling. Remember, darling. Now, sleep."

And then, with infinite patience, with caution, he extricated his limbs from her embrace, he found his clothes in the dark, he dressed in slow, deliberate motions. She watched him through one eye, opened to a slit, her head resting on its side on her folded arms. Barefoot, he came back to where she lay on the bed, and she wondered if she should speak. But no, she had already told him all he wanted to know; there was no way she could stop him from going. Both her eyes closed now, she concentrated on breathing with the regularity of sleep. She felt him hover over her silently, watching her back, her delicate shoulders, the tiny rise and fall of her exhausted frame. But he didn't speak, and he didn't touch her. Long after he had gone, she imagined him there, hovering, watching, guarding their love. She didn't sleep, not when the candle died, not when the first sounds of the predawn city began to stir the silence, not when the sun began to drift up against the black curtains, softening the gloom. So long did she lie, with so little movement, that when the time came, when it was nearly ten o'clock in the morning and she felt the life twist out of her, felt as if a fist had materialized inside the walls of her body and was now pulling its way out, felt as if she was being left an orphan, a friendless survivor, a widow, felt the need to rise up and stretch out her arms in a great voiceless keening, she was hardly able to move at all.

"He's dead," she said without tears or screaming or doubt. "Joey's dead." Whatever love she would know would always live in the shadow of this night that was now gone, chased by day and blood and madness.

EPILOGUE

They could have never gotten away with it. The roads were marked with an endless series of police checkpoints, the streets were filled with soldiers, the gate itself was manned by Arab Legionnaires, British soldiers, British and Arab members of the Palestine police. Mordecai drove the stolen police van, and Joey and Amos each had charge of one explosive barrel of TNT. Their plan was no plan: half a dozen cars from the garage drove out to tie up traffic around the gate, and then the police van was supposed to be free to let loose its murderous bombs and then go back where it came from.

But even before the stolen police van could get to the gate, they were challenged, and when they didn't heed the challenge, shots were fired into the air, and then directly at them, through the windshield, into Mordecai's face and chest and hands. Still, he managed to live long enough to crash up against the first barricade and swing the van about so that Joey and Amos could light their fuses and roll out their bombs. But as soon as the back of the van was opened, machine-gun fire sprayed the interior. Amos was killed instantly, his fifty-gallon barrel filled with TNT rolling onto his chest as the van skidded onto its side. Joey was hit too, in the belly and in the chest, but he felt no pain. There was no time for pain. He had to roll out his bomb, its fuse burning down to nothing, and he did this, effortlessly, letting it out into the mob of barricaders. There was fury out there, fury and fear and hatred, and he turned slowly now, without pain, though the strength was pouring out of him, the lifeblood, the electric current in his brain was dying, but still he remembered that the fuse on Amos's bomb was lit and sitting on the dead man's chest, and Joey tried to lift this, tried to set it in motion toward the source of guns and shouts and violence. He wished there was more time. Time would give him a moment of memory, a chance to bring back with clarity the love that had been given him last night, the love that fired his soul at that moment. He knew what Diana had said, but he knew too that she would learn to acknowledge his bravery, as she had learned to acknowledge his love. If there was panic in his heart, it had no chance to grow. The panic was only that he would not have enough time to picture her face, or the curve of her neck, or the texture of her hair, or the sweet breath of her tender mouth. And certainly his panic had cause, because the time ran out, almost at once; no alchemist could suspend the moment, could twist it out into an eternity of waiting. Reality was all about him, and he understood that he would die, and he held on to the memory of Diana that was ultimately best: the way she had feigned sleep so as not to disturb their wordless parting.

And then the second bomb went off in the van, and then the van was no more, and the people inside it, the two dead and the one who was dying, were no more either. They simply blew away, sending more death, in the shape of the van's tortured metal, into the crowd.

A dozen Arabs were killed in the two explosions. One hundred more were wounded. As a result of the explosions, negotiations between the Haganah and the British to arrange for a convoy of food into the Jewish quarter were suspended that day. But early the next morning the Haganah decided to threaten the British: the same sort of force that had wreaked such destruction would be unleashed again and again unless food could be sent into the besieged Jewish quarter. No negotiations about how and why and how many could enter or leave was necessary, explained David Stern. This was simple. Let food in, under British protection, or face the consequences of another violent act.

And so the British, via Joey's death, and David's words, decided to let the Jews have the food they needed to live. Food was convoyed into the Jewish quarter on a temporary once-a-week basis.

David was transferred into the new city a month later, where Diana was waiting for him. She told him at once about Joey: that she had loved him, that they had slept together, that she would never forget him. But she told David too that she wanted to be with him, and that she loved him; and this was true, though her love for David Stern was of a different order than her love for the young gangster from New York. David didn't get angry over this revelation. He never spoke about it again. When illegal arms shipments began to make it through the port of Haifa, he himself brought up Joey, and said that he would never cease to be grateful for his help and his heroism. Diana felt as if David was somehow glad that she remembered and loved someone else, because David's love for Diana was always in the shadow of his dead wife, martyred by the Nazis.

Prior to the proclamation of the state of Israel on May 14, 1948, the shipments of illegal arms coming from Haifa helped the forces of the incipient Jewish nation decisively. Still, they were not able to stem the violent tide against the surrounded Jews in the Old City. On May 27 the Jewish quarter was forced to surrender, and the Old City was closed to Jews until the Israel Defense Forces recaptured it in the 1967 Six-Day War.

David and Diana were married in West Jerusalem in December 1948. Marty Bernstein stood in for Diana's fathers—her busy adoptive father and her dead natural father—and gave away the bride. He took home to New York a photograph of a memorial plaque that Joey shared with Amos and Mordecai, as well as an inscription on parchment which detailed the new state's thanks for Marty's unspecified "contributions."

David and Diana settled in Jerusalem, brought three boys into the world, and named their eldest, Joseph, after Joey Marino. Joseph fought for the first time in the Six-Day War. At the age of eighteen he was among the youngest conquerors of the Old City. But more than most, he knew where he had come from, after whom he had been named, and what this sacred bit of earth meant to his people.